Under the Influence

ALSO BY JOYCE MAYNARD

FICTION

After Her

The Good Daughters

Labor Day

The Usual Rules

The Cloud Chamber

Where Love Goes

To Die For

Baby Love

NONFICTION

Internal Combustion

At Home in the World

Domestic Affairs

Looking Back

Under the Influence

Joyce Maynard

HARPER LUXE

An Imprint of HarperCollins*Publishers*

HarperCollins books may be purchased for educational, business, or sales promotional use. For information, please email the Special Markets Department at SPsales@harpercollins.com.

FIRST HARPERLUXE EDITION

ISBN: 978-0-06-225776-5

HarperLuxe™ is a trademark of HarperCollins Publishers.

Library of Congress Cataloging-in-Publication Data is available upon request.

16 17 18 19 20 OV/RRD 10 9 8 7 6 5 4 3 2 1

This one is for David Schiff,
a friend for life, whose integrity inspired me
to create the quiet hero of this novel.

Under the Influence

1.

It was late November, and for a week solid the rain hadn't let up. My son and I had moved out of our old apartment back before school started, but I had left it until now to clear the last of our belongings out of the storage area I'd been renting. With two days left before the end of the month, I decided not to wait any longer for dry weather. Worse things could happen to a person than getting a few boxes wet. As I well knew.

The fact that we had finally left this town was good news. Not long before, I'd finally paid off the last of my debt to the lawyer who'd represented me in my custody trial more than a dozen years earlier. Now Oliver and I were living in a bigger apartment closer to my new job in Oakland—a place where my son could finally have a little space, with a little work studio for me, too. After a long, hard stretch, the future looked hopeful.

Money being in short supply, as usual, and with Ollie off at his father's for the weekend, I was taking care of this last run over to Goodwill with a bunch of things we didn't need any more. Just about everything was soaked through, and so was I. I had pulled up to a four-way stop, waiting for my turn. All I wanted at that moment was to get out of town, knowing that once I did I would never go back.

Almost ten years had gone by since the last time I'd laid eyes on Ava Havilland. And then that day, I did.

There is this phenomenon I've noticed in the past: the way that, in a vast landscape containing so much visual information seemingly of no significance, your eyes will be drawn to one small odd thing among all the thousands of others—the thing that calls to you, and suddenly, out of everything else your eyes are taking in and disregarding, they'll focus on this one spot where something doesn't make sense, or maybe it spells danger, or it just reminds you of a time and place different from this one. And you can't look away.

It's the thing you don't expect. That fragment in the landscape out of keeping with the rest. To another pair of eyes it might mean nothing.

I remember a day I'd taken Oliver to a ball game—one of those endless attempts to construct a happy, normal time with my son within the unnatural confines of a too-rare six-hour visitation. Halfway up the rows of bleachers, in a totally different section of the ballpark—in among the thousands of other fans—I had spotted a man from my Tuesday night AA meeting holding a beer and laughing in a way that made me know it wasn't his first. A feeling of sadness had come over me—terror, actually—because just the week before, we had celebrated his three-year sobriety. And if he could slip this way, what did that say about me?

I had looked away that time. Turned to my son instead, made some comment about the pitcher—the kind of observation that a person who knew more about the game might say to her son at a moment like this, a moment when a mother wanted to share the experience of a ball game with her boy and forget about everything else. This would be the kind of mother whose child never had to see her hiding wine bottles under the cereal boxes at the bottom of the recycle bin, or led into the backseat of a police car in handcuffs—the kind of mother who got to see her child every night, not just for six hours, two Saturdays a month. For years, all I wanted was to be that kind of mother.

This was a long time back. I hadn't even met the Havillands yet. I hadn't met Elliot (who, when I did, would have given anything to bring my son and me to a ball game and be a part of our small, struggling family). A lot of things hadn't happened yet back in those days.

Now here I was at the wheel of my old Honda Civic, idling at that intersection in an unglamorous part of San Mateo where planes flew so low, taking off from the airport or coming in for a landing, that you sometimes got the feeling they'd skim off the top of your car.

A black car pulled up alongside mine—not a police car, but it looked like some official vehicle, not a limousine. But it wasn't the man in front whose face caught my attention. It was the passenger in the backseat. She was looking out the window through the rain, and for a moment her eyes caught mine.

In the few seconds before the black car pulled away from the intersection, I recognized her, and in the odd way the mind works—instinct not yet having caught up with experience—my first impulse was to cry out as a person would who'd spotted a long-lost friend. For a second there, this great wave of pure, uncomplicated happiness started to wash over me. It was Ava.

Then I remembered. Ava wasn't my friend anymore. After all that time, it was still an odd sensation seeing her and not calling out. Not even raising my hand to wave.

I let it go. Made my face stone. If she recognized me (and something in her eyes, staring out through the glass for those few seconds, suggested that she had; after all, she was looking at me, too), she showed no more inclination than I did to acknowledge all that we knew.

She'd changed a lot since the last time we'd seen each other. Not just because she was older. (Ava would be sixty-two years old now, I figured. Her birthday was coming up.) She had always been thin, but her face looking out the window now seemed skeletal—skin stretched over bone, and nothing more. She could have been a dead person, only they hadn't buried her yet. Or a ghost—and in many ways, that's what she was to me now.

In the old days, when we used to speak every day—more than once a day, as a rule—Ava always had a million things to tell me, though part of what I loved was how ready she was to hear what I had to say, too. How intensely she paid attention.

She was always in the middle of some project, and it was always exciting. More than anyone I'd ever known, she possessed this air of purpose and assurance. You knew that when Ava came into the room something was going to happen. Something wonderful.

The person I caught sight of in the back of the official-looking black car that day looked like someone for whom nothing good would ever happen again, a person whose life was over. Her body just hadn't taken in the news yet.

Her hair appeared to have gone gray, though most of it was concealed under an odd red cap of a sort the Ava I'd known would never have owned. It was the kind of hat you might buy at a senior citizens' craft fair, that some old lady had knitted out of polyester yarn, because that was cheaper than wool. "Polyester," she said to me once. "Can't you just tell from the name that the stuff is junk?"

But this was Ava, all right. Nobody else looked like her. Only the Ava in the car that day no longer sat at the helm of a silver Mercedes Sprinter Van. This Ava no longer presided over the big house on Folger Lane, with the black-bottomed swimming pool and that exotic rose garden, and a gardener on staff to tend it. There was no more Guatemalan maid to pick up her clothes from the cleaners and make sure they were perfectly arranged, by color, in her vast closet, with all the beautiful shoes in their original boxes, and the scarves, and the jewelry that Swift had picked out for her laid out on velvet trays. The woman in the backseat of the black car no longer dispensed gifts of cashmere shawls and socks for the lucky people she counted as her friends, and shepherd's pie from the backseat for homeless Vietnam veterans, and dog bones for strays. Impossible to imagine Ava without her dogs, but here she was.

Most unfathomable of all, this was Ava without Swift.

There had been a time when a day didn't go by that I didn't hear her voice. Nearly everything I did was directly inspired by what Ava told me, or didn't even have to tell me, because I knew already what Ava would think, and whatever that was, that's what I believed, too. Then came a long, dark time after she cut me out of her world, and the hard reality of that betrayal became—second only to losing custody of my son—the defining fact of my life. Losing Ava's friendship had left me unable to remember who I might be anymore without her. As strong a force as her presence had created, her absence was stronger yet.

So it was a surprise to realize, when I caught sight of her through the window of that briefly idling car, that a few weeks had gone by since I'd thought about her. And now that I did, I still registered a stab of sick, sad loss. Not that I wanted to go back to the old days at that house on Folger Lane. Now I only wished I'd never set foot in it.

2.

The house. I'll begin there. Someone else lives in the Havillands' house now; they've taken out the handicapped-accessible ramp and cut down Ava's camellias to make an additional parking space currently occupied by a silver hybrid SUV, from which I recently observed a pair of blond children emerging, along with a woman who appeared to be a nanny. And as much sorrow as I feel on those rare occasions when I pass the house, I cannot separate it from the other part, which was the way I used to feel every time I pulled into the driveway—the sense that I had landed at long last in a place that felt like home. I could breathe again, and when I did, the air was thick with jasmine.

I didn't live in that house. But my heart did. Ironic, saying this after everything that happened, but I felt *safe* at the Havillands'. No doubt it is a part of my story, and a reason why the place held such particular significance, that in the thirty-eight years before my first visit to Folger Lane, I had seldom if ever known such a feeling.

Back when Ava and Swift lived in this house, the first ones out of the Mercedes when she pulled up were always the dogs—three rescue dogs of indeterminate breed. ("They're rescue dogs," she'd point out to anyone who didn't already know.) The vehicle had been specially equipped with an electric lift that lowered her state-of-the-art wheelchair to the ground. More often than not, I'd pull up and there would be Ava wheeling toward me in her chair, with her free arm—the one not operating the chair—stretched open wide to greet me.

"I got you these fantastic leg warmers," she'd say. Or it could have been a mug, or a beautiful leather-bound journal, or honey made from bees who only frequented lavender fields. She always had some little gift for me: a sweater she'd picked up, in a color I never wore that was suddenly revealed to be perfect for my skin tone; a book she thought I'd love; or a vase holding a bouquet of sweet pea blossoms. I hadn't even realized that the tread on my sneakers was worn, but Ava had, and knowing my size and the brand I favored (or a better one, more likely), she'd bought me new ones. Who else would buy her friend a pair of shoes? And a pair of striped socks to go with them. She knew I'd love them, and she was right.

Sammy and Lillian (the two smaller mutts) would be licking my ankles then, and Rocco (the problematic one who always hung back, except when he decided to bite you), would run in circles the way he did when he was excited, which was always, his tail wagging crazily. And Ava, once she had a hand free, would take mine, and we'd burst into the house together as she called out to Swift, "Look who I brought home," though he'd know, of course.

Ava always fed me when I came over to Folger Lane, and I always devoured what she offered me. Somewhere along the line, over the years—without noticing, even—I'd lost the taste for food. Lost the taste for life, or close to it. That's what the Havillands gave back to me. I felt it every time I made my way up the smooth slate path to their open door, when the wave of good smells would hit me. Soup on the stove. Roast chicken in the oven. A bowl of floating gardenias in every room. And drifting in from outside, the smoke from Swift's Cuban cigar.

Laughter then. Swift's big, hearty explosion of it, like a macaw in the jungle, announcing his readiness to mate. "I'm making a wild guess it's Helen," he'd call out.

Just hearing a man like Swift speak my name made me feel important. For the first time in my life, possibly.

3.

S wift didn't go to an office anymore. He hadn't done that for years. He'd run a series of start-ups in Silicon Valley—the most recent, something to do with making it possible for high-end business travelers to procure last-minute restaurant reservations—which had made so much money that he'd quit. At the point when I met them, he and Ava were in the process of creating a non-profit called BARK that would find homes for abandoned dogs and provide funding for spay and neuter services. For now, he ran their foundation out of the pool house, where he also oversaw their investments. He was on the phone a lot, talking to potential BARK donors from his standing desk, in that big voice of his. But whenever Ava came home, he stopped everything and burst into the house, and then his hands were all over her.

"I'll tell you why Swift can relate so well to animals," Ava said to me early on. "Because he is one, himself. The man lives for sex. It's as simple as that. He can't keep his hands off me." Her voice, delivering this observation, suggested amusement more than irritation. Often, speaking of Swift, Ava adopted this tone, as if her husband were like a flea who'd landed on her, but one she easily flicked off. Still, I never questioned that she adored him.

And in fact, though she remained central in his universe, Swift had a number of other obsessions: his 1949 Vincent Black Lightning motorcycle (bought, after a long search, because he'd loved the Richard Thompson song and had to own one himself), the school he sponsored in Nicaragua for street children, his private qigong classes, his fencing lessons, his study of Chinese medicine and African drumming, and a seemingly endless parade of young Reiki practitioners and energy workers and yoga instructors who presented themselves at the house throughout the day for one-on-one sessions. Ava might have appeared to be the one in greater need of bodywork, but more often than not, when someone showed up at the door—generally a woman, probably a beautiful one, carrying a mat, or a massage table, or some odd and unidentifiable piece of equipment, it would turn out she was there to work with Swift.

The house on Folger Lane was the place where everything happened. Swift and Ava had a second home on the shores of Lake Tahoe, which they visited now and then, but other than that, and Swift's occasional trips to promote their foundation, they didn't travel. They didn't like to be apart from each other, Swift said. Or, Ava added, away from the dogs.

There was a well-loved son—his, not hers—but Cooper was off at business school on the East Coast now, and even when he came home, he usually stayed with his mother, though anyone who visited the house on Folger Lane could see, from the number of photographs lining the walls of Swift's library (of Cooper and his fraternity buddies heli-skiing in British Columbia, or horsing around on a beach in Hawaii with his girlfriend, Virginia, or with his father, hefting an oversize beer stein at a 49ers game) that Swift adored his son.

Ava's children were the dogs, she told me. And perhaps, I used to feel, it was the fact that she had no children that accounted for my friend's extraordinary generosity toward the people and animals she loved. It was understood that dogs held the primary position in her affections, but she had this uncanny ability to recognize when a person needed rescuing, too.

Not just me, though I came to occupy a unique position with Ava, but also strangers. I could be out with her someplace, having lunch at some little restaurant (her treat, naturally) and she'd see a man in the parking lot, sifting through the trash, and a minute later she'd be talking to the waitress, handing her a twenty-dollar bill and asking her to bring the man a hamburger and fries and a root beer float. If there was a homeless person standing by the side of the road with a sign, and that person had a dog, Ava always pulled over to give him a handful of the organic dog treats she kept in a large tub in the back of her van.

She'd made friends with a man named Bud who worked at a flower shop where we stopped in for the roses and gardenias—masses of them—that she liked to keep in a bowl next to her bed. Then we didn't see Bud for a while, and she found out he'd been diagnosed with cancer, and she was at the hospital that same afternoon with books and flowers and an iPod loaded with the soundtracks to *Guys and Dolls* and *Oklahoma,* because she knew how much he loved show tunes.

She didn't just go see Bud that one time, either. Ava followed up. I used to say about Ava that she was the most loyal friend a person could ever have. If Ava took a person on as a project, she was there for life.

"You'll never get rid of me," she told me once. As if I'd ever want to.

4.

I met the Havillands around Thanksgiving, at a gallery opening in San Francisco for a show of paintings made by emotionally disturbed adults. I was moonlighting to make a little extra cash, working for the caterer. I had turned thirty-eight two months earlier, had been divorced five years, and if you'd asked me that day to name one good thing about my life, I would have been hard-pressed to come up with an answer.

That gallery opening was an odd event, a fundraiser for a mental health foundation. The majority of the people in attendance that night were the emotionally disturbed artists and their families, who also seemed a little disturbed. There was a man in an orange jumpsuit who couldn't look up from the floor and a very small woman in pigtails and a great many plastic barrettes clipped to her bangs, who talked to herself nonstop and periodically whistled. Not surprisingly, Ava and Swift stood out in the crowd, though Ava and Swift would have stood out in any crowd.

I didn't know their names yet, but my friend Alice, who was working the bar, did. I noticed Swift first, not because he was conventionally handsome, or even close to it. A person might actually have described Swift as one of the homelier men she'd ever seen, but there was something fascinating about his homeliness—something primal and wild. He had a compact, muscular body and crazy dark brown hair that stood out in various directions. He had a dark complexion and large hands, and he wore blue jeans—some very well-cut brand, not Gap or Levi's, and his hand rested on the back of Ava's neck in a way that spoke of more intimacy than if he'd been touching her breast.

He was leaning close to Ava, saying something in her ear. Because she was sitting, he was bending over, but before he spoke, he had buried his face in her hair and lingered there for a moment, as if breathing her in. Even if he had been here alone, I would have recognized him as the kind of man who would never have noticed or paid attention to me. Then he was laughing, and he had a big laugh, more like a hyena than a person. You could hear it all the way across the room.

I hadn't spotted the wheelchair at first; I thought she was just sitting down, but the crowd parted and I saw her legs, immobile, in her silver silk pants, the exquisite slippers that never touched the floor. You wouldn't call her beautiful in the usual way, but she had the kind of face that people notice: large eyes, big mouth, and when she spoke she moved her arms like a dancer; the arms were long and lean, with every muscle defined as rope. She wore oversize silver rings on the fingers of both hands, and a thick silver bracelet that wrapped around her wrist like a handcuff. I could tell that if she were able to stand she'd be very tall—taller than her husband, probably. But even seated, you knew this was a powerful woman. That chair of hers was more like a throne.

Occupied as I was that night with my trays of appetizers, I allowed myself to consider, briefly, what it would be like to experience this crowd from the low elevation she did—with her face reaching to around chest level of most of the people surrounding her. If this bothered her, she betrayed no sign. She sat very straight in her chair, and she held herself like a queen.

I guessed that she was probably about fifteen years older than me, in her early fifties. Her husband—though he was in good shape, with taut skin and an abundance of hair—looked to be closer to sixty, which turned out to be right. I remember thinking, I'd like to look like that woman when I'm older, though I knew I wouldn't.

For my day job at the time I worked as a portrait photographer, which was a fancy way of describing hours spent standing behind a camera—in schools, malls, event venues—trying to coax smiles out of bored-looking businesspeople and recalcitrant kids. The hours were long and the pay was low. Hence my occasional catering gigs. Still, I was pretty accurate in my assessment of faces, and I knew the story with mine. Small eyes. A nose that is neither large nor small, but lacking definition. My body has always been normal weight, but nothing to write home about. Going on from there to the rest of me—hands, feet, hair—I'd have to say there is not one memorable thing about my appearance—which may be why even people who've met me several times often forget that they have. This made it all the more surprising that of all the people she might have spoken to in the gallery that night, Ava chose me.

I was circulating with a tray of spring rolls and Thai chicken skewers when she looked up from the canvas she was studying.

"If you were going to buy one of these artworks, knowing you'd be looking at it on your wall every day for the rest of your life," she said, "which would you choose?"

I stood there holding my tray as a blank-faced man (probably autistic) reached for his fourth or fifth skewer, dipping it into the peanut sauce, taking a large, messy bite, then dunking again. Some people might have been put off by this, but Ava was not that type. She dipped her spring roll into the bowl right after he did and finished the whole thing in a single bite.

"It's a hard choice," I said, looking around the gallery. There was a portrait of Lee Harvey Oswald, made on a piece of wood, with a long string of words written on the bottom that made about as much sense as a shopping list merged with your old chemistry textbook from high school. There was a sculpture of a pig covered in a bright pink glaze, with half a dozen smaller ceramic pigs, also bright pink, arranged around the pig as if suckling. There was a series of self-portraits of a large woman with bright orange hair and glasses—crudely done, but so success-ful in their evocation of their subject that I had spotted the artist immediately when she entered the room. The piece I liked best, though, I told Ava, was a painting of a boy pulling a wagon, which held a boy holding a similar but smaller wagon, with a dog in it.

"You've got a good eye," she told me. "That's the one I'm buying."

I looked down, too self-conscious to meet her gaze, though I had taken in the sight of her enough to know she was an extraordinary-looking person: that swan-like neck of hers, the smooth, tawny skin. I felt at that moment the way a child might when a teacher praises her. The kind of child who doesn't often meet with praise.

"I'm biased, of course," she added. "I'm a dog person." She extended her hand. "Ava," she said, looking straight into my eyes as few people did.

I told her my name, and though I hardly ever admitted this to anybody anymore, I said that I was a photographer. Or had been. Portraits my specialty. What I really liked to do, I said, was tell stories with my photographs. I loved telling stories, period.

"When I was young, I thought I'd be someone like Imogen Cunningham," I told her. "But this is more my calling." I gave a rueful laugh, inclining my head toward the empty canapé tray.

"You don't want to put that negative energy out there," Ava said. Her voice sounded kind, saying this. But firm. "You have no idea what you may be doing a year from now. How things can change."

I knew how things could change, all right. Not for the good, in my case. There had been a time when I lived in a house with a man I believed I loved, who loved me back, I thought, and a four-year-old boy for whom my daily, hourly presence was so apparently essential that he had once tried to make me promise that I wouldn't ever die. ("Not for a long time," I told him. "And by the time I do, you'll have some really terrific person in your life who loves you just as much as me, and kids, maybe. A dog." That was one thing he always wanted that Dwight never allowed.)

Dwight got mad when Ollie showed up in our bedroom wanting to get into bed with us, but I never minded that. Now I slept alone and dreamed of my son's hot breath on my neck, his small damp hand curled around me, and his father, on the other side, murmuring, "So I guess we aren't having sex tonight, huh?"

Dwight had a temper, and more and more, over the duration of our relationship, it was directed at me. But there had been a time when my husband, catching sight of me at a crowded party, or at a potluck at our son's school, would have grinned the way Ava's husband had when he'd spotted her across the room that night—smiled, then made his way across the floor to touch my back, or put his arm around me to whisper that it was time to go home, get to bed.

Those days were done. Nobody noticed the woman holding the tray. Or hadn't for a long time, until Ava.

Now she was studying my face so hard I could feel my skin turning hot. I wanted to move away and serve some other guest, but when you're talking with a person in a wheelchair that doesn't seem fair. You can get away more easily than she can.

"What's your favorite picture you ever took?" she asked. Not necessarily the best, but the one I loved the most.

"That would be this series I made of my son sleeping, the year he was three," I told her. "I stood over his bed after he went to sleep and made an image of him every night for a year. He looked different in every one."

"You don't do that anymore?" she said.

I wasn't usually like this—I was always a person to keep my problems to myself—but something about Ava, the sense that she actually wanted to hear what you had to say and cared when you told her, caused an odd reaction in me.

I didn't cry, but I must have had that look.

"He doesn't live with me anymore," I told her, shading my face. "I can't talk about it right now."

"I'm sorry," she murmured. "And here I am taking you away from your work, too."

She motioned for me to lean down, to bring my face level with hers. She reached out and dabbed my eyes with a cocktail napkin.

"There," she said, sounding satisfied. "Beautiful once more."

I straightened, amazed that this lovely woman had called me beautiful.

She wanted to know more about my photography. I hadn't taken my camera out of the case in a year, I told her. The work I did at my job didn't count.

She wanted to know if there was a man in my life now, and when I said no, she said we had to fix that. She said "we" as if there was already a team here, with two players. Ava and me.

The other part—the part about Ollie—was not a topic I intended to visit.

"I'm not suggesting that a man solves everything," she said. "But the other problems you have don't seem so overwhelming when you go to bed every night in the arms of someone who adores you." From the way she spoke, it seemed clear she had this with her husband.

"And then there's sex," she said. A little way off, I could see the man whom Alice had told me was named Swift. He was engaged in conversation with an odd-looking woman—one of the artists, no doubt—wearing a piece of what appeared to be aluminum foil around her neck. He was nodding in a way that suggested he was trying hard to grasp what she was telling him. Just at that moment he caught Ava's eye, and grinned at her. Perfect white teeth.

"You must never lower your standards," she told me. "Hold out for the real thing. If you don't feel totally crazy about him, forget it. And if the day comes when it's over, walk away. Assuming you can walk," she said, with a laugh free of bitterness.

Her remark suggested that I deserved something amazing and wonderful. An amazing and wonderful career, an amazing and wonderful partner and lover. An amazing life. I couldn't imagine why this would be so.

"You have to come over to the house," she said. "You need to tell me everything."

5.

Making the trip over to Folger Lane the next day—in Portola Valley, just two exits down the highway from my little apartment in Redwood City—I thought about Ava's instructions. *Tell me everything.* I was always good at stories, so long as they weren't mine. Not the real story, anyway. That one I kept under wraps, and the prospect that this woman who'd offered up such an unlikely invitation might seek it out had made me consider not showing up at all. Pulling my old Honda onto Folger Lane, I briefly considered making a U-turn and forgetting the whole thing.

I had never been inside a house like the Havillands'. Not that it was opulent in the way some houses are, like houses that you see in magazines, or even on the very road where Swift and Ava lived. There was a kind of joyful abandon to the house—the soft white leather couches covered with embroidered Guatemalan pillows, the collection of Italian glass, and the erotic Japanese etchings—the vases spilling over with peonies and roses, the wall of African headdresses, and the incongruously traditional chandelier scattering rainbows over everything, the bowls of shells and stones, a conga drum, a collection of miniature metal race cars, dice. Dog toys everywhere. And the dogs themselves.

There was so much evidence of life in the place—life and warmth. All of it seeming to emanate directly from Ava, as clearly as if the house were a body and she its heart.

In the front hall, on a sideboard, was the most wonderful object: a pair of tiny figures carved out of bone, no more than two inches high but perfect in every way, on an intricately carved base formed into a tiny and beautiful bed. It was a man and a woman, naked, entwined in each other's arms. I touched the piece with my forefinger, tracing the smooth curve of the female figure's back. I didn't realize it, but evidently I let out a long sigh as I did this. Ava noticed, of course. Ava noticed everything.

"There's that good eye of yours again, Helen," Ava said. "Those are Chinese, twelfth century A.D. In ancient China, figures like these were presented to royalty on the occasion of a wedding, as a talisman for good luck."

Lillian and Sammy were kneeling at the foot of her chair as we talked. Lillian was licking Ava's ankles. Sammy's head was in her lap. Ava was stroking it. Ava had instructed her Guatemalan housekeeper, Estella, to put Rocco in the car for a half hour. "He gets overstimulated," Ava said. This served as Rocco's time-out.

"I call these two figures the joyful fornicators because they look so happy together," said Ava. "So you should touch this piece every time you come over." *Every time,* she said. Meaning there'd be others.

Lunch that first day was served in the sunroom by Estella ("my helper," Ava called her), who set before us a tray of runny cheese, figs, and warm French bread, followed by a salad of pear and endive and a creamy roasted red pepper soup.

"I couldn't live without Estella," Ava said, as the housekeeper retreated to the kitchen. "She's a member of the family. *Mi corazón.*"

Sitting in her chair across from me looking out on the garden—the sound of water running over the rocks, and birds, and happy dogs, and off in the distance, Swift on the telephone, having a conversation that involved a lot of easy laughter—Ava didn't ask how, as someone who called herself a photographer, I'd found myself passing trays of spring rolls at an art opening. Or what had happened to the son whose sleeping face I'd once photographed every night for a solid year—the mention of whom, just one night earlier, had made me cry. When she offered me a glass of chardonnay and I told her I didn't drink, she made no comment.

I had dreaded the questions Ava might ask about my life. But she didn't ask about the past. Ava wanted to hear what was happening *now*. She wanted to know what we needed to do to make me a happy and successful person, as I clearly was not at the moment. Since she seemed so gloriously happy and successful herself, I decided that day to follow her instructions. On everything.

"We need to get you a life," she told me. As if she were suggesting the purchase of a blouse or some interesting piece of kitchen gear from Williams-Sonoma.

Here's what I loved: Ava seemed more interested in who I was at that particular moment than where I had come from or what had brought me here. And in fact, this was true of her, too. Somewhere along the line I gathered that long ago, she had lived in Ohio, but in all the time we knew each other, I never once heard her mention her parents. If she had brothers and sisters, they were no longer relevant. If I hadn't been so invested in keeping my own story under wraps, I might have paid more attention to this aspect of my new friend, but as things were, it was one of the many things I loved about Ava, that I didn't have to explain the old story. I could create a new one.

The Havillands collected all kinds of things. Art, certainly. They owned a Sam Francis and a Diebenkorn, a Rothenberg horse and an Eric Fischl (names unknown to me before, but Ava eventually taught them to me)—also a Matisse drawing Swift had given her for their anniversary one year and a trio of erotic etchings Picasso had made in the last years of his life. ("Can you believe it?" she said. "The man was ninety when he created this one. Swift says that's what he wants to be like when he's ninety. A horny old goat.")

But it wasn't just high-priced stuff that filled the Havillands' walls. Ava had a weakness for outsider art (outsider art, outsider people), particularly work made by the kind of people, like the man at the coffee shop and the homeless people with dogs—and me, of course—who showed signs of having gone through hard times. On a prime spot, just below the Diebenkorn, hung a painting by one of the autistic artists from the gallery where we'd first met—a fishbowl, with a woman inside, staring out.

Ava wanted to show me a collection of photographs they had acquired recently: a series of black-and-white portraits of Parisian prostitutes taken in the 1920s. Something in the face of one of the women, she said, reminded her of me.

"She's so beautiful," Ava said, studying the photograph. "But she doesn't know it. She's stuck."

I studied the photograph more closely then, trying to find the resemblance to myself.

"Some people just need a strong person in their life to give them a little encouragement and direction," Ava said. "It's just too hard, doing everything on your own."

I didn't have to say anything. My face must have said enough.

"That's why I'm here," she said.

6.

Ava was thirty-eight years old—the same age I was now, which was a great omen, she said—when she had met Swift. She'd never been married. Wasn't sure she ever would be.

"I wasn't in this then," she said, tapping the armrest of her wheelchair. "The day before I met him, I ran a marathon."

I might have asked what had happened, but I knew she'd tell me when she was ready.

"I had a great life," she said. "I traveled all over the world. I had some amazing lovers. But when I met Swift, I knew it was a whole different thing. There was this force field around him. I didn't just feel it when he walked into the room. Before I heard him pull into the driveway I'd know he was coming."

He'd been married before, to the mother of his son, and when he and Ava met, had only recently extricated himself from that miserable relationship. "If I told you how much money she got," Ava said, "you wouldn't believe it. Let's just say the house alone was valued at twelve million dollars. Then came the alimony and the child support."

But the main thing was, he had his freedom. And the two of them had found each other. What was the price tag on that?

"Two weeks after we met, Swift sold his company and gave up his office in Redwood City," she told me. "For the next six months, we hardly got out of bed. It was so intense I thought I might die."

I tried to imagine how that would work, staying in bed for six months, or even a whole day. What would you do all that time? What about things like food shopping and laundry and paying the bills? Considering all of this, I felt clueless and ordinary. Dull. I had always told myself I'd been in love with Dwight, and if I allowed myself, I could have summoned memories of times with him when the only thing that seemed to matter was being with him, but the woman I had become in the intervening years believed she would never again have a life of passion, and sometimes questioned if she ever really had.

"Just before my fortieth birthday we faced the first big test of our love," Ava told me, pouring a second glass of Sonoma Cutrer as I reached for my Pellegrino. "The baby question."

She'd thought she wanted a child. Swift knew he didn't.

"It wasn't so much that he had a child already," Ava said. "He just didn't want to share me. He didn't want anything getting in the way of what we had with each other. Anything that would dilute it. And in the end, I knew he was right."

Then came the accident. A car, I gathered, though I'm not even sure how I picked up that much. I heard the words "spinal cord injury," delivered in a tone that made me know all I needed. Any thought of getting back the use of her legs appeared to have ended for her, as did any thought of having children.

That was long ago, she told me. Twelve years. She adjusted the silver cuff bracelet on her slim, elegant wrist, as if signaling the topic was now closed.

"We have a fabulous life," she said. "And not because of this house, or the Tahoe place, or the boat, or any of the rest of it." She waved her long, slim arm in the direction of the gardens, the guesthouse, the pool. "None of that matters, really.

"Funny how it works," she said. "I never would have known what two people could experience together. The level of connection." She devoted herself to Swift now—to loving and being loved by him. And then there were the dogs.

Was there a dog in my life? she asked me. (Ava never used the phrase "have a dog." A relationship with a dog was a mutual one, with no ownership. Most human beings were unlikely to ever experience—even with a lover, a parent, or a child—the kind of unconditional acceptance and devotion a dog will offer to the human in his or her life. Though what she had found with Swift came close.)

There was only one problem with loving a dog, of course, and giving your heart to a dog rather than to a child.

Dogs died.

Just speaking these words out loud appeared difficult for Ava.

Promise you won't die, my son had begged me once. Well, no, I couldn't do that. I might like making up stories, but I wasn't a liar.

Out on her patio that day, her wheelchair angled toward the sun the way she liked it, Ava had not seemed to mind doing all the talking.

"Take Sammy," she said. He was eleven years old, the oldest of their three. Because of the care Ava gave to his diet—and the emotional health that came from being so well loved (a factor that should never be overlooked)—he would live many more years. Ava hesitated for a moment. Well, several, anyway.

But most people didn't have to live with the knowledge that they'd outlive their children. Whereas with a dog—she couldn't finish that sentence.

"We've had to deal with it in the past, of course," she said. This was when she led me into the dining room to show me the portrait Swift had commissioned for her of the two dogs—a boxer and a mutt—who'd preceded the current group. The painting filled most of one wall of the room, facing the long walnut table.

"Alice and Atticus," she said. "Two of the best dogs ever."

I stood there studying the painting and nodded.

"Come over again soon, will you?" she said to me. "I'd like to see some of your photographs. And maybe you can take some portraits of the dogs. You can have dinner with Swift and me."

I loved it that she was interested in my photography. But more than that, what made me happy was simply knowing Ava wanted to see me again. I put away the question as to why a person as extraordinary as Ava would want to be my friend. She said there was something she saw in me—something she'd seen in the face of that Parisian prostitute she'd pointed out to me. Maybe it was simply that I needed rescue, and Ava had a habit of taking in strays.

7.

When I was very young, and the other kids in my class would ask where my father was, I made up a story. He was a spy, I told them. The president had sent him on an assignment to South America. Then he was one of a small team of scientists selected to spend the next five years in a climate-controlled pod in the desert, doing experiments for the good of humankind.

Another time—different year, different school—I said my father had drowned in a tragic accident, rescuing American prisoners of war who'd been stranded on an island in the Pacific after the Vietnam War. He'd loaded them on a raft that he pulled single-handedly, holding a rope between his teeth and swimming through shark-infested waters off Borneo.

Later, in college, I was simply an orphan, left without family after a plane wreck of which I'd been the sole survivor.

The reason that I made up stories about my family was simple. Even when they involved great tragedy, the stories I invented were better—larger, more interesting, more filled with deep and powerful emotion, spectacular devotion and heroic sacrifice, and the promise of great things to come—than the actual details surrounding my origins. I preferred the idea of catastrophe or devastation to the truth, which was the dullest but also the saddest of all: the simple fact that neither of my parents took much of an interest in me. It was plain, early on, that I got in the way of their plans. If they had any.

Gus and Kay (I addressed them by their first names because that's how my mother wanted it) were young when they met—seventeen—and divorced by the time Kay turned twenty-one, when I was three years old. I retain virtually no memory of that time, just a vague image of a trailer with a fan that ran all day long but still didn't cool things down. Or Kay dropping me off at day care for such long days that the woman who ran the center kept a box of extra clothes for me in one of the cubbies. (Much as, in later years, I kept a toothbrush in my pocket in the hope that a school friend might invite me for a sleepover. Any place was better than where I lived.)

I remember a great many bologna sandwiches and granola bars. A Top 40 station playing seventies hits, and the television always on. Old lottery tickets piled on the counter, never the winning number. The smell of marijuana and spilled wine. Stacks of library books under the covers of my bed: the thing that saved me.

I didn't know Gus well enough to pick him out of a police lineup, which is where he'd been a few times in his life. He paid us a visit twice while I was young: once when I was thirteen and he newly out on parole (something to do with check fraud), and again a dozen years later, when he'd called me up out of the blue to say he'd like to get to know me. I had actually bought this line, so when he failed to show up as promised three days later, I was devastated. I allowed myself to get my hopes up and then be disappointed again the next couple of times, until it became clear he wouldn't be stopping by after all. (Other men, yes. They came to see Kay, not me. And nobody stuck around very long.)

If there was one thing I knew growing up, it was that I wouldn't be like the two people responsible for my birth. I wanted to go to college. I wanted to have a good job, doing something I loved. More than anything, though, I wanted to live in a real house, with a family. When I had a child of my own—and I knew I would—I would be a different kind of mother from the one who raised me. I'd pay attention.

As soon as I was old enough to ride a bicycle, I got myself to the library. They had these cubicles there where you could watch movies with headphones, so when I wasn't reading, that's what I did. As soon as we had a VCR of our own, I was always checking movies out at the library. When Kay was off drinking, or out with some man—which was often—I watched those tapes over and over, first in our mobile home and later, when we upgraded, at the apartment my mother and I rented off the highway in San Leandro. It seems obvious now that my love of movies had to do with the comfort I found immersing myself in a world and set of characters as far removed from what I knew as I could manage. Some days I'd be Candice Bergen, other days Cher. I particularly loved stories about loner girls, outsider wallflower types who catch the attention of some wonderful, kind, handsome man (rich, naturally) who sweeps them away from their dreary existence. Sometimes—if I'd been watching old movies late at night—I'd be Shirley MacLaine or Audrey Hepburn. Never myself.

After seeing *Sabrina*, I concocted the story that Audrey Hepburn was my grandmother. I doubt the kids at school even knew who she was, but their mothers did. One time I told the mother of one, who had come in to volunteer in our classroom, that I spent my summers at her house in Switzerland, and that as a child I had traveled with her to Africa, on one of her UNICEF trips. (A trick I learned early about lying well: You fill your story in with as many details as you can that will ring true with your listener. People might not know whether or not Audrey Hepburn had a granddaughter, but if they knew she worked for UNICEF, it wasn't such a big leap to the made-up part.)

Given how much time I spent with my made-up grandmother Audrey, it was not surprising that I spoke with an accent somewhat reminiscent of hers in *Sabrina* (part French, part British) and wore only ballet flats. One time I ran into a classmate and her mother at the community pool. (I reflected, as always, what it might feel like to have the kind of mother who accompanied you to the pool, and rubbed suntan lotion on your back, and brought snacks.)

She had expressed surprise that I wasn't in Switzerland. "I fly out next week," I told her. Then I stayed away from the pool.

Years later, when I was at college (I'd gotten a full scholarship) and word hit the news that Audrey Hepburn had died of cancer, that same woman sent me a note expressing her condolences. I wrote back to thank her, and to tell her my grandmother had left me a string of pearls, which I described as having been given to Audrey by one of the many men who'd adored her, Gregory Peck. I would treasure them forever, I said.

It would have been more difficult to maintain the illusion that my stories were true if I'd had good friends, but I didn't—and maybe it was the need to preserve my secrets that accounted for this. People on campus were cordial enough, but I didn't get close to anyone—and how could I? I was working very hard to maintain my grade-point average, which was important if I wanted to hold on to my scholarship. I was majoring in art, with a focus on photography, but I had signed up for a workshop in screenwriting. All my life I'd made up stories, so this made sense.

The workshop was taught by a writer-director who'd gotten one movie made, back in the seventies, and now ran screenwriting seminars at hotel conference centers. After it was over, he'd invited me for coffee—impressed with my knowledge of film history, he said. Coffee turned into dinner, which turned into a long drive to the ocean, on which he told me that he was fed up with the movie studios and the way they trashed his work, and all the shallow people an artist had to pander to if he wanted to get his movies made.

His last project was shit, he told me. His marriage was shit. Hollywood was shit. It was so refreshing, meeting a girl like me, who still possessed the passion he'd once had about films. I still called them movies.

Jake started calling me up from Los Angeles, writing me letters. I never even asked myself if I liked this man; I was just so amazed that he'd taken an interest in me. Amazed and flattered, of course. One day he said, "Meet me in Palm Springs," and when he sent me the plane ticket, I went. It had not occurred to me that I might make my own choices in life. I was waiting to see what the people around me wanted to do, and when someone offered a suggestion, I took it.

He said he was leaving his wife. Had left. Said we could make films together; he'd be my mentor. Said he'd drive north to my college campus to pick me up. He could attach a roof rack to his car—all I'd need to transport my belongings, I had so few. He'd be there by tomorrow morning. "I'm your family now," he said. "The only family you'll ever need."

A week later I had given up my full scholarship and moved out of my dorm room to go live with him. Six months after that, Jake was back with his wife. That was it for college. As a person who'd made up plenty of stories, you might have thought I'd recognize the signs when someone else was doing it. But I had trusted this man utterly, and for a while, after he left, I walked around in a state of shock, and the belief that I had evidently not deserved the love of this brilliant man. All failure and blame were placed firmly on my shoulders.

When I was with Jake, he had bought me a Nikon camera and taught me a little about light and composition, lenses and shutter speed. Now, to make money, I got a job taking photographs of camping equipment for an outdoor catalog. It was deadening work, but temporary, I figured, and the main thing now was being out of Kay's apartment and not having to go back ever.

Given that I had no money, no education, no connections to anyone besides the man who no longer returned my phone calls, the idea of working in the film industry now seemed unattainable. As soon as I had the money saved up, I bought a couple of good lenses and started learning how to use them. I figured I'd tell my stories one frame at a time. It turned out I was good at it, and I started getting jobs. They weren't great jobs, but I got to use my camera, and I earned enough money to get my own little apartment.

Back in those days, I'd spend hours just walking down random streets, shooting pictures. It was on one of my walks that I met Dwight. He was working as a mortgage broker in an office next to a mattress store in a strip mall along the highway. I'd pulled my car over because a young woman out in front of the store had caught my attention. She was one of those people companies hire for minimum wage to put on a ridiculous costume and dance around with a sign, trying to entice shoppers to come into their store.

Something about the dancing mattress girl had moved me, reminded me of myself. (That could be me, I thought. I could stoop that low.) Trying to get someone to pay attention, only they never did. I took out my camera.

That's what I was doing when Dwight approached me on the sidewalk. "Nice camera," he said.

It wasn't a particularly interesting opening line, but he was nice looking, and he had a kind of easy, back-slapping manner that came in handy in his line of work. Later, I'd realize the other side of his affable style: He was that way with everyone, at least until the person was out of earshot. Paid to make friends and spin numbers in the most positive light, he had cultivated a certain way of talking that left me wondering, later, if any of it was real. He was like one of those announcers you'd hear on AM radio. Always friendly, always upbeat. At least on the surface. What lay beneath was anybody's guess, though eventually I'd learn, and when I did, it wasn't good.

The first time Dwight took me out for dinner, he told me about his family in Sacramento—four other McCabe brothers and a sister, all of them close. His parents were not only still married to each other, they actually loved each other. Whenever the family got together—and they got together a lot—they did things like play charades and touch football, and exchange Secret Santa presents under the tree on Christmas Eve. They still lived in the same house where Dwight grew up, with pencil marks on the kitchen door molding recording the growth of all six children. It was my dream of a family.

"I told my mother all about you," Dwight said a couple of days later, when he called me to go out with him again. "I was telling her about how hard it was for you, growing up. Not having your dad around and all, and your mom not being there much, either. She made me promise to bring you over to the house for Sunday dinner with the family."

His parents would love me, he said. What a great storyteller I was. How much fun. Not to mention pretty, he said. Nobody had ever called me that.

That weekend in Sacramento I was so happy I couldn't eat—though I remember drinking more than I normally would, just to relax. Dwight's mother had made a ham with pineapple slices arranged over the top. I couldn't bring myself to tell her I was a vegetarian. That night I decided I wasn't anymore.

"Do you like to cook?" his mother asked me. From then on, the answer was yes.

The weekend after that Dwight brought me to his family's cabin in the mountains. He lit a fire and cooked us trout on the grill and that night there was no question we would be sharing the bed.

"I always wanted a girl just like you," he said to me.

I wanted to ask, what kind of girl was that? Whatever kind of girl he was talking about, that's who I would be. And maybe it was my own willingness to adapt to whatever the situation required of me that made me seem like his ideal partner. But I didn't understand that until later.

I didn't have a best friend, but I told my boss at the company where I was taking pictures of tech devices that I had met a man I wanted to marry. "So you're in love?" she said.

I told her yes. Even now, I'm not entirely sure whether or not this was ever so. I had developed, early on, the habit of low expectations, and of letting my life be directed by whatever person happened to come along who seemed to know better than I did what they were doing. The fact that a friendly, nice-looking, seemingly well-adjusted man showed an interest in me was reason enough to have an interest in him. Never having had anyone take any particular interest in me—not my mother or my father, and only briefly Jake, the screen-writing teacher. It was compelling when Dwight chose me as someone worthy of his attention and possibly even love. I felt not only lucky but supremely grateful—not simply for the love of this happy, apparently normal man, a person so accustomed to life going well that his favorite expression was "it's all good"—but almost as much so for his whole family, who seemed to embrace me as one of their own.

Six months after Dwight and I started spending time together, I found out I was pregnant. The idea of becoming a mother—having someone who would always be there, a family member of my own to bring to those wonderful dinners with the extended McCabe family in Sacramento, a child whose growth could now be measured alongside that of all the others on the kitchen molding—was the best thing I could have dreamed of. I did not give thought to the fact that, as had been true of so many significant events in my life, this one was not a choice I made, but something I allowed to happen.

The first time I ever saw my husband lose his temper, I was eight months pregnant. I had quit my job by this time. We were on the freeway, headed to his cousin's wedding in Los Angeles, and the car behind us had tapped our bumper. Dwight's face darkened then, and for a moment he just sat there, but I knew something was coming. He got out of our car and started screaming at the other driver, calling her an idiot and kicking the side door of her car. Who was this man I'd married?

I started to recognize a pattern. If Dwight was tired, or stressed—as he often was—he'd take it out on whoever happened to be around. Usually this was me. It might be nothing more than the discovery that I'd broken his 49ers beer stein or I hadn't remembered to buy peanut butter. Once he was set off, Dwight was like a drunk, without the liquor part.

But we had a baby. I decided that was enough. After Ollie was born, five months after our little Sacramento wedding, attended almost exclusively by Dwight's relatives, I believed there was nothing more I would ask for out of life than to be the mother to this child, to be part of this family. My mother-in-law had written my birthdate in a book she kept ("because you're a McCabe now," she told me). There was a place on the page to record things like dress size, favorite color—for future present-giving, presumably. I made sure to write down her birthday, too, and called her Mom, which wasn't difficult, not having called anybody else that before, including the woman who'd given birth to me.

By the time Ollie was six months old, Dwight had gotten a promotion at his firm, and not having had any kind of career before the baby, I was happy staying home—taking endless photographs of our son from every conceivable angle, engaged in every one of our small set of routines. (The walk. The bath. Playtime on the floor. Diaper change. Another walk. Another diaper change. Another playtime.) The ordinariness of my life now actually thrilled me. It wasn't that interesting to anyone else, probably, but I discovered I was really good at something, which was being my son's mother.

By this point, I had learned how to steer clear of my husband's temper, or shut it out with a glass of wine. And in an odd way, the times when Dwight wasn't angry were even more disturbing than the times he yelled, because at least when he was angry, the emotions he expressed felt real. It was his easygoing salesman's manner that left me feeling most alone. I'd hear him on the phone with one of his clients, or even one of his brothers in Sacramento, and realize with a chill that his tone of voice never changed. Even as he was delivering the news that a couple had been turned down for a loan, he adopted the identical upbeat tone. ("We'll

find you another package," he'd say. "It's all good.")
He was no different with me. Or with his parents. Even
with our son.

I was printing photographs I'd taken at a family
gathering when it struck me that in every image my
husband wore an identical expression. When he came
home from work, everything he said to me sounded
like something he'd heard on television. My marriage
had started to feel hollow. I didn't really know the man
I was married to. He certainly didn't know me. I doubt
he wanted to.

But I had fallen in love with our son. I couldn't
imagine being away from him.

Maybe it was that having Ollie revealed to me—for
the first time, I think—what real love felt like. It came
to me that what I had fallen in love with wasn't really
this man, but the picture of the life that being with
him made possible, and that made me as responsible as
Dwight was for the failure of our marriage. We probably didn't have much in common, if anything, when
you got down to it. I was just good at making pictures.
Inside the frame of my viewfinder. In life.

I was thirty-four—our son age two—when Dwight
came home from work one day to say he had some
news to deliver. He'd fallen in love with a woman he
met at his brokerage firm. He felt badly about this,

he said, but he and Cheri were soul mates. Even as he delivered this information, there was a bland predictability to his delivery: like a TV anchorman reporting on an earthquake somewhere, or the weather person predicting rain for an upcoming holiday weekend. "I wish it could have been different," he said to me, "but it is what it is. Life's funny that way."

As swiftly as Dwight had entered my life, he departed from it. His exit, whose warning signals I had missed, had evidently been in the works for a while, because he had moved out by that weekend.

By the time Dwight left, I had no illusions about our marriage anymore. The greater shock, probably, was discovering the effect of Dwight's change of heart on my relationship with his family. My family, too, as I had started to see them. Only it turned out they weren't. And most of all, the shock at realizing how easily I could be fooled, how poor my instincts were for spotting a fraud.

When I first learned the news, I actually called up Dwight's mother, imagining that she might convince her son to give our marriage another try. For Ollie's sake, at least. Short of that, she would comfort me.

"I hate to say this, Helen," my mother-in-law told me. "But we've all seen this coming for a while now. You can't leave your hubby feeling like an also-ran and then expect him not to notice if someone comes along and starts treating him like he's special again. No wonder he was getting short-tempered."

There were no more invitations to holiday dinners. Ollie paid visits to the relatives, but only with his father now, never with me.

My mother, Kay, was remarried by this point—living in Florida with a man named Freddie, who generally poured his first cocktail around 11:00 A.M. and kept going, which probably made her feel better about her own affection for gin and tonics. In the early years after Ollie was born, I'd chosen to spend Christmas with my husband's family rather than subjecting ourselves to the inevitable drunken nights and hangovers, but after Dwight left I made the trip to Daytona Beach to spend the holiday with her, out of some thin hope that maybe we'd pull off some kind of family closeness that had eluded us all those years. I even brought a bunch of my photographs along, hoping Kay might take an interest. She flipped through the images in my portfolio as if she were at the beauty parlor, reading an issue of *People* magazine. With less interest, probably. My son, who had always begged for a dog of his own, spent most of his time playing with my mother's shih tzu.

Two days into our visit, I returned to the condo after a trip to the store to find Kay, well into her third or fourth drink, from the looks of things, watching a video of a Quentin Tarantino movie, my son propped up on the sofa next to her, clutching his blanket.

When I told her this wasn't the kind of stuff I wanted Ollie to be seeing, she said, "You know where the door is."

8.

Maybe there was a family legacy here. If so, it was not a good one.

I had learned long ago that alcohol could help me feel relaxed and offer a certain short-lived comfort in a moment where little real comfort existed. But it was not until the long, chilly winter after my husband told me about Cheri and moved out that I got into my more serious drinking.

I always waited until Ollie went to bed, and in the beginning I only let myself have one glass. I didn't get drunk, but I liked how the wine took the edge off my day, the slightly fuzzy way things looked if I'd sipped a little cabernet. I felt looser, less anxious, and if the alcohol failed to take away the sadness, it made the feeling blurrier, the pain more of a dull ache than a sharp stab. This left me inclined to pour a second glass, and after I'd had a second glass, pouring a third was easy. Some nights I finished the entire bottle.

Often now I fell asleep on the couch with the glass on the floor beside me. When I got up, I'd have a headache, though I learned to avoid those by taking a Tylenol the night before.

I didn't drink during the day. Never when Ollie was awake. Unlike my mother, I was going to make sure my son had no doubt he was the most important thing in my life, and more than anything, I wanted him to feel he was safe with me.

With just the two of us there, it felt okay to eat our dinners on a tray table watching movies—not just Disney and cartoons, but Charlie Chaplin and Laurel and Hardy, whom he loved—or on the floor with a picnic blanket. Our dining room table was covered with art supplies and science experiments, and there were piles of library books around, and costumes we made from stuff we found at the Goodwill. Sometimes we went on photography missions—not to the usual places like the zoo or the beach, but a junkyard or a skate park or a plant nursery or his favorite, the pet store, to check out the puppies and pick which one we'd choose if they allowed dogs at our apartment complex. On weekends we cooked together—pasta or tacos, homemade pizza. But if we felt like it we might just make a big bowl of popcorn with butter and call that dinner. We'd curl up on my bed with blankets while I read to him—fantasy mostly, or our book of Shel Silverstein poems—and if he fell asleep, I'd let him stay there.

At first I only drank on the bad nights—if Kay had called up for one of her rare check-ins from Florida, or if my car had broken down and the bill wiped out my savings account. The night I learned the news (conveyed by our son) that his dad's wife, Cheri, was having a baby (and later, when the news came of her birth) I could feel that bottle calling to me.

I waited until I'd read Ollie his book and turned off the light. Then I took my bottle down from the top shelf of the cupboard. Peeling off the foil, turning the corkscrew, I could already feel the warm, comforting fog that first glass would produce in me. In the absence of an actual man in my life, the wine served almost like a companion.

Ollie was a few months shy of his fifth birthday when the big trouble happened. It was one of those nights—increasingly common now—that I'd polished off a whole bottle. I was half asleep on the couch, but one sound I never missed was my son's voice. He was calling out to me.

Ollie lay in bed holding his right side and groaning. Wine or no wine, I knew the story with an inflamed appendix. You had to get it out. I carried Ollie to the car and laid him in the seat next to me with a blanket. Buckled him in.

We were just a few minutes from the hospital when I saw the blue light flashing. My first thought: I'd been speeding. Once the policeman saw Ollie and heard where we were headed, he'd understand.

But the policeman wanted me to get out of the car.

"Let me see you walk a straight line," he said.

"I have to get my son to the hospital," I told him. "He's got appendicitis."

"You aren't driving this kid anywhere," he said. "If your boy's sick, I'm calling an ambulance."

He had me count backward from one hundred. He held a finger in front of my face and asked me to follow its movement back and forth with just my eyes. From the front seat, I could hear Ollie calling to me and moaning.

The ambulance pulled up a couple of minutes later. By this point the police officer had put me in handcuffs. As awful as this felt, worse was knowing my son was in pain and I couldn't be with him. Even hurting as he was, Ollie had seen the policeman snap the cuffs on my wrists.

Ollie knew about police from the movies, mostly, where the people they caught had usually done something terrible. "My mom's not a bad guy," he said. Sick as he was, and holding his belly, he was crying louder now, not only from the pain. The last thing I saw as they pushed me in the backseat of the police cruiser was Ollie lying flat on the stretcher as they slid it into the back of the ambulance and closed the doors. On the way to the station, the police officer asked for the phone number of my son's father.

So it was Dwight who was there for the surgery, and afterward, when our son woke up. His mother, my former mother-in-law, called me later. "I thank God he was looking out for Oliver, Helen," she said. "Because clearly, you weren't."

Four days later—with Ollie home again, while I was waiting for the suspension of my license to go into effect—I received the letter from a lawyer reporting my ex-husband's intention to file for full custody of our son. "Evidence of unfit motherhood," said the complaint.

A guardian *ad litem* was appointed to investigate— which meant Ollie had to be interviewed multiple times. As little as I could afford it, I hired a lawyer—a move that put me more than thirty thousand dollars in debt. I bought a suit for the day we went to court—the most conservative outfit I could find at the consignment store. Dwight arrived with my former in-laws and half a dozen other relatives whose charades teams I once played on, along with Cheri, heavily pregnant by this time. Greeting me outside the courtroom, my lawyer said he was optimistic. Since this was my first offense, the judge should allow Ollie to continue living with me, with weekend visits to his father.

The courtroom was hot that day. I could feel the sweat beading up under the jacket of my suit, the panty hose cutting into my waist. I'd purchased the wrong size because I hadn't bought a pair in years. Each of the lawyers spoke, though I was finding it hard to focus. I tried to pretend I was a courtroom photographer, imagined I was in this room to take pictures of these characters, as if it were just a job that brought me here and not my whole life as a parent that hung in the balance.

The guardian *ad litem* spoke first. In the report she presented to the court, she said it appeared to her that though my ex-husband expressed his desire to raise Ollie, she had the strong impression that it was actually his parents, more than he, who were pushing for custody. Oliver indicated that his father yelled at him a lot, and his stepmother apparently let him play video games all day when his dad was playing golf. Oliver's primary attachment was most definitely his bond with me, the guardian said. She went on to testify that if I made the commitment to attend regular AA meetings and counseling she had no doubt I could be a responsible parent. Her recommendation was that our son remain with me as the primary custodial parent, with regular visitation granted to Oliver's father.

Then it was time for the judge to speak, and from the moment he began I knew I was in trouble.

"It may be true that the mother has good intentions to do right by her son," he said. "I can only hope that she does. But she has already made it abundantly clear by her actions to date that she is sufficiently controlled by her addiction to alcohol as to remain incapable of acting on her good intentions. She placed her son's life in jeopardy. And not just the life of her son, but that of any citizen out on the roads."

He launched into a speech about drunk drivers then, complete with statistics. Though I was cold sober, of course—I hadn't had a drink since the night of my arrest—the room seemed to be spinning.

"I will step outside my traditional judicial role in this matter," the judge said, looking directly at me, "to convey a personal story here. Four years ago my wife of thirty-four years was killed by a drunk driver."

I looked at my lawyer. Wasn't this a moment when he was supposed to stand up and object? Evidently not.

"I considered long and hard," the judge continued, "whether my own personal loss required me to recuse myself from this case, but ultimately concluded just the opposite. My experience of the consequences of vehicular homicide, and the fact that the mother facing the court today could easily have taken a life, or even several lives, the night she got behind the wheel under the influence, serves to inform me as to where prudent judgment and justice may be found in a case such as this one."

There was more, but I had trouble taking it all in. Only the final words.

"I cannot allow a mother who places her son's life at risk to remain his custodial parent, and therefore award full custody to the father and his new wife, who have shown the ability to provide what the mother has not: a safe and stable home for their son."

I could feel the walls of the courtroom pressing in around me then, and my lungs struggling for breath. My lawyer touched my shoulder. Somewhere on the other side of the courtroom, I heard a familiar voice saying "Praise the Lord" and realized it was my former mother-in-law. Neither she nor any of the other members of Dwight's family present that day spoke to me as we left the courtroom. That day or ever again.

I was granted weekend visitation, conditional on my ex-husband's approval. No driving. No overnights.

Parenting classes were required. Also therapy. For me and for my son, who had experienced the trauma of living with an alcoholic parent.

When the judge was done speaking and the proceedings adjourned, I laid my head on the table. I didn't want to look up, to see the small, tight smile of my ex-husband's current wife, Cheri, as she sat there like a madonna, with her hands circling her belly, or the look of regret on the face of my lawyer, which may have had less to do with concern for me than the realization that it might be a while before he collected his fee.

I had already lost my driver's license; it was suspended for eighteen months. This meant I also lost my job. The only way I could get to Walnut Creek to see Ollie would be if I rode the bus and BART—as well as a taxi—or found someone to drive me.

At AA—where I attended meetings regularly, thanks to the kindness of my fellow AA members, who picked me up to bring me there—I learned plenty about the struggle most people have who've depended on alcohol to get them through the nights, or the days. For me, the decision to quit, and the ability to hold to it, came with stunning swiftness. Giving up wine was nothing compared to the other loss, the real one. My son.

9.

Outside of AA, I tried not to speak of what had happened. But that afternoon in the Havillands' sunroom on Folger Lane, with Ava across from me in her chair and the smell of gardenias from the cut-glass bowl on the table, and the beautiful cheese, and one of the dogs licking my ankle, it all came out. I hadn't planned on saying any of this. But by the time I left that afternoon—the sun low on the horizon, Ava pressing into my hands a jar of homemade soup and a sweater she said she never wore that was just my color, and reminding me that we were on for dinner that Friday at a certain Italian restaurant she and Swift loved—I had told her everything. My childhood. My marriage. The loss of my son. My brief, uncomfortable visits to his father's house to see him, and the fact that more and

more when I went there now, Ollie seemed aloof and
distant.

"I can't even think about another relationship at
the moment," I told Ava. "All I care about right now
is getting Ollie back with me. I know I need to hire
a lawyer, but I haven't even paid off the one I had
before."

"Things are going to improve," she told me. "When
I get to work on a problem, nothing stops me."

The floodgates opened that day. Ava was a great
listener.

I described to her the day my son moved out of our
apartment. I didn't want Ollie to see me crying when
we packed up his room, but when Dwight came to take
him away—greeting our son in the manner of a game
show host, as usual—I knew it was going to be impossible not to let him see how torn up I was.

"I'll see you before you know it," I told Ollie, standing on the sidewalk next to my ex-husband's car. Like
it was no big deal that my son's clothes, along with his
Legos and his rock collection and his stuffed pig, were
now boxed up in the trunk. Ollie himself sat stiffly in
the backseat with his hamster cage on his lap (his father's one concession: he could bring Buddy to Walnut
Creek) and his head turned aside in a way that made
me know he was sucking his thumb.

The court had ruled that I could see Ollie for six hours every other Saturday, contingent on his father's approval and my commitment to stay sober—but even if I'd had a license there was no way I could bring Ollie over to my apartment for those few hours and still get him back to Walnut Creek by dinnertime, and I wasn't allowed to keep him with me overnight. Ollie—the boy who used to sleep pressed up against me all night long, with his legs draped over mine and a piece of my hair wrapped around his finger—had become a person I saw now and then, if his father allowed it.

In the early days after Dwight had taken him to live in Walnut Creek, Ollie had clung to me when I went there for visits and begged to come home with me when I left, but lately, when I arrived at his father's house, he barely spoke to me.

I barely remember those early days without Ollie. I moved to a smaller apartment in Redwood City—very dark, in a sketchy neighborhood, but it was cheaper and closer to public transportation. I went to AA meetings every night, getting rides from my sponsor. I knit sweaters for my son that he probably never wore. I took portraits of other people's children—riding the bus to jobs, or sometimes, when I was really strapped, taking a taxi. I watched stupid television shows: *American Idol, Survivor, The Osbournes.* I went to the movies a lot.

I had one friend. I'd met Alice at a private party where I'd been hired to help out—work I'd taken on the side, in the early days after my divorce, back when Ollie still lived with me. Weekends when he was away with his father, I'd take on catering jobs to pick up extra money for the vacation I was planning for the two of us to see the dinosaur flats in Montana that we'd studied pictures of in *National Geographic*.

Alice was a few years older than me, also divorced (so long, she said, she'd forgotten what her husband looked like; so long, she said, there was probably moss growing inside her vagina, or barnacles. That was the way Alice talked).

Alice had a daughter in college, Becca, who hardly ever came home anymore. Becca's main presence in Alice's life seemed to take the form of large credit card bills that showed up in her mother's mailbox on a monthly basis for shoes and manicures and weekend trips with her friends, while Alice herself rented a room out in her house to a retired teacher (male, zero romantic prospect) and economized by cooking one stew in the Crock-Pot that lasted through most of the week, when stretched with rice.

In the old days, before I'd lost custody of my son, my friend used to come over for pizza nights, and the three of us—me, Ollie, and Alice—would play Monopoly or the Memory Game or pile up pillows on the couch and watch old movies or try to match Michael Jackson's dance moves in the "Thriller" video. After Ollie left, Alice and I used to go out to the movies together at least once a week, nights when we weren't catering some event, if I'd gotten my AA meeting in during the daytime hours. We'd buy a large tub of popcorn—buttered—and, for Alice, a box of Raisinets. Alice had pretty much given up on men some time back and no longer made any effort to stay in shape. She was always a big-boned person—tall, and never remotely interested in exercise or hiking—but over the six years I'd known her she'd probably gone from a size ten to a sixteen.

"I'm going to starve myself, just for the thrill of getting to have some idiot with a comb-over feel me up?" she said. "I'd rather have the butter."

She was one of those friends with whom not all that much that's exciting ever happens. She had a tough, hard edge to her, but she was funny and I knew she had a kind heart. I could trust her. After our movie, we'd go out for a drink together at a bar close to the theater—wine for her, club soda for me—and make it last a couple of hours. One time, two men had stopped by our table and asked to join us. There had been nothing particularly memorable about them, but they didn't look like total losers either, and if it had been up to me I would have said okay, but Alice had shaken her head.

"So, girls," one of them said, already sliding into our booth. "What do you say we buy you two a drink?"

I might have let it happen, but not Alice. "Why don't you save your money," she said, "and go buy some Listerine?"

That was it for our suitors, naturally. They probably hadn't expected that a couple of women like Alice and me—who weren't such prizes ourselves—would be that picky. But I had loved this about Alice: the way, unlike so many single women I knew, she never dropped a friend because a more promising prospect might present itself. Not that any such prospects had shown up for either of us, but that would be her policy, and I knew it.

Back before Ava, Alice and I used to have our coffee together over the phone almost every morning, and we checked in most nights, too. There was seldom much news to report, given the fact that we spoke every day, but it felt less lonely, having that voice on the other end of the telephone.

"I'm thinking about getting new blinds," she'd tell me. Did I think venetian blinds were horrible?

I talked a lot in those days about the custody mess— endlessly revisiting the scene in the courtroom that day, wishing I'd had a better lawyer, wishing I could get another chance. I had paid a visit to a women's social service group in San Mateo to look into legal aid lawyers, but they couldn't help me, and the one lawyer I'd consulted wanted a ten-thousand-dollar retainer up front.

Most often, now, when I went to see Ollie, he'd be in his room, on the computer. Dwight was usually off playing golf, or attending real estate open houses and handing out his card to potential clients. I knew the drill. When he came home, Ollie reported, he complained if there were toys on the floor. Dwight liked things tidy. I knew that part, too. And the anger that came if things didn't go his way.

"Bastard," Alice would say, speaking of Dwight. It wasn't the kind of talk that got you anywhere, but it felt good having someone on my side.

I'd make an effort to talk with Alice about other things besides the loss of my son, but it was hard thinking what those might be. I'd mention that I had a dentist appointment; she'd tell me about Becca's plan to go to Mexico on her spring break.

It was the kind of thing a person said to her partner, if they were married. The day-to-day. (Though later, once I got to know the Havillands, I could never picture Ava talking this way to Swift, or Swift to Ava, and the fact that this was so made me newly conscious of how ordinary and vapid my own life was. Or had been.) But as unexceptional as our exchanges might have been, Alice was a reliable constant in those dark days. The only one, probably, and she was loyal as the day is long, as loyal as a dog, she used to say. Times when I'd get to thinking about Ollie—how it sometimes felt as if he didn't even know me anymore—the number I'd call would be Alice's.

10.

After Ollie moved to Walnut Creek, I'd put into a closet all the things that reminded me of what we used to do together: the step stool he'd used so he could work next to me at the kitchen counter, his chalkboard easel, the art supplies I'd kept spread out on our table, his Spider-Man cape. Without my son around there was no reason to keep the aquarium, or to put funny sayings up on the refrigerator spelled out in alphabet magnets, or to play the old-timey music he loved that we used to dance to in the kitchen. When the CD player broke, I didn't get a new one.

I had an old digital camera that I let him use. One day I made the mistake of looking through the pictures we'd taken together—pictures Ollie had taken of his hamster, and his old room, and a cake we'd made where I'd let him squirt every color of frosting on the top. I never picked up that camera again.

Knowing his father's position on pets—that they made a mess and cost a lot in vet bills—Ollie had given up lobbying for a puppy. He got to have his hamster, Buddy, but that wasn't the same. Neither was the robot dog his stepmother had presented him with, which she claimed to have all of the good qualities of a dog without the trouble. All you had to do was buy new batteries now and then.

My son's life was filled with technology now. Every time I called his father's house to talk with Ollie, he seemed to be immersed in some video game. To the extent that he had a life beyond the computer, it was playing out in his new town now—school events, mostly. It was a worry to me that apart from those, and the occasional birthday party, I never got the sense that Ollie had friends.

"Cheri doesn't like having kids come over," he told me once. "She says we make too much noise and wake the baby." This was Jared, Ollie's half brother, born not long after Dwight gained custody of our son. Young as he was, Ollie had noted, early on, his stepmother's early preference for the baby. "She talks to me in this voice, like the good witch in *Wizard of Oz*," Ollie had said. He made a sound that resembled laughter but wasn't.

And then there were the Sacramento relatives—the grandparents and all those uncles and his aunt and cousins, one of whom always seemed to be having a birthday or graduation or a baby shower that would invariably be celebrated on a Saturday. How was I supposed to tell my son he couldn't be part of that? What did I have to offer that could even compete?

I made the trip to Walnut Creek when I could. Every other Saturday morning, if Ollie was free, Alice would drive me over so I could take him out. We'd visit the park and go for Mexican food or pizza afterward. Sometimes she joined us, sometimes she'd sit in the car with a book, waiting for me.

The truth is, Ollie never wanted to stay long at the park. He was getting too old for the jungle gym. We went bowling sometimes, but he mostly rolled gutter balls and got frustrated about that. "I like PlayStation better," he'd said. He'd just gotten this new NASCAR game.

What I longed for, more than anything, was time with my son that wasn't scheduled, meals that didn't take place in restaurants, times together that didn't have to be organized around some activity. I missed ordinary life: hanging out on the couch, sitting on the front step reading together, not even speaking sometimes, just driving to the supermarket with him, going on our photography shoots, buying him sneakers, look-ing in the rearview mirror and catching sight of his face. I had become a bowling alley mother, a woman who had the TGI Fridays menu memorized. I didn't do my son's laundry anymore, or get to dry him off when he got out of the tub. One day, when I took him swim-ming (using a Holiday Inn pool pass clipped from the newspaper), and I started helping him into his trunks, it occurred to me that I hadn't seen his small naked body in more than a year. But Ollie pushed me away. "I like to be private," he'd said.

I knew his father yelled at him a lot, but Ollie didn't talk about it. Or much else that was going on in his life. The absence of friends. The baby who seemed to occupy all his stepmother's attention. Back when he was five—after the divorce but before I lost him—we used to spend Sunday mornings taking pictures to-gether, but after he moved to his father's house he never wanted to do that anymore. Or anything else. Over the months—and then a whole year, and then two—it was as if Ollie were in some little boat and I was standing on the shore, watching him drift out to sea. Farther and farther away from me.

One day, not long after I'd gotten my license back, I pulled up to the house and didn't even recognize my son until he got close to the car. His face had that uneasy hangdog expression he wore almost all the time now, and when he caught sight of me, it didn't change. His father and stepmother had bought him new clothes, of a style I never would have chosen for him—shirts with sayings on them like LITTLE TROU-BLEMAKER and (from my ex-mother-in-law, evidently) MY GRANDMOTHER WENT TO LAS VEGAS AND ALL SHE BROUGHT ME WAS THIS STUPID SHIRT, and another one that suggested he must have been enrolled at some point in Vacation Bible School. They'd cut his hair—a bowl cut, with a wide margin of skin shaved clean around his ears. For some reason, it was that more than anything—the tender pink skin that left his ears looking even bigger and goofier than normal—that got to me. The haircut made Ollie look so small and vulnerable. Exposed.

"Do you like it?" he asked. By this point my son never confided in me about anything anymore, but he spoke to me in a way that made me know he was miserable about how he looked, and he was right.

"It'll grow," I said.

Even though I had my license back, Ollie never came over to my place—the new, dark apartment in Redwood City. My visitation time was too short, and even if we might have worked that out, Ollie didn't want to come over anymore. I knew he was mad at me for letting the whole mess happen in the first place and for my inability to fix it.

And he was different now, too. Sometimes, hearing Ollie talk, I would look across the table at him, at whatever chain restaurant we were eating at that night, and it occurred to me that the way he was speaking, the wary look in his eyes and his recently acquired habit of avoiding my gaze—looking at me sideways from under his long, feminine lashes—was not so different from how he'd looked on those awful visits to Florida to see my mother and her husband. I was that much of a stranger. Worse than that, even. An object of suspicion.

By this point I had gotten a job as a photographer for a company that took those school portraits of children that parents buy in packages for the relatives (one eight-by-ten glossy, two five-by-sevens, and a dozen wallet size). I had learned from working in this business for a while that parents tended to buy these photo packages out of some kind of weird guilt mixed with superstition, because their child might feel unloved if everybody else's parents had filled out the order form and sent in their money and theirs didn't, and because it almost seemed like bad luck if you didn't send in the check. My company deleted the files. And who wanted to picture the image of their child's smiling face—bangs recently cut, cowlick slicked down, front teeth missing, perhaps—ending up in their laptop trash?

Shooting three hundred children in a day for Happy Days Portraits, Inc.—times when I was lucky enough to get the work—had not been my original goal when I started studying photography. But I owed thirty-four thousand dollars to my divorce lawyer at this point, along with a few thousand dollars in credit card debt, not to mention my crazily high car insurance premiums. I needed the money badly, though the reasons for working as much as I did at the time went deeper. There was nothing harder or sadder to me than being alone with my thoughts, with enough free time to take in what a mess my life had become, how far away I'd gotten from the dreams of my younger days. I took whatever work I found.

My neighbors in my apartment complex were a young couple with a three-year-old and infant twins on one side, and an old man named Gerry who kept the television on all day and most of the night on the other. Gerry favored Fox News and sometimes liked to talk back to the set, which meant I might be reading, or trying to have a conversation with my son on the phone, and I'd hear him call out, "Damned liberals! Shoot 'em all, that's what I say." Then the twins might pipe up, or their mother, Carol, would start crying, and a minute later I'd hear the door slam, meaning her husband, Victor, had evidently had enough. Then more tears from Carol. Then Gerry again. "That's telling 'em!"

It never worked very well anyway, trying to carry on a conversation with Ollie on the phone. When I'd try to get him to talk about his day, what had happened at school, to tell me about a friend or his science project, there was a flatness to his voice. His responses, when I asked him a question, were monosyllabic, and I could feel his restlessness as he held the receiver. I'd hear Dwight and Cheri's baby in the background, or the television. Sometimes I could tell he was sitting at the computer while we spoke, the sound of zapping superheroes and monsters giving him away. *Beep beep beep. Crunch.*

"What game are you playing?"

"Nothing."

"What's Mr. Rettstadt been teaching you lately?"

"Poop."

"I miss you so much, Ollie."

Silence. Whatever he felt about this, there were no words for it in his vocabulary.

Then came the sound of my neighbors' twins again, or Glenn Beck or Rush Limbaugh spouting off.

In the old days, before the custody mess, Ollie might have actually found all the hubbub funny. We would have curled up on the couch with our Laurel and Hardy, and when Gerry would yell something in response to some report he'd seen on the television, we would have just laughed. Then Ollie would have pretended he was Gerry, shaking his fist at the TV, calling out, "That's telling them, Rush!"

Now, on nights when I was home alone, when the neighbors' voices filled my small dark living room—the crying babies, the angry man, the smell of take-out fried chicken seeping through the drywall—I just sat there, taking it in. I went to a lot of meetings, but I never stayed around for coffee hour. Most evenings, I'd call Alice, not that there was much to report. I edited my photographs from that day and went to bed early.

11.

Given how badly my life was going at this point, I couldn't muster much enthusiasm for finding a man. All I really cared about was staying sober and getting my son back. My social life mostly consisted of attending AA meetings. So when I signed up for Match. com, it was a distraction more than anything else.

They required you to put together a profile, of course. After creating a couple of versions of my story for the site, featuring a glamorous made-up history (something I was always good at), I opted to tell the truth—minus the DUI and the custody proceedings. Under "Hobbies" I mentioned photography and cycling, though I hadn't taken a photograph of anything besides other people's children for more than a year, and my bike was gathering dust. I gave my real age and noted that I had a child, though if that didn't totally scare a person off, and he read the rest of my profile, he would have learned that my son didn't live with me. For my profile picture I had not chosen—as so many appeared to have done—an image from my twenties, or a glamour shot of me wearing a cocktail dress or a pair of tight jeans and a come-hither look. I took my own picture, using a timer, with my camera set up on a tripod, in the kitchenette of my apartment, under fluorescent light.

After posting the bad self-portrait, I decided to include a couple of other images—not of myself, but pictures I'd taken on long-ago photography outings with Ollie of places I loved around the Bay Area: the Russian River, the Marin Headlands, Half Moon Bay. There was one picture, too, that had been taken by my ex-husband, of my son and me sitting in a booth at a diner together in Point Reyes after a long hike in the elk preserve. I included that one just because I usually looked so serious in pictures, and in this one I was actually laughing.

My online profile (under the moniker "Shuttergirl") sounded so boring I couldn't imagine anyone being interested. I posted it anyway, and found myself unexpectedly drawn into the process. Nights now, if I wasn't at the movies with Alice, at a meeting, or working a catering job, I'd be online, scrolling through my Match. com messages.

The results seldom yielded anything promising. Still I kept clicking through the profiles and the daily trickle of responses.

Hambone: "I saw your picture and you seem like a nice person. I'm looking for a friendly, kind-hearted woman who enjoys fishing and gospel music. I have what you might call the 'teddy bear' type of build, but with the right gal to inspire me, I plan to enroll in Weight Watchers."

Tantra4U: "My philosophy is that people should not be limited in their experience or tied down to a single person. I'm looking for an open relationship, without the restrictions society places on us that only limit our full potential to express our complete sexual identity. How about you?"

PeppyGramps: "Don't let my age discourage you from writing back." (The author of this message admitted to being seventy-four.) "I've got plenty of pep in my step, not to mention a drawer full of pharmaceuticals."

The vast majority of messages I left unanswered, but now and then—to my friend Alice's increasing chagrin—I'd write back to one of the men who had written to me, in which case there would probably be a follow-up telephone conversation. Most of the time I could tell in the first sixty seconds that the person on the other end of the line was not for me, but it wasn't always easy ending the conversation. Sometimes I just put it out there: "I don't think we're a match." Once, when I did that, a three-page response showed up in my inbox. The names its author called me shouldn't have bothered me, given that we'd never actually met, but even the words of strangers had a disconcerting power to unnerve me.

"Man-eating cunt," he wrote. (The guy called himself "Rainbow-Seeker.") "I know your type. Nobody's ever good enough for you. I wasn't going to mention this before, but it looks like you could stand to lose a few pounds, honey. Not to mention, you're no spring chicken. What's the story on your kid, anyway? What kind of mother doesn't live with her kid?"

Sometimes the men who wrote to me invaded my dreams. Most disconcerting was when the women did—the ex-wives they spent so much time talking about, years after the divorce. When this happened, I reflected that I'd probably like their ex-wives better than I liked them. I imagined what my ex-husband—living out in Walnut Creek with his new wife and baby son—would say about me if he were on a dating site. Or what he said about me to Cheri. Maybe even to Ollie.

She has a drinking problem. It's sad how substance abuse can ruin a person's life. She came from a screwed-up family, of course. If you met her mother, you'd understand why she's a mess.

He had a point. With the exception of Ollie, I didn't have a single relative I really loved. For that brief period of my marriage, I had believed myself to be part of a big, happy family. Then they were gone, and with them went my child. Besides my one friend, I was alone in the world.

That's how I felt when I met the Havillands.

12.

A couple of days after meeting Ava at that gallery that first time, Alice had called me up. "Who was that person you were talking to, in the wheelchair?" she said.

"Ava's an art collector," I told her. "She invited me over to see her collection."

"And you're going?" she said. I didn't tell her I already had.

"She has these original prints of some famous photographs of prostitutes," I told her. "She said I reminded her of one."

"Oh, great."

"She wanted to hear about my photography."

"Did she invite any of the retarded people over, too?" Alice said. There was that old bitterness to her voice. In the past it hadn't bothered me, but now it did. She almost sounded jealous.

"Developmentally disabled, not retarded," I said. "But no."

"Well, that's quite an invitation then."

"She probably just felt sorry for me," I said. "More than likely I'll never hear from her again." Only I would, I knew. I had written the date on my calendar the minute I got home, not that there was a chance I'd forget it. Dinner at Vinny's with Swift and Ava, that Friday night. Now, here I was, lying.

"I thought we were supposed to get together yesterday," Alice said. She didn't say more, but this was when I realized I'd forgotten. We'd planned to see the new Coen brothers movie.

"Oh, no," I said. "Things were crazy at work. I'll call you to reschedule as soon as everything quiets down."

"Sure," Alice said, but I knew from her tone she wasn't buying my excuse. My job was boring, but never crazy. "Just let me know when it's a good time."

But I didn't call her. And the next time Alice asked me to go to the movies with her, I said I was busy. Ava and Swift had invited me to have dinner with them at a different restaurant. Mediterranean, this time. The time after that, when Alice called to suggest we catch a movie together, I said no. The Havillands hadn't invited me anyplace, but I hoped they would. And that was enough.

"I guess you're one of the popular girls now," Alice said.

13.

"We might want to do something about your wardrobe," Ava said. It was a Saturday morning, and I had just shown up at Folger Lane to work on the photo project. Estella had already poured me a smoothie and set a carrot muffin on a plate for me, still warm from the oven. Swift was heading out to his qigong class. "Don't let her give you a hard time," he called out to me. "I happen to like sweatpants."

Even when she wasn't going anywhere, Ava always wore something interesting. That day it was a hand-painted silk blouse and a pair of linen pants with a silver necklace I'd never seen before, and earrings to match.

"I just threw these on because they were handy," I told her. I was wearing a faded T-shirt and stretched-out pants.

"It doesn't matter if all you're doing is passing appetizer trays, or even cleaning toilets," Ava said—not that she ever spent any time doing the latter. "It just makes you feel better when you've got a wonderful outfit on."

"I guess I never think about clothes much anymore," I told her. This wasn't completely accurate. I loved nice clothes. I just didn't own any.

"It's about valuing yourself, Helen," Ava said. "And letting the world know that's the kind of person you are."

Despite the number of times I'd been to their house, I'd never been upstairs, but now she took me there in her special elevator. "It's time you paid a visit to my closet," she said.

Ava's closet was the size of my whole apartment, more or less. One wall held the shoes. (Never mind that they never saw wear.) She must have owned a hundred pairs, which were arranged—thanks to Estella, no doubt—by color, with a row of handmade cowboy boots lined up along the floor. Then there was the scarf and hat wall, and the purses. One whole rack held nothing but sweaters in every shade of cashmere but yellow. Ava hated yellow. Then there were the silk blouses, and the Indian tunics, and the floaty silk pants she favored because they concealed how thin her legs were, and the long dresses. She owned more basic clothes, too—though of only the highest quality. This was the section she studied, for me.

"We need to find you some good black pants," she said. "That's a given. Black pants are a foundation of everything. You can build from there, but the pants are the starting point. Sort of like sexual attraction in a relationship. If you don't have that, it doesn't matter what other stuff you layer on top."

She pulled a pair of crisp black linen trousers from a hanger and held them out to me. "We're about the same size," she said. She pulled one of the cashmere sweaters off the rack then—a shade of blue somewhere between a robin's egg and the sky, and a scarf, mostly mauve and green, with a glittery blue thread running through it, unlike anything I'd ever worn or ever imagined wearing. She picked out everything, even stockings. Then a skirt—black leather—and a pair of boots, also black, to go with it.

"I couldn't take this," I told her, catching sight of the label and fingering the leather, the softest kid.

"Of course you can," she said, almost impatient. "This stuff is just hanging here. I'd love to see you put it to use."

There was more: a wrap dress ("a little conservative, but you might go on a date with some investment banker type someday") and another dress on the totally opposite end of the spectrum—short skirt, plunging neckline, draped to hug the body.

"One thing about this one," she said. "You can't wear anything underneath it. Panty lines."

I thought she'd probably leave me to try the clothes on by myself then, but she sat there waiting.

"Let's see," she said.

I felt a little odd, but I pulled my T-shirt over my head.

"Oh my god, your bra," she said. "You're way more buxom than me, so I can't help you with that one. But we definitely need to pay a visit to Miss Elaine." This turned out to be Ava's lingerie consultant. A good bra fitter made all the difference, she told me.

I stepped out of my yoga pants.

"You have a great butt," she told me. "But I knew that already. It was the first thing Swift said about you."

I pulled the pants up and buttoned the waistband. As she had guessed, they were too long by a couple of inches, but otherwise the fit was perfect. Same with the cashmere top. I ran my hands over the sleeves, taking in the feel of the wool.

"There's nothing like cashmere against your skin," Ava said. "Well, almost nothing."

I stepped out in front of the mirror, arranging the scarf. "Try these," she said, reaching into a drawer that turned out to contain earrings. She lifted out a pair of silver hoops and a cuff to go with them.

"Amazing," she said, as she snapped the bracelet onto my wrist. "You could almost be me." I had never seen the slightest resemblance between us, but I actually knew what she meant. "Me, if I were fifteen years younger with fabulous tits."

She laughed. A long, soft trill, like water over rocks. "And ambulatory," she added.

14.

At the time I met Ava, I had been spending time—
though not a lot of it—with a man named Jeff, a
bank manager I'd met on Match.com (moniker: "EZ-
DuzIt"). He hadn't divorced his wife yet, so I knew
this was going nowhere. But more than that he showed
so little enthusiasm about me—and truthfully, I didn't
possess all that much for him, either.

I told myself it was good to have the company, and
that at least when he was around, I was less likely to
do things like writing long letters to my ex-husband
that I knew better than to send, or crying on the phone
to Alice about missing my son, and about the court-
ordered parenting classes I still had to attend twice a
week, in which we were given lists of good activities
to engage in with a child. (*Do crafts. Read out loud*

together at bedtime. Attend library story hour.) One day at my parenting class they'd passed out recipes for fun and healthy snacks—hard-boiled eggs turned into clowns, carrots and celery sticks arranged on a plate to resemble stick figures, with a cherry tomato for the head. ("Ollie and I once made potato chips from scratch!" I wanted to cry out to the parenting-skills teacher, who looked to be around twenty-one. "Every Christmas the two of us made a gingerbread house.") As if my son was ever with me long enough for me to make him snacks, anyway. "You were always a great mother," Alice had said. "You were just depressed—which was understandable. And one night you had too much to drink. That's not such an unusual story."

"It was a little more than that."

"That cop probably never would have pulled you over if your taillight wasn't out. You weren't even speeding."

Making excuses was a negative pattern, our counselor told us. The first step toward sobriety was to own our behavior.

My name is Helen. I am an alcoholic.

Jeff used to come over to my apartment on Tuesday nights. We didn't have sex that first time, but later it became our Tuesday night routine. Thai food or pizza. Followed by a ball game on TV, then bed.

The Tuesday after I met Ava, I called Jeff at work.

"I can't get together tonight," I told him.

"What happened?" he said. "You sick?"

I didn't want to see him, I said. Not that night or ever. It confirmed what I already knew about Jeff that he accepted this news with about as much expression of emotion or curiosity as he had displayed in the rest of our brief relationship. He appeared to possess no interest in identifying the reasons for my choice or challenging it. I was off the phone in less than a minute, feeling an odd combination of anger at myself for ever spending time with such a person in the first place and relief that I wasn't going to do that anymore. I wasn't going to waste any more time with people who didn't matter. If I wanted to get my son back, I had to make a better life.

I credited Ava with my decision. Although I had seen her just a few times, I felt she had revealed to me a whole other way a person might live. As unlikely as it seemed that I, too, could accomplish this, the idea of having for one's partner a person whose presence in the room transformed it for you—someone who felt that way about you—seemed the only thing worth pursuing. If you couldn't have that, you'd do better on your own.

Before I met Ava, I had pretty much come to the conclusion that my situation was hopeless and it didn't much matter what I did—nothing would ever change. Ava offered a picture of my future as filled with promise, and there seemed no more convincing proof of this than that she and Swift wanted to be part of it.

It was early December when I met Ava, and Christmas was coming up. I had attended the holiday concert at Ollie's school, picking my son out of the lineup of second graders in Santa caps singing "Frosty the Snowman." But after, there was a party at the house of a boy in his class, and I didn't want to keep him from having fun with friends, so I only got to see him long enough to give him a hug. I wanted to wait and celebrate with my son on a day when we could actually spend some time together.

I knew what he really wanted, of course, same as he had all his life: a puppy. But there was no way Dwight was going to sign off on that one. I'd seen a man demonstrating a special kind of yo-yo on the street in San Francisco, doing amazing tricks, and at the time, the idea appealed to me of giving my son—a boy who now owned a few dozen video games—a present that didn't involve electronics. But when I got it home I couldn't make the yo-yo do any of the tricks I'd witnessed on the street. I hadn't even given Ollie the toy yet, and I already knew it would lie on the floor under his bed, untouched.

I went online and picked out a simple digital camera for him, smaller and cooler looking than the one I used to let him use back in the old days. I let myself envision the two of us exploring unusual places together the way we used to, taking pictures. Later, I could teach him about lighting and Photoshop. The idea of sharing those things with my son made me excited.

The next time I visited Folger Lane, Ava said she had a new project she wanted me to help her with. This involved photographing her art collection, which included not simply the work that hung on the walls of the Havillands' home but several roomfuls of drawings and paintings and sculptural pieces Ava had acquired over the years—some, like the piece she'd bought at the gallery that first night, possessing no significant value by conventional standards, others worth tens of thousands of dollars. There'd be a carving made by some old woodsman whose work Ava had spotted once on a drive through Mendocino, and propped up against the wall next to it a Lee Friedlander print with authentication papers stating its value at twenty thousand dollars. Beautiful things, stacked in piles that spilled onto the floor, including boxes that appeared to have been received months before, still unopened. And of course, there were all the artworks already on display to be cataloged as well. The Picassos. The Eva Hesse, the Diebenkorn. Those carved bone Chinese figures I loved so much—the joyful fornicators—which I positioned on a piece of black velvet when I took the photograph so they'd be shown off to the best effect.

I told Ava I wanted to do this job for her strictly as a friend. I liked the idea of being able to give something of value to a woman capable of such vast, almost boundless generosity to others. The fact that the job would require dozens of hours presented no problem. I had too much time in those days, and I already recognized that there was no place I'd rather spend it than on Folger Lane. But Ava insisted on paying me forty dollars an hour, which was a lot more than I made as a caterer or shooting student portraits.

"You're doing me a huge favor," she said. "I've been wanting to get this stuff documented for ages, but Swift is so particular about who comes over to the house that I haven't been able to find anyone he felt good about until now. He really likes you."

I was flattered, of course. For a man like Swift to notice me at all seemed surprising. But the person whose attention and interest mattered the most was always Ava.

15.

Weeks passed. Dwight and Cheri took Ollie and their son Jared to Disneyland, and then to Sacramento, and then to Cheri's parents somewhere in Southern California, and when I asked to see my son, Dwight reminded me Ollie needed to spend time with his grandparents, who weren't getting any younger. "I hate to say it, Helen," he added, "but Ollie's just not that comfortable with you right now. We think what's best for him is a secure family environment."

This was the kind of moment that would have sent me to the cupboard to open a wine bottle, in times past. But I didn't. Now I picked up the phone and talked to Ava. Or just drove over to Folger Lane.

Though a day hardly ever went by at this point that didn't include Ava, I tried Alice once, when a new movie adaptation of a Jane Austen novel came out, and I told her there was nobody else I'd rather see it with than her, which wasn't actually true. But Ava wasn't a Jane Austen type.

We had a nice enough evening at the movie, though I realized after I got home that my conversation that night had been all about the Havillands. Alice stopped calling, and I stopped calling her. Since accepting the job for Ava I was no longer taking catering work. So we didn't see each other there, either. Christmas—a time we always used to get together to give each other presents from the Dollar Store and dress up in tacky Christmas sweaters—came and went.

Now when I thought about Alice, I felt the way a person might who's cheating on a lover. I avoided places I might run into her. One time, her name showed up on my phone. I didn't pick up.

16.

It was mid-January when I finally got to see my son. As always when I arrived at his father's house on a Saturday morning, the television was on. Ollie was sitting on the floor with a bowl of cereal, eyes locked on the screen.

"It's a beautiful day," I said. "I thought we'd get an early start."

He didn't move or look up at me. Here was this person who used to melt into my body when I picked him up, a boy who started every day flying into my bedroom like a superhero, with a pillowcase around his shoulders for a cape, calling out, "Coming in for a landing!"

Now as I wrapped my arms around him, his body stiffened. His face was blank, and his eyes had a hardness to them. I had been the person he'd loved most in the world, but I was also the one responsible for the loss of that person.

"Where are we going this time?" he said. He sounded weary. Which would it be: the bowling alley, the children's museum, the batting cages, the movies?

"I brought your present," I said, my voice, even to my own ears, sounding falsely cheerful. "I thought we could try it out." I set the box with the camera down next to him. He didn't look away from the TV.

"I went on Space Mountain," he told me. "I didn't used to be tall enough but now I am."

"It's a camera," I said, indicating the box I'd set down in front of him, that he had yet to touch.

"I've got one already."

"Not like this," I said, taking it out of the case. "This one's got some really cool features."

"Uncle Pete took me to laser tag, too," he said. "I got a robot gun. There were lights flashing all over the place. Every time you zap someone, it energizes your battery pack."

"You can even take videos with it," I told him. Ollie reached for the box, but with about as much enthusiasm as if it contained medicine or socks.

"You could bring me to Lazer World," he said. He said it like a challenge. If I loved him, I'd bring him to Lazer World.

"I could. But I thought we'd have some quiet time."

"What for?"

"We haven't seen each other for a while," I said. I didn't want to sound needy or desperate. "I just miss you, and laser tag's so noisy I can't hear anything you say."

Silence. The whole time I'd been there, Ollie hadn't taken his eyes off the TV screen.

"We could pretend we're photographers for *National Geographic* and take pictures up on Mount Diablo."

He turned toward me then, and a sad, vulnerable expression came over his face. For a moment, it was as if a seawall had begun to crack, and you could sense the water pressing up against it, spilling out and flooding everything. This was the moment when my son might have fallen into my arms and said he missed me, too. He could tell me he wanted to come home. *Home* meaning with me. He might just have let his head fall on my shoulder for once, instead of holding his neck tight and his muscles tensed. He might have let me stroke his hair. But when I reached out to him he pulled away, and the hard, angry look returned.

"Taking pictures is boring," he said. "You never take me anyplace fun."

I gave him the yo-yo then. Also a shirt with a picture of otters on the front, because he had always loved otters, and a book of Shel Silverstein poems.

"Remember these?" I said. At one point, we used to read a poem from this book every night. We'd even memorized a couple of them.

He shook his head.

"Shel Silverstein. He used to be your favorite."

If he had any memory of the two of us reciting "The Land of Happy" out loud as we lay together in the hammock on warm summer nights, or later, when I tucked him in, he showed no trace of it. That must have been some other boy, some other mother, some other planet his spaceship had departed from long ago.

Somewhere inside the body of the boy who sat here now, eyes locked on the TV screen—his shoulders tense, back arched, eyes stony, mouth closed tight—there was a child who was my son. I wanted to grab him by both shoulders and dig my fingers in. *Come out, come out.*

"Laser tag, then," I said to him.

17.

It was March. Even if they were off at the Tahoe house or at one of the philanthropic events they were always attending, I went over to Swift and Ava's house several times a week now—often enough that even Rocco, though he didn't like me, seldom actually barked when I came through the door—he just let out his low, defensive growl. I could let myself in. I had my own key, attached to a hand-carved key ring Ava had given me with a medallion depicting the face of Frida Kahlo. I felt so proud that she and Swift trusted me this way.

But more often than not, the Havillands were around when I arrived. We had our routine down: the big greeting; Ava's presentation to me of whatever interesting item she'd picked up that day that seemed perfect for me; Swift's brief, explosive appearance, followed by his disappearance, back to the pool house or to whatever bodywork session he might be engaged in that day. We all knew I was Ava's friend above all else.

We'd settle ourselves in the sunroom then, or in the garden if it was warm enough. Wonderful food appeared on the tray. Estella knew by now that when serving drinks, she should fix me only Pellegrino with a little lime in it.

By this point my work for Ava had expanded to include a variety of other jobs besides cataloging art: having invitations printed for the party of some organization on whose board Ava or Swift sat, arranging for the donation of a great many boxes of Ava's discarded clothes to a halfway house for battered women, talking with the gardener, Rodrigo, about the placement of 150 tulip bulbs that had been special-ordered from Holland.

Sometimes when I got to the house, Ava's car would be gone, and I'd know she was off with the dogs, or at her special Pilates class with a personal trainer who'd modified the Reformer routine to work for a person with spinal cord injuries. After Pilates, she often stopped by the animal shelter to check in on the dogs. Then there was the family she'd adopted in Hollister—a single mother she'd read about in the paper a few months back, whose husband had been killed fighting wildfires in Southern California, leaving her with four children. Ava went over with groceries for them once a week.

One day I stayed an unusually long time in the back room, working on the art cataloging project—almost eight hours. Sometime over the course of that long afternoon, I became aware of sounds coming from upstairs, the other wing of the house from the one in which I was working. At first I thought it was one of the dogs, but then I realized the voice was human, and there were two of them. It was Swift and Ava, upstairs in the bedroom, apparently unaware of the fact that I could hear them. Or maybe they just didn't mind if I could.

It could have been yelling, or crying, or both. But more likely, knowing those two, they were having sex.

It was the one part of their lives that remained off-limits to me, and though I didn't want to, I found myself obsessed with their sex life. It was so mysterious and, it seemed clear to me, so far beyond anything I had experienced myself, or could even envision. As close as I felt to Ava by this point, I didn't know the particulars of the injuries that had put her in her chair—didn't know at which vertebra her spine had been injured or what if anything was left in the way of feeling, and I didn't ask, same as I didn't ask how it had happened, or if there had ever been a time (how could there not?)

when she'd viewed her situation with despair. The fact that she now relied on the wheelchair never seemed to slow Ava down or restrict her. If anything, she seemed more driven because of it, though I hadn't known her before. She accomplished more in a day than most able-bodied people I knew.

She had helpers, of course. Not only the gardener, but a pool man, and occasional catering staff. And now me. But the person who made everything run smoothly in the household was Estella.

Estella was probably around my age, though she looked older. I never knew exactly how long she had worked for Swift and Ava, but evidently she'd taken care of Cooper as a baby, so she must have worked for the first wife, too. She had come north from Guatemala when she was just a teenager and pregnant with her daughter, Ava had told me once—riding on the roof of a train through Mexico, making her way across the Arizona desert with a *coyote* who'd charged her three thousand dollars it took her six years to pay off—all so her baby could be born in America. That was her daughter, Carmen. The way Swift felt about his son, Cooper, was how Estella felt about Carmen.

Estella was at the house on Folger Lane seven days a week, generally—moving through the rooms with a dustcloth, doing laundry, ironing the sheets, arranging

Ava's wardrobe, picking up the groceries, walking the dogs. Her English was limited, so except for wishing each other *buenos días,* we didn't communicate much, though the first time we met she had shown me a photograph of Carmen, taken at her *quinceañera.* "This girl is U.S. citizen," Estella said with pride. "Not just beautiful. Smart, too."

I studied the photograph. It showed a lovely girl with dark brown skin and black eyes and a lively, intelligent face.

"My girl's in college now," she told me. "You got kids?"

Sometimes it was easier saying no than explaining, but to Estella—a Guatemalan woman, living illegally in the U.S., who probably knew something about mothers living away from their children—I nodded.

"He lives with his father."

Estella's English was limited, but she shook her head when she heard this and put her hand to her chest. "Hard," she said. "My Carmen, she is my heart."

In past years, when she was younger, Carmen had come to clean at Folger Lane alongside her mother, though Ava explained to me that it felt awkward having Carmen clean for them when Cooper was home. Carmen and Cooper were exactly the same age—born one month apart—and when they were very young, they'd played together in the pool or the game room. As he'd grown into his teenage years it had made Cooper uncomfortable seeing Carmen iron his clothes or vacuum his room, so Ava had decided it was best if Carmen didn't come around anymore.

"To be honest, I think Carmen had a little crush on Coop," Ava told me. "She was always sweet on him, but what could he do? He didn't want to hurt her feelings. And then—let's just say we started having problems with her."

Now Cooper was hardly ever home anymore, of course, having headed back East for business school, and thanks to Ava, Carmen had a job as a nanny for another family in the neighborhood. She had recently begun attending community college part time and was doing well there, I gathered. In another year she would transfer to a four-year school. That was the dream, anyway.

One day, when the family whose children she cared for was away, Carmen had brought her mother to work in their beat-up Toyota and set herself up in the laundry room with her books.

"*Mija* will get a good education," Estella told me. "Someday, she's a doctor. You see."

I looked in Carmen's direction—recognized the shirt she was wearing as one of Ava's that she had put in the discard pile the week before, a little tight around the bust. Carmen had a ripe, full body. She was beautiful.

I hadn't actually spoken with Carmen before, though I'd seen her once or twice, picking up her mother. Now she looked up from her textbook—something thick and dense like organic chemistry.

"My mom thinks I'm going to find the cure for cancer or something," Carmen said. "Or get a full scholarship to Stanford, at least. That's how it is with mothers, right? They all think their child is the most brilliant, perfect person."

Not necessarily, I might have told her, thinking of my own mother. But in Carmen's case, Estella's praise of her daughter didn't seem so extravagant. I had heard how she studied—eight hours straight, some nights, Estella said, after she came home from her nanny job. Weekends she attended classes.

She was a striking young woman, but there was more to the look of her than that long black shiny hair and tawny skin. She had a brightness and focus in her eyes as she bent over her books, a look of fierce intensity you didn't often see among the children who'd grown up on Folger Lane, for whom a college education was never a question.

"One day, my daughter will have a house," Estella said. "Not so big like this one. But nice."

"With a room for you, Mama," Carmen said. "And you won't even have to do the ironing."

"We find her a nice boy," Estella said. "Hard worker. Good husband. Good man."

"Suppose I don't want a good man?" Carmen said. "What if I want a bad one?" She laughed. Estella didn't.

18.

I called my ex-husband. "I was thinking maybe I could bring Ollie back to my place when I come to see him this weekend," I said, as if this wasn't such a big deal, just an afterthought, maybe. "If he spent the night, I could bring him home Sunday."

I didn't want to sound too desperate. Three years had gone by now since I'd been able to put my son to bed or be there when he woke up. I felt the absence of him every hour of the day. Sometimes as a stab of pain. Other times, a dull throbbing ache. Either way, it was always there.

"Or maybe I could come on Friday afternoon instead of Saturday morning," I went on. "I could bring him back Sunday."

On the other end of the line, Dwight was quiet, as if looking for the right script. I never got the feeling—on those rare moments when Dwight and I talked—that anything he said was natural or spontaneous.

"It could be a good thing for you and Cheri," I said. "You could get a babysitter for Jared. You two could have a date night."

"I don't think that will work, Helen," Dwight said.

"Or I could just come Saturday. Just have him for the one night this time." Was my voice going up an octave, or did it just feel that way? Later, maybe, I'd try for a whole weekend. I wouldn't be greedy. For now, one night was all I'd ask for.

I could hear Dwight drawing his breath in the way he used to when the two of us were together. It was something he did when he had some difficult news to deliver: that the baby's diaper needed changing. That he wanted to play golf on a Saturday. That he had fallen in love with someone at work.

"Cheri and I just don't think it's a good idea," Dwight said. "Every time Ollie sees you, he's all worked up for days afterward. We don't think he feels secure with you."

"We just need more time together," I said, trying not to let my voice rise, or to allow a note of desperation to come into it. His voice, addressing me now, was pure mortgage broker. Clearly I'd failed the credit report.

"Let's face it," Dwight said. "The last time you had our son for any length of time, he got to see you led off in handcuffs."

"That was more than three years ago, Dwight."

"Maybe down the line, things can change," he said. "But right now, that's where we stand."

I stood there, holding the receiver. I didn't trust myself to speak.

Then suddenly, he was back to his smooth radio-announcer way of speaking. As if I were a long-lost friend or a customer. No difference between the two.

"Tell you what," Dwight said. "If Oliver himself tells me he really wants to come spend a weekend with you, we'll let it happen. So far, that's just not the message I'm getting from him, but who knows what could happen down the line."

Then came his favorite expression. "It's all good."

19.

Ava and Swift were in the garden having lunch when I arrived at Folger Lane. "We get big news about Carmen yesterday," Estella said, setting down an extra plate. "First thing I say when she tell me is we got to tell the Havillands."

Carmen had been chosen to receive an award for a paper she'd submitted to a contest for college science students—a report based on an experiment she'd designed, proving that fruit flies that were fed organically lived longer than those that consumed conventional produce. She had been selected, along with just four other students (the others, unlike Carmen, from four-year colleges) to travel to Boston and visit the campus of Harvard University, where she would read her paper at a national science conference.

"When they see how smart she is," Estella said, "I bet they give her a scholarship."

We all said how wonderful this was, naturally. "Next thing you know that daughter of yours will be married off to some Boston Brahmin who talks through his nose and spends weekends on Nantucket playing polo," said Swift. Estella looked confused. She definitely didn't know what a Boston Brahmin was and probably had no clue about Nantucket, either.

"You're missing the point, sweetheart," Ava told him. "Carmen's not going to make her way by marrying some rich guy, like I did. She's going to make something of herself thanks to her own hard work and that great brain of hers."

"She don't have to pay for her ticket," Estella said. "Airplane. Food. Hotel. All free. They send her a shirt with the name of the school on the front to wear on her trip."

"Fantastic," said Ava. Estella's face glowed. I had never seen her so happy.

"She ask me if Boston is close to Cooper's school. Maybe he can show her the city."

Only a person who knew her well would have noticed, but I saw a tightness cross Ava's features then. Swift was back to reading his *Wall Street Journal.*

"Cooper's in New Hampshire, actually," said Ava. "Dartmouth. Maybe another time, though."

At this point I hadn't yet met Cooper, who was away at business school. But you couldn't spend more than ten minutes in Swift's company without his name coming up.

"My boy," Swift called him now, after Estella had returned to the kitchen. "My boy's got the world by the tail. He can do anything he wants in life. He's got the golden touch."

Just the weekend before, Cooper had flown to Las Vegas with his old fraternity brothers from Cal for the weekend. Now they were planning another trip—heli-skiing in British Columbia.

Though I had never met Swift's son, I'd seen pictures of him all around the house and I could tell that he was one of those people (like Swift, but even more so, probably) whom everyone noticed when they came into a room. He was a lot taller than his father, with the build of a rugby player, which it turned out he was. In every photograph he seemed to be laughing.

I knew from Swift that at the moment Cooper was trying to decide between a career in commercial real estate and the entertainment industry—putting together financing for movies, licensing, that kind of thing. He'd do great in the music business, too, Swift had said. Once, on a night out in San Francisco, a sportscaster for the local NBC affiliate had given Cooper his card. "I was watching you at dinner," he'd told Cooper. "You could have a career in television."

"I told him a job in television gets you great seats at Giants games," Swift said. "But the real money's in business. Once you make it there, you can buy your own season tickets."

"He's one of those people everyone loves the minute they meet him," Ava said. "Women in particular, of course. The apple doesn't fall far from the tree."

"That boy's going to be a millionaire before he's thirty," Swift added. "He's got that drive. He has success written all over him."

"Like someone else I know," said Ava.

Cooper had a beautiful girlfriend, of course. Virginia. She could be a model, but she was a medical student.

"If I was in a coma, and this girl bent over the bed, I'd wake up pretty quick," Swift said of Virginia. "The knockers on her—"

"Stop it, darling. You're terrible," Ava said. She was always telling him this, but you could tell it was part of their game.

"I'm just being honest," Swift told her.

"You're talking about our future daughter-in-law, sweetheart," Ava reminded him. "The mother of our grandchildren."

Everyone knew—had known for years, evidently—that Cooper and Virginia would end up married. They'd been together since they were sixteen, so seven years now, and they were perfect for each other. They were going to have a marvelous life.

I asked when he was coming home.

"It's always hard pinning Cooper down," Ava said. "He's got so many irons in the fire."

Swift stepped in then. "Cooper's been hired for a big internship at an investment firm in New York," he said. "You know how it is with these new account executives. They run them ragged until they've made their first ten million dollars."

I made no comment. I tended to keep quiet about all the things I didn't know, and there were many.

Swift continued, "One of these days when we least expect it, we'll be sitting out on the patio with the dogs and all of a sudden we'll hear this big ruckus, and he'll come bursting into the yard and do a cannonball into the pool or something. Or he'll pull up in a Maserati he convinced someone to let him take out on a test drive. That's Cooper for you. The guy moves at Mach speed. With or without a sports car."

"Sometimes I wish he'd slow down a little," Ava said. I heard a small note of worry in her voice. But then Estella was back with a plate of warm brownies.

More wine. The conversation about her daughter and Cooper appeared to be over.

"You be sure to tell Carmen how proud we are of her," Ava told her.

"This Harvard," Estella asked. "It's a good school?"

20.

Every night—before heading to my AA meeting, or if I went to an early meeting, after I got back—I called the house in Walnut Creek to speak with Ollie. When I did, I could almost see my son's hand on the mouse pad of his PlayStation as I tried to engage him in something that might pass for conversation.

"Yes."

"No."

"No."

"Maybe."

"I don't know."

"Whatever."

"Have you had a chance to try out the new camera yet?" I asked him. "I was thinking that maybe, if we had a little more time together, we could go do one of our photography expeditions like how we used to in the old days. If you spent the night over here, maybe."

"I don't know."

"We could make popcorn after and watch movies on the couch."

Silence on the other end. Then Cheri's voice, calling to say it was bedtime. Just seven o'clock, but Dwight and Cheri believed in early bedtimes.

When I put down the receiver, I usually cried. Those were the moments I most wanted a drink. I fixed myself a cup of tea instead. All I ever had to do, when I was tempted, was think about the one thing that mattered: getting Ollie back. Not just physically under the same roof with me again, though that was a big enough challenge. The hardest part was getting my son to trust me again. Or simply to know me. Or to let me know him. It was the loneliest feeling in the world.

And then there were the Havillands. I sometimes said that Ava and Swift were like my family. But they were not like my family—not *my* family, the real one—in any way imaginable, which was what I loved about them. Other than having Ollie, I had lived my life—with the brief exception of that handful of years when Dwight's family appeared to have taken me in as one of their own—like a stray dog or an orphan, and after my son left, that's more or less who I was once again.

"I was wondering whose name you keep in your wallet," Ava asked me one time.

At first I didn't understand.

"On that card you're always supposed to keep there, in with your driver's license," she said. "Where it says, 'The person to call in the event of an emergency is . . .' Whose name do you carry around with you?"

I didn't have a card like that, I told her. Or rather, the card that had come with my wallet, years before, had never been filled in. Not even when I was married.

There had been Alice once, of course. But even before she disappeared from my life she wasn't the type to make a big thing of our friendship. She was just sort of there.

"Now you can put our number there," Ava said. She reached for my purse and took out my wallet, and in her elegant script—using the special pen she favored—wrote her name on the back of the card, alongside her cell phone and home numbers.

"Maybe we should just adopt you," Ava said. "Like Lillian and Sammy and Rocco."

Some people might have been offended by this, but with Ava there was no better compliment than to find yourself compared to one of her dogs.

21.

After Ava and Swift came into my life, and I sent Jeff the bank manager packing, I had stopped checking out my Match.com e-mails with recommended dating prospects. I seldom even opened the occasional messages that came my way from men who'd seen my profile, suggesting we meet for a drink.

There was a time when I had yearned for the attention of a man, but the urgency I once felt to find someone with whom I might share my deepest sorrows and joys had diminished once my new friends appeared. If I did find a man, it was hard to imagine where I'd even find the time to see him, I was so occupied with affairs on Folger Lane. Or—even less likely—how would I ever find someone whose company compared with that of the Havillands? Above all there was this: If I ever managed to get my son back, I'd have even less time for a man.

But a few weeks after we met, Ava decided I needed a boyfriend, and that finding him would be her project. She made me upgrade my dating profile with a better picture (though she wasn't entirely happy with the new one, either) and had me take out the part about my son. ("You can explain about Oliver once some guy takes you out for a nice meal," she said. "One thing at a time.") I complied with this less for any remaining dream I might have of finding someone than for Ava. If she wanted me to go out on dates, then I would.

Now my perspective shifted. A new factor had entered into my online experience, though I don't believe I acknowledged it to myself: This was the desire to keep Swift and Ava entertained. The stories I shared about the men who wrote to me (and I always shared them with Ava and Swift) accomplished this. They loved my stories, the more depressing the better.

Most of the responses I received to my new online dating profile came from precisely the kind of men you'd expect to hear from if your picture showed a pale, faintly shell-shocked woman with her hair pulled back, wearing no makeup and standing in front of her refrigerator, who didn't drink and listed her favorite activities as photography and watching old movies, but added that she didn't get around to those things so much anymore.

The demographics of the men who wrote to me now were skewed to those in their late fifties, or who tended to be unemployed, or newly sober, or still married but planning to separate any day now.

There was a recent widower who devoted several pages (sent, I noted, a little after 3:00 A.M.) to the details of his dead wife's battle with ovarian cancer. Around page four he got around to the fact that she had left him on his own with four children all under the age of thirteen and not enough money to hire help. He was a terrible housekeeper, he wrote. Did I cook?

There was the ukulele player with the twitching eyelid (I found that out because I actually met him for coffee, or rather, chai), who was so worried about germs that he preferred not to shake my hand. Then came the guy who spent the entire duration of our walk together (my standard half-mile meet-and-greet stroll) describing in detail his struggle with eczema. There was a man—surprisingly attractive in his photograph—who had neglected to mention in our two-hour-long telephone conversation before we met that he was a dwarf. There was the one who wanted to hear (also on the first and only meeting) my attitude toward group sex.

"It makes you start wondering about your own self," I told Ava, when she asked (as I knew she would) for my preliminary report on the latest prospective boyfriend. "If everyone I meet turns out to be that much of a loser, what does that say about me? Because I picked out these people. We talked on the phone before I agreed to meet up with them. These men actually sounded reasonable to me at first. What's wrong with me?"

"So you're human," Ava said. "And optimistic. You're always ready to see the best in people. It's a nice trait."

More and more, then, I began to adopt the attitude that it didn't matter so much who the men turned out to be, because even if they weren't so great (even if the date was awful) it would make a great story for Ava and Swift.

Even when I was in the middle of dinner with some Match.com person, I'd find myself imagining how much fun Swift and Ava and I would have later, when I recreated the scene for them at one of their favorite restaurants. And what difference did it make, really? All I really cared about, anyway, was my son. Finding a great man might actually get in the way of that.

Ava saw it differently, of course. "The dwarf could have been interesting," she offered. "He's probably developed all kinds of amazing sexual skills to compensate. Might be an incredible lover."

"Watch out for a guy who cuts his hair too short in the back," said Swift, gesturing in the direction of the pool man, who had dropped by as we were discussing some recent dead-end date. "That's the sign of a rule follower. No fun in bed."

I said nothing. But I took in every word either of them told me.

Out in the Havillands' backyard, a bottle of zinfandel and my ever-present Pellegrino on the table, I described the real estate developer who had clutched me so tightly in the parking lot after our first (and last) dinner. I had the feeling if I'd tried to free myself he might break my arm, I told my friends. He had turned out to be a Vietnam vet. The war, for him, had not ended.

("I never sleep more than an hour at a time," he'd told me. "I have these dreams. If I had a woman like you next to me, I think I might stop having the nightmares." I couldn't say anything, he was clutching me so tightly.

"I want to marry you," he said. "I'll buy you anything you want.")

We were eating shrimp scampi prepared by Ava the night I shared my story about the Vietnam vet's proposal. Estella had come home from the farmers' market that day with the biggest shrimp I'd ever seen, and they were piled on my plate, covered in butter and garlic, over fresh pasta and peas, along with salad made with baby greens and Humboldt Fog cheese. I had never been a rosé drinker, but now, studying the wine in Swift and Ava's glasses, I felt the old urge to have a drink. This wine had the most beautiful color. Not pink, like the cheap rosé I'd observed Alice pouring in the past at certain lower-budget catering jobs, but a soft, peachy blush.

"It won't kill you to try," Swift said, indicating the bottle.

I shook my head.

"This guy," Ava said. "The vet. What did you say when he proposed?"

"I told him he had to let go of my arm," I told her. "But if he wanted to talk awhile, I'd listen. I said I couldn't marry him because I didn't know him, and he didn't know me, either. We ended up sitting outside the restaurant for another three hours while he told me the story of a raid he'd been part of, into a remote jungle where he and his platoon had to dig up the bodies of some American marines who'd been slaughtered. Then carry them ten miles out, on their backs."

"You've just got this big, open heart, Helen," Ava said. "There's this thing about you that makes people know they're safe with you. That guy might be a little

messed up, but he wasn't totally off base in recognizing something in you. And you trusted him, too. Some
people would have figured he'd take out a bowie knife
and slit your throat with it. But it never occurs to you
to protect yourself that way. Swift and I need to in-
still in you a certain healthy layer of skepticism about
human nature. Not that we don't love you the way you
are, mind you. We just don't want to see you getting
exploited."

"The world is full of sharks, Helen," said Swift. "I
think you may have found us just in time."

I looked across the table at the two of them, side by
side on the banquette. They were too young for this,
of course, but for a moment I let myself imagine they
were my parents. Not the parents I actually had. The
ones I wished I'd had.

"So this guy with the post-traumatic stress problem?" Swift asked me. Protective, still, in that way I
had not encountered before meeting the two of them.
"What was he driving?"

It was a BMW, I told him. Brand-new from the lot,
papers still taped to the window.

"You could do worse," Swift offered. "Maybe you
should reconsider."

"Stop it, darling," said Ava. "You're terrible. We
need to be offering Helen emotional support and

encouragement, not telling her to hook up with some crazy vet just because he drives a nice car."

"Of course," he said, showing those teeth again as usual. "For a second there I just forgot."

That time with the Vietnam vet, the truth was enough of a story to keep my friends enthralled. But somewhere along the line, after I'd started reporting on my Match.com dates to Ava and Swift, I realized that the real stories were generally boring. This was when I called upon my old habit of embellishing details or, if necessary, changing them completely so I could provide Ava and Swift with a night's entertainment. I considered this my contribution to all those expensive restaurant dinners. Not that it was the food I cared about. It was the Havillands, and the amazing fact that they had chosen me to be their friend. Ava and Swift were better company than any man I was ever going to meet online.

22.

There was just one story I did not share fully with the Havillands. The story about my son.

I had told Swift and Ava about Ollie, of course. They knew about the DUI and the custody case—the guardian *ad litem,* the terrible judge, and the fact that I went to Walnut Creek every other Saturday to see my son for a few hours, when he wasn't tied up with some family activity, though more often than not, he was. They knew that I still owed my lawyer a lot of money and that my ex-husband yelled at our son (though the worst part about Dwight, in Ava's eyes, was his refusal to allow our son to have a dog).

They didn't know that sometimes—not on my visitation day, just some random weekday—I actually drove the hour and fifteen minutes to Ollie's school, right when they let the kids out, just to catch a glimpse of him. I'd hold my breath when I caught sight of him coming out of the building with his too-large back-pack, trudging toward his stepmother's SUV, his face concealed behind the hood of his jacket like someone in the witness protection program.

When Ollie was little, he'd been the kind of boy who greeted strangers at the supermarket and ran up to other kids at the swings or the monkey bars to ask if he could play. Now when he emerged from school, he was nearly always alone. Though the steps in front of the school would be filled with other children, nobody ever seemed to call out to him.

He moved determinedly across the schoolyard toward Cheri's car, with no indication that he was eager to get there, or that anything would be better once he did. He kept his shoulders hunched, his head bent down, hands clenched—as if he were trudging through a wind tunnel or a hailstorm, as if some kind of trouble might appear around any corner and he couldn't let his guard down for a second.

If I managed to catch a glimpse of Ollie's face at one of these moments, what I saw was a tense, angry look, as impenetrable as a locked door. When he got close to the car, his expression didn't alter, even if—as was often the case—his stepbrother, Jared, was inside in the back, buckled into the car seat.

From where I'd stand watching, across the street, I could only see the back of Cheri's head, but it seemed to me that a woman picking up an eight-year-old from school would turn around, at least, to smile at him when he got into the car, ask him "How was your day?" or ask to inspect the art project he might have carried out—something involving toilet paper rolls and egg cartons and Popsicle sticks.

Only, she never did. The whole time she sat there in the pickup lane, Cheri faced the road, hands gripping the wheel. I kept my eyes locked on Ollie, meanwhile, as he slipped stiffly into the backseat, like a tired old man getting into a taxi at the end of a very long plane flight. I stood there, not moving, as the car pulled away. That was it: all I would see of my boy until Saturday.

I wanted to run over to him. I wanted to hear about every single thing that had happened in Ollie's day. I wanted to throw my arms around my son and bring him home with me, to take him out for a root beer float, anyway, where I would ask him to explain to me about the cardboard construction and laugh when he told me a corny second-grade joke. But it wasn't my legal visitation time, and anyway—this was the saddest part—I knew Ollie would probably show no more evidence of enthusiasm for my presence at that moment than he did for his stepmother's. He looked like a person who believed he was all alone in the world, and I knew the feeling.

23.

At least once a week, if I was over at the house in the afternoon and it got to be five thirty or six, one of the Havillands—sometimes Ava, sometimes Swift—would suggest that I stay for dinner.

"You're going to eat with us, right?" Ava said, the first time she invited me.

I never had plans. If I had any, I would have canceled them.

They'd feed me dinner. At a restaurant, or at home. Though always on the early side.

They went to bed by eight thirty. Not to sleep, just to bed, Ava added. Swift always gave her a massage first.

"We don't let anything get in the way of our alone time," Ava told me. "Not even the dogs."

I tried to imagine what it would feel like to end every day that way. With a man who adored me rubbing oil all over my body. And more, no doubt. The picture left me with a small, sad recognition that as close as the three of us were, there was a wall between the Havillands and me that would always exist. How could it be otherwise? I was the Little Match Girl, face pressed up to the windowpane, looking in at the warm table with the meal spread out, the glowing hearth. Not quite that, in fact: The meal would be offered to me. They would show me to a seat by the fire. It was the other part, that unimaginable intimacy those two shared, that I could not fathom.

Still, it was no small thing that they included me in their dinners as often as they did. And, of course, the meals were always wonderful.

It wasn't just Estella who prepared great meals at Folger Lane. Ava was a wonderful cook, too—the kind of cook who doesn't rely much on recipes, but just opens the refrigerator and puts things together in a way that seems nearly effortless and always results in a marvelous meal. Their refrigerator and pantry were filled with great options: every kind of vegetable from the farmers' market, fresh bread from the bakery, runny cheese and the best olive oil, aged balsamic vinegar, five flavors of hand-packed Italian gelato.

Nights when Ava wasn't in the mood to cook, Swift would suggest that the three of us go out. They weren't the types to go in for trendy restaurants in the city, but they had their favorite spots a short drive from Folger Lane—a Burmese place where the owner always gave us his special table that was easy to get into with Ava's chair and sent over interesting foods to sample that weren't even on the menu, and our other regular spot, Vinny's. Once the two of them had their wine—and I my mineral water—Swift would lift his glass and grin. I knew what was coming then. More questions about my dating life. My sex life, if possible. My experiences with the men I met online had become Swift's preferred topic of conversation, and because it was Swift's favorite topic it became Ava's, too.

I wasn't sure why, but this had started to worry me. I sensed that in some way I couldn't understand, the two of them derived pleasure and maybe even excitement from hearing about my depressing meet-ups. As miserable as my dating life may have been—all those meetings in Starbucks or Peet's, or at some bar where the first thing you had to do was figure out if the person sitting there was really the one you'd come to meet, even though he looked twenty pounds heavier and ten years older—the stories I recounted afterward never ceased to entertain Swift and Ava.

A problem arose. I didn't know how I could keep it up. I had recently been thinking I wanted to take down my dating profile, but if I did, I worried about what I'd have to tell the Havillands on nights like these.

"So, tell us about this guy you were going to meet last night," Swift said, settling into our usual booth at the Burmese place one Saturday. He had ordered a bottle of cabernet for him and Ava, and my usual Pellegrino. As he raised the glass to his lips, I knew I had to come up with a story. No doubt the reality would have been depressing, but for the Havillands I'd make it funny.

By this time my profile had been online for over a year, and the prospect of ever meeting a good man through a dating site seemed hopeless, even if I'd been more in the mood for a relationship. But I didn't want to disappoint my friends.

That night, when Swift started in with his question, an odd impulse took hold of me. Not totally unfamiliar, perhaps only dormant. Suddenly the old habit returned, my penchant for making up stories. I needed to create a picture of my life that was more enthralling than the real one.

"I don't know if I should tell you this," I said, lowering my voice a little and studying the corner of my napkin. "I don't want you to think less of me. It's a little . . . twisted."

A flicker of excitement crossed their faces. Ava reached for her drink. Swift set down his chopsticks.

"Twisted?"

I recalled the stories I'd told others over the years, to conceal the shameful truth about who I really was. I'd invented tragedies to explain the absence of my parents and extract both sympathy and admiration, and to create an alternative to the sorry reality. (My grandmother, Audrey Hepburn. The fatal illness that was going to cut my life short before I turned twenty-seven. The brother who'd rescued me when our canoe tipped over on a camping trip, then got swept away in a current. One time, on a date with a man I knew I had no interest in seeing again, I'd described this rare syndrome I suffered from: Whenever I had sex, my body broke out in oozing sores.)

Once again at the restaurant that night, I felt a shiver of anticipation, the desire to spin out for Swift and Ava the most wonderful story, for no purpose other than to make myself more interesting. I thought of the *Arabian Nights*—a book I'd read to Ollie long ago, curled up together on the couch—and the picture came to me of Scheherazade, spinning irresistible stories with the knowledge that if she ever stopped, the king would have her beheaded.

"I really shouldn't tell you," I said, whispering now, so the people at the table next to us couldn't hear. No one but Ava and Swift, who leaned in closer.

"I never did anything like this before. You might think I'm a terrible person."

Only they never would. These were my friends for life. The two people I trusted to accept and care for me no matter what.

"It's just so . . . bad," I said.

A look came over Swift's face—like a dog tasting meat, or blood. "Come on, Helen," he said. He said it playfully, but there was something more beneath the banter. *Urgency.*

"Okay, then," I said, but I hesitated. "It's just so hard—"

"Honey," said Ava. "It's *us* you're talking to."

Long pause again. I took a breath, then another.

"We were coming back from the movies," I said. "He was bringing me home, but he said he wanted to stop at Safeway before they closed, to pick up something. Lightbulbs. Don't ask me why."

Starting this story, I studied the tablecloth, as a person might who was too embarrassed to meet anyone's eyes, but then I looked up at my friends—seeing in their faces a kind of rapt attention and eagerness I would more typically have expected to give to someone else than to receive. It was one of the things I loved about her, the way Ava always took an interest in whatever I told her, but it was an unfamiliar experience, commanding undivided attention at the table as I felt I was doing at that moment. I *liked* this feeling.

"The store was empty, except for a couple of cashiers," I said, almost whispering. "When we got there, they had already started turning out the lights."

Long pause. I could feel Swift's breathing. I had him.

"He took me to the back of the store. The part of the store where they sell things like extension cords. And lightbulbs, of course."

Another pause. Now I was drawing in breath myself, as if struggling to get out the next words, only I managed.

"He put his hands under my skirt," I said. "He pulled an extension cord down from the rack and wrapped it around my wrists. He told me to bend over."

"In Safeway?" Ava said. "Right there in the aisle?" Her voice was hushed, excited. Next to her in the booth, Swift had his large hand on her neck, and he was stroking it.

"Nobody else was around. They were closing in a few minutes. It was pretty dark."

"Still."

"You were into this guy in a big way?" Swift said. "You'd been making out in the car a little first, maybe, as a warm-up?"

I shook my head. "Up until this moment he hadn't laid a finger on me. He was sort of cold, actually. Aloof. But all of a sudden, something changed. Even his voice. It got all low and sort of rough. He had reached for something else off the rack. A spatula."

"You've got to be kidding," Ava said.

"No."

"And then he did it?" Swift said. "The whole she-bang?"

Here's where I gasped and put my hand up to my mouth, as if reliving it all. "Like you wouldn't believe," I told him. "I never felt anything like that before."

I looked him dead in the eye then. I felt like a whole other person. Someone fascinating.

"I have to meet this guy," Swift said. "He sounds like a keeper."

Up until this moment, I'd managed to keep my face the way I wanted: very serious, earnest even, and a little pained. As if in some altered state. Now was when I lost it. I burst out laughing, and for a split second I wondered if I'd gone too far. I might have made Swift angry, to have made a fool of him this way. But no.

"You really had me," he said, shaking his head. Then he started laughing, too—that big laugh of his that I'd heard from clear across the art gallery that first night. "I've got to hand it to you, Helen."

Ava let out her breath then—for the first time in a couple of minutes, it seemed. "There's a lot more to you than meets the eye, Helen," she said. "I wouldn't have known you had it in you."

"You'd do great in a poker game," Swift said. "Or on Wall Street. You're the kind of person defense attorneys dream of, because they can put you on the witness stand and have you say anything they want, and you're going to sell it like every syllable's the truth. The God's honest truth." And his large hand continued, gently, to stroke Ava's delicate neck.

24.

All that spring, every couple of weeks, the Havillands threw a party, and with a few exceptions the
guest list was always the same group of regulars. This
now included me.

The odd thing was that though the members of this
group had just about nothing in common besides friendship with Ava and Swift, the parties always turned out
to be amazing. One time, Ava hired a psychic who went
around the room making predictions about everybody's
life—with an emphasis on the sexual. Another time a
helicopter landed out by the pool, and four reggae musi-
cians got out and started playing on the steel drum and
guitars already set out for them. There was a fire-eater,
and a pair of break-dancers Ava had seen on the street in
San Francisco and hired on the spot. One time Swift and

Ava attached the names of famous people to our backs and we had to go around the room asking questions of our fellow guests until we figured out the name of our person. I was Monica Lewinsky. Swift was Ted Bundy, the serial killer. One time they hired a magician who somehow ended up with Ava's bra inside his top hat, and another time they hired a rock band that could play any hit you named from the last forty years. Each of us was supposed to take the microphone and sing the song of our choice. I chose Cyndi Lauper's "Time After Time."

If not for the Havillands, I would never have known any of these individuals in Swift and Ava's inner circle, but now that I did, we shared this odd bond. Not friendship, precisely, but a mutual recognition of our extraordinary good fortune in having a couple like the Havillands for our friends.

One person always present at the parties was Ava's massage therapist, Ernesto—a huge, swarthy man who dressed in black and had hands the size of ten-pound hams. The thin, pale woman who dispensed Swift's Chinese longevity herbs, Ling, came with her husband, Ping. I was never sure whether he spoke English, because he never spoke. There was a lesbian couple, Renata and Jo, who worked as building contractors, and met Swift and Ava when they'd done the handicapped-accessible additions to their house. Though he lived two hours away, in Vallejo, Swift's oldest friend from childhood, Bobby, always showed up with whatever woman he was dating at the moment. (That was Swift for you, I reflected. A man who never turned his back on his friends. It didn't matter that Bobby worked at a stone yard, operating a forklift truck, and lived in a one-bedroom studio. He and Swift were best friends and always would be.)

Always near the head of the table was Swift's attorney, Marty Matthias. Marty came from somewhere back East—Pittsburgh, maybe—and even after twenty-five years in California, still had an air of the coal mines about him. He didn't play tennis. Would rather submit to water torture than go for a hike. When I asked him once what kind of law he practiced, he said, "Whatever kind my buddy here needs to keep him out of trouble." He had a doglike devotion to Swift, and Swift returned it.

"This guy," Swift said once, at a party, making a toast to Marty to acknowledge some brilliant legal maneuver he'd pulled off recently on Swift's behalf. "This guy would chew a person's ear off and swallow it before he'd let me pay an extra nickel to the IRS. Right, Marty?"

Then there were Ava's friends Jasper and Suzanne, stylish and beautiful art dealers in the city. Most recently—but before they'd taken me under their wing—the Havillands had befriended a woman in her late seventies named Evelyn Couture, a widowed fellow dog lover who owned an enormous house in Pacific Heights. On party nights, Evelyn Couture would be brought to the house by her driver. At first glance she seemed an unlikely member of these gatherings, but she appeared to love Swift, and he always seated her near himself at the long, linen-covered table. The night he'd hired the karaoke band, Evelyn got up and sang "How Much Is That Doggy in the Window?"

In addition to the regulars, you could always count on some newcomer—a person Ava had met on one of her walks with the dogs or in line at Starbucks whom she'd taken a shine to. I might have been one such person myself, except that I had quickly and magically been elevated to the next level, of those not simply putting in a one-time guest appearance, but installed as a regular. I worried that I wouldn't have anything to say, but it wasn't a problem. Most everyone liked to talk about themselves so much, they were happy to have someone who'd listen.

Although both Estella and Ava were excellent cooks, Ava always had these parties catered to cut down on the stress. All Estella had to do was prepare and pass around platters of olives and salami and cheese and roasted artichokes from North Beach and caviar on great bread. Estella usually brought along Carmen to help out with the postparty kitchen cleanup, and when she came to work, Carmen always had her textbooks from community college with her, in case there might be a lull in the kitchen that allowed her some time for studying. Even when she was washing dishes or mopping the floor, she had earphones on, listening to some book on tape. She was trying to improve her English, she told me. She didn't want to have an accent, and she didn't.

The first time I attended one of Ava and Swift's dinner parties, I brought a bouquet of gerbera daisies, not understanding that Ava would have ordered elaborate floral arrangements for every room in the house. The next time, when I asked what I could do to help, Ava suggested that I bring my camera.

"I've always wanted to make some kind of record of our gatherings," she said. "Nothing posed. More documentary style. Black and white. Like that photographer Sally Mann, who took all those great, raw photographs of her children naked over the years they were growing up."

I obliged, of course. A place had been set for me at the table, but I barely sat down that time, or at any party after that one, because I was always taking pictures, and I wanted to catch the unexpected shots. I'd wander into the kitchen as Estella and Carmen cleared away dishes, or go out by the pool, where the guests hung out sometimes, or into the library, where Ava liked to sit by the fire, catching up with one person or another who might have some piece of news to confide that couldn't be shared with the whole group. Unlike Swift, who loved the group dynamic of parties, Ava was more interested in having a very long and deep conversation with one person at a time.

And because I knew how Ava felt about her dogs, I also followed Sammy, Lillian, and Rocco, trying to get images of them that might differ in some way from the hundreds that already existed. As Ava had once pointed out, I was very good at becoming nearly in-visible—a skill I possessed even when I wasn't taking photographs. With the exception of Rocco, who still growled when he saw me, nobody seemed to notice I was taking their picture, or even that I was there.

For Cinco de Mayo, Ava procured a ceremonial Mexican dress for Estella to wear when she served the mole. (She was Guatemalan, of course. "Close enough," Ava said.) Jasper and Suzanne brought one of their gallery's stable of artists with them—a very beautiful young woman named Squrl. Sometime after dinner I headed out to the pool house, with the idea of getting a shot of the festivities from a distance. As I stood outside the pool house framing my shot of the party a few dozen yards away, I heard a sound behind me from inside. I turned and peeked through the French doors, the curtain only partly covering the glass.

Only moments before, I'd been back at the main house snapping photographs of Suzanne's husband, Jasper, as he held forth on their upcoming visit to Art Basel. Now, through the curtain, I caught sight of Suzanne and Squrl, sprawled on the deep-pile Tibetan rug, both nearly naked, their arms and legs entangled in a passionate embrace. I figured the image of Suzanne and Squrl was probably not the kind of shot Ava had in mind when she mentioned Sally Mann's photographs of her children, and left before either of them was aware I'd been there.

I saw other things through my lens: At one end of the garden, I witnessed what looked like a pretty unpleasant argument between Ling and Ping. I saw Estella slipping a rib eye steak into her purse. Possibly the strangest thing—which I took in, by accident, while trying to capture a portrait of Lillian—was the sight of Ernesto's meaty hand, viewed from under the table, resting without opposition on the thin white thigh of the herbalist, Ling, as her husband soundlessly chewed his meat in the chair directly next to her.

I didn't share any of this with Ava. As interesting as the photographs might have been, I didn't record these images with my camera. My own life might be fair game for amusing conversation over cocktails or dinner with my dazzling friends, but the intimate secrets of others were not my business, and so on the rare occasions when I'd snapped something I shouldn't have seen, I deleted the image. A photograph—once captured—held more power than most people knew.

One night, as the group of us gathered around the long teak table on the patio, Estella set down at its center a golden platter bearing a dish called Bananas Foster. Ava reached her long, thin, well-defined arm across the table and, with a very long match, ignited the dish, so flames leapt up around the edges.

I watched Ava's face then: the way the light hit her cheekbones and how beautiful she looked as it did. I tried to take all this in with my camera: the flaming bananas, the looks of amazement on the faces of the assembled guests. Fingers of smoke curled around us all, as if we were passengers on a glamorous ocean liner, making our way through the Strait of Magellan or circling a Greek island with every light on the deck illuminated. The ship's captain, obviously, was Swift.

There he sat at the end of the table, presiding over everything, leaning back in his chair with his white teeth clamped around a Cuban cigar and his hand caressing some part of Ava's body (knee, elbow, earlobe), almost as if we were their children gathered around, and they were the parents who'd given us life. Which, in a way, they had.

One night, as Carmen was clearing away the dishes—the bottle of Far Niente, the shells of a few dozen lobsters—Swift instructed us to step away from the table and into the garden, where each of us was presented with a gas-fired flying lantern, the size of a small kite, which we lit and then released. Our lanterns floated slowly upward—first above the roof, then beyond the trees, and higher into the night sky, until it seemed to me that we had created a whole new constellation, right there on Folger Lane.

None of us asked how (fire codes being what they were) this was possible. In Swift and Ava's world, everything seemed possible. Somewhere off in the kitchen, a Guatemalan mother and her American-born daughter scraped the remnants of our fabulous meal into the garbage. (Leftovers were never a good idea for the dogs. Too rich.) The rest of us just stood there in the darkness, around the glowing turquoise of the pool, watching our flickering lanterns float slowly toward the stars. They continued to stay aloft, and to glow, for many minutes. When the last one finally burned out, we all returned to the house for a glass of champagne and individual chocolate soufflés, with a cloud of crème fraiche on every plate and one perfect raspberry. Then gradually, one by one, we said our good nights and retreated to our own small lives, away from the strange and beautiful Shangri-la created by our amazing friends. I think we were all grateful to have touched down for a few hours, like weary travelers washed up by good fortune on that remote and glittering shore. For all the hundreds of pictures I took there—thousands—no photograph could capture what it felt like to find myself at that place, in the company of that magic couple.

25.

I had started to dread reading through the responses to my online dating profile, they were so uniformly discouraging. Then one spring day, right around the time Ava's tulips were coming out, I opened my laptop and there was a short note, different from the others.

The man who'd written it (JustaNumbersGuy was his moniker) said he'd studied my profile carefully and ("based on my rigorous analysis") thought there was a slim possibility ("keep in mind," he wrote, "this is a pessimist speaking") that we might get along. Or at least, he wrote, a meeting between us might be somewhat less dreadful than the rest of them were.

It was hard to know, reading his note, whether he was a total nerd, or whether he was being funny. Possibly both.

His name was Elliot, and he was forty-three—a good age to go with my thirty-eight, it seemed to me. Divorced, no children.

"To be honest, I didn't think that was a great picture you posted of yourself," he wrote. "I suspect it did not do you justice. But I liked your face right away, and I also get the feeling you are the type of person who downplays her good qualities. Maybe I sensed this because I'm that way myself."

If his photograph were to be believed (as the profile pictures for so many of the men I'd met so far were not), Elliot was a nice-looking man—even handsome, in that nerdy kind of way, basically thin, though with a hint of a belly: the kind of man who probably owns a drawerful of white tube socks on the theory that by doing so he avoids any problems of matching them up when doing the laundry. If his picture was to be trusted, he appeared to be in possession of most if not quite all of his hair. He reported that he was six feet tall. ("You mentioned that you enjoy dancing," he wrote, "and I see you are five foot five. I trust your own petite stature won't cause you to rule me out as a dance partner, and will simply offer encouragement that this may not be a problem, since I am told my posture is not the best.")

I smiled reading this. But not, for once, out of a sense that the author of this note appeared to be a comically ridiculous candidate for my affection or a great subject for entertaining Swift and Ava at our next dinner together. I actually *liked* the sound of Elliot.

"I'm not rich, by the way," he wrote, "but I own a nice little place in Los Gatos, and it's unlikely I'll get fired from my job any time soon since I'm my own boss."

He worked as an accountant, he told me. "I know," he said. "Boring, right? Next thing you know I'll be telling you I'm interested in genealogy. Guess what? I am."

He had been divorced for seven years, following a marriage that had lasted twelve, he went on. The good part was that absolutely no drama existed there. He and his ex-wife, Karen, remained good friends. "We just grew apart," he wrote. "That's probably a boring thing to tell you, too, but in this case, I'd rather be boring than have one of those stories where the two people are leaving anonymous hate mail on the doorstep and dreaming up ways to murder each other.

"I am going to guess that despite your characteristic dismissal of your finer qualities, you are a good photographer," he wrote. "I arrived at this conclusion not from your profile picture, but from a number of the images you posted on your page, that I deduce may have been taken by you.

"As for that picture of you and your friend," he wrote, "well, what can I say? Something about the look in your eyes has caused me to return to it half a dozen times this evening. Looking at you in that photograph, I actually said out loud—though there was no one in the room but myself—'I like this woman.' More significant, perhaps, is the fact that as I was looking at your profile, I registered an unfamiliar sensation around the edges of my lips that suggested to me that I was smiling.

"I have to tell you," he wrote, "you are a beautiful woman."

Maybe he's gotten me confused with Ava, I thought for a moment. Because Ava looked stunning in that picture, of course. Ava always looked stunning.

Then I read the next line of his note to me, written as if in response to my thought.

"And don't think I have you confused with your friend, either," he wrote. "Though I'm sure she's a lovely person. But I'm talking about you, the quiet one, in possession of what I detected as a certain sadness, along with a true capacity for joy. The one on the right"—this would be me—"is the one I am hoping to persuade to have dinner with me. Soon, I hope."

26.

When contemplating a blind date with someone encountered on a dating site, my general rule was to have a phone conversation first. You could tell a lot from a person's voice, including some things that made it clear you wouldn't want to meet him. (A lot went undetected, of course, which accounted for my many disastrous blind dates.)

But when I wrote back to Elliot after receiving that first note, he suggested that we bypass the usual phone check-in and move directly to dinner. It reassured me when he told me that he was actually busy that night (because it had begun to occur to me that maybe this was some kind of weird stalker; after all, he admitted he'd spent an entire evening clicking back to my photograph at regular intervals). I wanted a man who had friends.

"I'm tied up tomorrow, too," he wrote, "though I'd much rather be having dinner with you. So how does Friday look?"

Friday was one of the nights Ava and Swift and I often got together, so I hesitated. Then I stopped myself. It was a little ridiculous, I knew, to turn down a dinner invitation with a totally reasonable-sounding and not-unattractive man who seemed for whatever reason to have genuine interest in me, on the chance that my married friends might decide at the last minute to include me in their plans.

"Friday's fine," I said.

"I'd like to pick you up," Elliot said. "But I also understand it might feel a little creepy for you to have a total stranger know your address. So let's say we meet at the restaurant this time."

I recognized him the minute I walked in the door. Often, the men you met from dating websites barely resembled their photograph. But Elliot looked just like the profile picture he'd posted. As I approached the table he stood up. Bad posture: He'd been right about that. But he had nice hair and his eyes looked kind. He pulled out the chair for me.

"I can't help it," he said. "I just have to tell you. I've been looking forward to this ever since I first saw your picture."

We were the last ones to leave the restaurant that night, and when he walked me to my car he took my arm, but not in the manner of the Vietnam vet with the marriage proposal. Firmly, but tenderly. "I would like to kiss you," he said. "You have to tell me if that's a problem."

"Not a problem," I said.

After, he stood there looking at me. "I want to remember this moment as clearly as I can," he said. "Not that I'm likely to forget."

"I had a good time, too," I said. Normally by this point, I would long since have noted at least one red-flag issue that discouraged any future exploration of a relationship. But the only ominous thing about Elliot was the surprising intensity of his feeling for me. It made no sense that I would have an effect like this on a man. I never had before.

There was another surprising element to my evening with Elliot. For the first time since I'd gotten into the routine of my dinners with Swift and Ava, I had not spent the evening taking mental notes of all the funny and ridiculous things I could tell them about later.

Elliot asked if getting together for dinner again the next night would seem too soon. "I could pretend to be less eager," he told me, "but I can't think why I'd do that."

Tomorrow would be fine, I said. I had been hoping to make a trip to Walnut Creek that day, but as usual,

Dwight had e-mailed me that afternoon to say he and the rest of the McCabe family were meeting up in Sacramento to celebrate Jared's birthday. Bringing Ollie, of course.

"I don't want to scare you off by saying this," Elliot said, "but this was the best date I ever had."

"I need to tell you something before we go any further here," I told him, still in the parking lot. We had covered a lot of ground over dinner but not this one large fact about me that mattered most.

"I have a son. Eight years old. He doesn't live with me, but I wish he did. I lost custody of him a little over three years ago. I wouldn't blame you if that gave you second thoughts about me."

For a long moment, Elliot just stood there. He took his time responding. "All this tells me," he said when he finally spoke, "is that you've had a big hard loss in your life. Like most of us, if we're honest. Next time we see each other, I hope you'll feel you can tell me the story."

"I'm trying to fix things between Ollie and me," I told him. "But it's a difficult situation."

"Listen," Elliot said, "I'm a man who prides himself on being sensible. But I'd better tell you now. I'm going to be crazy about you. I probably am already. The only thing in question for me is whether you could feel the same way back."

27.

Ava called me the next morning.

"So?" she said. "It's already nine thirty. Why aren't you over here? Swift and I want details."

"I thought you two might still be at the farmers' market," I said. This was not wholly accurate. The truth—and this was unprecedented—was that I had forgotten we'd talked about getting together. I had been thinking about my evening with Elliot.

"We got back ages ago," Ava was saying. "I've been listening for your car. Even the dogs miss you. Well, not Rocco, but the other two. You have to get over here immediately and tell us everything. The whole sordid story."

There was her laughter. Swift had probably come up behind her and was more than likely doing something not simply sexually suggestive but explicit.

"I'm trying to concentrate!" she said. Then, "Disregard that! I was talking to Swift. You know how incredibly irritating he can be."

Untypically for me, I had been lying in bed when Ava called. I had been reading an e-mail from Elliot. Two of them, actually—one written the night before, after our date, the second written that morning.

"The last time I remember feeling this excited," he had written, "was back in 1992, when they came out with the renewable energy production tax credit."

I liked it that he had not felt a need to write "LOL" here, or type in a colon followed by a parenthesis, to make sure I knew he'd made a joke. I liked a lot of things about Elliot.

"It's a little out of character for me to say something along these lines, being as I am a bit of a pessimist," he wrote. "But I think we might have something really good here."

I drove over to Folger Lane that afternoon. Ava had a cappuccino waiting for me, and croissants Estella had brought home from the good bakery, whose proprietor Ava was friendly with. On one of our recent trips she'd stopped there to deliver a hydrangea plant that she thought the woman would like, because the color matched her awning perfectly. That was Ava for you: errands that required parking the car, getting out, going into a place—the kind of thing that people who don't have spinal cord injuries might regard as too much of a nuisance—never bothered her. Ava was always making stops, buying gifts for people, delivering them.

"Well?" she said, handing me the croissant.

"I liked him," I told her. "He's taking me out to dinner again tonight."

"That soon?" said Ava. "Doesn't that feel a little excessive?"

Swift had been out on the patio, but now he joined us. "No weirdness this time?" he said.

I shook my head.

"Is he short?" Ava said.

"Normal. Tall, actually. Nothing wrong with his teeth, either."

"Did he let you split the check?"

"No."

Ava asked me where he was taking me this time. I named a restaurant where I knew the two of them often ate, though not with me. Pricier than the Burmese place where we generally went.

"Not too shabby," she said.

Swift asked about the kissing, how far he'd gotten.

Though up until now I had told the Havillands everything that happened on my dates, this time I felt an unfamiliar reluctance to share the details of my evening with Elliot. I could have made up one of my stories, but I didn't feel like it.

"It was good," I said, my voice a little flat, though maybe I was trying to make myself sound that way. "All good."

"That's wonderful, honey," said Ava. But I picked up something else in her tone then—or maybe it was only later that I registered this, and maybe I was only imagining it. She sounded faintly disappointed.

"The guy isn't still married, is he?" said Swift.

I shook my head. "Divorced for ages. No terrible stories about the awful ex-wife."

"Something happens to men who've been on their own too long without a woman around," Ava said. "It's the old-bachelor syndrome. They get rigid and stuck in their ways."

"But he was married for twelve years," I told her. "He and his ex-wife are good friends."

"Friends? Really?" she said. "I don't understand how that could be. If Swift and I ever split up—which would never happen—I'd need to slit his throat. Maybe this Elliot person just isn't the passionate type in the first place."

I started to say something, but stopped. Ava hadn't even met Elliot yet, and already I was defending him.

"I think he's just a really nice person, is all," I told her.

"That's great," she said. "If *nice* is what you're looking for."

28.

Elliot and I had an even nicer time the second night. Hearing myself describe it that way—over at Folger Lane on Monday morning, having coffee in the garden with Ava—I registered immediate regret.

"Not just nice," I said. "Terrific, actually."

Ava seemed dubious. "I don't want to throw ice water on this," she said. "But when it's right, you want to feel hot. Excited. Sweaty. Like you might die if you don't see him again. And it had better be soon."

This was just the second date, I told her. "It's not like I'm marrying the guy. Believe me, after some of the men I've been meeting, nice is no small thing."

"The night I met Swift, we went back to his apartment and we didn't get out of bed all weekend," she said. I had heard this before, of course—though in the original version it was six months. That probably came a little later.

"Don't get me wrong, honey," she said. "I think it's great that you've found someone you can spend time with. I just know you're a person who has sold herself short in the past. You may think this Elliot person is the best you can expect, when he might not be."

"I'm not selling myself short," I told her. "He's great. And anyway, I just met him."

"Well, good for you," she said, gesturing for Estella to take our cups away. "I think that's wonderful. And if you still like him a week from now, you know we're going to insist that you bring him over here, so we can check him out."

I did like Elliot even better a week from then, when he brought me over to his house on Sunday and we cooked dinner together. The day before, after I came back from seeing Ollie, we'd gone to the movies.

We were kissing a lot, but we had not yet slept together. Elliot was a deliberate man—the kind of person who read all the reviews of a particular model of car before even taking a test drive. We had talked about sex. "I want it to be just right," he said. "I'd like to feel, at that moment, that you're going to be the last woman I make love with. For the rest of my life."

"That's a pretty heavy responsibility," I said. "Unless, of course, the experience kills you on the spot."

I'd intended to make a joke, and as a rule, Elliot had a good sense of humor. But not where this topic was concerned.

Two weeks after we met, Elliot invited me to drive up to Mendocino with him for a long weekend, and I said yes, even though this would mean missing one of Swift and Ava's parties. They were bringing in a sushi chef and had hired a group of Kodo drummers to play in the pool house.

"You could have taken the most amazing pictures," Ava said. "The drummers wear the traditional costumes from the thirteenth century. You should see the muscles in their arms. Not to mention the rest of their bodies."

The Mendocino weekend was when Elliot and I finally had sex. It wasn't some mind-altering experience, but it was good—though later, driving home with him along Highway 1 past a beach where Ava and I had once brought the dogs, I found myself hearing her voice in my head, and it left me unsettled. I remembered the two of us sitting together in her sunroom that first time, Ava telling me about how it had been when she met Swift and she was so much in love she forgot to eat. "He had this really long hair back then that he sometimes tied in a ponytail," she said. "One time, when he was sleeping, I cut a piece off."

I studied Elliot's face as he drove—keeping a strict eye on the road as always, but smiling in a way that had to do with me, I knew, and the weekend we'd just spent. "Have you ever thought about not cutting your hair so short in the back?" I said.

"No. What made you bring that up?"

"Nothing in particular."

The next day, back at Folger Lane, Ava wanted to hear all about the weekend, of course. This time I was careful to convey another side of Elliot—something that revealed him to be more than a blandly nice person who wasn't an ax murderer. I had taken a bunch of photographs of him on my phone, and I scrolled through them, looking for a good one.

"He's very playful and spontaneous," I said, aware that none of the images on my phone conveyed that he was actually a good-looking man. "When the two of us were over at his apartment last week, making paella together, he put his arms around me and started dancing." I told her about another time, the week earlier, when I'd come over after one of my trips to Walnut Creek to see Ollie, he'd had a bath ready for me, with candles all around and bath salts in the water. He left me alone in the bathroom, but after I got out of the tub, we sat together on his couch—I, in his old chenille bathrobe—and he rubbed my feet. We weren't even lovers at that point—technically speaking. But no man had ever made me feel so loved.

"Mm," said Ava. But I knew she wasn't changing her opinion. "So how's the sex?"

Always in the past, I would have been quick to volunteer everything. Ava was closer to me than any man, so I'd been quick to fill her in on even the most intimate details. But this time felt different. I registered a small but clear desire to keep certain parts of what went on with Elliot to myself. Though I hoped what I offered up was enough to suggest that things were good.

"We found this creek bed, up in Mendocino, leading to a hot spring," I told her. "There was a spot where we sank into the mud up to our ankles. Nobody was around, so we stripped down to our underwear and slathered mud all over each other and just lay out in the sun till it dried, then jumped in the water."

"He must have looked pretty funny, with those skinny legs and that little potbelly of his," Ava said. I'd been the one who'd described his physique this way to her, of course.

Still, the minute she said this, I felt something shift in me. At the time Elliot and I had slathered the mud on each other, it had seemed wonderful and sexy and romantic, lying almost naked with him that way. But hearing Ava's take on it, the picture was suddenly different. Seen through Ava's lens, all of a sudden Elliot looked faintly ridiculous. Pathetic, even.

I wished I hadn't told her about his belly.

29.

Now and then, if I was over at the Havillands' by myself working on the art-cataloging project, an odd and disconcerting feeling came over me. Some possession of Ava's would catch my eye, and it occurred to me how easy it would be to take this object home with me. Nobody would notice it was gone.

Though they left twenty-dollar bills all over the house, I never pictured myself stealing a cent of the Havillands' money. I knew where Ava kept her rings and the diamond pendant Swift had given her, and all the rest of the serious jewelry. I never would have touched those. And there were all those artworks—not the outsider art, but the insider stuff. The Diebenkorn. The Matisse. There were pieces in that house worth more than I'd earn in my whole life. I would sooner have given up a finger, or more, before I would have touched those.

But sometimes I'd be alone on Folger Lane—Ava at Pilates, Estella out buying groceries, Swift off in one of his sessions with Ling the Chinese herbalist or the fencing instructor, or meeting someone about his foundation, and the urge would come over me—not so different from how I used to feel when it was that bottle of wine in the top cupboard that I couldn't stop thinking about—to pay a visit to Ava's enormous closet. After that first time she'd brought me there, I couldn't stop myself from thinking about it. There were so many beautiful things there I'd never seen her wear. I imagined how it would feel to have one of them hanging in my closet. Or a pearl necklace. Or just a pair of earrings. Or less.

There was a ring I loved, in the shape of a fish. (Not a dog, for once. This was unusual for Ava.) There was a pair of earrings with a single red stone encased in a little golden cage. One time, alone in the closet, I held them up to my own lobes. I didn't even know if they were rubies; I wasn't that familiar with precious stones. I just loved the look of these: the red stones, the fine gold filament that held them in place. It would have been so easy to slip them in my pocket. My mind taunted me with the picture.

Or I'd be in the kitchen fixing tea, and the thought would come to me: I could just take this one silver teaspoon—part of a set, each engraved with a different wildflower. In the same drawer, there was one spoon meant for a left-handed person. Ava and Swift weren't even left-handed, but I was. If that spoon were mine, I'd make oatmeal every morning just so I could eat it with my special spoon.

For one whole week, I couldn't stop thinking about Ava's bone china tea light holder—a little dome that sat over a candle on a matching bone china plate. It didn't look like anything much until you lit the candle—preferably in a darkened room. Then a whole scene was revealed, carved into the china: a village lane, a horse and wagon, a cozy farmhouse in the woods, all glowing from the candle tucked under the china dome. I knew just where I'd set the tea light holder in my apartment, if it belonged to me.

One night, when we were having dinner together, Ava had set this candleholder on the table. Thinking maybe I'd buy one for myself, I'd asked where she got it.

"God only knows," she said. "Someone probably gave it to us as a favor at one of those awful events we used to have to attend when Swift still ran his company. I've got drawers of that stuff."

I never would have taken the tea light holder. Or anything else. But if I had, I knew that unlike Ava, I would have treasured it.

Ava didn't pay that much attention to possessions, was the truth. She cared about the people she loved, and her dogs.

This was a refreshing quality, in many ways. Though you could also have viewed her as spoiled for having so much stuff, individual objects—even treasures—held little meaning for her. Not even her expensive clothes—her leather jacket from Barneys, her velvet cape, the Fendi boots, the cashmere robe that hung next to her Jacuzzi. She was always dropping things off at dry-cleaning places, then forgetting about them. She did this so often that one day she put a couple of hundred-dollar bills in my hand with the instruction that I drop by every dry-cleaning place in town, just to see what items they might have that belonged to her.

This took hours. It turned out some of the clothes I picked up that day had been sitting over a year. There was a linen skirt I particularly loved. If I brought this one back home to my apartment, instead of to Folger Lane, I thought, she'd never know. "Stop it," I said out loud—same as I once did while reaching for a bottle.

Sometimes I asked myself what it was about me that made those thoughts come into my head all the time, of stealing something from the Havillands. I considered whether this meant I was a terrible person.

But it wasn't as if I ever actually took anything. I knew I would never do anything to betray the trust of my friends, especially after all they'd done for me. I would never have risked losing the two of them, as I might if they knew about my covetous urges. I just loved Ava, and I loved the world she'd made, full of beautiful things. I wanted to be part of her world. I wanted some part of her world to be mine.

30.

Though Ava liked to say that Swift's main purpose in life was loving her—and he said plenty, himself, to promote this idea—he seemed to be closeted in his office more and more these days. He appeared to have become increasingly involved in their project of creating the nonprofit animal organization, BARK. With the help of a number of friends—including Ling and Ernesto, surprisingly, and several young finance types who stopped by often these days, and a buddy who'd sold his startup around the same time Swift had, for even more money, and Marty Matthias, naturally—he'd been having a lot of meetings designed to win funding for the group among some heavy hitters from his old days in the tech world. Evidently Evelyn Couture, the Pacific Heights widow, was talking about making a major bequest to the foundation, and he had met with her lawyers about that.

By this point I'd come to understand that as much as Swift liked making phone calls and having meetings, of the two of them, the one who actually made everything happen was Ava.

"Sending him off to schmooze up donors is a good way to keep Swift out of my hair," she told me. "The boy loves sitting in a cigar room and shooting the breeze about the 49ers, and he's great at getting people to take out their checkbooks. But you want to know something? He doesn't know the first thing about creating a nonprofit."

Meanwhile, Ava was taking the project to an even higher level, she said. She had hired a web designer and a marketing team to get the concept of the charity out to potential donors all over the country. Though he hated flying, now she was sending Swift off to New York for a meeting, and another time to Palm Beach. Also Atlanta, Boston, Dallas.

Sometime in late spring, when I showed up at their house for the usual combination of a walk with Ava and the dogs, plus work, followed by dinner—Ava was waiting for me in front of the house.

"I had this fabulous idea," she said. "I couldn't wait to tell you about it."

It turned out that Swift's birthday was coming up that October; he was turning sixty. ("Pushing sixty with a short stick" was how he'd put it.) Ava was planning to throw a big surprise party.

He'd know she would never let his birthday pass without some amazing celebration. But she had an idea that would make the whole thing much more meaningful. She'd tie the launch of the first BARK spay-and-neutering center, to be located in San Francisco, to the birthday night, with a big announcement, a short film maybe. And—here's where I'd come in—with my help, she'd create a commemorative book of photographs celebrating Swift's career and his dedication to rescuing dogs, along with documenting the lives of the very dogs the BARK foundation would be serving.

"Wouldn't he need to know about something like this in advance?" I asked her. "If you're planning to go public with the entire foundation that night?"

Ava laughed. "Oh, honey," she said. "You really are a babe in the woods. Swift never pays any attention to details. Set him up with one of his old fraternity brothers and a bottle of Macallan's, and he's happy. Particularly if there's a good-looking cocktail hostess nearby."

Ava, on the other hand, was a worker bee. And so was I.

I was to go through all the old family photographs and digitize them. Then Ava and I would select the images that best told the story of Swift's life—scrappy go-getter, entrepreneur, family man, dog lover. And lover of Ava, of course. Simultaneous with the presentation of the book at the birthday celebration would be the opening of the first of what Ava envisioned as hundreds of free spay-and-neuter centers to be built around the country. The party would be the social and philanthropic event of the season, guaranteed to be written up in the society and financial pages of all the major news outlets. With Swift's face—as captured by my camera—grinning over it all.

"Here's what came to me in the night," Ava said. "We'll combine the photographs with pictures of all the dogs his charitable contributions have saved in shelters that we've been supporting around the Bay Area and Silicon Valley.

"You'll take the portraits, of course," she said.

"I'm not an animal photographer," I told her.

She shook her head. To Ava, there was no meaningful distinction between dogs and humans, except that dogs were nicer. If you were a portrait photographer, you could take anybody's portrait, including that of a dachshund or a mutt.

"It would be like the pictures you take now of the children at all those schools," Ava said. "Except instead of children, you'd be capturing images of rescue dogs. And of course, being you, you'd do it in a way that made people fall in love with every dog and want to take out their checkbooks, the way Swift has. And we'd combine the pictures with the photographs you've been assembling of Swift over the years as a way of putting a human face on the foundation."

"I don't know anything about animal photography," I said again. "It's a very specific art."

"You'll learn."

Ava never had much patience for potential problems. "This would be a gorgeous, coffee-table-size book, a special limited edition only available to our guests at the party and big donors to BARK. I know you'll do an amazing job," she said. "This book will make the connection between human beings and animals, and show how interrelated our lives are."

But what about logistics, I asked her? It wasn't like at a school, where they gave me a room with my lights set up, with a team of classroom aides shepherding my subjects into the room one by one.

Ava would make all the arrangements for me; employees of all the Bay Area shelters knew her well already. It was up to me to capture the essence of each dog I photographed, the same way I did with school-children.

Just like that, it was settled. Ava had an uncanny ability to infuse every one of her projects with potential and promise. In her eyes, at least, everything she touched would be not simply successful but the most successful ever. Before I knew it she had me set to work on the first step of the undertaking: sorting through more than twenty boxes of family photographs. Some were from Swift's family, dating back to his childhood in New Jersey and his days in high school, where he was evidently a star wrestler. More came from his first marriage: his wedding, the birth of his son, trips to Disneyland and Europe. My job was to go through all of these, locate images that didn't include his ex-wife, Valerie, and select the ones that should be converted to a digital format. In some cases, I might actually be able to crop the image to exclude Valerie from the frame.

"I guess that might sound harsh," Ava said. "But if you knew her, you'd understand. I have no use for that woman."

"We'll want pictures of his years at his company, of course," she added. "Swift taking Cooper to ball games. Meeting me. Pictures of Swift in the pool and on his boat, all the things he loves. Ending up with the two of us and our dogs."

"I even thought up the title for our book," Ava said. "We'll call it *The Man and His Dogs*."

It turned out to be an enjoyable project, working my way through the pictures, observing all the stages Swift had gone through before he married my friend. (*My friend.* Just calling Ava that still thrilled me.) It was interesting to see what an awkward-looking kid he'd been—shorter than virtually all his classmates, with too-curly hair and glasses and, later, what appeared to be a bad case of acne. Around age sixteen he must have gotten into wrestling and his body changed. He was still short, but his arms were thickly muscled now, and his calves bulged. The photographs suggested that he carried himself differently, too: not swaggering, but confident.

In photographs from later in Swift's high school career, he was nearly always grinning, with a succession of unusually pretty girls on his arm, most of them taller than he was. Then came college; he joined a fraternity and bought a car. A beat-up Mustang first, then a Corvette. Then a Porsche.

Swift was a man on the move. Even when he was nineteen years old, you could tell that about him. Nothing was going to get in his way.

Well, maybe the marriage had, for a while. The first one. But Ava had instructed me to get through that part of the story in a single page. That left plenty of space for the part that mattered. Her.

31.

Ava said she'd love to accompany me on my shoot-ing expeditions, but there was a lot going on at home now having to do with the foundation. The sur-prise was that Elliot, whose schedule was flexible since he worked for himself, said he would come along with me to help.

Unfortunately, Elliot was allergic to dogs, but he said it would be worth enduring a few minor sinus issues to accompany me to the animal shelters just for the time we'd get to spend together in the car. While I was shooting, he could look over files on his laptop or catch up with his reading.

"I can't think of anything I'd rather do," he said, "than spend a bunch of afternoons driving around with you, helping you do something you love."

We had a lot of time to talk on those car rides, to places like Napa and Sebastopol and Half Moon Bay. We'd talked plenty already, but this was different. Maybe it was being off in the car that way, just the two of us, that made the difference. We talked about things we hadn't up until then.

When Elliot was growing up, in upstate New York, outside of Buffalo, his family had a farm where they raised dairy cows and chickens. His father's younger brother came to work on the farm one year. Uncle Ricky. Everybody loved Ricky, including Elliot. He was one of those people who simply by walking into a room was able to command everyone's attention, making them forget who they were talking to before.

"I know the type," I said, thinking of Swift.

"My dad was a quiet guy," Elliot said. "Like me. Boring, I guess you could say. If you were stuck on a road in a snowstorm, he'd be the guy you'd call to come with his truck and get you out of there, or the one who'd stay up all night with a cow having a hard time birthing a calf. But he wasn't what you'd call a live wire the rest of the time, like Ricky."

Ricky managed the books at the farm, handling the sale of milk and cream, the payroll. This was a pretty big operation at the time, had been in the family for five generations, and while nobody would have called their farm a gold mine, they made good money.

"Young as I was," Elliot said—eyes on the highway, as always, with both hands on the wheel—"I could feel something was going on between my uncle and my mother, though I was not of an age to understand what that might mean. I just knew she acted different when she was around him. Happier. But distracted."

Elliot's father must have noticed, too. There was a fight one night, and a lot of yelling. Next morning when Elliot got up, Uncle Ricky was gone. A while after that, Elliot's sister Patrice was born. Nobody said anything, but it occurred to Elliot later that very likely his father always wondered if she was his, or, more likely, knew she wasn't. Not that he treated Patrice any differently. Their dad was not the kind of man to favor one child over another, no matter what the story was surrounding that child's birth.

"Not long after Ricky left," Elliot told me, "we found out that he hadn't been paying any of our creditors. We owed more than sixty thousand dollars at this point, and back taxes on the farm. A whole lot of money that should have been in the revenue account was missing."

They all knew who was responsible, of course. They just didn't know where he was. Then or ever again.

"We lost the farm," Elliot said. "My dad went to work at a hardware store and my mother stopped getting out of bed. If it happened today, we'd understand my mother was suffering from depression, but back then all I knew was that she hardly ever got out of bed or said anything anymore, or if she did, it was something weird, like telling my father we needed to stock up on Campbell's soup in case there was a nuclear attack. She had this thing about Bob Barker—that he was hypnotizing people through the TV, and if you watched *Truth or Consequences* something would happen to your brain. One day it hit me: The guy was a ringer for Uncle Ricky.

"I stopped bringing friends home after school," he said. "My dad just poured himself a beer when he came home from work and sat in front of the television. If there was going to be dinner, I was the one who made it."

I put my hand on his shoulder. I knew what it was like to be so embarrassed about a parent you never wanted anyone to see where you lived.

We drove along in silence for a while then. I knew Elliot had more to say but figured he'd speak when he was ready.

"The year my sister entered high school, my mother killed herself," he said. "Closed the garage door, got in the car, turned on the ignition."

I asked Elliot if his father ever remarried. He shook his head. "I don't think he ever stopped loving her," Elliot said. "He was that type."

"I guess I never knew anyone like that," I told him. I was better acquainted with men who left than those who stayed.

"You've met one now," Elliot said, putting his arm around me.

"You've come a long way from farming to accounting," I told him.

"You know why?" he said. "I never got over the way my father lost every cent he had, just because he didn't know anything about his own finances. He hadn't kept good books, or any books at all. He let everything he loved slip through his hands because he was too busy taking care of the day-to-day running of things to keep an eye on the books. And then there was nothing left to run and no more land to take care of."

"So you decided you'd get really good at numbers," I said.

"I know it's just about the most unglamorous career there is, in most people's eyes," he said. "But an accountant can be a hero, too, if he saves his clients from financial ruin."

"It's a fine thing," I said. Though that perception of accounting as a boring profession filled with passionless bean counters was precisely the one Ava had expressed to me. And truthfully, it was one I'd held, too.

"I guess you could say I'm obsessed," Elliot said. "Because when I open up a person's taxes or their business records, I don't want to miss a single decimal point. I'm the guy who reads annual reports for fun. Always on the lookout for something that doesn't add up."

I studied his face then: not the kind of face that would inspire anyone to look twice if he walked in the room, even if he was wearing something other than his baggy Dockers and button-down shirt, though if you looked closer, he was actually a good-looking man. But he was not a person who needed anyone to notice him, or one to draw attention to himself.

"I wish I could be more of a hero in your eyes, Helen," he said. "Or a guy like your friend Ava's husband there, who can probably fly her to Paris for Valentine's Day, or just build them an Eiffel Tower in their backyard if it's too hard for her to get there. Maybe it will be enough for you one of these days that I'm an honest man who loves you with all his heart."

"I wasn't comparing you to Swift," I said. Though I had done that.

"But I was," he said. "And I'm aware of all the ways I fall short in the eyes of people like those two."

Something about the way he said it—"those two"—
made me stiffen. This should have been where I'd tell
him he was wrong, that they'd said he sounded like a
terrific guy for me and they couldn't wait to meet him.
Only they hadn't said that. All I could say was how it
was for me.

"Swift and Ava have been wonderful to me," I said.
"I owe them so much."

"I just hope they don't try to collect at some point,"
Elliot said.

32.

It was June now, and I hadn't been over to Swift and Ava's for a while. Normally I was there almost daily, working on my photography project for Ava, but the Havillands had been off at Lake Tahoe, and then I'd been over at Elliot's house in Los Gatos. He'd been on vacation, and I'd had no jobs, either, so we'd driven up the coast and gone camping for a few nights. That Saturday, when we got back, we'd gone bike riding, and the next night he'd invited a few of his friends over and barbecued chicken. Nothing like the kind of gatherings that took place on Folger Lane, but we'd had a nice time together. *Nice.* I couldn't think the word now, let alone say it, without hearing Ava's voice in my ear.

Just nice?

The morning after I returned from our camping trip, I headed over to the Havillands' to get back to work on the book project. But above all, I wanted to see Ava. She was there in the driveway to greet me, calling out my name even before I got out of my car. Lillian and Sammy raced in circles around me like long-lost friends.

"Do you have any idea how much I missed you?" she said. "I know I used to get along fine without you, but honestly I don't know how."

She reached out her long, sculpted arms to throw around my neck. I breathed in her gardenia perfume.

"Estella just came back from the market with the croissants and they're still warm," she said. "You have to tell me everything."

There wasn't a lot to say. When I was going on awful dates, I'd had a million stories for her. Now that I was spending time with Elliot, there was only one.

"I'm happy," I told her. "I know it sounds crazy, but I think I might actually love this man."

"That's great, honey," she said. I couldn't say why, but something in her response left me feeling faintly deflated. I had the sense I'd disappointed her, fallen short of her hopes. As if I was her child, and I was telling her I'd gotten into a program to become a dental assistant, when she'd expected me to be a cardiac surgeon.

I had thought Ava might like to hear more about my trip to the Sierras. Or that we might talk about Elliot and me. I had been looking forward to telling her more, though not so much the intimate details.

In the past, I had always told Ava everything. But I felt a new and unprecedented sense of protectiveness around this relationship. Still, I had pictured the two of us sitting in the garden, maybe out by the pool, sharing iced coffee and discussing our men. Planning a dinner—just the four of us, maybe. Though early on in my relationship with Elliot the Havillands had professed a desire to meet him, nearly two months had passed since we'd started seeing each other, and they had yet to follow up with an invitation.

"Listen," Ava said now, when we got in the door. "I'm hoping you can do me a favor. You remember Evelyn Couture?"

This was the rich widow from Pacific Heights whom Swift had befriended somehow, who'd shown up—with her driver—at the Havillands' last couple of parties. An unlikely friend for Ava and Swift, but you never knew who those two would take under their wing. I figured they'd noticed she was lonely. Maybe she had no family, or the family she had only wanted her money.

"She's moving out of her house on Divisadero and moving into a condominium in Woodside," Ava said.

"And she's just overwhelmed, trying to figure out what to do with all her things. I volunteered to help her."

Ava never acknowledged any limitations created by being in the chair, but I had to ask her. It seemed unlikely that the house would be handicapped accessible. What was she planning to do?

"Those Pacific Heights mansions are impossible!" she said. "Maybe she'll have some lovely giant of a houseboy to carry me up the stairs and set me on one of her velvet couches. More likely I'll need to drop you off. I know you'll be amazing at calming her down. Evelyn needs help making a plan. She has so much stuff in that house, she'd never know where to start."

There was no houseboy, of course. Ava left me at the house on Divisadero and went to Pilates, in a building that was handicapped accessible, and did some other errands in the city—hair, brows, therapist. I spent the rest of the morning and part of the afternoon with Evelyn Couture, helping her sort through the clothes she'd be donating to an upscale resale shop, the proceeds from which would benefit the ballet. Before I left (Ava having pulled up in front to retrieve me), Evelyn presented me with a brooch in the shape of a butterfly and a pair of earrings still in their Macy's box with the price tag attached: $14.95.

"That's so Evelyn," Ava said, when I showed her the earrings. "Let's just hope she's more generous with her donations to our foundation. We've got high hopes."

We both knew the big moment for that would be Swift's sixtieth-birthday party, when the Havillands would go public with their plan for free spay-and-neuter clinics in all fifty states. The Havilland Animal Centers, under the auspices of BARK.

"Just because I asked you to help Evelyn out today, I don't want you to think that I don't recognize your professionalism as a photographer," Ava said as we were driving back to Portola Valley from the city. "This book you're making for us, it's going to be a real artwork. Today was just greasing the wheels. You know the kind of thing you sometimes need to do, when people have a lot of money and you want to keep them happy."

33.

"I have these friends," I had told Elliot the first night we met. "Wonderful people. The best friends I ever had. They sort of took me under their wing. They're like my family."

The weekend we went to Mendocino I had told him the whole story about what happened with Ollie. That terrible moment in the courtroom when it felt as if the building were crashing down over me, and after, packing my son's belongings in cardboard boxes and trash bags. My worries about Dwight losing his temper with Oliver and Cheri ignoring him. My hope of someday—when the lawyer was finally paid off—hiring a new attorney, a better one, and trying to get the custody order changed. But all that seemed like an impossible goal.

"You're not the first person on earth to get a DUI," Elliot said. "You go to AA. You don't drink anymore. Can't you at least bring your son over to your apartment sometimes?"

"I keep asking, but Dwight never allows Ollie to spend the night at my place," I said. "It's like going to the principal's office. Every time I stand on Dwight's doorstep to see Ollie, I feel like this pathetic loser."

"Never mind what they think about you," Elliot said, "so long as you get to spend time with your son."

"But Ollie never seems to want to see me anymore," I said, quieter now. "I think he's angry at me. Even though he's not close with his father, I'm the one he blames.

"Then there's the whole thing about the Sacramento relatives," I continued. "He's always getting invited to these elaborate birthday parties on weekends. Bouncy houses and magicians and trips to a water park."

"One thing Ollie doesn't get over there," Elliot said—he took my hand here—"is you. He might not even know it yet, but he needs his mother. Once you get to spend some real time with him again—not just an hour here or there—you can rebuild his trust."

An idea had occurred to me, in fact: something that would entice Ollie to make an overnight visit, if his father okayed it and we could find a weekend when he wasn't all booked up with social engagements. I'd bring him to Swift and Ava's.

In the years since my marriage had ended, I'd come to feel that what I offered Ollie now—because it didn't come with the trappings of family life—was no longer enough. But at the Havillands', family life was always going on. I knew the house on Folger Lane would be just about irresistible to an eight-year-old boy, with the pool and all the things Swift had bought for Cooper when he was a kid: the jukebox, the pinball machine, the professional-quality air hockey table, the DJ turntables and mixing board. What were a bunch of PlayStation games and a Wii compared to that? And I could offer my son Ava and Swift—Swift in particular, who was in certain ways just like a boy himself.

Ollie would love Swift. And as a boy who had asked for a puppy since he was three years old, I knew he'd love the dogs. As the son of a father who always seemed to be yelling at him for not cleaning up his room, Ollie would love the relaxed, easy way life went on Folger Lane, where a person's one responsibility was to have fun.

The next day, over lunch in their garden, I asked the Havillands if I could bring Ollie over one weekend day. "I'd love for you to meet him," I told them. "I know he'd love it over here. And he'd love you."

No need for convincing. "It's about time we had a kid over here again," Swift said. "With my boy off at that expensive business school of his."

"We have a kid here," Ava said. "I'm looking at him. What Swift really means is, he could use a playmate. So by all means bring Ollie over, Helen. The sooner the better."

That night I called my ex-husband to suggest that Ollie spend the night with me the following weekend. "If you want to ask Oliver, be my guest," he said. He put our son on the line. "Your mother has something to ask you," he said, handing over the receiver.

"I have these friends who've got a pool," I told Oliver. It was a bribe, and I knew that, and I didn't care. "Also they've got a boat. I was thinking it might be fun, if you came over here next weekend, we could spend some time over there. Maybe have a cookout or something."

"I don't know how to swim," Ollie said. His voice was flat, wary, as it nearly always was now when I talked with him.

"It could be a good opportunity to work on that," I said. "And they have dogs."

He hesitated.

"Three of them," I said. "Their names are Sammy and Lillian and Rocco. Sammy loves playing Frisbee."

Partly I hated it that I was using the Havillands and their dogs as bait this way. But I just wanted to get Ollie back with me, one way or another, someplace where we could settle in with each other a little.

"Okay," Ollie said.

We set a date for the following weekend. I'd be picking Ollie up Saturday morning, bringing him over to Ava and Swift's. Swift would grill burgers. Ava would make her homemade ice cream. There was no telling what else Swift would come up with, but I knew it would be something Ollie had never experienced before, something wonderful.

What I didn't feel I could do—because I didn't want one thing to go wrong, or risk upsetting Ollie—was include Elliot. I was nervous telling him, but he said he understood.

"You're wise not to introduce your son to the man in your life until you feel really sure of where you're headed," Elliot said. *The man in my life.* He was calling himself that.

"It's okay," he said. "I'm a patient man. Meeting Ollie means a lot to me. I want to do this right. I plan to be in your life—in both of your lives—for a long time."

34.

The weekend came.

I changed four times before making the drive to Walnut Creek to pick my son up at his father's house. Dress, shorts, dress again, jeans. In the end I decided that the best idea was to look as if I hadn't been trying so hard, which was what brought me to the jeans. I had also noted, the last time I'd attended one of Ollie's games, that his stepmother, Cheri, appeared to have put on weight, so I liked it that I was thinner than usual, myself, and definitely slimmer than the woman for whom my husband had left me.

"I hate it about myself that I still care about looking good when I go over there," I told Ava.

"You're human," she said. "Look at Swift and me. I don't have a doubt in the world that he adores me, but on the rare occasions when I know we're going to run into the monster woman"—this would be Swift's first wife, Valerie, Cooper's mother—"I go and do something crazy like get my hair blown out.

"It's not about anything between Swift and me. It's about me and the ex-wife," she offered. "Same as it is for you, probably. You probably want to look good around your ex-husband, but more than anything I bet you just want to look better than his wife. And make sure she notices that."

"I hate how women can get with each other," I said. "It's like we never graduated from junior high."

"You know one of the things I love about our friendship?" Ava said. "There's none of that kind of crap between us. I never worry about you that way. We don't have this sick competition going on. And I know you're not after my husband the way so many other women are. With you, it's just not an issue."

I knew this was supposed to be a compliment, but thinking about what she'd said as I drove along the freeway to pick up my son, I couldn't help but feel, as I often did, small and colorless. So invisible I could be jumping off a diving board naked and the most sex-obsessed man I ever met wouldn't even look up.

There was one who would, though. Elliot. He wasn't like Swift, but to him, for some reason, I was the most desirable woman on the planet.

"I'm not going to be the kind of jerk who calls you a dozen times a day," he said to me, on one of the many occasions when he did call me. "But I just want you to know, that's how often I feel like calling. Not to mention how often I think about you. Which is constantly."

We had spent the night together two nights in a row that week, but now we wouldn't be seeing each other all weekend.

"I might be an idiot in some ways," he told me, "but one thing I'll never do is interfere in your relationship with your son. That's the most important thing in the world for you."

I kissed him then. One thing I could always count on from Elliot (in fact, there were many) was his understanding.

"I just want you to know," he said. "I'll be missing you like crazy this weekend. I'll probably have to drown my sorrows in rereading the tax code, or watching every *Thin Man* movie."

That was Elliot for you, I thought. It could be the most beautiful day outside, and he'd be happy holed up in his study with the blinds down, watching old movies or working on his laptop. Whereas someone like Swift would be off on his motorcycle. Or taking a seminar on tantric sex. Or just practicing it.

I registered a small, tight feeling then, like a constriction on my heart. When a relationship was really good, you didn't think critically about your partner the way I was inclined to do. You didn't compare him to your friend's husband, or find yourself observing, as he stood there in his old bathrobe, making the coffee, that he really did have terrible posture and a poochy belly. Or that the bathrobe was made out of this cheap kind of terry cloth, the kind your friend's husband would never be caught dead wearing.

But there was this other part, and it confused me: Hearing Elliot say how much he'd miss me that weekend, it occurred to me that I would miss him, too. As much as this was true, I also felt a kind of relief that Elliot wouldn't be around for my weekend with my son. If he were, I'd be worrying about what the Havillands thought about him.

And who was I, anyway? I, who owned an equally unstylish bathrobe, and probably looked as ridiculous in mine as he did in his. I, who also loved old movies, and would have liked to spend a whole afternoon—even a sunny one—watching three in a row with him. If I had felt more confident about Elliot's ability to be enough for my son, I could have suggested that he be the one—he, and not Swift—who could come along with us on fun excursions and cook out together, to help Ollie get past that hard, bitter place he inhabited, in which he viewed his mother as a person who'd abandoned him. I would have chosen Elliot, not Swift, as the man to hold out to my son that weekend with the message: *See, you can have a good day with your mother. And if there's one, there can be more.*

But the truth was, I knew my son wouldn't be that impressed with Elliot. The lure for Ollie would be Swift and the picture of life on Folger Lane. The pool, the dogs. But mostly Swift.

At the time, I admitted none of this—not even to myself. As guilty as I felt for looking critically at Elliott, I felt equally guilty for being as contented with him as—more and more, when we were alone together—I was. Sometimes, now—remembering all Ava had told me—I found myself worrying that there might be something wrong with me for being so satisfied with someone so seemingly ordinary as Elliot. As if I had made the choice to have a smaller, lesser life. Opting for simple, uncomplicated contentment over large and extraordinary passion.

Don't settle, Ava had said. When I was with Elliot, I didn't feel I was doing that. But every time my car pulled up in front of the house on Folger Lane, the doubts returned.

35.

Cheri was on the phone, as she often was, when I got to my ex-husband's house to pick my son up for our weekend together—the first in over three years. My son's stepbrother, Jared, sat on a booster seat in front of a half-eaten Pop-Tart, gesturing with an uncapped felt-tip pen. Seeing me in the door, Cheri pointed in the direction of the living room, where I could hear the sound of cartoons. Dwight was out golfing, probably. Ollie was on the couch in his pajamas. He looked pale, and his neck, in the stretched-out pajama top, seemed skinny and pinched, birdlike. There was a bowl of cereal on the coffee table and a bunch of toys on the floor that must have belonged to Jared. My son didn't look up.

It was never my style to make some big, dramatic entrance, even when I had been aching to put my arms around him. I'd learned, over the course of the sad gray months, then years, since he'd moved away to Walnut Creek, that it took Ollie a few hours—sometimes as long as a day—to get comfortable with me again after we'd been apart. It no longer surprised me as it first had to see his blank, impassive expression when I came to pick him up. I knew that when I hugged him, his body would be taut and wary. Sometime later, if I was lucky—right around the time I had to say good-bye—he'd fold into me in the old familiar way, and I'd glimpse for a moment the way it had been before between us. Then it would be time to bring him home, and I'd feel the armor come up.

"Hey, Oll," I said. "Good to see you." I lowered myself onto the floor beside him.

He was sucking his thumb, a habit I knew he was trying to break because kids at school teased him about it. When he was alone, or anxious, he reverted to his old ways.

"Want me to help you get your stuff together?" I said. I could be irritated at Cheri, or Dwight, for not having taken care of this, but what was the point?

"I want to finish my show."

I sat down next to him on the couch, resisting the impulse to pick him up, to press him up against me. I rubbed his back. Ran my hand over his hair. Sometimes, when I came to pick him up, he'd have a buzz cut—for convenience, I figured—but this time Ollie was overdue for a trip to the barbershop, and his toenails were long. He looked like a boy whose mother had not been watching out for him as closely as she should.

Although Ollie had been going back and forth between his father's house and my apartment for three years now, somehow we'd never gotten around to buying him a real suitcase or duffel bag for his stuff. With Cheri on the phone still, I reached under the sink for a plastic trash bag to gather his belongings for the weekend.

Two sets of underwear. Two pairs of socks. In the old days, when he lived with me, we used to make a game of matching the pairs, but now they were all thrown in the drawer together. All white. Cheri probably found that easier than keeping track of all the interesting designs—cars, dinosaurs, Transformers—that I used to buy for him.

I reached in the drawer for his Boston terrier shirt that he loved, though it was too small now, and a couple of others—one long-sleeved, one short.

"We need to bring your swim trunks," I told him. "At the friends' house where we're going, they've got a pool."

"Nobody ever showed me how to swim," he said. The implication was clear enough: I should have taught him.

214 • JOYCE MAYNARD

"I'll be in the water with you," I said. "They'll have a noodle."

"You said they have a dog," he said. Wary as usual.

"Three of them."

"Do they get cable?" he said.

"Wait till we get there," I told him. "We'll be having way too much fun to watch TV."

"I was going to watch a show about robots," he said. His voice had a quietly resentful tone I knew well. As if every wrong thing in the world right now was my fault.

"Cheri has a DVD player in her van," Ollie said, once he'd buckled himself into the backseat of my Honda. I hated it that the law now required children to sit in the backseat, instead of up front next to you, where you could talk. Evidently this was safer, but driving this way, with Ollie behind me, I always felt more like a chauffeur than a mother.

"Well, I prefer to have a conversation," I said. "I haven't seen you in two weeks. I want to hear what's going on at school. What's Mr. Rettstadt been teaching you lately?"

"Nothing."

"I don't believe that. Tell me one thing."

"Blah blah," he said. "Blah blah blah blah blah. Blah blabaddy blabaddy bladda bladadda blah."

"I went to the library," I told him. "I got a stack of books for us. There's one about insects."

"I hate insects."

That didn't used to be so, back when he lived with me, when we'd spent the better part of an hour studying an anthill. But this was not a point to win.

"There are other books," I told him.

"I hate reading."

In the end, he fell asleep on the drive. I had thought we might stop at a park we sometimes went to, where he liked to ride his scooter, but by the time we made it across the bridge it was past noon, and I knew Ava would have lunch ready for us, so I headed straight for Folger Lane.

"I think you'll like these friends," I said when he woke up, a mile or so from their house. "They've been looking forward to meeting you."

I hated the sound of my own voice, saying this stuff. I sounded like a flight attendant.

"Ava, the wife, can't walk," I told him. "She has a wheelchair. She's got a special car that lifts her up into the seat."

"What time is it?" Ollie said. Thumb in mouth then. Eyes glassy, staring out the window. "When do we go home?"

Pulling into their driveway, I was thinking I'd made a terrible mistake. My son would not allow himself to have a good time. Ava and Swift would try their best, but later, after we left, they'd look at each other and say, "Thank God that's over." They'd be kind, but agree not to ever invite us over again. They might even come to the sad but obvious conclusion that it was probably for the best that I did not have custody of my son.

Then Ava was throwing open the door for us. Lillian came right over to Oliver and started running around in circles the way she always did when she met someone new, and Sammy wagged his tail, making a happy yipping noise. But the big surprise was Rocco, who usually growled at everyone who wasn't Ava, but appeared to take an immediate liking to my son. From the moment Ollie walked in the door, Rocco was licking his hand and following him.

"Pleasure to meet you, Oliver," said Swift, offering his hand. "Can I get you a drink?" Like Ava, he was one of those rare people who do not adjust their tone of voice in any way when speaking with a child.

"Do you have to put money in that?" Ollie asked. He had noticed the pinball machine, which Swift had been smart enough not to point out. Better to let Ollie discover things for himself here.

"For you, buddy, it's free," said Swift. "My son Cooper used to play that all the time. When we first got it, he was too short to reach the controls, so we got him that box there.

Ollie climbed up on the makeshift step stool. He was stroking the controls. Then he looked at me, as if I might tell him not to touch it.

"It's fine," I told him. "These are our friends. You can do whatever you feel like."

After lunch, he wanted to see where the dogs' beds were. Then Swift showed him the den, where he had taken out Cooper's old Ninja Turtles.

"Is your kid around?" Ollie asked.

"He's big now," Swift told him. "The only kid around here now is me."

Ollie looked at him hard. Sizing him up.

"You can make yourself at home, bud," Swift told him. "The one place you've got to be a little careful is by the pool. Ava made this rule, there has to be a grown-up around if I'm going in the water. This would apply to you, too."

"But he's not a kid," Ollie whispered to me.

"You got me there, buddy," Swift told him. "But I misbehave a little now and then, same as kids do. The only difference is, nobody sends me to my room."

We walked outside. They stood at the side of the pool for a moment, the two of them looking down at the water, Swift darkly tanned—he never believed in sunscreen—Oliver's legs, under his too-big shorts, the color of milk.

"I don't know how to swim," Ollie said. His voice was low and husky. Back when my son still lived with me, I'd taken him to two different sessions of swimming lessons, but Ollie had always been afraid of the water.

"You don't say?" said Swift. "Maybe it's time we did something about that."

He picked up my son and threw him over his shoulder. Still holding onto Ollie, he jumped in the water. I thought Ollie would cry, but he came up laughing.

In the end, the two of them spent most of the afternoon in the water. By four o'clock, Ollie was jumping off the edge backward and doing dead man's float from one end of the pool to the other.

"You were kidding me, right?" said Swift. "When you told me that stuff about not swimming. You're a natural. You'll be a champ."

"I didn't know I could swim!" said Ollie. "I never came over to your house before."

"Well, now you know what you need to do," said Swift. "You have to come visit us more often."

My son's face took on a serious expression. As if Swift had just offered him a job, and he, after consideration, was accepting the offer.

"Do you think your kid will mind if I play some more on his pinball machine?" Ollie asked. Swift had shown him a photograph of Cooper hang gliding over the Arizona desert, and another of Cooper in the skybox at a Giants game.

"I think he'd like you to do that," Swift said. "Maybe one of these days when you come over, he'll be here, too, and you guys can hang out together."

Ollie played pinball for a while and tossed the Frisbee to Rocco out in the yard. Then Ava made us smoothies and let Ollie throw every single thing he wanted into the blender. A little before dinnertime we all got in Swift's Range Rover and drove to the park to take the dogs for a walk. Rocco stayed next to Oliver the whole time.

We went out for hamburgers. Swift ordered Ollie a root beer float. Sitting with me in the backseat, with Rocco on his lap, Ollie leaned close to me. "I wish we didn't ever have to go home," he whispered.

My son fell asleep in the car. This gave Ava and Swift a chance to get caught up on what was happening with Elliot, though—even with Ollie sleeping—we avoided some of the specifics.

"So you really like this guy?" Swift said.

I told him I did. "It's not some huge deal," I said. "But it's always easy with him."

"Easy," said Ava. She sounded skeptical.

"And how does he feel about my little buddy here?" said Swift. "Because this little guy deserves to have a great guy in his life. The best."

"Let's not jump the gun, darling," said Ava. "Helen's just dating this Elliot person. It's not like they're getting married."

"It's a fair question," said Swift. "Helen needs to think ahead."

"Well, Elliot probably wouldn't be a natural with kids, like you," I told Swift. "But hardly anyone is."

"But good in bed, right?" he said, grinning as usual.

"Hush," said Ava, gesturing in the direction of Ollie. *"Her son."*

It was past ten o'clock when Ollie and I got back to my apartment. Though he was too big to carry up the stairs, I managed—it felt so good, getting to do this again, and afterward, laying him on the air mattress I'd set up for him and unlacing his shoes. The last thing he said, drifting off, was to ask if we could go visit our friends again tomorrow. He called Swift Monkey Man.

The next morning Ollie asked again if we could go back to Monkey Man's house, but I'd promised to have him back at his father's by noon. We sat outside on the little balcony off my living room—looking out over the parking lot—and I gave him a haircut. I could have stood on that balcony forever, my son in the chair with a towel around his neck, me with the scissors, clipping his wispy blond hair. I didn't want it to end, and though I might have been wrong, it seemed to me that he was happy, too. His shoulders—so tense just one day earlier—weren't hunched up in that way they often were. He was singing "Yellow Submarine," one of the songs he'd heard on the jukebox the day before at Folger Lane.

On the car ride back to Walnut Creek, he was already talking about what he wanted to do the next time we went over to Monkey Man's house. Play with the dogs again. Try out the air hockey table. And go swimming some more with Monkey Man.

"Is that guy a superhero or something?" he asked me.

"You could say that," I said.

The Monday night after I brought Ollie back to his father's in Walnut Creek, Elliot took me out to dinner.

"I hope this won't sound needy," he said. "We only went three days without seeing each other. But I just missed you so much. I can't even remember what it was like before you were in my life." I could have felt happy that he felt this way, but instead I registered a certain irritation. As if he had nothing else going on.

"I totally respect your decision not to introduce me to Ollie yet," he said. "I just look forward to the day when you feel sure enough about the two of us that you can do that."

I didn't know what to tell him. The truth was, my reluctance to introduce Ollie to Elliot was only partly about the relative newness of our relationship. The other part came from my fear that if the two of them did meet, Elliot wouldn't know what to say to Ollie. And that Ollie would think he was a dork. It came from recognizing that Elliot would be nothing like Swift. And Ollie would wish he were.

And it wasn't just my fear that Ollie might not think much of Elliot that had kept me from including Elliot in our time at the Havillands'. I also worried about Ava and Swift's judgment of Elliot. I worried that Elliot might embarrass me in front of my friends. Or worse, embarrass himself.

"I'm sure you two will meet up before too long," I said. "I just want to find the right moment."

Hard to say what moment that would be.

36.

Usually Swift would be out in the pool house talking on the phone when I came over to Folger Lane to see Ava or to work (in secret, of course) on the birthday book. If he was around, he'd joke with me for a minute or two before disappearing. But the next time I saw him, a few days after Ollie's visit, he wanted to talk about my son.

"You've got a great kid there," he told me.

"He loved hanging out with you," I said.

"It's totally fucked up that his father took him away." Swift was chewing on a turkey leg as he spoke. He ate like a caveman. No fork. "He won't admit it, but a boy that age needs his mom. As much as my ex-wife drove me crazy, I knew that when Cooper was a kid."

"Believe me, my son's father is nothing like you," I told him.

"Well, you're a great mom," he said. "Ollie should get to spend a lot more time with you."

It had seemed to me that the person my son wanted to spend time with that last weekend had been Swift. But that was still good news. So long as Ollie wanted to visit Swift and Ava's house, he'd want to visit me. So long as the Havillands were around, I had a family to offer him.

"So when are you going to get that boy back over here?" Swift said. "I miss him already."

"I was thinking about trying to get some more time with Ollie over summer vacation," I told Swift. "But his father's not likely to be very supportive of that, and if he doesn't agree to it voluntarily, there's no way I can go back to court right now to force the issue. The legal aid lawyer I talked to last year still hasn't done one thing on my case."

Not to mention, I said, I hardly had any time off all summer. In addition to the work I'd been doing for the Havillands, I'd taken on extra work, doing some low-paid catalog shoots down on the peninsula, which meant I'd hardly have any free time for being with Ollie. Never mind Elliot.

"Listen," Ava said. "Oliver's happy over here. And Estella's always around. If you can just get your ex-husband to agree to let him spend a few weeks this summer with you, Swift and I are happy to have him come over here when you're working."

I couldn't say anything. I was stunned by their generosity. I let myself imagine setting up an air mattress for him. The Legos back on the living room table. Popcorn on the couch.

"I'll teach him to swim," Swift said. "We'll have that kid doing the butterfly by Labor Day."

"I'll talk to his father," I said.

37.

I called Dwight to ask if I could keep Ollie with me for a few weeks that summer. With less argument than I'd anticipated he agreed to a two-week visit, by far the longest amount of time I'd gotten to spend with my son since losing custody.

"If I hear one word about you drinking, we won't be doing this again," he said.

I wanted to say something back, but I didn't. All that mattered was getting time with Ollie. I'd waited a long time for this.

Over the phone the next night, Ollie told me his plans for the visit. He was going to teach Rocco a trick, he said. And he was going to work on his swimming. That day he'd gone into the pool with Monkey Man, they'd decided to have a swim race on Labor Day week-end. Now, Ollie said, he could start training.

"Maybe if I'm in a good mood I'll give you a head start, buddy," Swift had told him. "But I don't think you'll need one. You're a lot younger than me. Do you know how old I am?"

"Twenty-five?" Ollie had guessed. He was sketchy on ages of adults, but Swift really did act like a twenty-five-year-old.

It wasn't only Ollie who seemed excited about the summer plan. So was Swift. He had bought seats for a Giants game, and he was looking into how old a person had to be to go drive the Formula 4 go-karts he'd seen at a track off of I-280, with an eye toward a field trip for himself and Ollie. Not only that: Cooper's old batting cage, which had sat neglected in the yard for close to ten years now, would be refurbished. Swift understood that I probably wouldn't want Ollie riding on the back of the motorcycle. But how would I feel about it if he got a sidecar? he asked me.

"I want to bring the kid to Tahoe," Swift told Ava and me. "Take him out on the boat. The Donzi."

I'd heard him mention the boat before. It had been a graduation gift to Cooper. A number of the photographs lining the walls of the house featured the two of them on a highly streamlined speedboat. Laughing, as always.

"We're not talking some old Boston Whaler," Swift went on. "This baby's an original 1969 Donzi cigarette boat. Colin Farrell drove a Donzi in the *Miami Vice* movie. Think our boy Oliver might go for a ride in that one?"

"Let's not forget the point here, sweetheart," Ava said, as Swift listed his many plans for things to do with my son that summer. "This is about Helen and Ollie getting to see more of each other. Not you getting a fresh chance to share all your toys with a little boy again."

"I know, I know," Swift said. "I'm just talking about all the stuff I'll do when Cooper and Virginia start popping out rug rats. This will be good practice."

Hearing Swift say this, I felt a rush of gratitude and affection. As if it weren't enough that the Havillands had adopted me as they had, now they were including my son in that warm embrace. It might be true that I was using Swift and Ava as a way of getting Ollie to spend time with me, but if so, was that so terrible? We had to start somewhere.

"I'm not sure I feel old enough to be a grandfather," Swift added. "Call me an uncle. A rich uncle." He let loose his big crazy laugh. "We're going to have a ball."

"Just keep in mind, darling," said Ava, "this is supposed to be Helen's time with Oliver. Who knows, I might even like to see some of you myself this summer."

"Which part of me were you planning to see?" he said.

38.

The person whose name did not come up in our discussions of the summer activities was Elliot, whose existence remained unknown to my son and the object of a certain quiet but unmistakable judgment to my friends. With Ollie back at my apartment—for those two weeks, anyway—I'd have to curtail my new practice of spending two or three nights a week in Los Gatos with Elliot. But having that time with Ollie was a precious, long-awaited opportunity to rebuild our relationship. I would let nothing get in the way of that.

When I told Elliot I wouldn't be able to sleep over at his place anymore, once Ollie came to stay with me, he took the news with kindness, as usual. He was happy for me that I'd get to see more of my son. If things went well over the summer, who knew what might follow?

As for the rest: We'd take things slowly. Once he and Ollie met, he knew things would work out.

"I know I'm a nerd," he said. "But I think once we get to know each other he'll be able to tell that I mean well. And I care about him."

I already had the inflatable bed, but with a longer visit approaching I bought a folding screen to give my son a little privacy and stocked up on his favorite cereal and Popsicles. Rather than subject Ollie to yet another uncomfortable transfer of his possessions, I bought a giant set of Legos and set the box on the living room table, along with a fresh box of watercolor markers and (because the Havillands' pool would be a big part of his time that summer) a new pair of swim trunks. Nights now, counting down the days to picking Ollie up, I allowed myself to imagine us together again, finally. I would never let anything bad happen again. Nothing— not even this very good man I'd grown to care about— would get in the way of my time with my son.

I picked Ollie up at the end of June, two days after school got out. He was out in the yard waiting for me when I pulled up, and for the first time I could remember since the move to Walnut Creek, he was smiling. From inside the house, I could hear my ex-husband yelling. It sounded as though Jared had been giving him a hard time.

"He just spilled a box of cereal," Ollie said. "You know how Dad gets."

A few moments later Dwight came out to the driveway. As Ollie climbed into the car and started fiddling with the seat belt, my ex-husband leaned down and spoke in a low voice into my ear. "Just remember what I said about the drinking. One slip and it's over."

He straightened up and turned his attention toward Ollie in the backseat. "Don't forget, son, if you have any problems, you can always give Cheri or me a call. Even if it's the middle of the night." Then he stepped back from the car and waved, a tight smile on his face. From the doorway, I could see Cheri standing there, with Jared on her hip. No flicker of emotion there.

The moment we got to my apartment, Ollie wanted to go over to Monkey Man's house. Every day after that was the same. He liked Ava and he loved the dogs, but he was crazy about Swift. The first thing he said when he woke up in the morning was "When do we get to go see Monkey Man?"

I still had to work—though it never felt like work, helping Ava with the book project, and the best part was I could do this with my son nearby. Sometimes Swift went in the pool with him, but if not, Ollie would follow him around the house, stand watching his qigong lesson, or join in. If he got bored, he'd head outside with the dogs.

I worried sometimes that my son might overstay his welcome, become a nuisance to the Havillands, but Swift told me he loved having Ollie around. "This guy's my number-one sidekick," Swift said as the two of them headed out to the pool. "After Ava, of course."

Ava had taken to speaking of them as "the boys"— and pretty swiftly, they developed a routine together. Sometimes the two of them went on errands in Swift's Range Rover. Or they played air hockey. Swift was teaching Ollie how to play cards, and said he had a knack for bluffing. "You know the best way to get people to believe you when you're lying?" Swift said. "You fill in the fake part of your story with true stuff. Then they believe everything."

He showed him how to read the NASDAQ, and to make it more interesting, bought him three shares of Berkshire Hathaway, so he could follow what was happening to his stock. He had done the same thing with Cooper, years before. Sometimes Ollie brought his Legos out to the pool house where Swift worked and lay on the floor for an hour or two, just building, while, in the back room, Ava and I laid out photographs for the book—now well along—or talked.

But the big thing was the pool. After all those years of being afraid of the water, Ollie couldn't get enough of swimming, so long as Monkey Man was with him. Within a week his skin had turned brown and I could see muscles developing in his formerly skinny shoulders.

As much as possible, I wanted to spend time with my son, too, of course—not only during the days at the Havillands' but back at our apartment together in the evening. And we were having good times there, too, though my work for Ava seemed to be occupying more and more time. Sometimes it would be seven or eight o'clock before we made it back to the apartment for Ollie's bath time and our book.

The project of cataloging Ava's entire art collection had been set aside for the time being, so Ava and I could direct the majority of our energies to the secret birthday book—*The Man and His Dogs*. And my job description appeared to have expanded. More and more often, Ava was finding other tasks for me, little jobs she might once have assigned to Estella. She'd ask me to untangle a drawerful of necklaces or organize the perfume bottles on her vanity.

"Maybe Estella would like this job," I said once. "Or if Estella's too busy, Carmen."

"I used to ask Carmen to do things like this for me," Ava said. "But I've got to be honest. I don't trust that girl anymore. One time when I came home, I found her coming out of the laundry room with a guilty look on her face. But the deal breaker for me had to do with Cooper."

I asked what she meant.

"Back in high school, he earned this ring for rugby. The most valuable player. One day, a year or so after that, Carmen left her purse open on the table, and I saw it. That ring. She must have taken it."

"What did you do?" I asked her.

"Reached in and took it back, naturally. We never told Cooper. It would have broken his heart. He was always so fond of Carmen."

Ava told me that the additional work I did would free up more of her time. But more often than not, she'd end up sitting with me in the room where I worked, editing or arranging or organizing. I could hear my son and Swift outside splashing in the pool or hitting balls out by the batting cage. Ollie was so enthralled with Monkey Man that I started to worry that he and I weren't getting in as much time together on our own as I'd hoped for.

"I was thinking Ollie and I might take off a little early today," I said one afternoon, a week or so into Ollie's time with me. "Maybe take our bikes out together."

"I'm just so anxious about having the book ready for Swift's sixtieth," Ava said. "And anyway, you don't need to worry about Ollie. He and Swift are having a great time. Swift's always been like the Pied Piper where kids are concerned. It's like he hypnotizes them. They'd follow him anywhere."

Just then came the voice of my son, calling up from the pool house. "Hey, Mom. Monkey Man invited us for dinner. We can stay, right?"

"Of course," I told him. What plans could I have more exciting than that?

39.

As good as things had been with Elliot before the start of summer, I didn't think about him much once Ollie came back to stay with me. I was just so happy to have my son with me. And our days were filled with the Havillands. Things were going so well that Ollie had asked Dwight if he could stay another week, but the answer came back, no. Still, it was a good sign to know my son wanted to be with me. Even though I knew a big part of his reason was Swift.

Once and once only during that time, Ava asked me about Elliot. We were up in her office, looking through photographs for the commemorative birth-day book.

"You still seeing that guy?" she said. "Evan? Irving? The accountant?"

"We haven't had a chance to get together since Ollie's been with me," I told her. "But yes."

"When I first got together with Swift, we couldn't
be apart even for five minutes," she said. "I'm thinking
the sex is just average?"

I didn't really want to discuss it, but with Ava it was
hard to say no. Elliot was a sweet lover, I told her—
not wild or aggressive, and lacking a certain imagination, maybe, but slow and more tender than anyone I'd
ever known. When I got out of the tub—I was thinking back to earlier times, before Ollie's arrival—he put
lotion on my elbows and knees—a brand he'd sworn by
all his life, he said, one that farmers used.

"Mmmm. Sounds wonderful," Ava said. Dubiously.

It was true, I admitted: Elliot was not romantic in
any of the ways people think of when they're talking
about romance. But once, when I had three days off
in a row, we had driven up to Humboldt County and
camped in a secluded spot by a natural hot spring; he
had brought along his telescope, and we studied the
constellations. On the way home it had occurred to me
that though he was not one of those people who knock
you off your feet when you meet them, every time I
saw him I cared about him a little more. But, I told her,
I just didn't see how to have Elliot in my life as well as
my son. And I wanted my son more than anything.

I never said I was in love with Elliot, or that I felt that kind of all-consuming hunger to be with him that Ava described having known with Swift. (And still did, apparently.) In fact, almost nothing in the way Ava would speak about how things were between herself and Swift bore any resemblance to what I would have said about Elliot and me. Things were just easy and comfortable with him. I felt happy when he was around, but hadn't missed him now that he wasn't. He was always kind to me. I trusted him completely—more than I trusted myself, possibly.

"Kind is good, I guess," said Ava, with a certain hesitation in her voice. It was clear enough, without her saying more, that she expected more from a relationship than this.

As much as Swift alluded to how mind-blowing things were for the two of them, Ava never spoke of the particulars. They made no effort to conceal the books about tantric sex they kept around, or the erotic limited edition Hiroshige prints lining the second floor. But what actually went on between the two of them, and what was actually possible for Ava with her spinal cord injury, was a topic we never went to.

One night back at my apartment, I went online and googled *paraplegic sex,* which brought up all kinds of websites with information about catheters and positions for lovemaking in a wheelchair. Just doing that search left me feeling guilty, as if I had opened up the door to a room that should have stayed shut. Whenever Ava spoke of her intimate connection to Swift, she was vague, saying only that what went on between the two of them was beyond anything most couples ever imagined.

"Swift and I have no secrets from each other," she said. "It's like we're part of the same body. Maybe that's why I don't see it as a tragedy that I'm in this chair. He's not, and that makes me feel whole."

Talking about Elliot, I said, "We're very different. But it feels good, having this very steady man at my side. I never had a partner before that I trusted this way."

As always, when I spoke about Elliot, Ava's responses felt like damning with faint praise. "No doubt he's a really great guy," she said. "Just make sure you're not in the market for a brother or a pal. Speaking purely for myself, of course, I'd rather have a passionate love affair."

At the time, the idea of having a passionate love affair seemed inconceivable, anyway. Ava didn't have children, and maybe that was the difference between us. I had my boy back in my life. There wasn't room for much more than that.

40.

Ollie and I finally had something like a routine during those two weeks—the first time since he was five years old that I'd had a rhythm with my son. Because my apartment had only one bedroom, I'd set Ollie up in the living room, on an air mattress, but most mornings he'd come into bed with me sometime before sunrise, bringing a stack of library books with him, and we'd pile up the pillows and read till the sun came up. I'd make French toast or pancakes, and we'd play a round of a card game called Anaconda that Swift had taught him. Ollie usually won. Then we'd get dressed and I'd bring him over to Swift and Ava's, where he'd spend most of the morning playing with the dogs and swimming in the pool with Swift while I got a few hours' work in.

"I've got an idea," Swift said. We were out by the pool. I was taking a midmorning break to have a snack. Ollie was stretched out on a beach chair after a game of Marco Polo with Swift, listening to Swift's iPod. Ava was reading a magazine. Estella had just brought out the Bloody Marys and my own nonalcoholic version of the drink.

"It's been way too long since we had a party over here. Let's invite the boyfriend over for dinner."

"I don't know about that," I said. In fact, I'd been missing Elliot, but Folger Lane didn't feel like the best place for getting together with him after almost ten days of not seeing each other. And besides, Ollie would be here.

"It's about time we met this guy," Swift said. Ava knew his name, of course, but she always referred to him as "the accountant." Evidently Elliot's name hadn't registered with Swift either. "Why don't you call him up and see if he's free for dinner?"

When did he have in mind, I asked.

"Now."

"I don't think it's such a great idea," I said. "Elliot's never met Ollie. It might be better to do one thing at a time. First let Ollie spend a little time with just Elliot and me. Then we could all get together."

"You overthink things," Ava said. There was a sharpness in her voice I rarely heard in her, usually only when she was speaking to Estella, if she came home with the wrong kind of dog food or missed a spot vacuuming. Or—as had happened recently—when she'd told me about Carmen stealing Cooper's ring.

"It'll be fun," she said. "We can all head over to the yacht club and have dinner on the boat."

Not surprisingly, Elliott was free that evening, but as happy as he was to hear from me, he raised the same concern that I had earlier—though now, hearing him wonder if this was the right time and place for him to finally meet Ollie, I dismissed it with a certain sharpness of my own. "You overthink everything," I told him. "And you worry too much."

"I worry about things that matter to me," he said.

"How about we just have fun for once, without analyzing every-thing?"

Elliot was quiet. "I thought we'd been having plenty of fun," he said. "I just take this seriously, that's all. Meeting Ollie means a lot to me."

"It'll be fine," I said, sounding like Ava. "Swift has a grill on the deck of his boat. We can have hamburgers, and Ava will make s'mores. Swift will probably let Ollie steer the boat."

We decided that Elliot would meet us all over at Folger Lane that afternoon. We'd have a drink, and a swim for those who wanted, then head over to the yacht club for dinner on the Havillands' sailboat.

"The Donzi?" Ollie asked. He'd heard all about Monkey Man's speedboat by now.

Swift shook his head. "That one's at Tahoe, buddy," he said. "But don't you worry. I'm getting you out on that boat soon. And when we do, look out, baby." He made a motion like a cowboy twirling his lasso.

We were out by the pool when Elliot showed up. Swift was in his swim trunks, Ava in one of her long gowns. Ollie was in the water—his swimming having progressed to the point where he was no longer in need of an adult at his side, though we kept close watch.

I registered Elliot's clothes first. A button-down shirt and baggy khakis, penny loafers. He must have gotten a haircut since I'd seen him last. This left a strip of neck exposed, pink and vulnerable, and a naked place around his ears also. I didn't want this to bother me, but it did.

I got up to greet him, put my hand on his shoulder, but didn't kiss him, though in other circumstances I would have wanted to.

"I want you to meet my friends," I said. I figured it was best if we handled one introduction at a time. Swift and Ava first, then Ollie, once he got out of the water.

"I've heard a lot about you," Elliot said, extending his hand over the table, which held a nearly empty bottle of wine. Swift was already opening a new one.

Elliot had brought wine to contribute to the meal, too, but I knew it probably wouldn't pass muster with Swift.

"We know all about you, too," said Ava. "Well, maybe not everything. But you might call this 'meeting the parents.'"

"It's great that Helen's had friends like you two looking out for her," Elliot said.

"She's the kind of person someone could take advantage of," Swift said, looking Elliot in the eye. "There's a lot of sharks in the water."

"I'm not one of them," Elliot said. Meeting Swift's gaze.

"Of course you aren't," Ava said, reaching a hand up to pat Elliot on the arm. "A mouse would be scarier than Elliot."

They laughed. I didn't.

Swift tossed a towel to Elliot—thick pile, oversize, with a blue racing stripe on the bottom that matched the logo of one of the companies Swift had started. Back in the days when he still worked in Silicon Valley, Ava told me once, they gave these out as Christmas presents, along with matching, personally monogrammed bathrobes.

Now Swift was handing Elliot a cigar from his humidor of Cubans. Elliot's face took on a faintly pained expression.

"I hope you brought a change of clothes, pal," Swift said. "We're going out in the boat later."

"If not, we can give you something of Swift's," Ava said. Elliot was a good four inches taller than Swift, and their builds were entirely different, but Elliot made no comment.

"It's a rule around here," Swift added. "When a person doesn't go in the water on his own, we throw him in." He let out his big hyena laugh. I looked at Elliot, who wasn't smiling.

Ollie was on the diving board now doing cannonballs, calling out for Swift to watch. "My husband has turned this kid into a fish," Ava told Elliot.

"Next comes wrestling," said Swift.

Later, when he got out of the water—in that moment that always clutched at my heart: the sight of my little boy, skinny and shivering, dripping by the side of the pool, teeth chattering but happy—I wrapped Ollie in one of the blue striped towels and brought him over to the table where the adults had gathered.

"There's someone I want you to meet," I said. "This is Elliot."

I could see my son taking him in: the shirt, the dorky pants, his pale white ankles and pale white hands. Elliot had not gone in the water.

"He's your boyfriend, right?" Ollie said to me.

Swift let out one of his big laughs again. "This guy doesn't miss a trick," he said.

"Your mother and I are good friends," Elliot said. "But I'm not going to lie to you. Sometimes if I'm lucky I get to take her out on a date. I was hoping we might get to go someplace fun with you sometime, too."

"I don't want to go someplace else," Ollie said. "I like it here." He turned to Swift. "You want to play foosball?"

"I will destroy you," Swift said. "Destroy, and then pulverize." He lifted Ollie up over his head then and carried him—shrieking and laughing—to the pool house, where the games were.

This left Ava and me alone with Elliot. She started to pour him a glass of wine but he stopped her.

"I'm not much of a drinker," he said.

She set down the bottle. "Oh my," Ava said, and laughed a little, as if this were an astonishing thing. "No swimming. No drinking. Do you *ever* have any fun?"

"Yes, actually," he said.

"I hope you like dogs, anyway," she said.

"I love dogs," he said. "I'd have one myself, if I wasn't allergic."

I studied Ava's face.

"Isn't it odd," she said, "that nobody ever says they're allergic to people?"

41.

An hour or so later the five of us piled in the Range Rover with a cooler of steaks in the back—also oysters, wine, a bunch of take-out salads, and hamburger meat and buns for Ollie—and drove to the private marina where Swift kept his sailboat.

"I'm actually more of the speedboat type than a sailor," he said. "But I keep the fast boat up at Tahoe. That's where we really crank up the horsepower."

"Can we do that soon?" Ollie asked him.

"Do dogs piss on fire hydrants?" said Swift.

Swift and Ava sat in the front seat of the car with Ollie between them, so he could play with Swift's iPod. Elliot and I sat in the back. Since Swift had introduced him to Bob Marley, reggae had supplanted the albums that used to be Ollie's favorites—late-eighties and nine-ties music favored by his father.

"I shot the sheriff," he was singing, off-key but loud. "But I didn't shoot no deputy."

From the backseat, Elliot mentioned that he'd seen Bob Marley live, at a concert back in the seventies. I could feel how hard he was trying to come up with something Ollie might find worthy of notice.

"I was down in Jamaica one time with a buddy," Swift said. "We got invited to a party at Bob's house. Crazy place."

"You *met* Bob Marley?" Ollie said.

"We played soccer. Only Bob called it football."

Elliot didn't say anything about this, but I knew he got seasick sometimes. I wasn't too worried about sun-burn, because it was past four o'clock when we set out onto the bay in Swift's boat, *Bad Boy*, but Elliot had slathered himself with sunblock. Luckily, he hadn't brought along the hat he sometimes wore when we went hiking—designed to protect not only a person's face, but also his neck, with a string that went under the chin. It always reminded me of the bonnets worn by the little girls on *Little House on the Prairie*. That day he had his Oakland A's hat with him.

"I'm a Giants man myself," Swift said.

"Me, too," Ollie volunteered, though this was news to me.

It was gorgeous out on the bay, but the water was choppy. "I don't want to be a party pooper," Elliot said, "but aren't we going to put a life jacket on Ollie?"

"I'm a great swimmer," Ollie said. "Monkey Man said so."

"Even good swimmers wear life jackets on open water," Elliot offered. "In fact, I was just about to buckle one on myself." He reached for a life jacket that was attached to the wall along the outer deck of the boat. "Better safe than sorry, right?"

Ollie looked at Swift. The grin on Swift's face was one I recognized from a few hundred photographs I'd sorted through for *The Man and His Dogs*—a wide, toothy smile suggesting his allegiance with Ollie and their mutual recognition of the absurdity of Elliot's suggestion.

"It's good we have some people like you in the world, man," Swift told Elliot, "to keep people like me from getting too wild and crazy. We need a few rule followers to counterbalance the outlaws. Some people might say if you get hung up on life jackets, you're a pussy. But what's the harm?"

"I just want to make sure Oliver's safe," Elliot said.

Swift took a puff on his cigar. "I hear your point, my man," he said. "But I just can't get into wrapping some piece of Day-Glo orange Styrofoam around myself out here on the bay." He picked up a life jacket himself then, waved it over his head like a lasso, and tossed it in the water. "Cramps my style."

"Yahoo!" Ollie shouted. "Life preservers are for babies."

"He hasn't been swimming that long," Elliot said.

"It's probably a good idea," I said. My head was throbbing. "I think Elliot's right."

Swift put a hand on Ollie's shoulder. "You heard your mom, buddy," he said. "Her boyfriend's got a really good point there. That guy's a lot more sensible than your old pal Mr. Monkey Man."

"Did you make Cooper wear a life jacket when he was my age, Monkey Man?" Ollie asked. Though Ollie had yet to meet him, Cooper occupied a legendary status for him. Now he held Monkey Man's son up as the standard for coolness in all things. Cooper and Swift, both, like a couple of rock stars.

In the end, I buckled my son in his life jacket, tying the extra length of straps into a series of bows, which he undid, so the jacket—though nominally attached to his chest—would have offered scant protection in the event our boat capsized or if Ollie fell overboard.

I considered making an issue of this but decided against it. He was mad enough already. He blamed Elliot for having to wear the life jacket, though really, I should have thought of it myself.

"So I hear you play tee-ball," Elliot said to him. "How's your team doing?"

"The season's over, but anyway, tee-ball's stupid," Ollie told him, eyes on the water. "It's a baby game. All the dads are the pitchers, and they just throw these puffballs. Some of the kids on my team are so bad they just stand there and don't even swing. The dads have to throw the ball so it hits their bat."

"You've got to start somewhere, right?" Elliot said. "Pretty soon you'll be old enough for Little League. That gets more challenging."

"I hate Little League," Ollie said.

"What do you want to be when you grow up?" It wasn't a great question, but Elliot was trying hard.

"Garbageman. Or bad guy. I'll probably rob banks."

"If you're going to take people's money," Swift said, "you want to do it the smart way. Create a start-up."

Out on the bay, the water was dotted with sailboats. The sun was low on the horizon. "What do you say we cook up these babies?" Swift said, pulling four steaks out of the cooler, along with a couple of raw hamburger patties Estella had prepared for Ollie.

I could tell from the look on Elliot's face that he was feeling sick, but he said nothing.

Swift asked Elliot how he liked his steak. "I go for rare meat myself," he said.

He and Ava exchanged looks. It often seemed that the two of them imbued all comments—whether made by them or anyone else—with sexual connotations. When it was just the three of us together, I didn't mind—and in fact, I got into the game with them. But with Elliot around, not to mention Ollie, the heat that always filled the space between them left me uncomfortable.

"Come to think of it," Elliot said, "my stomach's a little off at the moment. Maybe I'll just stick to bread."

Swift reached for one of the raw oysters Ava had set out on a platter with horseradish and lemon and a bowl of mignonette. He lifted the shell to his mouth and sucked down the oyster with a groan of pleasure.

"Nothing better than this," he said. "Well, one thing, maybe." He gave another meaningful glance in Ava's direction.

At that moment Elliot swung around, with a suddenness I was unaccustomed to from a man who generally moved with deliberation. He took a few steps to the side of the boat and doubled over, his head over the water. It took a moment for me to understand. He was throwing up.

42.

Something shifted after that. Of course I had told Elliot all about Swift and Ava's plans for their non-profit, and their devotion to dogs, which Elliot seemed to accept as one of those things very rich people do with their money. But after our disastrous sailing trip, it seemed that Elliot developed a new obsession: studying the inner workings of BARK.

We were nearing the end of Ollie's time with me, and to mark it, Swift had taken Ollie to the go-kart track in Mountain View for a final blowout day. It was a field trip I would have liked to share with my son, but Ollie had made it plain he wanted this to be just the two of them, him and Swift. Meanwhile, I took the opportunity to drop in on Elliot.

It was the first time I'd seen him since that evening out on the Havillands' sailboat, and it had been much longer than that since I'd visited Elliot in Los Gatos. The last time I'd been over to his place, it had been immaculate, as usual, but that day his dining room table was covered with papers, and Post-it notes covered one whole wall. Scanning the scene, I spotted a paper with the name *Havilland* on it, and another referring to the BARK foundation.

"What are you doing?" I asked Elliot. "You're not even Swift's accountant. Is going over information about people's companies some kind of weird hobby, like stamp collecting or Ping-Pong?"

"It's public information," he said. "They've registered as a nonprofit."

"Don't you have anything better to do than snoop around in my friends' finances?" I knew my words were stinging, but I didn't care.

"Something's not right about all of this," he said.

"You're just jealous," I told him, "because I'm spending so much time with my friends."

"I'm just concerned," he told me. "You know how photographs can tell a story? Numbers can, too. And it's not always a good one."

"Do you understand how much they've done for me?" I said. "And now for Ollie, too? He adores Swift."

Elliot was silent for a moment. "Don't you think I'd love to have the chance to form a friendship with your son, too?" he said, finally. "If you gave me a chance."

"I'm sure the opportunity will come up," I said. "You two just didn't get off on the best foot."

"I'd cook us all dinner," he said. "We could take my telescope out to a spot I know where the ambient light is minimal. I'd show him Mars."

"Maybe next time I get him," I said.

"When the planets are aligned," Elliot said, with a certain tone of bitterness. He was not talking about the sky.

43.

I t was Ollie's last day with me, and he wanted to spend it at Monkey Man's house, of course. He was in the pool, practicing his freestyle for the big Labor Day race while Swift held the stopwatch, timing him. Swift had promised Ollie they'd go up to Lake Tahoe if he won. They'd take the Donzi out—my son's dream. Though going anyplace with Monkey Man was good enough for Ollie.

Ava had been off at Pilates. I'd been up in the office for a couple of hours working on the invitations to the birthday party—still early, but Ava wanted to make sure everyone saved the date. I came downstairs to join Swift, Ava, and Ollie for our usual lunch.

We were standing by the edge of the pool, watching Ollie swim his laps. "He's some kid," Swift said. "You've done a great job."

I shook my head. "I can't take any credit at the moment," I told him. "You know I've barely gotten to spend any time with Ollie for three years. These past two weeks have been the best I've had with my son since he was in kindergarten."

"I've been wanting to talk with you about that, Helen," Swift said. He sounded more serious than usual. "Ava and I have discussed this and we're in total agreement. We'd like to pay for a lawyer so you can get your boy back where he belongs. We need this kid around."

"I haven't even come close to paying off my old lawyer," I told him. "I could never accept a gift like that."

"What's family for?" Swift said. "I'll call Marty Matthias. We'll get you a meeting."

That night Swift and Ava took Ollie and me out to dinner at a Japanese restaurant. To her credit, Ava had suggested that I might like to invite Elliot to join us— she even used his name—but when I called him to suggest the plan he'd said he was busy.

It was one of those places where the waiter comes to your table and cooks everything in front of you on a sizzling griddle, while waving a samurai sword over his head. Of course Ollie loved this.

"I'm going to miss you a lot, buddy," Swift told him. "You'd better promise to come back soon."

Afterward, my son and I drove back to my apartment. He put on his pajamas. I climbed onto the air mattress next to him. I didn't want to make a big deal out of his leaving, even though I dreaded saying goodbye the next morning.

"I've been thinking," I told him. "I was wondering how you'd feel if we talked to your dad about the possibility of you coming to live here for third grade. Just to give it a try."

Oliver had been flipping through the iPod Swift had given him at the restaurant that night. He looked up at me. Not with that old wary sidelong glance, but directly, looking straight into my eyes. "I'd like that," he said.

"I'm not saying you'll be going out to restaurants and getting fancy presents like this all the time," I told him. "I'm talking about regular life. School. Homework. Chores."

"I know," he said. I wasn't sure if he even realized it, but he had draped one leg over mine, and his head rested on my shoulder. At that moment, nothing else mattered but the hope that I might have my son back for good.

Later, other things occurred to me. I hadn't told Ollie that Elliot would be a part of our lives, too, if he came to live with me again. But I wasn't going to risk it. Having come this far with my son, I wasn't prepared to lose him again. What we had here seemed way too precious and fragile still. And the truth was, after that evening on the boat, I was uncertain of my future with Elliot, or whether I even had one.

44.

The day after I brought Ollie back to Walnut Creek—mid-July, with all of Ava's roses in glorious bloom—Elliot left me three messages. I told myself I'd call him back as soon as I wasn't so busy, then I didn't get around to it.

He called again, close to ten o'clock on a weeknight.

"I know you're probably in bed, but we need to talk," he said.

"Okay."

"Not over the phone. I was hoping I could come over."

I could tell from Elliot's voice that this was important. We hadn't spoken about it, but ever since I'd introduced Elliot to Ava and Swift and to Ollie, something had changed in my feelings about him. Knowing

Elliot, he probably felt this, too, but hadn't wanted to ask anything of me during my last precious few days with my son. Now here he was on the phone, wanting to talk.

Ava hadn't said anything much about Elliot since that day they'd finally met, but that in itself said plenty. Swift had observed, afterward, that Elliot was probably a great guy to have in your corner if you ever got audited. Ollie had not even brought up his name.

Thirty minutes after I put down the phone, Elliot was at my front door. I had been wearing my bathrobe when he called and hadn't changed out of it.

"I know your friends don't think much of me," he said, still standing in the doorway, clutching a brown paper sack that turned out to hold a loaf of the four-grain bread he made sometimes. He handed this to me. As usual, it could have served as a paperweight.

"I was trying to distract myself from thinking about you by baking," he said. "It didn't work."

"My friends like you fine," I told him. Then stopped myself. One thing I treasured about the time I spent with Elliot was how we always told each other the truth. He told me about the time he had gotten a panic attack climbing Half Dome at Yosemite, and had to turn back. He told me that before the first time we met for dinner he had written down five interesting things to talk about, to avoid being tongue-tied. I had told him about how I sometimes made up stories, though I never did with him. I was a more boring person with Elliot, probably, but an honest one.

"I don't care what my friends think," I said. Then I stopped myself again. I *did* care. He knew this.

"The thing is, I'm in love with you," Elliot said. "And I know that's not going to change, but if you tell me you don't want to be with me, I'd better find out now, before I get in even deeper and it's even worse to lose you."

I did not tell him I loved him back. I had never said that. I stood there, studying his kind, good face—the deep lines in his cheeks, around his eyes. His hair was mussed up from his habit of running his hand over his head when he felt worried about something, which was most of the time.

"Why don't you come in?" I said. He took a deep breath. He looked around the room in a way that suggested he was memorizing this place. As if this was going to be the last time he'd be here. He lowered himself onto the couch like a man who has walked a very long way to get here. Straight up a mountain.

"I know you probably think Ollie would never be able to get close to me," he said. "But you're wrong. I'm the type of person that people tend to appreciate more as time goes by. I think your son would figure that out over time. If you and I were together. If you'd give me a chance."

I still couldn't say anything. I stood there, the brown-paper-wrapped doorstop of bread cradled in my arms.

"He'd see I was making you happy," Elliot said. "Because I believe I would. I think you'd appreciate me more, too, as time went by."

"I appreciate you now," I said. "You're the best man I've ever known." This much was true. I had other reservations about Elliot—mainly, that my best friends didn't think much of him—but I never doubted the goodness of his heart.

"Some people seem really great at the beginning," Elliot said. "I was never that type. The type people always want to be around."

"You're a lot of fun to be around," I told him. "That time we took the portraits of the pit bulls? And the Chihuahua who kept humping my leg? That was a great day."

"I would help you take pictures of dogs seven days a week if I could," he said. "I'm always happy when I'm with you. Almost always. I wasn't happy on that sailboat, I have to admit."

I had put the bread on the table and sat next to him on the sofa. "And I loved it when you brought me to the

Academy of Science for the insect exhibit that I didn't think would be so interesting," I told him.

"I wish we could have brought Ollie with us to that one," he said.

"We had a good time, just the two of us."

"I've never felt as happy with anyone as I am with you, Helen," he said. "*Was* with you. I haven't gotten to see much of you lately."

"I was going to call you back. I just got busy."

He shook his head. All of a sudden he looked terribly sad. There was no point, ever, pretending with Elliot.

"It shouldn't feel like a chore, calling me. Or some kind of obligation."

My friend Alice used to say she never trusted a man whose hands were too smooth. Elliot's were surprisingly rough. Maybe from his farm days, though that was long ago. Maybe just from puttering around in his garden, where he had been laying a brick patio. If any man I knew had soft hands, in fact, it was Swift, the one who'd suggested that Elliot might be a little tame and boring for me.

"I needed some time to myself," I said. "To be with my son." But this wasn't the whole story, either, and he knew it. I never minded being around other people if those people were Ava and Swift.

"I know you care a lot about your friends," he said. "But at the end of the day, they're off together in that big house of theirs, having all this mind-blowing tantric sex, according to them, and you're here all alone in your bed." He stood up and looked at me, and his back—so often stooped—was straight.

"I'm the man who wants to be here with you."

He did something surprising then. He reached for me—my face, my hair—and held on tight, with a kind of urgency that I'd never experienced from Elliot before.

He pulled me to my feet. He was kissing me. My mouth, then my neck, my eyelids. His hands were in my hair, and he was saying my name in a deep and hungry voice, almost growling. *Helen. Helen. Helen.*

For once we weren't talking. I kissed him back. Once, and then many times. His hands pressed into my shoulder blades and down my back. He pressed his face into my neck and remained there for a surprising length of time before looking into my eyes again.

"I know I didn't get off to a great start with Oliver," he said. "But I could be a good man for you. For both of you."

For once I didn't hear Ava's voice in my ear. I didn't even think about my son at that moment. I reached out my hand to touch his and stroked his fingers. I pulled him down onto the sofa. I lay my head on his. I felt my whole body soften, and a long sigh came out of me, like the feeling when you finally get to take off tight shoes or unzip your dress, the feeling of pulling into your own driveway after a long time on the road.

"We could be a family," Elliot said.

45.

A week after Ollie went back to Walnut Creek, a surprising thing happened. Dwight called to suggest that our son move back in with me for the rest of the summer.

"We're going through a rough patch," he said. "He's just gotten so defiant. No respect for authority. All of a sudden he's saying things like 'piss' and 'badass,' and when I call him on it, he just mouths off more. I guess it's a stage, but Cheri's concerned that Jared's picking up Oliver's bad habits now. If you want to tackle it, be our guest."

I didn't say anything, but I knew where our son had acquired his new vocabulary. Swift was always telling Ollie that the guys who got someplace in the world were the rule breakers, the outlaws. Once, when we'd been over at the Havillands, Ollie had told a story about his second-grade teacher, Mr. Rettstadt, and how he made them march all the way back to their bus, when they were on a field trip, because some of the boys started break-dancing in the line.

"What a pussy," Swift had said. "He was probably just jealous he didn't have any cool moves of his own."

Now in the car, bringing him back to Redwood City with me again, I tried to talk with my son about what was going on with his father and Cheri.

"Cheri's stupid," he said. "All she ever does is talk on the phone."

As much as I might have disliked Cheri, too (might have, and did), I knew I couldn't let that one go.

"You know I wish you could be with me all the time," I told him. "But when you're with your father and your stepmother, it's important to try and get along, and you need to be kind. Kids don't know everything. That's why they have parents to take care of them."

Ollie was quiet for a while as we drove over the bridge, with his clothes and his hamster on his lap.

"It's not like Dad wants to get rid of me or anything," he said, in that way children have of naming their worst fear, in the hope that someone will tell them it's not real. "He just thought it would be a good idea for me to have a change of pace," Ollie told me.

"Jared's always getting into my stuff. Little kids are a pain."

Ollie's face had that tough, diffident look I recognized well at this point. I knew him well enough to recognize what it concealed, which was hurt. "Plus I think I get on Dad's nerves," he said. This part was spoken so softly I could just barely hear him.

"I've been thinking about some fun things we can do together now that we've got more time," I said. "Go camping maybe. Visit the Monterey Aquarium."

He looked at me warily. "What about Monkey Man?" he said. "I get to go over there, right?"

"Some of the time," I said. "But some of the time I thought it might be fun if we hung out with Elliot, too. Remember him?" I didn't call him my boyfriend. I called him my friend.

"I want to hang out at Monkey Man's pool," Ollie said. "I need to practice for our race. And we're going to Tahoe and ride in the Donzi."

"Ava and Swift will probably want their privacy sometimes," I said. "But you and I will have plenty of time for adventures."

Ollie looked out the window for a while, studying the cars on the bridge. He'd been keeping count of how many were Mini Coopers. Every minute or two he'd call out that he saw another one.

"People don't like to have kids around when they do sex," he said. He didn't look at me when he said this, just kept staring out the window, tracing imaginary letters on the glass.

"Making love is private," I told him. "Someday when you're older, you'll have someone you feel that way about. You'll want to be private, too."

"Like going to the bathroom," he said.

"Not so much. But the privacy part's the same."

"My dad and Cheri do it when they think I'm asleep," he said. "They don't know I know."

I thought a moment before addressing this one.

"Racing stripes," Ollie called out. Another Mini Cooper for his count.

"People do that when they love each other," I told him. Or not, I might have added, but didn't.

"I'm glad you didn't get married to anybody," Ollie said. He announced this as if it was a done deal I'd be alone forever.

"Right now, I'm not married to anybody," I said. "But you never know. Maybe someday."

"That would be dumb," Ollie said.

"Well, anyway, I don't have any plans to get married to anybody anytime soon," I told him. This might have been a moment to mention Elliot, but I didn't.

46.

July was almost over when Ollie came back to spend the rest of the summer with me. I didn't bring him over to Folger Lane that first night he returned. Nor did I invite Elliot over. I thought we should have some time together for just the two of us, the way it used to be.

But the next day there was no keeping my son away from the Havillands' house. He wasn't past the door before Swift put him in a wrestling hold. "What took you so long, buddy?" he said.

Then came the sound of Ollie's laughter. Swift had pulled his shirt up and was tickling him. Around his ankles, all three dogs were barking. Rocco was actually licking his hand.

"I hope you like brownies," Ava said.

"You think I'm sharing your special brownies with this no-good bum?" Swift said to her. He had Ollie in the air now, upside down.

"Say uncle. Say uncle," Swift told him. "Then I'll let go. Maybe."

More shrieks from Ollie. Happy ones. "Uncle!" he yelled. "Uncle!"

"All right," Swift said. "I guess I'll release you. But you must understand, I am your mighty and all-powerful leader. You do as I command." He set my son back on the floor. His voice was deeper than normal and his eyes narrowed.

Ollie was bent over from laughing so hard. I worried he might wet his pants—a problem in the past—but he didn't.

"Repeat after me," Swift said. "'I promise to obey you, my all-powerful leader!'"

"I promise to obey—"

"—all-powerful leader," Swift reminded him.

"All-powerful leader."

Ollie was still catching his breath, though I knew he loved this. He had the same look I sometimes observed on Sammy when Ava took out his leash and the special tool she used to throw his tennis ball farther than normal, meaning he would be going to the park. Excitement, not fear. Though I knew what this amount of excitement would bring about later, back at our apartment. I wouldn't get Ollie to sleep tonight until way past his bedtime. He'd be too wired.

The table was set for us out on the patio. At Ollie's place there were two packages: a snorkel mask and fins, and a watch.

"It's waterproof," Swift told him. "Good up to a hundred meters. That should do until you and I get into some serious scuba diving. Cooper and I did a lot of that when he was just a few years older than you."

Ollie had ripped the packaging off already. He was trying to set the time.

"And there's a timer," Swift said. "So we can clock your speed from one end of the pool to the other. Or holding your breath."

"I always wanted a watch like this," Ollie said, his voice a husky whisper.

This was news to me. But Swift revealed a whole new side to my son I had not experienced before. A kind of swagger and bravado. Around Swift, he even seemed to lower his voice when he spoke, though he was still a few years from the age when it would happen on its own.

The next day was Sunday. Elliot showed up at my apartment at eight thirty in the morning with a gift for me: a staple gun. He'd noticed I didn't own one. I was in the shower, so Ollie answered the door.

"That guy's here," my son called out. "The one that threw up." I pulled on my bathrobe and went out to the living room.

"I thought I'd take you two out for breakfast," Elliot said. "I know a place that makes the best French toast."

Ollie was still in his pajamas. He'd been eating cereal and watching cartoons on television. I had promised myself that while Ollie was with me we'd have our meals at the table, not sitting in front of the TV, but for now I was just happy to let him hang out and relax.

"Good morning, Ollie," Elliot said. He offered his hand. My son looked up at him a little blankly, but shook it.

"We weren't expecting you," I said. He was trying to be spontaneous, probably—a little crazy, like Swift—but it didn't come naturally. Elliot had to plan his spontaneity.

"I already ate," Ollie said.

"Well, how about this, then? We load the bikes on the back of my car and go for a ride? I brought mine along."

"I think Ollie might like to hang around at home for a while," I said. "Actually, so would I."

He had set the staple gun down. I looked at the coffee pot. Empty.

"I could make another pot," I said.

He shook his head. "I should have called first," he said. "All I was thinking was how much I wanted to see you two."

"Why would you want to see me?" Ollie said. "You don't even know me."

"Well, that's true," Elliot said. His voice, which had been, very briefly, playful, returned to the usual somber tone. "But I wanted to *get* to know you."

47.

From the moment he heard about the Donzi, my son had been after Swift to take him out on that boat. He'd never even heard of *Miami Vice* or Colin Farrell before meeting Swift, but now Ollie reminded me this was the same boat he drove in the movie. The Donzi could go faster than a speeding bullet, Ollie told me. Warp speed.

When Ollie had asked Swift if he could drive the Donzi, Swift had given him an uncharacteristic response. "When you're older, you can," he told Ollie. "But you really have to know what you're doing to drive the Donzi, or you can get into trouble. That's why I waited till Cooper was seventeen until I bought it, and even then I wouldn't let him take the controls unless I was right there next to him."

If Ollie was disappointed by this, he didn't show it. Swift's words on the subject only added to the Donzi's mystique.

"The Donzi used to belong to bad guys that used it to carry drugs from other countries to America," Ollie told me. We were driving over to Folger Lane when the topic of the speedboat came up, as it frequently did.

"Also machine guns," Ollie added. "Then they got arrested, and the police sold the boat, and Monkey Man bought it."

I didn't know this, I told him. Leave it to Swift to take ownership of a cigarette boat formerly owned by cocaine smugglers with guns.

"When I grow up I want to be like Monkey Man," Ollie said. He made his voice go low and narrowed his eyes, checking his reflection in the mirror.

As I saw my son do this, a realization came to me. Though I had been the one who introduced Swift into Ollie's life—and though I loved spending time with Swift, and called the Havillands the nearest thing I had to family, I didn't want my boy to be like him when he grew up. Swift entertained and amused me, and I had come to count on his generosity and protection, but I realized with a sudden clarity that I didn't entirely respect the man. If I were still working at that catering job and he'd attended some party where I was passing around the trays of appetizers, my old friend Alice would probably have written Swift off as an asshole, and I probably would have agreed with her.

Now in the car with me, heading over to the Havillands', my son was once again launched into a discussion of Monkey Man's speedboat.

"Monkey Man says the Donzi can go a hundred and fifty miles an hour," Ollie said. "One time he was going so fast, this girl on the boat lost her bikini top."

My hands tightened on the wheel. "If we go up to Tahoe with Swift and Ava someday, and you ride on that boat, I can tell you he won't be driving that fast with you," I said. "I'll make sure of that."

"You're not the boss of him," said Ollie. "Nobody's the boss of Monkey Man."

48.

My ex-husband had agreed to let Ollie stay with me for the remainder of the summer, with occasional visits back to Walnut Creek. All of this sounded so civilized, I was actually thinking I might not need to enlist the services of Marty Matthias at all, which may have been just as well since Swift seemed not to have gotten around to calling him yet. Maybe, after Labor Day, Dwight and I could sit down and have a reasonable, friendly conversation about custody, and we could talk about the possibility of Oliver coming to live with me again.

"It sounds as if Dwight might be open to that," I told Swift and Ava. "Maybe he and Cheri are a little burned out from juggling a toddler and an eight-year-old."

Meanwhile, the defiant behavior Dwight had complained about was not in evidence with me. Every night now, when we got back to the apartment, Ollie would have his bath and then climb into bed to read with me, as if all the old bad times had never happened.

On the first weekend in August, I drove Ollie up to Sacramento for a visit with Dwight's family. The McCabes, who had once embraced me as their new daughter, stayed inside when I dropped him off at their house.

That same weekend, the Havillands were going up to their Tahoe house. In the past, Ava would have asked Estella to watch the dogs, but Rocco had taken a strong dislike to her—stronger even than his dislike of me, which had actually lessened over time—and anyway, Ava said, the idea that Carmen might accompany her mother to the house had left her uneasy about having Estella over on her own for a whole weekend. So Ava asked if I'd stay there.

I knew Elliot would have welcomed this opportunity to spend a couple of nights with me. This was true with or without Ollie on the scene, but Ollie's presence that summer—and my reluctance to be around Elliot when Ollie was there—had severely curtailed our time together, and virtually eliminated any possibility of sex.

I could have called Elliot and invited him to join me at the Havillands'. But when I thought about it, I realized that what I really wanted was to be alone in their house.

As always, I offered to take care of whatever errands or odd jobs Ava might need done, but other than walking the dogs and checking in with Evelyn Couture to make sure she was doing all right, she told me not to bother, just to enjoy myself. "Take a nice long soak in the Jacuzzi and slather yourself with La Mer," she told me. This would be her three-hundred-dollar face cream. "And I left a great piece of wild salmon in the refrigerator."

"Give me a job to do," I told her. "I might as well be useful."

"Just pick up my dry cleaning," she said.

On my way over to Folger Lane from the cleaners', I turned the radio up high to a hard rock station. Not my usual choice, but I liked the feeling of singing at the top of my lungs. I stopped at the market where Ava shopped and picked up a couple of imported cheeses and a baguette. No doubt the Havillands' refrigerator was already well stocked with great delicacies, but it felt good to choose for myself. I added a large slice of dark chocolate cake to my purchases and a croissant for the morning.

I had considered the possibility that Estella might have dropped by, so I was glad to see that mine was the only car in the driveway when I pulled in. With the pile of clothes over my arm, I turned the key in the lock, bracing myself slightly for the dogs I knew were on the other side. As usual, Lillian and Sammy jumped all over me with excitement as soon as I stepped into the house. Rocco hung back, but no longer growled at the sight of me, though he bared his teeth in a way that always set mine on edge.

Something came over me then: the knowledge that for once I could do whatever I wanted in this house.

I set the clothes down. Opened the refrigerator.

I'd sat on the patio with Ava and Swift a hundred times while they drank wine without it bothering me, but for some reason this evening, the sight of their French rosé and the good chardonnay chilling beside it made me hesitate a moment. For just a few seconds, I let myself imagine how it would feel to sit out by the pool by myself with the runny cheese and a plate of Ava's special crackers and a large, chilled glass of wine. I closed the refrigerator.

With Ava's clothes in one arm and a bottle of Pellegrino in the other, I made my way up the stairs to Ava's dressing room.

I was going to just pull the plastic off the clothes I'd picked up and hang them on a hook for Estella to put away later on, then head downstairs to cook my fish, but something made me linger. I let my hand pass over one of the cashmere sweaters. I kicked off my shoes. Counted out loud, in high school French, the number of silk blouses in Ava's collection. *Quatorze.*

I studied a particular gown from among those I'd just picked up, which Ava had recently worn to a dinner in the city—one of the intimate gatherings Swift had hosted for BARK benefactors. This dress was made of hand-painted silk, with diaphanous butterfly sleeves. The dress went down very low in the back, though because she had been in her wheelchair the whole time she wore it, this feature must have been lost on her tablemates. Only Swift and I would have known Ava's dress was backless and that she'd worn no underwear to accommodate it.

"Sometimes, driving home," she'd told me, as I helped her get ready, "he takes his right hand off the wheel to touch me."

"On the freeway?" I said.

"Only his right hand. He's a good driver."

There was a stereo in Swift and Ava's bedroom, naturally, with a stack of compact discs beside it. I picked up the top disc. Andrea Bocelli. That blind Italian singer.

I put the disc into the player and turned the music up loud, so I could hear it in the dressing room. Andrea Bocelli was singing in Italian, of course, so I had no idea what the words meant, but it had to be about love—passionate, possibly desperate. This was the kind of song that probably made Andrea Bocelli's fans throw themselves at his feet and beg to go back to the hotel with him, even if he was blind. Maybe that made it even better.

I touched the sleeve on a velvet jacket and brought it to my cheek. Took a sip of my mineral water, imagining it was champagne.

I wondered how one of the fourteen silk blouses from Paris would feel against my skin, especially if I had nothing on underneath. I considered what I'd wear with it. A pair of the Thai silk pants, maybe. Or nothing else. Just the delicate, beautiful blouse.

The shirt I was wearing came from the Gap—cotton, button-up, white, basic. I unbuttoned it. Took another swig of the Pellegrino. Dropped the shirt on the floor. Unhooked my bra.

My breasts were fuller than Ava's, but if I left the top three buttons undone, the French blouse would fit. I started to lift it over my head, then realized I should have unbuttoned the cuffs first.

I pushed my hands through the cuffs and a button popped off. Not a Gap shirt button. This one was mother-of-pearl.

Andrea Bocelli was on to another song now, even sexier and more tragic sounding than the one before, if this was possible. I sang along with him, as well as a person can who doesn't speak Italian and had never heard the song before.

The shirt was tighter on me than I'd expected, so I unbuttoned it all the way. I placed my hand on the part of my skin left uncovered by the shirt and stroked my left breast. Brought the Pellegrino to my lips again. Pretended I was in Italy.

The song on the CD wasn't exactly danceable, but I started dancing anyway. I must have reached for one of the cashmere sweaters—the arms, both of them. I pulled them toward me as if there were a person inside, embracing me.

"Tesoro, Tesoro!" I sang. *"Ti amoro fino alla fine dei tempi."*

I had no idea what I was singing.

I kicked off my shoes. Stepped into a pair of green kid leather slippers. Pulled a scarf from one of the accessories drawers. Twirled around the room, making the silk of the scarf flutter like a kite string.

I made my way into the bedroom. Ava and Swift's room. I lay down on the bed, crosswise. One slipper fell off my foot. A person might have thought I was drunk, but I was just feeling a strange and wonderful kind of freedom, all alone in this house I loved.

At first, all I saw when I opened my eyes were the dogs—all three of them lined up like a panel of judges. Lillian's head was cocked slightly to one side. Sammy was barking. Rocco just bared his sharp little teeth in that way he had that made you imagine the row of bright red blood spots they'd leave if they sank into your skin.

Then I realized there was a person in the room too. Estella.

"I was just fooling around," I said to her. "I didn't mean anything."

"We don't go in Mrs. Havilland's room," Estella said. "This room is special."

I knew that, too. Nobody ever had to say it. You could just tell.

"I was putting away the dry cleaning," I said. No point in continuing. There had been no need to linger in the bedroom.

"I don't say nothing," Estella said. "I know how it goes sometimes. You see all the dresses. Me too, some days. I stand here with the iron and I wish my daughter has a blouse like that for graduation. A special necklace. Nice shoes."

A wave of relief washed over me. For a moment I had imagined Estella telling Ava about her crazy friend

Helen, dancing in the closet with her four-hundred-dollar sweater. Lying on her bed in the room no one was supposed to enter besides Ava and Swift. How could she ever understand, after all she'd done for me? But it turned out Estella did.

"Ava's so generous," I said. "She's given me so much. And Swift, too, of course."

"Mr. Havilland. He's not like her," Estella said. "Be careful your boy don't get too close."

"Ollie loves Swift," I said. "I know he acts crazy sometimes, but he's got the biggest heart."

"Mr. Havilland is my boss," she said. "Not good to talk about it. I just tell you be careful."

49.

When Swift had first offered to hire Marty Matthias to file for a change in custody of my son, I had held out a hope that maybe we could work things out in time for Ollie to start the new school year with me in Redwood City.

But that wasn't realistic. And as far as I knew, Swift had not yet placed a call to Marty. I longed to remind him of his promise, but I didn't want to pressure him. Swift was just preoccupied with the foundation, I told myself. He'd get around to it soon, and in the meantime, I was getting to see a lot more of my son than I had in three years. We still had a full week left before he had to return to Walnut Creek for the start of third grade.

Labor Day weekend was coming up. To my son this meant only one thing: the big swim race. Himself versus Monkey Man.

Ollie came back from Sacramento. The Havillands returned from Lake Tahoe. With Oliver still sleeping on the air mattress, Elliot and I barely saw each other, though one night he brought ice cream over and we sat in the kitchen, sharing the pint and speaking in whispers. Ollie was a sound sleeper, but I worried what he'd think if he woke up and saw my boyfriend there.

"I don't like it that we have to pretend to your son that nothing's going on between you and me," Elliot said. "Like being together is something to be embarrassed about."

"Ollie's gone through a lot," I said. "And things are good now. I just don't want to rock the boat."

Elliot didn't say anything.

"Maybe we can take our bikes and have a picnic," I said. "Somewhere flat, with no traffic, where Ollie can ride along with us. The bike path by the reservoir. Just not quite yet."

"Maybe you need to stop protecting your son so much," Elliot said quietly. "Did it ever occur to you that having me in his life could actually be a good thing, instead of some big problem for him to deal with?"

In fact, it had not.

In the end, I agreed to let Elliot come over one night and cook us dinner. The surprise was that the three of us actually had a good time. We played charades, with Ollie on both of our teams, and made popcorn. Ollie didn't know there was another way to make popcorn that didn't involve the microwave, he told Elliot. Hearing this, Elliot looked very serious—which he was good at—and said maybe he should reconsider our relationship.

"But my mom makes great peanut butter cookies," Ollie told him.

"In that case, I'll stick around," Elliot said. "She hasn't made those for me yet."

Afterward, we put on a movie. Elliot had brought over a DVD of his all-time favorite movie, *Old Yeller*. Ollie said it didn't look too exciting, and that he liked action movies better, but he cried at the end. "This part always gets me, too," Elliot said, putting an arm around Ollie. In the past, Ollie might have stiffened at a moment like that, but he showed no sign of resistance, and when he fell asleep, a few minutes later, with his head on Elliot's shoulder, Elliot said he didn't want to get up because he didn't want to wake Ollie.

"You can't just sit there like that all night," I told him. A rush of tender feeling came over me. Not heat or passion, or the drug that came from a certain element of drama and danger in a relationship. This was something different, that I couldn't name.

"There are worse things than having your sleeping son leaned up against my shoulder," he said. "In fact, there are not a whole lot of better things."

50.

With two days left before Ollie was scheduled to return to his father's house, it was time for the big swim race.

"I know I said I was going to give you a head start, pal," Swift told Ollie when they got out of the pool that afternoon. "But I have to take that back. You're just too fast. You don't need an advantage."

I had brought my son a towel, and was wrapping it around him. It was things like this—small moments—that I had missed the most since he'd gone to live with his father. Ollie settled himself in my lap while I dried him off. Applying the sunscreen. Getting to watch, from one day to the next, how his frame was changing over the summer: how he'd lengthened, how his body fat was disappearing. Buying milk by the gallon instead of the quart, knowing he'd be around long enough to finish it.

"Not that I won't pulverize you, understand?" said Swift. "I just mean, we will conduct this race fair and square. No baby stuff."

The one thing Ollie hadn't mastered was his flip turn for when he got to the end of the pool. Swift had shown him how to do it, but he still had trouble, and sometimes when he tried it he'd come up gasping and coughing, which slowed him down.

The race was set for Saturday, Ollie's last day with me. Swift and Ollie spent all morning working on Ollie's flip turn. Ava and I sat on lounge chairs, taking in the sun, while our two boys—Ollie and Swift—moved endlessly back and forth, up and down the length of the pool, flipping, reversing direction, flipping again. By lunchtime Ollie had it down.

"Tonight," said Swift. He placed a hundred-dollar bill on the table. "Ten laps. Winner take all." He held up his palm and Ollie slapped it.

"I thought you said if I won you'd take me out on the Donzi," said Ollie. He was doing that thing again with his voice, when he spoke to Swift—cool and tough, as if none of this mattered so much to him, though I knew this race mattered to Ollie more than just about anything.

"No question about that, pal," Swift told him. "I'm just figuring it may be a while before you and me can make it up to the lake. This is just a little cash on the barrelhead, for now. But only if you beat me, understand?"

The race was scheduled for six o'clock. Ava had invited a few of their friends over. Following the race there would be a cookout. Ava was making her homemade ice cream with berries from the farmers' market, to be served with Estella's biscuits. When I had asked Ava if Elliot could join us, she said of course, though as always when his name came up, I noted a hint of disapproval in her response.

"Whatever you want," she said.

Early that evening, the friends started to arrive: Renata and Carol, the lesbian contractors; Swift's childhood friend Bobby, who had made the long drive from Vallejo; Ava's massage therapist, Ernesto; and a new friend of Ava's, Felicity, whom I'd been hearing about but hadn't yet met.

Ava had run into Felicity at the vet's office. She was probably around my age. She had recently lost her husband to cancer and now had to sell her house and find a job. On top of all that, her dog needed surgery. Ava ended up paying for that, of course. Now Felicity was standing alongside the pool in a long green dress

I recognized from Ava's closet. She was holding her Cavalier King Charles spaniel in her arms.

"Oh, Felicity," Ava said when she saw her new friend in the green dress. "You have no idea how beautiful you are." It turned out she had a cashmere shawl in just the right shade to go with the dress; they'd go upstairs after dinner and get it.

I stood by the side of the pool, looking around for Elliot—aware, to my surprise, of how much I wanted to see him. Just after six, Swift emerged from the pool house wearing a monogrammed bathrobe, arms held up over his head like Muhammad Ali entering the ring. Ollie trailed behind, in a bathrobe monogrammed with the initials CAH that must have belonged to Cooper when he was younger. My son had thrown back his shoulders and puffed out his chest, but I knew he was anxious about the race—afraid of not doing a good job, with everyone watching. Afraid of disappointing Swift, most of all.

The two of them lined up at the edge of the pool and took off their robes—Swift with his broad, hairy back and muscled shoulders; my son beside him, skinny and shivering.

Swift owned a miniature cannon (of course he would) that used real gunpowder. Ernesto lit the fuse, and bang: The two of them dove into the pool.

I had been wondering how Swift would play this one. Knowing the differences not only in their age and strength, but also that just three months earlier, Ollie had been afraid of the water, it seemed unlikely that Swift would put up a real fight in this race. Of course he wouldn't want to let Ollie know the race had been handed to him, but I was sure he'd let Ollie win.

But when the two of them hit the water, Swift launched into his freestyle no differently than he might have if his opponent had been another adult swimmer, not an eight-year-old boy. When he reached the end of the pool, he was already a good five meters ahead of Ollie, and his lead was widening.

Ollie was giving it a real fight. I'd never seen him swim so fast, or so intently, but the flip turns were slowing him down. That, and the fact that he was a child who'd only recently learned how to swim.

Only once, when he came up for air after a flip turn, did my son look over to check where Swift was, but he couldn't have determined anything from that one quick glance. As it happened, Swift was alongside him, but a full three laps ahead in the race.

As Swift was closing in on the finish, he stopped. Three meters from the end, he flipped over on his back, then started treading water. Ollie was coming up behind him, stroking for all he was worth, but with another two laps to go. Swift looked out to the group of us standing on the sidelines of the pool and grinned. Only when Ollie approached the finish line on his final lap did Swift resume swimming.

Ollie touched the edge of the pool just one stroke ahead of Swift. From the side of the pool, all of us cheered.

I had never seen a look on my son's face like the one he wore as he pulled himself out of the water. His body was shaking, and for a moment, he covered his face with his hands, as if the whole thing was too much for him.

"Did I do it?" he said.

Swift was pulling himself up out of the pool now too, alongside Ollie. "You were amazing, little buddy. I thought I had you there for a while, but in the last crunch, you pulled out all the stops."

I was sitting next to Ava a few feet back, taking it in: my beaming son, the unmistakable hoot of Swift's laughter as he slipped the medallion they'd gotten for him around Ollie's neck. Standing beside Swift, Ollie was still trembling all over and shaking his head, looking stunned. "I can't believe I did it," he said. "I still can't believe it."

Beside me, Ava touched my sleeve. "That's Swift all over," she whispered—a tight smile on her lips.

"He knew Ollie had to be the winner, but he couldn't help himself from competing. Swift *hates* losing. *Anything.*"

Over by the pool, Ollie was still in a state of disbelief over his victory. "Now I get to go up to Lake Tahoe with you, right?" he said to Swift. "And ride in the Donzi."

"Absolutely," said Swift. "As soon as we get a nice long weekend, that's where you and me are headed."

"This meant so much to Ollie," I said to Ava. "You two made his summer. Mine, too."

"Swift is basically a boy, too," she said. "Just a larger one, who's gone through puberty."

"Ollie worships him," I told her. Not that she didn't know.

"Don't we all," Ava said.

Afterward, Swift dried off and put on one of his crazy Hawaiian shirts. He presented one to Ollie, too—decorated with monkeys in banana trees. The shirt was miles too big, but Ollie put it on anyway, displaying his victory medallion outside the shirt. When Swift asked him if he wanted a burger or a steak, Ollie said he was still too excited to eat.

Elliot came up to me. He had been standing off in the shade with Evelyn Couture—after Elliot, the most unlikely guest at the Havillands' parties.

"What were you and Evelyn talking about?" I asked him. It was hard to imagine an odder combination than those two.

"She heard I was an accountant," he said. "She was telling me about moving out of her house in the city. Evidently she's donating the property to Swift and Ava's foundation."

I hadn't heard this. Whenever I was over at Evelyn's, we were always boxing up donations of clothes and antiques for various charities—the ballet and Junior League resale shops—with most of her furniture headed for an auction house. I had assumed the house would be going on the market.

"That's wonderful," I said.

"You probably greased the wheels with all the help you've been providing," he said.

"I doubt that," I told him. "People don't decide what to do with their five-million-dollar house just because somebody's friend comes over to help them pack."

"That house of hers is worth a lot more than five million dollars," Elliot said. "From what she told me, I'm guessing more like twenty. That's a lot of dog spaying and neutering."

I was accustomed to a consistent tone of tenderness in Elliot's voice whenever he spoke to me, but at this moment all I heard was skepticism.

"I'd like to know who's on the board of directors of this nonprofit of theirs," he said.

"Just a bunch of rich people who love dogs, no doubt," I said. "Why does it matter?"

"You know me," he said. "I can never resist a good spreadsheet. Going over figures is probably my favorite thing in the world."

I was going to make a joke, but he suddenly looked even more serious than usual. "Actually, that's not true," Elliot said. "My favorite thing is being with you."

51.

The next day I drove Ollie back to his father's house. He didn't cry when I dropped him off, and I knew he wouldn't. I had learned long before that this is how a child of divorced parents protects himself, the way he closes off the feelings that go with leaving one parent's world to enter the other.

Earlier that morning, while I was helping him pack, I could tell Ollie was gone already. When I put my arm around him, he stiffened in that way he had. I knew not to push it.

"You said maybe I'd get to stay here with you," he had said the night before, when I put him to bed for the last time on the air mattress. "But it didn't happen."

"I'm working on it," I told him. Or Swift was. I hoped he was, anyway. I had to talk to him about it.

Ollie wanted to bring his swimming medal and the hundred-dollar bill from Monkey Man back to Walnut Creek. That last night, after we got home from the race, he had slept in that shirt. Now he placed it on a hanger, studying the fabric as if he was memorizing it. For reasons he did not explain but ones I felt I understood, my son had chosen not to bring the shirt to his father's house.

"We can still go over to their house when you come for visits," I said, studying my son's face as he touched the collar.

"And we're going to Tahoe together," Ollie told me. "He promised we'd go out on the Donzi."

"I'm sure you will," I said. "Maybe not right away, but eventually, for sure."

When we got to Dwight and Cheri's house, I said good-bye to my son out on the sidewalk.

"I'm going to see you very soon," I told him—my words inadequate. I got down low and put my arms around him.

In times past, my son's body would have stiffened at such a moment. Now I felt him melt into my arms. He held on for a long minute. I didn't want to let go.

I was not yet home when Ava texted me.

"Come have dinner with us," she said. It was a funny thing about those two, how they never asked if I had

other plans. As it happened, I did have other plans—
sort of. I'd told Elliot I'd call him when I got back that
evening, and that we could get together if I felt up to it.
But now all I wanted was to be at the place where I'd
spent so much of that happy summer with my son: the
Havillands' house.

I texted Elliot:

**Sorry. Not feeling so hot after leaving Ollie. OK
to beg off tonight?**

He responded a few minutes later, kind and understanding as always:

**Of course. Take it easy and know I love you. See
you soon.**

I headed over to Folger Lane.

When I got there, Swift and Ava were already well
into the wine. I had let myself into the house, knowing they'd be out in back, having guacamole. Ava said
nothing when I reached them. She put her arms around
me. Swift poured me a Pellegrino. For a moment, I
almost asked him to give me a glass of wine. I was feeling awful about Ollie leaving, and I wanted a drink.

"I'm going to miss that kid," Swift said.

I couldn't say anything. Just the sight of the pool made me sad.

"I was really hoping he could go to third grade here with me," I said.

Now was the moment for Swift to bring up his promise about the lawyer. Filing papers. Applying for a new evaluation based on change of circumstances, my perfect record of sobriety, character references from Swift and Ava and others. From across the table, I studied their faces.

"Swift's grilling salmon tonight," Ava said. "Felicity's joining us."

52.

Now that I no longer had Ollie with me, one would think I'd be spending more time with Elliot. But I didn't. For one thing, we were getting closer to the date of the big surprise party for Swift, and I needed to finalize the book layout and get it to the printer. Ava wanted my help deciding on the menu and other party details. But that was not the only reason I was putting a little distance between me and Elliot.

After I introduced Elliot to Swift and Ava—the day of the disastrous boat ride—my friends had made it clear that they didn't think he was good enough for me. Since then, I'd tried to keep my life with Elliot separate from my time spent with the Havillands. They asked about him occasionally, but it seemed that as far as Ava and Swift were concerned, it was out of sight, out of mind. The one other time I had allowed these two important spheres of my life to intersect—the day of the big swim race—the tables seemed to have turned. Whereas in the past it had been Swift and Ava who registered reservations about Elliot, now it was Elliot doing the same about them.

"How much do you know about the way Swift made his money?" Elliot had asked me shortly after that party, where he'd met Evelyn Couture.

"We don't talk about business," I said. "It's not that kind of friendship."

"I'm just curious because I spent a little time online, checking a few things out," he said. "This nonprofit of theirs is a privately run concern. Three board members: Swift, Ava, and Cooper Havilland."

"There's no law against that, right?" I said.

"None at all," he told me. "Just curious."

Over the weeks that followed, Elliot kept asking more questions. I never knew the answers and I felt irritated that he was bringing them up. What would I care about Swift selling shares of stock to the foundation, or an insurance company in the Cayman Islands?

I assumed Elliot's research about BARK fell in the category of his research into genealogy, or the *Consumer Reports* ratings of the various models of car he was considering to replace his Prius—the idle curiosity of a number cruncher with too much time on his hands—and so I was increasingly impatient with Elliot's obsession. I couldn't see what the big deal was whether BARK had three board members or thirty, or how they'd arrived at their bylaws, and the fact that Elliot cared so much about all of this seemed to confirm Ava's opinion of him as a man with nothing better to do than hunch over a stack of spreadsheets.

One morning at his apartment, I'd gotten up to find him already at his desk scrutinizing figures again. It couldn't have been later than 6:00 A.M. From the look of his hair, I could tell he must have been running his hands over his head a lot in the way he did when he was thinking really hard about something. Three empty coffee mugs surrounded his yellow legal pad.

I could hear Swift's term for accountants in my head: *bean counter.* And Ava's question to me: *Just nice?*

"What are you trying to accomplish here, anyway?" I asked him.

"I just want to figure this out," Elliot said. "How this whole thing works."

Not all at once, but like a person caught in a strong and steady current that's taking her downstream, I felt my perspective changing. It was as if a piece of grit had gotten stuck in my eye, and as much as I wanted it gone, it affected the way I looked at everything. Most particularly the way I looked at Elliot.

The care he'd always taken—that I buckle my seat belt, or apply antibiotic cream if I got a cut—had once seemed the characteristic of a tender and loving man. Now I heard Ava's voice in my head calling him "fussy" and "anxious." I found myself getting irritated by Elliot's dogged attention to detail. We still had good times together—just the two of us, snuggling over a cross-word puzzle, eating popcorn in bed while watching old black-and-white movies, trying off-the-beaten-path restaurants that Elliot had read about online. As long as it was just us, in our own little bubble, it was as close to perfect as I'd ever experienced. But when he brought up the Havillands, I shut down. Elliot was on a mission to locate evidence that something was wrong with how Swift conducted business. More and more, I was left to conclude that there was simply something wrong with Elliot.

53.

One night late that September Elliot called to say he had to see me and that he was coming over. I'd been avoiding him the past few days, helping Ava with the increasingly elaborate details of the upcoming birthday party. I was exhausted, and I wasn't up to fending off more annoying questions from Elliot about the financial structure of BARK.

I didn't make any effort at fixing myself up. I was in my pajamas when I opened the door. "I look awful," I said.

"You look wonderful to me," he said. "You look like yourself."

In many ways, Elliot was an old-fashioned man. He was standing there in a suit holding a bunch of roses in one hand—the kind you get at Safeway, not a florist's, which was just like him. I once told Ava that Elliot must have been absent the day they handed out the rule book on romance. One time he brought me bath salts from CVS. Another time, when we were heading to the Sierras for a camping trip, he brought me long underwear.

That night, it turned out he had bought me a ring. It was a surprisingly large diamond for a person who was always careful about his money, in an absolutely traditional setting—the kind of ring your father might have given to your mother forty years ago, if you'd had a different father from mine. Even the first time I'd met him, on our blind date, he hadn't looked as anxious as he did now.

"I know you probably won't say yes," he said. "But I urge you to consider this carefully. I can be a good husband for you. I won't just adore you. I'll watch your back. I don't think you ever had that before."

Consider this carefully. This was Elliot for you. Even at the moment of greatest personal significance, when it might be supposed that passion would overrule intellect, his orientation was always to take the quiet, sensible, contemplative route.

"I know I don't come across as Mr. Stud," he said. "But there's one thing I do know. Nobody could ever love you more than I do, Helen. I'll never do anything to hurt you. You can count on me."

I had always been a person who let other people—very often, men—decide what I should do with my life. That night, looking into Elliot's kind and anxious eyes, at the cellophane-wrapped roses, the deep lines in his face, the blue velvet box, I knew I loved this man. He moved me. And I trusted him. I pictured him at the jewelry store, picking out the ring in its old-fashioned setting, and a wave of tenderness overtook me. I imagined him then driving over to my house—going around the block a few times before he parked, maybe, with the awareness that in the likely event I'd turn him down these might be the last hopeful moments he'd know. I wouldn't break the heart of this good man.

"Marry me," he said.

I sat there, studying his face and his large, surprisingly callused hands, which still looked as if they belonged to a dairy farmer, and remembered how whenever we got into the car, he'd reach across the seat to buckle me in, and how he had waited patiently for as long as I needed—two hours, sometimes, or even three—to get the photographs I needed of all those dogs.

I looked up at Elliot, standing there in his rumpled shirt, still holding the box with the ring.

"Okay," I told him. "I'll do that."

Even as I said it, I saw Swift's face that time on the boat with the life preserver, heard Ava's voice. *Low expectations.*

"You've made me the happiest man," he said. "Well, as happy as a man like me ever gets, anyway."

I accepted the ring. But I didn't put it on my finger. I held it in my palm for a moment, then returned it to the velvet box. "I'm not quite ready to tell people yet," I told him. "I just want to get used to this a little while first."

Really, though, I knew the reason I didn't want to wear the ring yet. I was afraid of what Ollie might say if I told him I was getting married again. Specifically, that I was getting married to Elliot, whose most enduring impression for my son had been that of a man determined to see him wearing a life preserver and leaning over the side of Swift's sailboat, throwing up. In their brief interaction since then, Elliot had made some progress with Ollie, but the truth remained that in my son's eyes, my accountant boyfriend was no Monkey Man.

Most of all, though, my reluctance to put the ring on my finger had to do with Swift and Ava, with whom Elliot had made no progress whatsoever. I didn't put on Elliot's ring because I didn't want to have to justify my decision to the Havillands.

54.

Almost from the moment I said yes to Elliot, I began avoiding him.

Sometimes I'd see his name on the screen of my cell phone and just let it ring. Nights when I got home from Swift and Ava's, or after dinner with them at our Burmese restaurant or Vinnie's, or after a day in the city helping Evelyn Couture, I'd usually find a message from him.

"It's me," he'd say. First hopeful but later, anxious, and eventually, discouraged. "Your fiancé?"

Sometimes I called back. When I did, our conversations were surprisingly brief. I could hear him on the other end of the line, wanting to connect in the way we had done in the past—talking about work, or something he'd read in the newspaper, or a doctor's appointment he'd had that day—the kind of thing people who are in a couple talk about. Ordinary life. As he spoke, I'd scroll through my e-mails.

"I'm thinking about getting an all-electric car," he said to me. "Once we move in together"—this would be at his place—"we could put solar panels on the house and give up buying gas."

"Sounds good," I said.

More often now, when I got home at night, I'd send Elliot a text that I was just too tired to talk, that I'd check in tomorrow. Then the next day would come and I'd be off at the Havillands' again, putting the final touches on the birthday book, or driving into the city to help Evelyn Couture with her endless packing, or picking up something for the party—antique Chinese lanterns, a bubble machine, the special place mats Ava had ordered featuring a giant picture of Swift at the center of each one so he'd be grinning up at you as you sat down to eat . . . at least until the caterers set down the plates, which were also special ordered and featured ten different breeds of dog.

Finally, after five straight days of messages, I called Elliot back. "I know I should have gotten back to you sooner," I said. "It's just been so crazy with all these arrangements. Especially having to keep everything secret from Swift."

"Do you really think Swift hasn't figured out there's going to be a party?" Elliot said. "The man's turning sixty. He's an egomaniac. He knows his wife would never let an event like this pass without a massive celebration. It wouldn't surprise me if she tried renting Candlestick Park."

Ava had, in fact, considered a number of extravagant venues for the party, but in the end she decided to rent tables and set them up under a tent in the extensive grounds behind their house. They'd have more freedom then, she said. "If someone wants to tear off their clothes and jump in the pool, for instance," she said. We both knew who that person would be.

After considering many options for the theme of the decorations, Ava had finally settled on one. Knowing how much Swift loved Lake Tahoe—in winter most of all—she had arranged to have a machine brought in to blanket the entire backyard with snow. In addition, she'd commissioned a life-size ice sculpture of Swift, posed like Michelangelo's David, but with champagne pouring from one crucial appendage.

Elliot wanted to know, of course, how Ava intended to keep this all a secret.

"She's arranging for Swift to leave town the day of the party," I told him. "That way she can get him out of the house while the final preparations are made."

"I thought Swift never wanted to go anyplace?" Elliot said. "Particularly without Ava."

"She's organizing a special guys' trip to the Monterey Aquarium with Ollie," I said—though this was a trip Elliot and I had planned on taking with my son. "The place Ollie really wants Swift to take him is Lake Tahoe, of course, but that's way too far for a day trip, and anyway, I don't want him going all that way without me. So we settled on Monterey."

"Mr. Magician," Elliot said drily. "The guy waves his wand and makes your dreams come true. If Swift were here, of course, he'd make a joke about his mighty wand."

I decided to ignore this.

We'd have to work fast to get everything set up in a single day, of course. Our goal was to make sure that when Swift and Ollie walked in the door all the guests would be there, ready to party. Outside, a reggae band would be set up by the pool house; a fire pit would be blazing in the middle of the snow-covered yard; and various performers, including a fire-eater and a pole dancer, would lend additional drama to the extravaganza, just in case there wasn't enough.

During the cocktail hour, servers would pass foie gras, oysters, Dungeness crab, caviar, and flutes of Cristal champagne, to be followed by a sit-down dinner of rack of lamb, potato gratin, haricots verts, and an endive, pear, and walnut salad. At every guest's place (more than a hundred of them, mostly high rollers with the ability to write very large checks, as well as all the dinner party regulars) there would be a copy of *The Man and His Dogs*. We printed a thousand copies so the Havillands would have extras on hand to give out later as their foundation grew.

I had described all of this to Elliot over dinner at a restaurant in the city—a rare event. Now we were sitting across from each other drinking coffee. I had put the ring on my finger for the occasion, but the air felt tense between us that night, though we were both trying to act as if everything was fine.

"If this is how they celebrate Swift turning sixty, I'm trying to imagine what Ava's going to pull off for seventy," Elliot said. "Assuming these two are still together."

"What are you talking about?" I said. "If there's one relationship in the world I'd bet on, it would be the Havillands. I never saw two people more in love."

"Love doesn't always display itself in the obvious ways," Elliot said. "Not everybody has to announce to the world all the time how incredible their relationship is. Some people show how they feel by how they behave."

55.

I had come over to Folger Lane to show Ava the final page proofs of the birthday book, due at the printer the next day. Just as I turned into the driveway, Ava's Mercedes pulled up next to me. Estella was in the passenger seat.

"I took her for a mani-pedi," Ava said, when they were out of the car. "Can you believe she's never had one?"

I could, actually. Now Estella was holding out her hands—her short, work-worn fingernails gleaming with bright red polish. Red toenails peeked out of a pair of those paper flip-flops they give out at nail salons. Her own shoes—an old pair of Nikes—were tucked under one arm.

"I tried to talk her into something a little less flashy," said Ava. "But our girl wanted to go for the whole piñata."

I leaned over to take a closer look.

"How's Carmen liking her classes?" I asked her.

"She's doing good," Estella said. "This girl of mine, she's going to be a doctor. Take care of her family."

"You don't have to worry about that, Estella," said Ava. "No matter what Carmen decides to do, you know Swift and I will always take care of you."

"Carmen graduates, we take care of ourselves," Estella said. "I got a smart daughter."

"Medical school's pretty tough, Estella," Ava said. "I hope she makes it, but don't give up your day job."

"Yes, Mrs. Havilland," Estella said as she started toward the house. The hopefulness in her tone from earlier seemed suddenly subdued.

"Besides," Ava added, "what would we ever do without you?"

56.

Ava and Swift needed to take care of some things up at the Tahoe house. They had a property manager who normally looked out for their place, but he'd been giving them problems. They needed to find a new person to handle the job.

"I could probably work this out over the phone," Ava said, "but that place is so special to us, I don't want to hand the keys over to someone we don't know."

She asked me to drive up to the house myself and interview a couple of property management firms. "You can make a vacation of it," Ava said. "Bring a stack of magazines. Interview the guys who answered our ad and see who you like. Swift and I trust you totally to make the best choice."

That wasn't all. Evidently Ava and Swift were thinking of doing a total renovation sometime in the spring. As soon as the big birthday event was behind her, Ava was going to start talking with architects.

"What we were hoping is that you'd bring your camera up and take a bunch of pictures of the place," she said. "To give our architect a preliminary idea of what he'll be working with before he makes the trip up himself."

She waited for a moment, then added, "You could bring along that boyfriend of yours if you wanted." It was odd how she and Swift never said Elliot's name.

I told her I'd go. But by myself. I hated that this was so, but I wasn't in the mood to spend time with Elliot. What I really needed was some time alone.

I'd never been to Lake Tahoe before. I wasn't a skier, for one thing—though neither was Ava, of course. But more than that, the place always sounded to me like a spot for people from a world I didn't belong to— people who grew up snow-skiing and water-skiing and playing tennis, and knew how to sail and had fast boats. Just the way they called it *Tahoe*—never *Lake Tahoe*—suggested a certain familiarity that I couldn't pretend to.

But after all these months hearing about it from the Havillands, I wanted to experience the place. And I felt proud that they trusted me with the decision of hiring a new property manager. While I was there, Ava suggested, maybe I could have the rugs cleaned, and the curtains, and arrange for someone to come take a look at the dishwasher, which had been acting up the last time they were at the house.

The part of my responsibilities at the house that appealed to me most was the photography, naturally. It had been a while since I'd done anything but shoot portraits of dogs and schoolchildren, one after another, for my day job. I loved the idea of having a whole day to wander through the rooms of the Havillands' lake house and the grounds beyond it, shooting photographs on my own timetable.

It took me more than four hours to get there, but I didn't mind. I was thinking about Swift's promise to talk with his lawyer about reopening my custody case, and the fact that he never seemed to get around to following up on it. I had been hesitant to pester Swift about it, but a couple of days earlier I'd brought the subject up, afraid he might have forgotten. "I'm working on it, babe, don't you worry," Swift said, patting my arm. I wasn't so sure, but what could I do?

By now more than three years had passed since my DUI and I hadn't had a single problem. I wasn't out of debt, but at least I was earning reasonable money. And most important, my son himself was saying he wanted to come live with me. Maybe part of what fueled his desire was his hero-worship of Monkey Man. Maybe partly it was about how much he loved playing Frisbee with Rocco. But it was about his wanting to be with me, too. We had come a long way over the summer. My son trusted me again.

I was considering all of this as I made the long drive up to the town of Truckee and then the fifteen miles or so beyond, to the house Ava and Swift owned on the shores of Lake Tahoe. The plan was to settle myself in and relax after the long day of driving and wait till morning to go into town and meet up with Ava's candidates for the property manager job. If I left home by noon, I'd still get to the Tahoe house in time to shoot my pictures of the property during the golden hour.

I passed a lot of big lakefront estates on my way to the Havilland house: large, no doubt expensive, custom built, with all sorts of amenities, but none was remotely charming. Then came the turnoff for Swift and Ava's property.

There were more magnificent houses, but nothing that came close to the charm of Swift and Ava's. My first thought, seeing the place, was to wonder why anyone would want to change a single thing about it. The house was situated at the end of a long driveway, with no other houses in sight, trees all around, and a mossy path that led down to the beach. The house itself was a good size, but it gave the feeling of a cottage more than a mansion, with a porch that wrapped around on all four sides and a stone chimney rising up from the roof.

The house was shingled, with red shutters, and the trees surrounding it weren't like the ones at those other places I'd passed along the road, that had the look of having been planted recently by some high-end land-scaper. These were mature pines and redwoods, grow-ing out of a carpet of ferns. There was a hammock strung between two of them and, facing the lake, a glider swing.

The other buildings on the property included the guest cottage and a boathouse, where I gathered that Swift and Ava kept their kayaks and paddleboards, along with a birchbark canoe Swift had specially built by a man in Canada, and the water-skiing equipment. The boathouse was also where Swift kept his pride and joy, the Donzi. I knew all about this boat from my son, of course: how much horsepower it had, how the men Swift bought it from had eluded the authorities on a crazy five-hour chase somewhere off Florida, with a couple of million dollars' worth of drugs on board, along with an AK-47. Telling me this story, Ollie displayed a tone of awe. "Then the bad guys went to prison," Ollie said. "And Monkey Man got the Donzi."

Even before I turned off the ignition I could see the lake, glittering blue against the horizon. Not many boats out now, and probably not a single one as fast as the Donzi.

"I've got the most badass boat on the whole lake," Swift had told Ollie.

For me, it was the piece of land where the house sat, more than anything else, that was most dazzling—a spot where the year might have been 1900, there was that little evidence of modern life.

I brought the car to a stop in front of the house and got out, taking in the view. It was five thirty or six by now and the light was hitting the lake at the perfect angle. I reached for my camera.

Something happens to me when I start shooting. Everything else falls away. There could be a forest fire raging, but if it didn't show up in my viewfinder, I might not even notice. Now I was transfixed by the sight of the sun going down over the lake. I spotted a loon gliding over the water, illuminated by that perfect golden light.

He dove under. I caught him just as he surfaced.

Who knows how long I stood there. It could have been five minutes or half an hour. But suddenly I became aware of music coming from the house—some kind of hip-hop. I looked away from my camera, up toward the main house, and took the place in for the first time up close.

That's when I saw it: another car in the driveway—a yellow convertible, top down. Now I could also see that there was smoke rising from the chimney, and the sound of laughter coming from an open window.

I should have been frightened, I suppose, but the idea of someone invading Swift and Ava's precious, perfect space must have banished whatever fear I might otherwise have experienced. All I registered was fierce protectiveness.

An unlikely impulse hit me then. I raised my camera. If, as I was now thinking, someone had broken into the house, it seemed important to record the license plate number of the yellow car, so I did. Then, too stunned to feel fear, I approached the door and turned the knob. No need to take out the keys. The door wasn't locked.

At first all I could see was a suitcase, which was leather, and expensive looking. On the floor next to it sat a worn backpack. No one was in sight, but I could hear the crackling of a fire and smell the woodsmoke coming from what must have been the living room. Like a person in a dream, I made my way down the hall into the room, with its old velvet sofas—the kind that are so much nicer than new ones—a couple of leather club chairs, an oak rocker, a southwestern-style rug, and a piece of art I recognized as made by the same outsider artist whose dog painting had inspired my first conversation with Ava.

I could smell something cooking. Meat. Now I heard voices, too—one high-pitched, giggling, and a lower one. A familiar laugh, but different, too. By now I realized that whoever was in this house was not a burglar.

I was standing there, trying to figure out what I should do next, when the door on the other end of the room swung open. It was Swift's son, Cooper, holding a martini glass. Though we'd never met, I recognized him immediately. Beside him, wearing nothing but an unbuttoned man's shirt, was Estella's daughter, Carmen.

57.

For a few moments, at least, we all stood there. I didn't say anything, and neither did Cooper, who was holding a very long and slightly bloody barbecue fork in one hand, his drink in the other.

The three of us just looked at one another. The last I'd heard of Cooper, his parents were toasting his engagement to beautiful Virginia. The last time I'd seen Carmen, she'd been cleaning the toilet.

I studied their faces. They took in mine.

Then I turned around. I walked out the door and down the steps, back to my car. I set my camera on the front seat, though not—once I was partway down the driveway and no longer in view—before taking a photograph of the property. I had promised that to Ava and Swift. I had told Ollie I'd get a picture of the

Donzi, too, but there was no way I'd head down to the boathouse now.

It was a long drive back to Portola Valley. Sometime around eight thirty my cell phone rang. Ava.

"Let me guess," she said. "You're curled up on the couch by the fire with a glass of that Pellegrino you insist on substituting for the really good cabernet you could be drinking," she said. "And you probably were crazy enough not to bring the boyfriend along, even though you're going to be sleeping in what may be the most romantic spot on the entire lake. Which may possibly tell you something about what's lacking in your relationship. Not that I intend to belabor that point."

"I'm on my way home, actually," I told her. Though making up stories had never been difficult for me, I had not yet had time to figure out how I'd explain to Ava my premature departure from the lake.

She wanted to know what happened, of course. "I'm feeling kind of nauseous," I told her. "It must be some stomach bug."

"In that case, you're coming straight over here as soon as you hit town," she told me. "We're putting you to bed with a hot-water bottle and a cup of mint tea. I'll wait up."

"I'll be fine," I told her. "I just need to get home."

"You're coming here," she said. "No argument. We need to take care of you."

It was nearly eleven o'clock when I pulled into the driveway at Folger Lane. The lights were on. The dogs were waiting. Ava met me at the door.

"Okay," she said, ushering me into the living room. "What's going on? Because I just don't buy the upset stomach line. You never get sick."

She was right, actually. This was one of the many moments that reminded me how well Ava knew me, how close we were.

"Let me guess," said Swift, coming up behind her, holding a drink. "You brought the accountant with you to Tahoe after all. Then you had a big fight. I'm thinking you tried to play an illegal word in Scrabble and he was sticking to the rules. You had to get out of there."

I shook my head. I couldn't let them believe I'd had a fight with Elliot. How could anyone fight with Elliot?

"It's just—female trouble," I said. I figured that would be enough to send Swift out of the room, and it was. I had learned long ago that nothing gets rid of a man faster, if that's what you want, than some vague allusion to the menstrual process.

"Okay," said Ava, once he was gone. "Now you're going to sit down and tell me the real story. This is me, remember? Your best friend. We don't have secrets from each other."

She had never actually called me her best friend before, but now, hearing those words, I fell apart. I collapsed on the couch. Ava leaned forward in her chair to put her arms around me. "You can tell me," she said. "It's going to be all right."

"It was Cooper," I said. "He was up at the house and I walked in on them. He had Carmen with him."

Almost imperceptibly—to a degree that would have barely been discernible to anyone else, probably—Ava pulled back slightly to right herself in her chair. Her beautiful long arms returned to their armrests. She looked at me with that steady, cool-eyed gaze of hers.

"That's it?" she said, her tone a combination of irritation and amusement. "The big catastrophe?"

"They were cooking a meal together," I told her, as if any further information were necessary. "She was wearing his shirt. *Just* his shirt. They were *together*."

I couldn't read the look on Ava's face. She was nodding her head with a kind of smile on her lips, though not the kind she'd exhibit if one of the dogs had laid his head on her lap, or if Swift had come up behind her to bury his face in her hair.

"Listen," she said. "Whatever was going on between Cooper and that girl"—*that girl,* she said—"it doesn't mean anything. He's just being a boy."

"He's engaged," I said. "I thought he was getting married to Virginia."

Ava didn't laugh, exactly, but she came close. "Everything that matters is still the same as it ever was," she said. "Cooper will graduate from business school next June and go to New York. There'll be a big wedding. He and Virginia are going to have a very nice life."

Nice. That word she'd questioned when I'd used it to describe Elliot.

"I doubt Virginia would see it that way," I said.

"She already does," Ava told me. "You think she doesn't know that Cooper plays around now and then? You think this is the first time in the eight years they've been together? That's what men do, Helen."

I might have argued this point, but I was past that.

"But what about Carmen?" I said. "She probably thinks it's something else. She's probably in love with him. And Estella . . ." I didn't know what the rest of that sentence might be. But however it was that Ava had managed to justify Cooper's behavior, I knew it wouldn't fly with Estella.

"It's not your job to look after Carmen," Ava said. "Not yours, or mine. Or Cooper's, for that matter. Carmen's a grown-up. She can make her own decisions, and evidently she's doing just that."

"Does Swift know?" I asked her. I was still reeling from her reaction. Ava looked vaguely impatient.

"He might, he might not. Either way, it wouldn't be a big deal to him. And it shouldn't be to you, either." She adjusted the wheels on her chair in a manner that indicated she was ready to make her exit from the room.

The conversation was over, clearly.

"You'll spend the night, right?" she said to me. "After that long drive? We've got a bedroom all ready for you."

I told her I'd just as soon get back to my apartment. She didn't try to convince me to change my mind.

"I guess all of this happened before you had a chance to take care of things up there?" Ava said as I was heading toward the door.

"Take care of things?"

"Interviewing the property managers. And taking those photographs to show our architect."

"I only got one shot of the exterior," I told her. "Sorry."

There had been a few others—the sunset, the loons, the license plate on the yellow convertible. None of those would be helpful in any way.

"Don't worry about it," Ava said. "No big deal. Let's just concentrate on the birthday party now, shall we? Can you imagine the look on Swift's face when he walks in and sees snowdrifts in the backyard? He's got to know I'm cooking something up for his birthday, but I've never put on a party like this one before."

Driving home that night, it wasn't the party I was thinking about. Or Swift. I was thinking about the look on Cooper's face when he'd emerged from the kitchen of the house at Lake Tahoe earlier that evening.

A different kind of person might have displayed fear or even horror at being discovered in such an awkward situation, but that wasn't what I saw on Cooper's face. He was a young man who even now, at just twenty-two, seemed in possession of total assurance that the world would go his way, and if other people had a problem with his behavior—if, for instance, his parents' trusted friend caught him in a compromising position with their housekeeper's daughter not long after the announcement of his engagement to someone else—that was her problem, not his.

Cooper knew who I was, evidently. He had actually grinned a little when he'd seen me. A little lopsidedly, in a way that suggested he'd had a few drinks, although it might just have been his usual boyish grin, with which he was accustomed to charming people. If there was one thing that might have bothered Cooper about my impromptu visit, it was probably just that I disturbed the mood. Because the other person in the room—Carmen—had looked the way a person might (her mother, for instance, years back, crossing the desert into Texas from San Ysidro, confronting the border patrol).

Cornered and terrified.

58.

I should have gone right to bed when I got home, but I didn't. I didn't even go straight home, to tell the truth.

On the road between the Havillands' house and my apartment was a liquor store. I must have passed the place a thousand times and barely noticed it. But this time, I pulled in. I bought a bottle of cabernet and set it on the seat next to me beside my camera. When I got back to the apartment, I took out my corkscrew and poured myself a glass. After all that time, sitting at meetings, crossing off the days of sobriety, it was gone that fast.

After the bottle was empty, I stood in front of the mirror and studied my face to see if I looked any different. Maybe I did, but at the time, given the amount of alcohol I'd consumed combined with the fact that I hadn't eaten anything all day, it would have been difficult for me to make a clear assessment of anything.

I did an odd thing then, though it seemed to make sense at the time. Maybe I wanted to make a record of the moment, so I'd remember to never let it happen again. Maybe I did it out of the despairing recognition that I hadn't managed to change my life after all.

I set my camera on a stack of books, the same as I had when I took my picture for my Match.com profile, and set the timer. I stood in front of the viewfinder and waited for the click of the shutter.

Then I picked up the telephone. I might have called my sponsor, but the person to call in an emergency was Ava now. If I hadn't been drunk, I would never have called her at this hour, but I was, so I did. As it always was—even at this hour, even though I had clearly awakened her—Ava's voice on the other end of the line was full of compassion and concern.

"I blew it," I said into the receiver. "I got drunk.

"I am Helen," I said, out loud, the way we did at meetings. "I am an alcoholic."

The next morning, I tried to forget about the whole thing. The trip to Tahoe. What I saw there. Ava's response. Most of all, the drinking—though I had to acknowledge it at my meeting the next day, and I did.

Up until then, I'd had 1,086 days of sobriety. Now I was back to zero.

Before I could put the whole event out of my mind, though, I had to do one thing: I printed the photograph I'd taken of myself wasted, the night before. I placed it in my underwear drawer so I'd see it every day, to serve as a reminder to never let anything like what took place the night before happen again.

After I got rid of my headache, I drove over to Folger Lane. I had decided to ask Swift point-blank if he still planned on helping me hire an attorney to help me get Ollie back. Once he placed the call he'd promised to make to his attorney, I'd get to work assembling my bank statements and credit report, and character references. Starting with Swift and Ava, of course. And maybe Evelyn Couture.

Just then it occurred to me: There was just about no part of my current life anymore that didn't come directly from the Havillands. My friends, my livelihood, my prospective lawyer, even my clothes. Swift and Ava were responsible for everything, with the sole exceptions of the son I gave birth to and the man I was sleeping with—though not even that so much anymore. In some ways, they had claimed Elliot, too, by always showing me his shortcomings so that, after a while, I no longer saw his strengths.

This was baffling, even to me. Having learned from Ava about the apparent disregard of her stepson, his father, her stepson's fiancée, and herself, for the concept of fidelity to a partner, I might have felt renewed respect for Elliot, who was loyal as the day was long. But all I could see was that aligning myself with Elliot put me in direct opposition to everything Swift and Ava represented. And Swift and Ava were the ones who had made my new life possible—including Oliver's willingness, finally, to open his heart to me again. Whatever unease I might feel now, emanating from my discovery at Lake Tahoe, there was no place for any of that if I wanted to get my son back.

59.

I still hadn't told anyone about my engagement to Elliot. There weren't that many people to tell, but Ava and Swift would have been two, of course, and then there was Ollie. I didn't want to deliver the news to my son until he'd gotten to know Elliot better.

There was another important factor driving my decision to keep my engagement to Elliot a secret: my impending court motion to regain primary custody of Ollie. If Ollie knew I was getting married to a man he didn't hold in much regard, he might not want to come live with me. I had already told Elliot this was the reason why I didn't wear the ring he'd given me (though I spared Elliot the part about Ollie's low opinion of him). I said that Ollie simply didn't know him well enough yet, and that before we broke the news, my son and Elliot should spend more time together. "Once he knows you, he'll love you," I told Elliot. Though privately I had my doubts.

As hard as it would be to tell Ollie about Elliot and me, the thought of delivering the news to the Havillands seemed even more daunting. There was nobody else in my life I felt a need to tell—certainly not my mother, Kay. But for some reason I felt I needed to get their okay, if not their blessing, before I fully committed to such a big step. They were that important to me.

Thinking about sharing my news, I realized that, with Alice gone from my life, there was nobody to tell but Ava and Swift. Now, knowing that I couldn't put off the announcement much longer, it seemed important that the four of us have dinner together, and since the Havillands had made no further mention of a dinner with Elliot since that first disastrous trip out on Swift's sailboat, I decided that, for once, I'd take the lead.

"I know Swift's not wild about going out, but I'd really like you to get to know Elliot better," I told Ava. "So I thought I'd be the one to make us all dinner, for a change. Nothing fancy. Just roast chicken and my special potatoes. Caesar salad maybe? With the birthday coming up, it would give you a night off cooking."

"I'll try to persuade him," Ava said. "But you know Swift."

Amazingly, they agreed to come over to my tiny apartment. I didn't plan on telling them about the engagement just yet, but I hoped that if things went well—and I wanted to believe they would—there could be other dinners after this one, during which my friends would grow to see Elliot's good points: how funny he could be—in his deadpan way—and above all, how good he was to me.

I spent most of the day preparing, though the meal itself was a simple one. I bought flowers and candles, and rearranged the furniture in the living room to make space for Ava's wheelchair. I studied the bathroom, wishing for some way to make it look less shabby, and since there wasn't one, I put an orchid on the back of the toilet and stuffed my cosmetics under the counter. I put out an expensive scented candle and pretty hand towels. I framed and hung a print of a Boston terrier that had been a gift from Ava.

"These are your *friends*," Elliot said, observing my preparations and the anxiety surrounding them. "You shouldn't have to worry about all this stuff. They're coming here to have an evening with us, not to critique your apartment."

Or to critique him, I hoped. Or for him to do the same to them. Because as harsh as Ava could be on the topic of Elliot, Elliot had revealed his own surprising capacity for sharp, critical assessment, too, where the Havillands were concerned. I had not shared with him the details of my experience at Lake Tahoe, of course. Had I done so, he would have closed his mind forever to the possibility of a friendship with Ava and Swift. But even without his knowing about Cooper's betrayal of his fiancée and the ease with which Ava dismissed it, I knew Elliot didn't think much of my friends. And now, in addition to everything else he appeared to dislike about them, he had become seemingly obsessed with the inner financial workings of BARK, which were evidently a matter of public record for whatever crazy individual had nothing better to do than read through a pile of boring documents. An individual like Elliot, for instance.

The idea that the man I'd promised to marry now suspected my friends of some kind of sketchy business dealings made me sick, and the fact that he would never have embarked on his tireless study of the BARK foundation if he hadn't known me, and if I hadn't been their friend, left me feeling guilty and ashamed.

Swift and Ava arrived on the dot of five thirty. When the doorbell rang, I asked Elliot to let them in. I was in the kitchen, no more than five steps from the door, but I hung back to convey that we were a couple and to help Elliot feel like a part of things. When Swift handed him the bottle of wine—a very good red—I asked Elliot to open it and pour everyone a glass. Everyone but me, of course.

As I knew she would, Ava noticed the print she'd given me right away. Swift made a comment to Elliot about the Giants, who'd had a good season, evidently.

"I've got to admit I'm not much of a baseball fan," Elliot said. "Though I'm even worse about basketball. The playoffs always take place in the busiest period of tax season."

"That would be reason enough for me to consider a career change," said Swift. "But of course, you're talking to a bum who doesn't go to any job any more. All I have to do now is sit around thinking up new ways to give my wife an orgasm."

I was accustomed to hearing Swift talk this way, but I could see Elliot having a hard time responding. Ava came to the rescue, sort of.

"It's not all that difficult," she said.

"Anything I can do to help in the kitchen?" Elliot called out. I knew he was hoping the answer would be yes, but it wasn't. I wanted him to get to know my friends. More than that, I wanted them to get to know him.

I'd shared so many happy evenings with these people—with Swift and Ava, and with Elliot, too. Just not all of us gathered together as we were then, around my small table, with that chicken in the middle, like a burnt offering, while I tried to reveal to Swift and Ava just how good and lovable a man Elliot was. And I wanted badly to persuade Elliot that just because at least one of my friends (meaning Swift) kept doing and saying mildly obnoxious things, while the other (Ava) kept making vaguely condescending remarks, did not mean that my friends were obnoxious or condescending.

"Tell Swift about the time when you were growing up on the farm, when all the cows got loose," I suggested to Elliot, because it was a good story and he'd told it really well a few weeks earlier, and because it showed him taking charge in a way I thought even Swift could recognize and admire.

"You're a farm boy, eh?" said Swift. "You ever engage in any hanky-panky out in the barn?"

"My family got out of agriculture when I was seven," Elliot said. "We sold the farm and moved to Milwaukee, where my father got a job at a brewery."

The full story had a lot more to it than that, I knew. But Elliot wasn't going there. His goal that evening seemed to be to keep his conversation as bland and terse as possible. But Swift, ever the frat boy, couldn't let it go.

"A brewery, huh?" said Swift. Beer was a topic he could get into. "You get into that line of work yourself?"

"Actually," said Elliot, "I fell in love with the accounting field pretty early on. I love the clarity of numbers. I've always loved the way a ledger book can tell a whole story. Not always a good one, mind you. In our case it was a disaster. We lost our farm."

"Sorry to hear that," Swift said, reaching for the wine.

"That's when I learned the importance of keeping a close eye on the balance sheet," Elliot said. "My father didn't, and it cost him the land he loved, which had been in our family over a hundred years."

"To each his own," Swift said. "Me, I see a calculator or a spreadsheet, I head for the hills. I leave that to the people who work for me."

"I hope they're doing a good job," Elliot said.

I had made a cake, but it took longer to bake than I anticipated, and the Havillands didn't stay to try it.

"You know how we are, honey," Ava said to me as she was pulling on her jacket. "Early to bed. It's like Swift's religion."

"To bed," he said to Elliot with a wink. "Not necessarily to sleep."

After they left, when the cake had cooled, I cut Elliot a piece. I wasn't in the mood myself.

"I know you love those two, and I intend to respect that," he said. "But doesn't it ever seem to you like whenever they're around, all of a sudden you feel kind of small? That Swift takes up all the air in the room?"

"I don't know what you mean," I said. "Swift and Ava always take an interest in what's going on in my life. Swift spent hours this summer teaching Ollie to swim."

"But what do they know about *you* that doesn't involve them?" Elliot said.

"They're very interested in me," I said. "They always want to hear my stories. They find me entertaining."

"Entertaining," he said. "Sort of like the court jester?"

I had never heard Elliot speak this way. Up to now, I'd always seen him as a gentle man. What I saw in his face now was contempt. Not for me, but it might as well have been.

"You're threatened by our friendship, aren't you?" I said. "You want me to choose between Swift and Ava and you."

He shook his head. "I'd just like to see you choosing yourself, Helen," he said. "Instead of racing off every time Ava snaps her fingers to do some errand in support of maintaining the amazing Swift and Ava road show. The ongoing performance of their wonderfulness."

I'd never heard so much anger in Elliot's voice. Hearing him now, I felt dizzy.

"They've done everything for me," I said. "They're basically my family."

"I was hoping *I'd* be your family," Elliot said. "Ollie and me. The kind of family members who don't walk out the door at eight o'clock to give each other massages."

"They're passionate people, is all," I said to him. "They have this intimate connection that most people can't understand."

"He's a narcissist," Elliot said. "Whatever her gig is, I haven't figured it out. She's his pet paraplegic, maybe. The woman who will always look up to him, no matter what, because she's stuck in a chair twenty-four seven."

Of all the things he'd said up to now, this was the worst. I could feel my body turning cold. I had a sick feeling in my stomach.

"Ava's spent the last twelve years in a wheelchair, for God's sake," I screamed. "You think that hasn't been hard? Who are we to judge how they live their lives?"

"The thing is," he said, scarily quiet, "the thing is that they're judging mine. They've been doing it since the day they met me. And they decided within the first ten minutes I wasn't worth their time."

"They don't *know* you. That's why I wanted them to come over. So they would. But all you wanted to do was talk about accounting."

I had practically spit out that last word, pronounced it as if it were an obscenity. "Numbers. Columns. Balancing the budget," I said. "I can't imagine why they didn't find all that as *fascinating* as you do."

"I'm sorry if I'm not as exciting a person as you'd like me to be, Helen," Elliot said. "But the exciting people aren't always the ones you can count on."

"Ava and Swift love me," I said. "Swift's going to pay for the lawyer who'll help in my custody appeal. I don't even know how much that will cost, but I know it's a lot."

"I thought Swift was supposed to get that going ages ago," Elliot said. "Since he doesn't seem to be following through, why don't you let me help with that?"

"Swift's busy, that's all," I told him. "He'll come through. He and Ava are my best friends in the world."

"You don't know a good friend when you have one," Elliot said. "As for love, if you can't trust in mine at this point, I don't know what more I can do to convince you."

In the past, one thing I could always count on was the tenderness in his voice when he spoke to me, even about difficult things. But there was a hard edge to

Elliot's tone now. His face betrayed none of the old gentleness.

"I know good friends don't sneak around checking up on someone's finances, like they're just looking to find out something terrible about them," I said. "They don't go around thinking that everyone's hiding some deep terrible secret, and it's their job to uncover it."

My voice had been rising over the last few minutes. With Elliot, the opposite had taken place. His was growing quieter, and his words, when they came out, had a tight, strangled quality, as if it were painful to speak.

"I hear a lot of emotion in what you're saying to me here, Helen," he said. "But I'm not picking up much in the way of love."

"Well, right now it's not that easy to feel loving toward you," I said. "You just attacked two people who have been kinder to me than anyone else ever was."

Elliot's voice was so quiet now I could just barely hear him. "Love doesn't come and go, when it's real," he told me. "Love is supposed to be constant."

Up until this, the two of us had been facing each other at the table, the barely touched cake between us, the candles I'd bought that afternoon—so anxious to make everything perfect—burned out, leaving little pools of melted wax on the tablecloth. Now Elliot got up slowly and stood in front of me, with his too-short haircut and his baggy pants. This was the moment when I might have wanted him to grab my shoulders firmly and press me against his chest, tell me I was being unfair and that he deserved better. He could have raised his voice, even, and told me I was making the wrong choice. Maybe a part of me knew that, even.

But fighting wasn't Elliot's style. So, very slowly, as if every muscle and nerve ending in his body hurt, he put on his suit jacket, like a hundred-year-old man with a bad back and arthritis. He made his way to the door, as if this was the longest walk he'd ever taken.

"I wanted to be your partner, Helen," he said. "I would have been true blue. I would have loved to have gotten to know your son, if you'd let me. I wanted to be his stepfather, whatever that might have looked like."

"True blue," I said bitterly, "so long as I abandon my friends. What have you done for us, besides putting them down? And not just putting them down, either. Snooping around in their finances as if they're criminals. I was at rock bottom when Swift and Ava came into my life. They saved me."

"You actually believe that, don't you?" he said. Whispering now. "You're breaking my heart, Helen."

I stood in the middle of the room watching him. I knew if I said one word that conveyed regret, he'd turn around and come back to me, but I didn't. I let him go.

60.

That night, after Elliot left, I went to a late-night meeting. It wasn't my normal Tuesday night meeting, so there was a group of unfamiliar faces in the room that night—people who didn't have to be home for young children, from the looks of them; people who used to hang out in bars and called AA their new nightlife. Because it was a young crowd, most of the stories they told didn't relate all that much to where I was anymore, or where I'd been even back when I was drinking. Ten minutes into the meeting I asked myself what I was doing there.

Most of the people in the room were in their twenties. They looked to be the kind of drinkers who had gotten fake ID cards when they were fifteen, hung out in front of liquor stores waiting for someone to buy them a cheap flask of gin, or drove around in cars with a few six-packs of beer. I didn't see anyone in this group who looked like the kind of person who had waited until her son went to sleep before taking out the wine bottle, and drank it—the whole thing—alone in her apartment with the knowledge that come morning, when the alarm went off, she'd be getting him ready for preschool again. These weren't people familiar with custody fights and guardian *ad litem* interviews, or court-ordered visitation schedules.

Afterward, though, as I was headed for the door, a woman in her early twenties approached me.

"You know the Havillands," she said. More statement than question. The look on her face made it clear that she knew them, too.

Hearing their name in this place caught me up short. I never associated Ava and Swift with my meetings. This was the dark side of my life—my real life, probably, though not the one I would have preferred. With Ava and Swift, I got to pretend none of this went on. No DUI. No guardian *ad litem* report. No handcuffs.

"How did you know that?" I said.

"My friend that I came with waits tables at Vinnie's. When you came in tonight, she recognized you. She knows the Havillands, too."

It was no surprise that Swift and Ava would have made the acquaintance of a young woman. Ava made friends everywhere. I'd seen that already. Still, I asked what the connection was. Art, maybe? Dogs? Or perhaps—this seemed likely—she was one of the dozens of people who had at one time or another been the beneficiary of Ava's kindness.

She looked unsettled. "I know their son. *Knew.*"

"Cooper," I said. "Seems like everybody loves him."

"Yeah, well. Depends who you talk to. His father definitely thinks he walks on water and pisses perfume."

I could feel now that something was wrong here. As many people as there were who would tell you that Swift and Ava were two of the kindest and most generous human beings they'd ever met, this young woman was not going to be one of them. I didn't want to hear the particulars of why, but she kept standing there in front of me. I felt as if she were staring me down.

"I'm Sally," she said. "They might not remember my name. Not that I'd suggest you ask."

There was a flatness to her voice, a bitter quality that made her seem a lot older than she looked.

"Cooper and me used to drink together. When he came home from college on break, a bunch of us would hang out. He called us his townie girls. We even went up to his parents' crazy expensive house at Lake Tahoe a few times, snuck into Squaw together. He wasn't my boyfriend. Just one of the guys I did shots with."

Then this one time, they'd driven out to the beach together. Sally and her two girlfriends, Savannah and Casey, Cooper and two of his college buddies.

"We were out on the dunes with a fifth of Jim Beam and some crème de menthe," she said. "They must've given us some kind of drug. When Casey and Savannah and me woke up, our underwear and jeans were gone. All we had was our T-shirts. No cell phones, no money to get home."

"How do you know it was Cooper and his friends that did it?" I asked her. Maybe they'd left and someone else had come along. You never knew.

"There was a picture of me. Looking"—and here she looked down—"the way you'd think. He texted it to a bunch of his friends."

"If something like that really happened, you could've pressed charges," I said. "If this was true, why didn't you go to the police?"

"We did," she said. "But then the Havillands' lawyer got involved. Some killer asshole. They were going to say all these other things about me. How I got picked up for shoplifting in junior high. I told them I didn't care; that was a long time ago. Then they dragged my dad into it. He's a contractor, and he'd been building spec houses, with a lot of loans out. All of a sudden, the banks were telling him he had to pay up."

I just stood there, taking this in. All around us people were putting away folding chairs, turning off lights. I didn't want to hear anymore. I wanted to go home.

"Then *poof*, there was no more problem. Cooper's dad made everything go away."

Including Cooper. He was back at Dartmouth in time for the start of classes.

"Those people get what they want," she said. "It must be pretty great being their friend. You just don't want to be their enemy."

61.

It was a Wednesday, only four days to go until the big birthday celebration. As we'd planned, Oliver was coming for a visit with me that weekend. Ava instructed me to let Oliver in on the plan. He was excited about it. "Kind of like I'm a secret agent," Ollie said. Only Monkey Man wasn't one of the bad guys, of course. Monkey Man was the hero, as always.

When Ava had presented the Monterey idea to Swift, he'd made no objection. We'd been out for dinner together when she broached the plan to him. "You know how you promised Ollie back in the summer you'd take him someplace great if he won the swim race?" she said. "Well, time to pay up, buster. And since Tahoe's a little too far to take him without his mom, we were thinking a day trip to Monterey would be perfect."

I'd already had a long talk with Ollie about not telling anyone about the surprise party. I didn't tell him expressly not to tell Dwight, but Ollie seemed to understand early on that certain aspects of life on Folger Lane were best not discussed with his father and stepmother. Besides, Ollie would never spoil Swift's surprise.

The afternoon before the big party, a Friday, I drove to Walnut Creek to pick up Ollie. We'd spend the night at my apartment and on Saturday Ollie would go off with Swift on their road trip to Monterey, with strict instructions to be home no later than 7:00 P.M.

That night, back at my apartment, I ran a bath for Ollie. As he peeled off his clothes, I reached for the bin of toys I kept for his visits: a G.I. Joe, a handful of plastic dinosaurs, his pirate ship.

These days Ollie wanted privacy in the tub, and he was old enough that I let him have it, but I sat outside the door with a magazine, listening to him. It was something I'd always loved, and one of the ten thousand things I had missed since he no longer lived with me: the sound of my child taking a bath.

I loved all the things little boys do in the bathtub when they're alone, like making the dinosaurs talk to each other. One—a female evidently—was lecturing the other about being mean to his little brother. "Did not," Boy Dinosaur said. "Did so," Girl Dinosaur said back in a high voice. "You're mean," said Boy Dinosaur. "You get on my nerves," said Girl Dinosaur. "If you say that one more time, I'm going to slap you."

Then there were bubble noises—Ollie briefly submerging himself, as he liked to do, then the splash when he came up for air. Now he was making the sound of an engine—the boat, I guessed. The high-pitched female dinosaur, calling out for help. G.I. Joe to the rescue.

At that moment, I wished he wasn't going away with Swift the next morning. I wanted to keep him home with me, here in this safe place where I could read to him and play Memory Game and make him macaroni and cheese, and afterward, tuck him in to bed and listen to the sound of his breathing. I wanted him to stay being a little boy, and it suddenly felt that the time in which he'd be one might be almost over. The thought came to me then, as clearly as a billboard on the side of the highway: *Don't let him go with Swift.*

If I told Ollie that he couldn't make the Monterey trip, he'd never forgive me, of course—any more than he had ever completely forgiven Elliot for insisting he put that life jacket on. (*Elliot.* Thinking of him now left a small hollow feeling in my heart. Ever since the night of the disastrous dinner party, I'd kept my cell phone close by and charged, just in case he called. It was ironic, I suppose, considering how I'd avoided his many calls to me all those weeks before. I'd thought about calling him, but I couldn't bring myself to do it. I had said such terrible things to Elliot; why should he forgive me? How could he? Even more ironic was that Ollie asked me where Elliot was. Even though Ollie adored Monkey Man, it seemed as if my son understood, too, that there had been something comforting in the solidity and steadiness of Elliot. For Ollie, as for me, it may only have been after he was gone that it became clear how good he had been for us.)

But now Ollie was with me again, and if what he wanted was to go off on a road trip with his hero, I wasn't about to tell him no. The two of them would have a great time, watching the dolphins and the sharks and the seals together—and then they'd drive home just in time for the big surprise. The party. Ollie loved it that he had such an important role in pulling it off. Getting Swift out of town so we could set things up was essential.

Swift was due to arrive at six on Saturday morning. I packed Ollie's bag the night before: a change of clothes, a few granola bars, a Baggie filled with Goldfish, some books to look at (though I doubted he would). He had asked me to charge up the digital camera I'd given him for his birthday so he could take pictures of all the cool stuff he'd see at the aquarium.

Ollie was up and dressed by five, wearing the San Francisco Giants jacket that Swift had given him over his monkey shirt, which was tucked in so it wouldn't hang to his knees. We were standing on the doorstep in the dark when the Land Rover pulled up and Swift rolled down the window.

"Yo, sport!" Swift called out to him. "You ready for some serious guy time this weekend? I brought along a couple of machetes, in case bad guys hijack us along the road."

Swift tied a bandanna around Ollie's head. And another around his own. "Don't mess with us," he announced, with that big hyena laugh of his. "We're pirates."

Ollie looked at me. He knew Swift well enough to understand this could be a story, but he wasn't sure, and he didn't want to get it wrong.

"He's kidding, honey," I told him. "There won't be any bad guys."

"Just this one," Swift said, leaning over to open the passenger door and biting down on his cigar. "Hop in, bud."

"We're a couple of pirate guys," Ollie said as I buckled him in.

"Tone it down a little, okay, Swift?" I said to him, as he was unzipping the soft top. "You've got precious cargo."

"Don't I know it. I'll treat him like he was my own boy."

62.

All that morning I resisted the impulse to call Swift's cell phone and ask to speak to Ollie. My son wanted guy time, not check-ins from his mother. And anyway, I knew those two would be having too much fun for Oliver to want to spend one minute talking to me.

After I'd had my coffee, I headed over to Folger Lane, where preparations for the party had gotten under way the moment Swift's car pulled out of the driveway. Now there were three trucks parked outside, delivering flowers, tables, linens, glassware. In the kitchen, the team of caterers was setting out trays.

Ava had called the day before to tell me the books were in—*The Man and His Dogs,* all one thousand specially printed copies.

"I can't wait to see how they turned out," she said. "But I didn't want to take them out of the boxes without you."

Ava was waiting for me in the large laundry room just off the kitchen. Close to a hundred corrugated cardboard boxes were stacked up against the far wall. Somehow Ava had managed to have the book cartons brought in through the back door without Swift's knowledge, to be stored until the party in the one place in the house Swift never ventured. This was Estella's exclusive domain and he had no idea how to use a washing machine, anyway.

We slit open the first carton. I lifted a volume from the top of the stack, felt the weight of it in my hand, ran my fingers over the embossed letters on the cover. Ava had selected the most expensive option for the cover: red leather with gold stamping. It took me a moment before I realized the mistake.

There was a misprint. The subtitle read as intended: *The Amazing Life of Swift Havilland.* But instead of *The Man and His Dogs*—the title Ava had selected— the letters read *The Man Is a God.*

I looked at Ava's face, to see how bad this was. But she was laughing.

"Well, that's not so far off base, is it?" she said. "The man *is* sort of a god. He may not have created the whole world. He just thinks he did."

Estella came in to see what we were doing. She picked up a copy of the book and turned the pages, studying each photograph carefully.

After she went back out to the yard, Ava shook her head. "I'm such an idiot," she said. "All those months of putting our book together, with all those pictures of parties and friends, and I forgot to include a single picture of Estella."

"She's not the type to take offense at something like that," I told her. In fact, there was no picture of me in the book, either. It would have seemed odd, putting one in myself, and Ava had never suggested it.

There was a lot of work to do, but I wanted to take a few minutes to study the book. I took a copy out to the garden with a glass of lemonade. As many hours as I'd spent on this project—as familiar as I was with every photograph—I wanted to imagine I'd never seen the book before. I was some guest at the party—Swift's motorcycle repairman, or his massage therapist, or Evelyn Couture, perhaps—picking it up for the first time and curious to know: *Who is this man?*

Page one: the face of a baby, the image bleeding right out to the edge. Even at six or seven months old, the features were recognizable. His mouth was open wide, howling with laughter.

For my husband, lover, and soul mate for all time— the dedication. *In celebration of his first six decades on Planet Earth. The Milky Way Galaxy will never be the same.*

That was followed by a couple of pages of images from Swift's childhood. Ava had decided that this part shouldn't occupy a lot of space, and the photographs suggested the reason behind her decision. Swift had been a homely child who hung back in all the early pictures. An older brother and a younger sister appeared in the pictures too. (Curious, I had thought, while assembling the images for the book, that I'd never even heard their names. They were not on the guest list for the party, either. Neither was any other member of Swift's family, if they existed, besides his son. Or any member of Ava's family, for that matter. About whom, it had occurred to me, I knew nothing.)

There was one formal family portrait from Swift's growing-up years. Swift's father looked like a hard man: square jawed, with dark narrow eyes and a stance that suggested military training. Beside him—but not touching, not even grazing her hand against his shirt— stood Swift's mother. She was thin, nearly bony, with hollow eyes and a look of defeat, her mouth open in the photograph, as if gasping for breath. One hand rested on her younger son's shoulder, less with an air of tenderness than control. She was keeping him out of trouble. She would not succeed very long.

Then came adolescence, also skimmed over lightly. Swift was short and undeveloped looking, with a bad haircut and bad skin. One photograph showed him on what must have been some kind of school trip, in which the students had evidently gone camping—standing in a lineup, against a backdrop that appeared to be Yosemite, with a pack on his back. By now he had adopted the expression of the class clown, perhaps having realized that all the best roles had already been taken. He had one arm behind the back of the boy next to him—Bobby, who still attended all the Havillands' dinner parties—and his hand was raised over Bobby's head (not easy; the guy had a good six inches on Swift), his fingers forming a devil sign.

The transformation came after. The wrestling team. Better acne medication, maybe. A date to the prom. (Not the hottest-looking girl. But she had large breasts, and even in what appeared to be their official prom portrait Swift seemed to be eyeing them.)

The next picture showed Swift taking off for college with a couple of Samsonite suitcases and a bass guitar. (He'd played in a rock band for about ten minutes. A move also aimed at improving his standing with girls, maybe, considering the fact that the Swift I knew displayed little interest in music.) He was wearing tight pants now, with long sideburns and the top three buttons of his shirt left open. Standing stiffly beside him: the younger sister and his parents, looking baffled to be related to this person. By now the older brother must have moved on.

This was the last image in the book in which Swift's family of origin appeared. From all I could gather, this was pretty much the last time they existed as any kind of significant factor in his life.

What followed was a surprisingly rapid rise. Fraternity membership. A good-looking girl on his arm. A better-looking one. The Corvette. A whole string of pictures depicting fraternity-style pranks (Swift dressed up as a woman, Swift mooning out the window of a Mustang convertible, Swift in a hot tub with three women. All drunk, from the looks of it.)

But there were also signs now of the beginnings of the career that earned him this house, and the ex-wife's house, and the ability to host a party like this one, and everything else. He wore a suit now. The first one looked cheap. The next one didn't.

Then came his marriage to Valerie, the mother of Cooper. She appeared in exactly two photographs: their wedding portrait, and a second taken years later, after she had clearly put on weight. She held a baby, Cooper, in the second photo, and she looked deeply unhappy. A little ways off stood Swift, smoking a cigar, and clowning for the camera as usual.

The rest of the story unfolded as a person might expect. A succession of cars and postdivorce girlfriends (more photographs of those than of the ex-wife). Cooper growing taller. (As instructed, I'd Photoshopped his mother out of these pictures.) The lease on his first building in Redwood City. The announcement of his company, Theracor, going public. Then Ava.

There was a picture in the book of the two of them not long after they met—it had to be early, because she was not yet in the chair. As I'd guessed, she had been taller than Swift, with beautiful legs. Her body was a lot rounder and fuller, more voluptuous, than it was now. I had noted, after seeing this photograph and others from the first days of their relationship, how much the accident must have aged her. Him, not so much.

It had been Ava's idea to alternate the pages featuring images from Swift's life with my portraits of dogs from the shelters she and Swift supported around the Bay Area—the photographs I'd taken on all those happy road trips with Elliot. When Ava had initially presented the concept to me, of combining photographs of Swift with photographs of rescue dogs, it had seemed a little odd, but I'd tried to give some thematic structure to the presentation. Therefore, the dogs whose portraits I featured after the divorce seemed happier; the dogs in those earlier pages were lovable, but with a melancholy air. Opposite the page depicting Swift with his parents, I'd placed a basset hound and a one-eyed mutt. Next to the page in which Swift was shown dressed in a devil suit, announcing the sale of his company to Oracle, I featured a photograph of a dog we'd found at a shelter in Sonoma, who looked like a cross between a pit bull and a lion. No question this was an alpha dog, though of the two subjects facing each other on opposing pages, the one who was licking his lips was not the dog, but the man. Swift.

As I was turning the pages of the book, Ava came up behind me. I smelled her gardenia perfume first, felt a long, slim arm circle my neck, and the silver cuff against my skin. She stroked my hair, then maneuvered her chair up alongside mine.

"You did a wonderful job, honey," she said. "You really captured the essence of Swift."

"I just put the photographs together," I told her. "They were all there already. It's more about who he is than about anything I did."

I looked over at her. I hardly ever saw Ava without her makeup on, but at the moment she was wearing none. I was startled by how old she looked. Her legs, which she normally kept covered, were exposed to just above her knees. I was shocked at how wasted they were, lacking all definition. Two sticks, set onto the footrest of her chair, decorated in useless though expensive shoes.

"I couldn't manage without him, you know," she said. Her voice sounded different. Softer and more vulnerable than I'd ever known Ava to be.

"You're strong, too," I said. She didn't seem to hear me.

"It's like the two of us make up one person now," Ava said, and for a second I might almost have described her tone as bitter. "Like conjoined twins sharing a single heart. If one dies, so does the other."

63.

It was midday and I was helping the caterers carry in the plates and silverware when the snow-making equipment arrived. The idea was to transform Folger Lane into a replica of their Lake Tahoe home in winter, down to a giant snowdrift in front of the house. As the machine spit out the snow, Ava explained to me that because we were doing this for Swift, it would not be enough simply to create a pretty scene of a winter wonderland. Once the snowdrift was complete, there would be a large and prominently positioned squirt of yellow food coloring, to give the appearance that a dog had recently peed there.

As for the real dogs, Ava had sequestered them in her bedroom, with an assortment of dog treats, largely so Rocco—always the high-strung one—wouldn't have to deal with all the people and the frenetic pace of party preparations. Huge faux icicles hung along the eaves of the house, and along the front walk, snow sculptures of penguins. (Not exactly native to the Lake Tahoe habitat, but Ava was taking more than a few liberties.) There were more lights in the trees, and an igloo, which would be lit from within in a way that gave the thing a wonderful and mysterious glow.

Ollie would love this. Ollie, who was probably at the aquarium right about now, checking out a barracuda or a manta ray. Tamer fare than Swift's usual, but I knew that loving Ollie as he did, and knowing how much Ollie would enjoy it, Swift would get into the whole thing. I suddenly wished I could have been the one introducing Oliver to the aquarium. Or Elliot and me, together.

Elliot. No more of that.

"I can't wait to see what the igloo looks like in the dark with the lights on," Ava had said, when the men had finished building it out of pale blue ice bricks. "It reminds me of my little bone china tea light holder."

Ava had commissioned ice sculptures of the three dogs to go in the living room: One depicted Sammy and Lillian, curled up together on their dog bed; the other was of Rocco on his own. Mouth open, as usual. Barking.

Out behind the house, by the rose arbor, two men wearing jumpsuits with MELTING MEMORIES printed on the back were setting up another ice sculpture, in which photographs of Cooper had been embedded—almost as if he were an avalanche victim, buried and frozen, grinning out at the world of the living from some frigid eternity. At the far end of the pool, a plasma screen was set up, with an all-Swift video loop: Swift performing qigong, Swift running, Swift swimming, Swift dancing. Swift in warrior pose, Swift tossing a Frisbee to the dogs, Swift reclining on a floating lounge chair, cigar and drink in hand. The largest of the ice statues had been placed at the center of the garden—the life-size naked ice sculpture of Swift, whose penis contained a tube that dispensed champagne. Another utterly Swift-like concept.

"Someone's going to make the crack that the penis seems out of proportion to the rest of the sculpture," Ava said. "And Swift will probably feel a need to prove them wrong."

"Speak of the devil," I said. "I was just thinking I should call those two. They should be heading home soon." I was proud of myself for holding out this long before calling to check on Ollie.

No answer. "They probably lost track of time," Ava said. "I figure they should be rolling in around seven thirty."

I tried not to worry. Ava was right; the two of them were probably just having so much fun they'd lost track of time, but they'd show up by party time.

The work continued. It was amazing to see Swift and Ava's yard transformed. Among the ice sculptures and lights, Ava had arranged, somewhat incongruously, to install a fire pit, where the fire dancer was set to perform. There would also be a pole dancer, for no reason besides the fact that Swift loved pole dancing. A dozen tables had been set up with the custommade place mats featuring a grinning image of Swift, biting into an exceptionally long cigar. At every place, wrapped in silver paper and tied with an ice-blue bow, was a copy of the book, *The Man Is a God*, along with an envelope containing a form guests could fill out to accompany a donation check in the honor of the birthday boy and made out to BARK. Suggested contribution: $2,000.

At four o'clock, Ava called Swift, but got no answer. "Those two are probably having such a great time they want to spend every minute they can fooling around together," she said. "I bet they stopped at this Mexican place Swift loves, for a giant burrito."

"They've still got plenty of time to get back here by the time the guests arrive," I said, though I was aware, as I said this, of a small but insistent worry. I was wishing that whatever plan Ava had cooked up to get Swift out of town had not involved my son.

Cooper's fiancée, Virginia, arrived—beautiful though oddly forgettable looking. Virginia had spent the weekend with her parents in Palo Alto, working on wedding plans. Cooper had stayed in New York, she told us, working on some big deal, but his flight to SFO was due to get in that afternoon. He'd rent a car at the airport and drive straight from there.

Virginia went off for a pedicure. Estella took the dogs for a walk. Ava emerged with one of her special collagen-activating masks on her face. "Swift's still not answering his phone," she said, looking vaguely worried. "Bad cell service, probably."

Now I got scared. I was trying not to, wanting to give my son the gift of a day with his idol. Why hadn't I bought Ollie one of those cheap disposable cell phones he was always begging for, to stay in touch?

The guests began arriving at seven. Ava was obviously distracted now by her inability to reach Swift, as I was, knowing Ollie was with him.

Virginia had gotten back from the manicurist's long ago with her mother—the two of them now floating around the garden in blue and silver gowns, showing off their matching silver nail polish. But Cooper had yet to arrive.

"You know Cooper," Ava said. "He's always late."

Swift's friend Bobby was one of the first guests to show up, with his latest age-inappropriate girlfriend, this one named Cascade. Ernesto arrived early, too, along with the woman who had worked as Swift's personal assistant at his last start-up, Geraldine. I said hello to Ling and Ping, Swift's herbalist and her husband, and a bunch of others I didn't recognize—old business associates, probably. Renata came, without Carol, who had evidently left her recently for another woman. Ava's new protégée, Felicity, came dressed as a snow bunny. Evelyn Couture wore a vintage gown that looked like something Nancy Reagan might have owned during her White House years.

The mariachi band—also a little incongruous, given the winter setting (but Swift loved mariachi music) had started playing "La Bamba." The pole dancer had set up her apparatus over by the pool, having been instructed to begin her act the minute Swift came through the door. The caterers, assisted by Estella, were circulating the first of the appetizers: raw salmon on thinly sliced rye bread with crème fraîche and caviar. Lillian and Sammy were wearing special birthday collars for the event. Because Rocco was upset by crowds, Ava had him contained upstairs in the master bedroom, with a very large bone to occupy him. "He can't handle the stress of all these people around," Ava explained. "But he needs to know I'm nearby."

No sighting of Cooper yet.

"This is so like Cooper," Ava said, checking her watch. "He wants to make sure everyone's already there when he arrives, so he can make the most dramatic entrance." But I knew the person whose absence really concerned her now was Swift. For me, of course, it was Ollie.

At half past eight, Ava made her way over to the statue of the naked Swift and held her glass under the champagne-dispensing penis fountain, then tapped it—the glass, not the penis—with a spoon.

"As everyone knows," she said—the light catching her silver beaded full-length gown—"we're here to celebrate the birth of my amazing husband. This is supposed to be a surprise, though seeing your cars will probably give him a clue when he pulls up, as I know he will any minute now. Until he gets here, I just want to encourage you to take a look at the book our amazing friend Helen and I have put together for you all, commemorating all of Swift's great work on behalf of rescue animals throughout the Bay Area and, soon, all over our nation. Welcome to our home."

I scanned the grounds. The guests appeared enraptured. All our weeks of planning had paid off, from the look of things.

"So many of you have asked what you could possibly give to a man who has so much," Ava continued. "The answer is: You can give your support to our foundation, BARK, whose website we're launching tonight. With your help, dogs all over California and across the nation will be able to receive free spay and neuter services."

"And hump each other to their hearts' content, with no consequences!" Swift's friend Bobby called out. "That's a cause dear to my buddy Swift's heart."

"So thank you for joining us. And drink up." Ava raised her glass in the general direction of the ice-sculpture penis. I reached for my mineral water.

The mariachis resumed playing. People had mostly gathered near the pool now to admire the talents of the pole dancer, to whom Ava had given the instructions that she might as well start. Cooper's fiancée Virginia was checking her phone.

Estella emerged from the kitchen, but not with a tray this time. She was holding Ava's cell phone, wearing an expression I had never seen before. Whatever this was, it wasn't good.

I knew the moment Ava took the phone that it must be about Swift, and that meant it was about Ollie, too. I ran over to her.

She was still holding the phone. Just listening, but shaking her head. The mariachi music was so loud, it was hard to hear anything. I was screaming now.

Tell me. Tell me.

There had been an accident. Not in Monterey, but at Lake Tahoe. That's where my son and Swift had gone, evidently.

Someone was saying something about a boat.

64.

The drive from Portola Valley to Lake Tahoe takes four hours and twenty minutes. Three and a half hours, if Swift were driving. We made it in Bobby's car in three and a quarter.

The first details the police had given Ava over the phone had been confusing. Sometime that afternoon, Swift's boat had collided with a Jet Ski out on the lake. All together, four individuals had been involved in the crash—two males, one young woman, and a child. Someone had sustained a life-threatening injury, but the officer who'd spoken to Ava had been unclear about the identity of that person.

"Your husband's at the hospital," he told Ava. "We suggest that you get here as soon as possible."

"Ollie!" I said to her. Screamed, more like it. "What about Ollie?"

She didn't seem to hear me. "We need to go now," she said—not to me or to anyone. She had already begun to wheel her chair toward the door, like a person in a dream. A bad one.

Then Ernesto was lifting her into the front passenger seat of Bobby's car—for once, Ava showed no sign of objection to the help; she just wanted to get going. I dove into the back; Ernesto stowed Ava's chair in the trunk. Some of the guests were asking what had happened, but Ava seemed not to hear, or if she did, had no breath to respond. In the brief moment before the car door closed, Estella had put her arms around me.

"I pray for your boy," she told me. There was more, but in Spanish.

"Just drive," Ava told Bobby. He tore out of the driveway so fast the tires screamed. Behind us, the white lights glittered over the fake snow, but we weren't looking back.

What I remember of those three hours and fifteen minutes: Ava dialing her cell phone, not making any sense. Me reaching for mine—only who was I going to call? Not Swift. I dialed the police station in Truckee,

California, but when I got a live person, I realized I couldn't hear over the sound of Ava's weeping.

"I'm looking for news about a boy," I said. "Eight years old. He may have been involved in an accident."

"Are you the mother?" A woman's voice on the other end of the phone, barely audible over Ava's moaning. "They have him at the hospital. It would be best if you get here as soon as possible." More calls then. No clear word. Bobby was going ninety, but it still didn't feel fast enough.

We did not speak on the drive up. Bobby, at the wheel, had at first tried to offer a few words, but Ava told him to be quiet, and after that nobody said anything. I was aware, as we sat in the darkness, tearing up the highway, that in a terrible and unavoidable way, each of us must be praying it was the beloved person of the other who had been injured. Not the one belonging to us.

65.

Bobby had driven up to the emergency entrance. I jumped out of the car before it came to a full stop. I didn't consider this at the time—didn't consider anything but whether my son was all right—but afterward it occurred to me that this must have been one of the moments in Ava's life when her inability to use her legs revealed itself most brutally. I could run into the hospital to talk with someone, finally. She had to wait for Bobby to get her chair out of the trunk and unfold it, then lift her onto the seat. Though I think if he'd taken another five seconds she would simply have flung herself on the ground and dragged herself up that ramp through the double doors.

No child by the name of Oliver McCabe had been admitted to the hospital. There was no Swift Havilland, either.

"The accident?" I said. "The boat crash?"

"You'll have to speak to someone else about that," the woman told me. "I don't know anything about a boat crash. I just came on duty."

Someone told me to go to the third floor. That's when I found them finally: my son and Swift, sitting with a police officer. Also—here came a shock—Cooper.

Swift and Cooper sat side by side at a table, the officer to one side taking notes. Swift had one Band-Aid on his forehead, nothing more. Cooper's right arm was in a sling.

I ran to Ollie, of course—slumped alone on a couch on the other side of the room. He had no visible injuries, though one look told me that something had happened to him that had left him deeply shaken. He was staring straight ahead. He was wrapped in a blanket, but even so his whole body was trembling.

"I hate that boat," he said. "I'm never going on any more boats."

"It's okay now," I said. "I'm just going to hold you for a while." Now that I'd seen him, and he was alive, the particulars of what had happened didn't seem that important, though later they would be.

Oliver couldn't stop shivering. I looked over at Swift now, speaking with the police officer. His expression, unlike Ollie's, remained remarkably unchanged from any other day—calm, reasonable, sober—though his trademark grin was absent. He appeared to listen intently to what the officer was saying, though Swift was doing most of the talking, with occasional interjections from Cooper.

What was Cooper doing at Lake Tahoe? (What were any of them doing at Lake Tahoe?) The last I knew, Cooper was supposed to be flying into SFO from New York. (Renting a car. Showing up at the party to meet up with his fiancée and deliver the big birthday toast to his father.) Now he was leaning back just a little on the molded plastic chair, legs spread wide apart in that way a certain kind of man is likely to sit, that always seemed, to me, to announce the presence of their manliness. *Here is my cock. Here are my balls. Any questions?*

He had a Coke in one hand, cell phone in the other. He was wearing a pink polo shirt, with the little alligator appliqué on his left chest, his Ray-Bans suspended from his neck on a rubber cord, a two-day growth of beard in no way diminishing his handsomeness. The way he looked reminded me of one of the photographs of Swift I'd included in the *Man and His Dogs* book, taken when Cooper was sixteen or seventeen and had been named Prom King, class of 2000.

I would have expected to have spoken with Swift when I reached the waiting room—or he to me—but strangely, given our many months of apparently close friendship, he seemed not to acknowledge my arrival, or, stranger still, the presence of my son. We remained on separate sides of the room—he with his son, I with mine. The unspoken message was clear: This was how things were going to stay. If I could have picked Ollie up right then and run away with him, I would have. Through the blanket, I could still feel his whole body trembling, though after those first syllables when I'd taken him in my arms, he had not spoken another word.

I looked back to Swift. Though he was not smiling, for once, his face seemed strangely placid. I thought fleetingly of Elliot, and how when he was anxious or upset he ran his hands through his hair and how crazy it looked. Elliot, who was normally so calm, acted agitated when he was upset. Swift, who was usually so outrageous and loud, seemed chillingly composed, at a moment when you might have supposed he'd be unsettled.

I missed Elliot. I wished he were here.

With my arms wrapped tightly around my son, I watched Swift talking with the policeman. He was gesturing with his hands, but without any hint of distress, as if he were telling the gardener where to plant the tulip bulbs, or recreating for a friend the workings of a particular play enacted by the 49ers at last Sunday's game. Beside him at the table, Cooper looked earnest, thoughtful, concerned. Now and then, as his father spoke, he nodded, and other times he shook his head—not as a person would who takes exception to what the other is saying, but simply by way of conveying how regrettable things were.

"He's just a little kid," Cooper was saying, his voice level, reasonable. All evidence of the frat boy absent now. "It's not his fault."

Cooper and Swift exchanged glances then. I had never recognized before how much they resembled each other. It came to me, they were speaking about my son.

"You have any kids, Norman?" Swift was saying now. Somewhere along the line he'd picked up the officer's first name. "You know how they are at that age."

The police officer looked over at Ollie. Whatever else Swift was saying then, I didn't hear it. All my focus went to Ollie.

Just then, Ava came into the room in her wheelchair. She went immediately to Swift, seeming not to notice me and Ollie. "Finally!" she said. "Nobody could tell me what floor you were on." She reached her long, thin arm—still in the silver beaded gown—to stroke his chest and smooth his hair. The way she touched him reminded me of how she would pet one of their dogs.

"You're okay," she kept saying to Swift. "The only thing that matters is you're okay."

A second officer came into the room. "Please, ma'am," he said. "I know it's hard, but we need your husband's attention. We're trying to get a statement."

A doctor entered, wearing surgical scrubs.

"She made it through the surgery," he said. "But there was a lot of pressure on her brain. The impact was pretty severe. We won't know the extent of the damage for some time."

"Who is he talking about?" I asked the second police officer, the new one.

"Ms. Hernandez," he said. "I understand she was employed by the family. Or her mother is? She was thrown off the back of the Jet Ski. That young woman is lucky to be alive."

Carmen.

Later now. I had lost track of the time, but it was early morning and we were at the police station now—my son asleep, at last, on a cot they'd provided, with a blanket over him, and a second blanket because he was shivering so badly, which had nothing to do with the temperature. One of the officers had offered me a cot, too, but I couldn't sleep, so I just sat on the floor next to Ollie, with my arms still locked around him.

Sometime around dawn, the officer came in to say he'd finished his report—"just the initial findings"— and that he was ready to tell me what appeared to have happened, based on his interviews with Swift and Cooper, neither of whom had spoken to me directly.

"We'll want to have a talk with your son, too, naturally," he said. "But he's in no shape for that now. We might want to have a child welfare officer present, just to assess how much of this he can handle."

I didn't want to leave Ollie, but he finally appeared to be sleeping soundly, so I followed the officer into the other room and sat down across from him at his desk.

Reynolds was the name on his badge. "So," I said. "What can you tell me?"

"I understand that Mr. Havilland had brought your son Oliver up to the lake to give him a ride in his power boat," Officer Reynolds offered.

"This wasn't the plan," I said. "They were supposed to be spending the day in Monterey."

"According to Mr. Havilland," Officer Reynolds said, "he'd wanted to surprise your boy. I gather this was something the two of them had talked about for a long time."

"They were supposed to be going to the aquarium," I said. For whatever that was worth. Nothing, evidently.

"Unbeknownst to Mr. Havilland, his son Cooper had chosen to pay a visit to the house sometime earlier—the day before—and brought along a friend of his, Ms. Hernandez," the officer continued.

Described this way—based on his interview with Cooper, I gathered—the whole thing sounded wonderfully uncomplicated. A cookout on the grill. A dip in the lake. A little card game. (A little fooling around, too, no doubt. But that was not a police matter.) Then, on Saturday afternoon they took out the Jet Ski. The younger Mr. Havilland thought he'd show this young woman around the lake.

Sometime in the late afternoon Mr. Havilland, senior, had shown up with Ollie.

Late afternoon? The two of them had set out at six that morning. What took them so long to make what should have been a four-hour trip? What was Swift thinking, arriving at Lake Tahoe late in the afternoon, with full knowledge that he needed to be home in time for dinner that night?

No answer for any of that. All the police officer had to say was that Mr. Havilland arrived, by his own account, sometime around 4:00 or 5:00 P.M. He had not been concerned to see another car in the driveway already, because he recognized the vehicle as the yellow Dodge Viper his son Cooper liked to rent whenever he flew home to San Francisco. He figured Cooper had come west to surprise him on his birthday and was taking an extra couple of days to enjoy the lake house. He had his own key, and it was not uncommon, he had said, that he'd use it this way, as a getaway.

"Since there was no sign of the younger Mr. Havilland on the premises, Mr. Havilland, senior, deduced that his son must be out enjoying the lake, as he and your son intended to do," Officer Reynolds continued.

"This was confirmed when he recognized that one of the two Jet Skis was missing from the boathouse. So he drove down to the landing for the purpose of lowering his speedboat"—he consulted his notes here—"the *Donzi* . . . into the lake."

I was listening, but only partly. It was hard to focus, knowing Ollie was in the other room. I didn't want to leave him by himself. If he woke up afraid, or had a bad dream, I wanted him to know he wasn't alone. But I was having trouble making sense of the officer's account of the events of that afternoon. Or what Cooper and Swift could possibly have been thinking, heading out onto the lake for a boat ride, and a Jet Ski ride, on the afternoon of the day when they knew they were due back on Folger Lane by seven thirty. At least one of those two—Cooper—knew a big party would be under way at which his presence, not to mention his father's, was expected. Even Swift had to have realized something was up for his wife to have been so insistent that they make it home no later than eight. We had both known, as he set off on the trip, that he was humoring her when he acted as if there were nothing unusual in Ava's insistence that he go away for the day with Ollie.

"Apparently your son and Mr. Havilland rode around on the boat for no more than fifteen or twenty minutes before the trouble occurred," the officer continued. "Mr. Havilland explained that this particular model of speedboat is capable of getting up to speeds as high as eighty miles per hour. But he had made it plain to Oliver that they would not be doing that kind of racing. This was meant to be strictly a child's pleasure trip."

I nodded. More numb than in agreement. The Swift I knew would not be averse to taking a boy on a thrill ride.

"Mr. Havilland has made it plain to us that he is adamant about water safety," the officer went on. "At first his plan had been only to take Oliver out on the smaller dinghy with the outboard motor, or the kayak, but your son was so insistent about going on this bigger boat that he finally acquiesced."

They'd driven up there to ride the Donzi. That was the whole point of the trip. Those two didn't travel over four hours for a ride in a dinghy. I didn't say this. I just thought it.

"Unfortunately, your son evidently displayed a strong resistance to wearing his life jacket," Officer Reynolds continued. "I gather he had been somewhat argumentative and oppositional for much of the day, but Mr. Havilland attributed this to the boy being overtired."

"He may have been tired," I said. But none of the rest made any sense. If Ollie hadn't wanted to put on his life jacket, it was hard to picture Swift making an issue of it. It was even harder to imagine Ollie ever being argumentative—or "oppositional"—with Swift. Every time I'd seen those two together, Ollie behaved like the most obedient and loyal puppy.

"As you would expect, Mr. Havilland took a firm position. He explained to your son that there would be no ride in the boat unless he agreed to wear the life jacket. At this point, Ollie reluctantly complied."

The crash, I thought. Tell me about the crash.

"But evidently your son kept giving Mr. Havilland a hard time about the life jacket," the officer said. "You know how mouthy kids can get."

Maybe I did. But not Ollie, not to Swift.

According to this police officer, Ollie continued to "mouth off" to Swift about the life jacket. He had used an epithet describing the kind of person who wears life jackets.

"I don't want to repeat this epithet, Ms. McCabe," he said to me. "Let's leave it that the word begins with 'P.' Then Ollie starts asking if he could drive the boat. Mr. Havilland says no. Under no circumstances. They were rounding the point just south of Rubicon Bay, if you're familiar with that area."

I shook my head. "I've only been to Lake Tahoe once before," I told him.

"This was when Mr. Havilland noted a Jet Ski on the starboard side. Coming at a reasonable speed but close enough that it was important to keep a close watch. The Jet Ski gets closer, and to Mr. Havilland's surprise, the Jet Ski is being driven by his son, Cooper. Naturally, then, the two wish to pull their two crafts up, one alongside the other. They'd almost reached each other," the officer continued. "Close enough that they could speak to each other. Mr. Havilland, senior, calls out to his son, does he have sunscreen?"

Here the officer interrupted his story with a detail from Swift's account of the events. "Mr. Havilland, senior, wanted number fifty," he said. "He explained to his son that he had twenty-five, but out on the water, it wasn't enough."

At this of all moments, Swift had been talking about sunscreen. What was that about? A memory came to me of Ollie playing cards by the pool, and Swift instructing him on the secret of winning at poker.

You want to make a lie sound like the truth? Swift had said to Ollie. *Surround it with smaller details that are real.*

I knew this, too, from the stories I made up. It had been true that Audrey Hepburn worked for UNICEF. It was true, she made a movie with Gregory Peck. She just wasn't my grandmother.

"They were evidently close enough that Mr. Havilland, senior, reached to grab the tube of sunscreen from his son. It was in this moment, when he looked away, that your son Ollie wrested the helm from Mr. Havilland and proceeded to gun the engine."

I drew in my breath. I looked at the officer hard. I didn't know this man, but I knew my son. He wouldn't do something like that. I thought I knew Swift, too, but I'd been wrong. He was lying.

Swift never wore sunscreen. He had told Ollie that sunscreen was for pussies.

"When Ollie gave it gas," Officer Reynolds continued, "the boat shot forward, full throttle. That's when the boat rammed into the Jet Ski. Mr. Havilland's son was knocked off his seat, sustaining only the minor injury of a sprained wrist.

"Unfortunately, the injuries incurred by Ms. Hernandez were much more severe. When she was thrown from the Jet Ski it appears that she sustained a head injury. She lost consciousness. It was no doubt due to the efforts of Mr. Havilland—the senior Mr. Havilland—who dove into the water to rescue her, that this young woman is alive at all.

"Given what he was facing," the officer concluded, "I'd call that man a hero."

I asked if there was any more information about how Carmen was doing. "Has anyone contacted her mother?" I asked.

"The doctors are saying it's too early to tell much," he said. "Her mother's on her way up now."

"Of course we understand that Oliver is too young to be held responsible for this," the officer went on. "He couldn't have anticipated the consequences."

"My son wouldn't have done anything like that," I said. "My son worships the ground Swift walks on. I can't picture him grabbing the helm of a boat and trying to drive it himself. He doesn't have that kind of confidence. That's more the kind of thing Swift would do. Or Cooper."

"With all due respect, Ms. McCabe," Officer Reynolds said, "mothers never seem able to view their sons with a totally unbiased eye. My wife would be the same where our son was concerned."

"It's not like that," I said.

"Of course we'll be speaking with your son about all of this, when he's ready," the officer said. "Meanwhile, given his age, no charges will be filed against him. What he did, according to Mr. Havilland, was a prank. A stupid prank, with terrible repercussions for the young woman involved, though we can thank God nobody else was seriously injured. And nobody's suggesting that Oliver injured Ms. Hernandez intentionally."

"He didn't do it at all," I said.

"In Oliver's case, we understand your son has had a lot of traumatic experiences," Officer Reynolds went on. "We managed to reach his father by telephone earlier this evening. He was deeply troubled, of course, but confirmed that Oliver has displayed a lot of anger lately, particularly to authority figures."

They'd spoken with Dwight. The walls seemed to be closing in on me now. Not unlike that courtroom, three years earlier. But worse.

"Kids from divorced families can often act out," the police officer said. "Your DUI arrest was probably confusing to your son. Seeing an authority figure placed under arrest."

"Who told you that?"

"Mr. Havilland explained to us that your drinking is no longer an issue. I understand you're in AA."

This wasn't happening. No, *this was.*

Maybe I would have said something, but I heard Ollie calling out for me and I went back in the other room.

They wanted to talk with Ollie, of course. He wasn't in good shape for that, but it seemed important. Particularly after the account I'd heard—Swift's account—of what had happened out on the lake.

First they got him a Coke. The officers sat him down in a comfortable chair. This time there was a female police officer, and someone I figured must be some kind of child protection officer. I was not allowed in the room.

"I'm sorry about this," Officer Reynolds told me. "It's just policy."

He was gone only briefly—five minutes at most. When Ollie emerged from the room—his face pale, his eyes hollow in their sockets—the female officer took me aside while Ollie was in the bathroom.

"He isn't responding to our questions," she said. "All he could do when we ran over Mr. Havilland's account of what happened was to stare out the window and nod his head. Mostly he just kept saying 'I'm sorry' over and over again."

"Ollie's eight years old," I told her.

"Of course he's feeling guilty and responsible. He asked if he was going to go to jail. I made a point of reassuring him that we understand he didn't realize the consequence of his actions. It's not like we're going to be charging someone his age with a crime."

"Ollie agreed he gunned the engine?" I asked her. "He said *he* was the one who crashed the boat into the Jet Ski?"

"He isn't speaking at this point. But he concurred with everything Mr. Havilland and his son had represented."

"He's exhausted," I said. "He's confused."

"Right now your son is a very troubled boy," she said. "I'm sure you'll want to consult a therapist not only about the underlying issues surrounding his anger but what is likely to be his ongoing sense of guilt and shame concerning this event. The thing to remember is that he's just a child. We all recognize that."

Later, there might be more questions, but for the moment there was no further reason to stay around. I'd heard that Estella was getting a ride to the hospital with a friend of hers, but there wasn't much I could do for her. She'd have her family around, and even if I spoke Spanish, what could I say? The doctors were waiting for the results of a bunch of tests they'd done on Carmen, who was still in the intensive care unit, not yet having regained consciousness.

Until now, I had not had the time or space to consider this, but now I did: In all the time that transpired between our arrival at the hospital and now—at least eight hours—neither Swift nor Cooper nor Ava had exchanged a word with me or my son. Wherever they were now—at their house on the lake, taking a shower and putting on fresh clothes, or in a car headed back to Folger Lane—they had disappeared without any acknowledgment of me or Ollie.

And what now? I had no idea how we'd get home, even though this was the least of my worries at the moment.

When I tried to think of who to call—a person willing to drive more than four hours to pick up a desperate woman and a messed-up child at Lake Tahoe on a Sunday afternoon—it struck me how, taking Swift and Ava out of the equation, there was nobody.

"Think of me as the person to call in the case of an emergency," Ava had told me that day, and she'd written her name down on the card I kept in my wallet. This no longer applied.

Once it would have been Alice, but I'd burned that bridge when I abandoned our friendship in favor of my two more glamorous friends.

Then there was Elliot.

He picked up the phone on the first ring. He was home, of course, as he usually was, even on sunny days. I could hear a movie playing in the background. I pictured him sitting on his old corduroy couch in his baggy pants, with the blinds shut to keep the light out, watching *The Lady Vanishes* for the hundredth time. Or *High Noon*.

A wave of love washed over me. Love and regret.

"I wouldn't blame you if you hung up right now," I said when he answered the phone. No need to say who it was calling. He'd know.

"I wouldn't ever hang up on you, Helen," he said.

"I'm in a tough place," I said. "Ollie and me both. I was wondering if you could come get us."

66.

He arrived a little before sunset, with an apple for me and a bag of peanuts for Ollie.

"You're probably hungry for some real food," he said, lifting Ollie into his arms. It surprised me that my son showed no resistance. "But I figured this would tide you over."

It wasn't cold, but he had brought a blanket and a pillow for Ollie. "You can tell me about it if you feel like it," he said to me after he set Ollie down in the backseat. "Or not."

But Ollie was there. And where to begin? The truth was, I didn't even know what had happened—only that it was terrible and the whole world looked different now.

"You were right," I said.

"Right?"

"About my friends. The people I thought were my friends."

"If you think it makes me glad to hear that, you're wrong," he told me. "I'm just sorry you got hurt."

We drove in silence after that. After a while, Ollie fell asleep in the back. I still didn't want to chance saying anything he might hear, so I kept to safe topics.

"It's good to see you," I said. "How have you been?"

"Oh, Helen," he said. "How am I supposed to answer that?"

It was dark when Ollie woke up, an hour or two down the highway. Elliot asked if he was hungry and he shook his head.

"I think I'll pull into this diner I know, anyway," he said. "You can get something, too, if you change your mind."

It turned out Ollie was ravenous. He finished off two chicken tacos and a bowl of chocolate pudding, and when that was done he asked Elliot if he could have one more taco. I realized it had probably been a very long time since anyone had given him anything to eat. He had a glass of milk, and then another one.

"I guess the last time you ate was probably lunch with Swift," I said to him.

He shook his head. "We were going to have lunch after the boat ride. Only then all the other stuff happened."

"So, you went out on the boat in the morning?" I asked him. "Before lunchtime, even?"

"I was excited," Ollie said. "The minute we got to the lake Swift and me took the Donzi out."

"But it was still dark when you left home. You would have gotten to Lake Tahoe pretty early," I said, doing the math in my head. Ten o'clock, maybe. If they stopped for breakfast, eleven at the latest.

"We didn't stop for breakfast. Monkey Man and me had a banana in the car on the way to the lake."

"I don't understand," I said. "You mean you spent all morning driving the boat around the lake? And the afternoon too?" I was confused. It had been almost six when the 911 call came in from Swift's boat.

Oliver was looking uncomfortable now. He started playing with the saltshaker, pouring little piles of salt on the diner table and driving the pepper shaker through them. It was the kind of thing he used to do when he was four or five—the kind of thing he'd done during his guardian *ad litem* interviews—and the fact that he was doing it now signaled that Ollie had reached his limit with the current conversation, for the time being, anyway.

Once we were back on the road, I couldn't stop thinking about what Ollie had said—that he and Swift had taken the boat out before lunchtime. It didn't make sense. I knew he didn't want to talk about it anymore, but I was still trying to understand. I started in again.

"I don't get it, Ollie," I said. "It was still morning when you and Monkey Man got to the lake. But the emergency rescue guys said it was six o'clock when they got the call about the accident. What were you and Monkey Man doing all day? You had to have been driving for hours and hours."

Up until now, Ollie hadn't said anything about his day with Swift or their time together at the lake. But suddenly the words exploded out of him.

"We only drove the boat a couple of minutes," Ollie said. "Then we crashed, and after that we didn't drive anymore."

"But it was starting to get dark when the rescue guys got there."

Elliot and I enchanged glances. From where I sat in the front, I could see Ollie, in the seat behind us, examining the tread on his sneaker.

"I hate that boat," Ollie said, yelling now. "I never want to ride on any more boats."

He put his hands on his ears. He started to sing. Not real singing. Just yelling out notes. *Blah blah blah blah blah.*

"I know you don't want to talk about this, Ollie," I said. "But I need to know. What went on all that time, between going out on the boat and when the rescue guys showed up?"

I had been looking at my son's face in the rearview mirror, but now I turned around to face him, belted into a corner of the backseat of Elliot's car, huddled under the blanket. "What were you doing all that time?" I said.

Ollie put his hands over his ears. "I wish I never went on that dumb boat ride," he said. "That's when everything went crazy."

"You can tell me what happened," I said. "Whatever it is, it's okay."

"She just kept lying there," he said, so softly I could just barely hear. "Her eyes were open and there was blood coming out of her." Finally, then, he started to cry.

Elliot pulled over by the side of the highway. I got out of the front seat and into the back, where I could put my arms around my son and hold him.

It was a couple of minutes before Oliver calmed down enough to speak again, and when he did, his voice was different, a whisper. Almost as if he was afraid someone other than the two of us might hear.

"Monkey Man said we needed to rest," Ollie began. "Cooper was throwing up, and doing all this stupid stuff like singing 'Ninety-nine Bottles of Beer on the Wall,' only he kept getting the numbers wrong. He said twenty-seven bottles. Then he said forty-two bottles. Then he was back to ninety-nine again. He sounded crazy."

"What about Monkey Man?" I asked him. "What was he doing?"

"Monkey Man was making Cooper drink all this water. Monkey Man kept telling him to drink more water and rest."

"You mean, you were taking a rest *before* the crash happened? Cooper was drinking this water and you were having your rest, and then the crash happened?"

Ollie shook his head. "The crash happened first. We were supposed to rest after. We rested a long time. Monkey Man kept saying we had to wait for the girl to wake up, only she didn't. She was looking funny, and she wasn't moving, and Monkey Man kept making Cooper drink more water, but he was acting like an idiot."

I looked at Elliot. He didn't know the story yet—neither did I, really—but he had gathered enough to know this was a far cry from Swift's version.

"I was really hungry. I fell asleep. After a long time, Cooper wasn't acting crazy any more and Monkey Man said we could call some people to come get us."

Once again, I looked over at Elliot. He wasn't the type to take his eyes off the road, but his face said everything.

"The girl still didn't wake up. She still looked funny."

"Did you tell this to the police?" I asked Ollie. "The part about taking the rest, and the girl? The part about drinking all the water?"

Ollie shook his head. He was studying a piece of thread on the blanket, twirling it between his fingers. "Monkey Man said not to tell that part," he said. "He said everything would get messed up if I told."

From where he sat next to me, Elliot reached over to take my hand. "It's going to be all right," he said. "Thank God he let you know."

I knew that tomorrow I'd have to call Officer Reynolds and tell him there was more he needed to know. As hard as this would be, I'd need to bring my son back to Lake Tahoe to speak with the police again. This time, Swift wouldn't be in the next room. Not then, or—I knew now—ever again.

67.

When we got back to my apartment, I asked Elliot if he'd like to come upstairs with us, but he shook his head. "You need to take care of Oliver," he said, and he was correct about that, of course. We'd talk later.

Although Ollie had slept most of the way back in the car, the first thing he wanted to do once we got home was to go lie down in my bed. Five minutes later, he was asleep.

I looked around the apartment. For a long time, all I'd done in this place was sleep. There was no food in the refrigerator, and in the cupboards nothing but a couple of bags of popping corn and a bottle of canola oil. My whole life, for almost a year, had been lived on Folger Lane. No more of that now.

I placed a call to the hospital up at Lake Tahoe to ask about Carmen. Because I wasn't family, no one could tell me anything. I wished I had Estella's number. Though if I had, what would I say? I remembered how she was that day in Ava's closet, folding laundry, telling me her dreams for her daughter. *Mi corazón.*

I thought about my camera. I had left it at the party when I ran out to Bobby's car after hearing the news of the accident. At some point I'd need to go back and get it.

From the other room, I could hear the sound of Ollie's breathing—steadier now than it had been at the police station. Whatever dark and troubling images swirled around in his brain, he seemed to have calmed down, finally.

As much as I resisted it, I knew I would have to call Dwight. I'd promised to have Ollie back in Walnut Creek by bedtime, and there was no way this was possible now. I needed to keep our son with me longer. Evidently the police had already reached Dwight and told him enough that he felt obliged to share with them the story of my DUI. But I didn't have the luxury of being angry with him about that. We had to talk about what had happened. Though I had not yet figured out what I would say to him or to our son.

Sometimes people really disappoint you. Even grown-ups. Especially grown-ups, maybe. There can be a person you love a whole lot, and you think you can trust him and still he lets you down. That doesn't mean you shouldn't ever love anyone. You just need to be careful who you love.

None of this was what I would have wanted to tell my eight-year-old. Only now I had to.

My doorbell rang. I figured it had to be Elliot—and as bad as things were, I felt a certain lifting of my heart that he'd come back. But when I opened the door, Marty Matthias was there, in golf clothes—bright yellow shirt and bright green pants, but carrying a briefcase. How did he even know where I lived?

He stepped in. "Nice place," he said, though we both knew it wasn't. He set his briefcase down. "Cute.

"I got a call from our friend Swift this morning," he told me. "He wanted to let me know we should go ahead and file those papers to reopen your motion for custody of your son."

My custody case. Now?

The detective Swift had hired a while back to investigate my ex-husband—all news to me—had evidently come up with some incriminating information. "Seems your ex-hubby lost his job. He hasn't been keeping up on his mortgage payments for quite some time now," Marty said. "He's on the brink of foreclosure."

Foreclosure. I was having a hard time focusing.

"But it gets better," said Marty. (Marty, the attorney Swift had described to me once as capable of biting off a person's ear, if they ever threatened his client. Meaning Swift.) "Seems the guy has a little problem with anger management. A while back the wife placed a domestic violence call to the authorities in Walnut Creek. She didn't press charges, but it's on the books."

That Dwight had anger issues was not a surprise, of course. Only the part about Cheri reporting him. "You need to keep your voice down, Marty," I said. "My son's asleep in the next room."

"Gotcha," he said. "Isn't it something, when you finally get them down for their nap? And you can live a little?"

I just looked at him.

"So things are looking very good for you, Helen," Marty continued. "If we take this stuff to court, I'm confident we'll get your kid back where he belongs. Though my guess is we won't ever have to even put any of this in front of a judge. Once the ex hears what you've got on him, he's likely to give us what we want pretty quick. Particularly given the guy won't have money for attorney's fees. Unlike you."

It was a strange thing. For almost three years now, all I'd really cared about was getting my son back, being able to have a life with him again. Now here was this lawyer telling me it was going to happen—soon, probably. And all I felt was numb.

"Swift has already taken care of the detective," Marty went on. "As you know, the Havillands are very generous people."

We were still standing in the foyer of my apartment. I had not invited Marty in to sit down. As little as I understood about what was going on, I knew this was not a simple friendly visit.

"Now of course there will need to be a significant retainer for ongoing legal services."

A retainer.

"I'm guessing we can take care of this matter for under thirty K," he said. "Not that you have to worry about any of this. Swift is happy to cover the full amount.

"We just need to be sure, before we move forward here, that we're all on the same page concerning the events at Lake Tahoe this weekend. With your son."

I didn't say anything. I knew Marty would let me know exactly what he wanted.

"It would be unfortunate if any discrepancy were to arise concerning the details of the accident," Marty said. "Not that any of us anticipates this. But given how confused young children can be about things, I wanted to clarify. You can understand that it would not be possible for our friend to make such a generous offer to you if there were any question that you or your son might offer an account of what took place the other day that could conflict with that of Swift and his son. And of course, they were the ones who were actually present."

"So was Ollie," I said. "He's very upset."

"Kids get all kinds of crazy ideas, don't they?" Marty said. "It's so great, their big imaginations. Not that they've got any proof to back up the stories they tell. But you got to hand it to them. They sure can be entertaining. And I gather you're quite a storyteller yourself, by the way. Swift was just telling me about some of the wild yarns you yourself have spun on occasion."

"I wouldn't ever lie under oath, if that's what you were suggesting," I told him.

"Of course not."

Marty seemed to be heading for the door then, but he turned around. He had picked up one of Ollie's stuffed animals. Now he was taking his time, studying the toy. "Ava tells me you had a little slip with your drinking problem recently," he said. "But I see no reason to worry about that. The Havillands are the only ones who know. We certainly wouldn't want that information getting out."

"Ava told you that?" I said.

"One thing to know about me and the Havillands, honey," said Marty. "They tell me everything."

68.

I didn't call Officer Reynolds the next morning. I did call my ex-husband, who had heard from the police that there had been an accident in which our son had been involved. Perhaps for the reasons Marty Matthias had now revealed to me, Dwight offered no resistance when I told him I felt I should keep Oliver with me for another day or two, rather than bringing him back to Walnut Creek that night. If, in fact, Dwight was now faced with losing his house, this might have explained how distracted he seemed when I tried to fill him in on what I knew.

"Keep him all week if you think it will be good for him," Dwight suggested, sounding almost relieved.

The next day, Monday, I called Elliot. I hoped that what had taken place the day before might have changed something between us, but it was clear, hearing his voice on the other end of the phone, that the kindness he had shown Ollie and me after the accident had come strictly out of a place of friendship and compassion. Nothing in his tone suggested that he saw us getting back together. Elliot was loyal to the ends of the earth, but he could not forget my profound betrayal. I had recognized how wrong I'd been to attack him for his distrust of the Havillands. But this happened too late.

Now, though, out of kindness, he offered to drive Ollie and me over to the Havillands' house to pick up my car and my camera.

When we got to Folger Lane, Elliot got out of the car, but only long enough to open my door for me. He stood next to the driver's-side door and with an unmistakable air of finality, he reached down to shake Ollie's hand.

"You're a fine young man," he told Ollie. "Whatever happened up there, don't let it change your opinion about what kind of a person you are."

It was the kind of thing a person says to another when he does not expect they'll see each other again.

To me he said, "Take care of yourself, Helen." He put his arms around me, but very briefly, and stiffly. He got into his car and left.

My son and I stood in the driveway, watching him drive away. Then I turned to look at the house: the camellias and the jasmine, the tinkling wind chimes, the sign, ALL DOGS WELCOME HERE. AND SOME PEOPLE. It was a sight that used to lift my heart every time I pulled into the driveway. Now I felt relief that from the looks of it, the Havillands weren't around. No sign of either of their cars, though I recognized the van of a cleaning company, and another belonging to the party rental company, who must have come to take away the chairs and tables and whatever else remained of the wrecked birthday celebration.

"I don't want to go in," Ollie said.

"That's okay," I told him. "You can wait outside. I'll only be a minute."

He opened the door of my car and lay down on the backseat. I made my way up the path to the front door. On either side of me were the puddles left by melted snowdrifts and the remnants of the ice penguins that had lined the walk just a day and a half earlier.

Estella would be at the hospital with her daughter now, of course, waiting for Carmen to wake up. Cooper must have taken off with his fiancée—back to business school and the rest of his life. I figured Ava and Swift were probably staying up at the Tahoe house a little longer, preferring to avoid Folger Lane until the last remnants of the disastrous party were safely cleared away. No problem with that: What did I have to say to them? Now or ever again? About as much as they intended to say to my son and me, evidently.

Every other time I had shown up here, the dogs were there to greet me. (Lillian and Sammy, anyway. While somewhere, lurking behind them, Rocco growled.) But there were no dogs in evidence. As I opened the door—unlocked—I was met with an unaccustomed sound. Silence.

Somewhere out by the pool there must have been workers packing up, but here in the house, no one. There were pools of water everywhere from the melted sculptures, and a few place mats blowing around with Swift's face on them. Unopened presents had been piled on the living room table, along with a basket filled with the envelopes that must have contained the contributions made by the birthday guests that night to the Havillands' foundation. Stacks of extra copies of the book we'd produced, *The Man Is a God.*

I picked up a copy and flipped through the pages. As familiar as I had become with every image between the covers—as well as I knew all the players—I was curious to see if, studying them now, I might discern something in their faces that I had failed to detect before. Maybe it had been there in the pictures the whole time: the essential truth about the man with whom I'd spent so many hours over the course of so many months, who had finally revealed his character to me just twenty-four hours earlier. Maybe it had been here in these pages the whole time and I'd just missed it.

I was just setting the book down again when I heard a voice behind me.

"They're such amazing people, aren't they?" I turned around. It was Ava's new friend, Felicity.

"They're unbelievable, all right," I said. "I never met anybody like those two."

I did not add that I hoped I never would again.

"It's just such a tragedy, what happened," she said. "They've been so kind to me. Meeting Ava changed my whole life."

"She does that," I said. "Is there any news about Carmen?"

"Carmen?" said Felicity. "Who's that? I was talking about the Havillands' dog."

"Their dog? Which dog?" I asked. What was she talking about?

"Rocco," she said. "I thought you knew. It's just unbelievable that those two wonderful people would have to endure this after everything else. As if having the whole party ruined wasn't enough. I don't know if Ava will ever get over it."

Rocco. In my mind's eye I saw his sharp little teeth, which he bared whenever he saw me. More than once, they'd drawn blood. I continued to stare at Felicity. Baffled.

"After all hell broke loose and you and Ava took off, Rocco got out of the bedroom where he'd been left for the party. You know Rocco, always getting into things. He came downstairs and ate the entire birthday cake. Chocolate. Must've made him thirsty, because then he drank champagne from that crazy ice sculpture. We found him yesterday afternoon, dead on the laundry room floor. Who knew chocolate and alcohol are poisonous to dogs?"

She went on to explain that Ava and Swift were at the crematorium now, making arrangements for Rocco's ashes. Lillian and Sammy were with them, "to help them understand and say their final good-byes."

All I could do was shake my head.

From the kitchen, I heard the phone ringing. "I bet it's Ava," Felicity said, running to pick it up. "This is such a difficult time for her."

My camera was where I'd left it, on the chair by the door, but for once, I felt no impulse to record the scene photographically. No need for a picture. I'd remember, though I might wish I didn't.

I stood alone in the middle of the room then, just taking it all in—this place where I had believed, for almost a full year, that I'd finally found my home. I looked out at the garden—the paper lanterns, the strings of snowflake lights still blinking because nobody had thought to turn them off, the last of the melting snow and ice—and breathed in the eucalyptus candles. Noted the cashmere sweater Ava had given me once, draped over a chair. Left it there.

I was just heading to the door when I spotted the little carved bone Chinese figurines of the man and woman: the good-luck charms, the happy fornicators, stretched out blissfully on their tiny carved bone bed. I slipped them in my pocket and headed out to my car, back to my son.

69.

That night, I made Ollie the most comforting dinner I knew: macaroni and cheese. Afterward, I ran him a bath and, as was his preference now, let him be by himself in the tub, though I sat just outside the door, listening to make sure he was okay.

At first all I heard was the sound of water running, and then Ollie making sounds like a motor. Often, at bath time, he would take out his Matchbox cars and run them along the edge of the tub.

"Faster, faster!" he was yelling. "Yeehaw!"

Then his voice changed, so what I heard sounded like a man, or a child's imitation of a man, anyway. One of his plastic action figures must have entered into the drama now. "Slow down, buddy," the voice said.

Then a different voice, also male, but deeper, tougher than the first. "You want to see how fast this baby can go?"

"I want to go home," said a third voice. Higher, softer. Ollie's voice. "I don't like it here."

No response from the deep male voice. "What are you, a pussy?" Followed by an eerily familiar laugh.

"I'm scared," said the smaller voice. "I'm going to throw up."

The laughter grew louder, like something in a fun house.

"Are you a baby?" the deep voice said. "I thought you were a big boy."

Then came another sound. Vowels and consonants all mixed together. The soap dish clattered against the side of the tub. The sound of metal hitting metal—the shower wand, maybe, hitting the faucet, then splashing, followed by a high voice. My son's rendition of a girl.

"Help, help! I'm drownding!"

More. A weak cry, followed by a raucous sound from the male voice.

"Ninety-nine bottles of beer on the wall."

"I told you to rest."

"I want my mom. I think we should call the police."

"Shut up."

"Are you okay in there, Ollie?" I called to him through the closed bathroom door.

"I'm fine," he said, his voice back to normal again. Just my son again. My small, pale, anxious son.

After I dried Ollie off, I put on a DVD. I chose one Elliot had given us that Ollie had loved: Laurel and Hardy pushing a piano up a mountain and across a bridge. He'd watched this DVD a dozen times, but he laughed every time at the part where Hardy dangles off the side of the bridge. This time he was strangely silent.

When the movie was over and he'd brushed his teeth, I tucked him into bed.

"You don't have to talk about what happened up at the lake if you don't feel like it. But it might make you feel better."

"If I told, you'd be mad."

"I won't be mad. I promise."

"I don't want Monkey Man to get into trouble," he said. "He made me promise not to tell."

"It's okay," I said. "You get to tell me. A kid should always get to tell his mom."

So he did. The whole story this time, including everything he'd left out in the car driving home from Lake Tahoe. And unlike his mother, my son never makes up stories. What he says has always been the pure and unsparing truth.

70.

They had gotten to the lake house just after ten on Saturday morning. Ollie knew this because he was wearing the watch Monkey Man had given him, that he never took off—his special diver's watch, good up to a hundred meters underwater.

The minute they pulled into the driveway, they realized that Cooper must be there. That bright yellow sports car.

"They call that baby a Viper," Monkey Man told Ollie. "You got to promise me, bud, that you'll never be caught driving a boring car."

He promised. When he grew up, he would drive a Viper, too, just like Cooper.

They thought he'd be in the house but he wasn't, though it was clear he had been. ("Sort of like with

Goldilocks and the three bears," Ollie said. "When they say 'Someone's been sitting in my chair.' ")

Monkey Man offered to make Ollie breakfast—his Tahoe tradition—but Ollie said no. ("No *thanks*," he told me.) They'd had a banana in the car already and anyway, he wanted to get out on that boat. He had been waiting a long time for this day.

So Ollie and Monkey Man went down to the boat-house. One of the Jet Skis was gone, which is how Monkey Man knew Cooper must be out on the water. But the Donzi was there.

"It was like a rocket ship," Ollie told me. Even now, after everything that had happened, he spoke of the boat with awe. Awe mixed with horror.

Monkey Man said they'd take a quick ride first, find Cooper, then come back to the house and make a nice breakfast.

"We were going to have bacon and flapjacks," Ollie said, "then go back out on the boat."

Because it was late in the season, there were hardly any other boats on the water that morning. "That's good news," Monkey Man told Ollie. "It means we can really crank this baby up to warp speed."

"I should probably put on my life jacket," Ollie told him. "I promised my mom."

"Sounds like a plan, bud," Monkey Man said. "Me, I was never one to do what my mom told me, but if you're that type, good for you."

Ollie had brought his camera along. Monkey Man had brought a cooler on the boat. He popped open a beer. "You want a taste?" he said.

"I'm too young for beer," Ollie told him.

Then Monkey Man started up the Donzi, and they were flying across the water—so fast, Ollie said, that he felt like his cheeks might blow off his face, so he put his hands on them. His Giants hat blew off, and Monkey Man told him not to worry, he'd get him another.

They tore around that way for a couple of minutes. Monkey Man was laughing and waving his hand in the air. Ollie wanted to yell something, too, but he was actually feeling sick. He was worried he might throw up on the boat.

Actually, Ollie hated being on that boat. He closed his eyes tight, holding onto the railing, wishing it was over.

"I didn't want Monkey Man to think I was a baby," Ollie said.

"Monkey Man kept yelling stuff like 'Banzai,' like we were cowboys or paratroopers or something, and I tried to yell, too, only I couldn't catch my breath," he told me. "I was just wishing it was over."

That's when they spotted the Jet Ski. Even from a distance, Monkey Man could tell this was his son, Cooper. Possibly because of the way he started zigzagging around when he spotted the Donzi.

He was headed toward them, coming up from behind, and there was someone on the back of the Jet Ski, though Monkey Man couldn't tell who it was. Ollie was just keeping his head down, trying hard not to throw up.

Just at the point where the Jet Ski got close to the Donzi, Cooper started doing this crazy thing, Ollie said. "He was making it go all wobbly, to get the Jet Ski to ride over the big waves the Donzi made. When he hit one, the Jet Ski seemed to lift right out of the water for a second, like he was flying. Then it crashed back down onto the water, smack. Then more zigzagging, to do it again. Cooper was shaking his head back and forth and he was laughing, the same way Monkey Man did, but even more than that."

He took his hands off the handlebars of the Jet Ski. He was close enough now that Ollie could see it was a girl riding behind him. She was yelling at him to put his hands back on the handlebars.

Monkey Man started doing the zigzagging thing, too, Ollie said. Like the two of them—the boat and the Jet Ski—were dancing with each other or playing tag.

Then the Jet Ski veered toward them, and it was like Cooper had given it an extra shot of power, because it was coming faster than ever, right toward the Donzi. Too fast and too close for Monkey Man to get out of the way.

Then came a crashing sound. Ollie got knocked on the floor of the boat. The Jet Ski turned upside down, and its engine sputtered and stopped. Cooper fell in the water, but he came up a second later, not even looking like anything bad had happened, just rubbing his hand. He wasn't laughing anymore, but he was smiling.

The girl had fallen in, too, but she didn't come up. She yelled something one time, but then she was under the boat and they didn't see her anymore.

"I think she hit her head," Cooper said. He was talking in a funny voice, like he had marbles in his mouth.

"She didn't have her life jacket on," Ollie said. "I was waiting for her head to come back up, only it didn't."

That's when Monkey Man turned off the Donzi's engine. He dove into the water. There was a lot of splashing, and a few seconds later Monkey Man came up, holding the girl, keeping her head above the water, which wasn't so easy because she was all floppy.

Cooper was still lying there against the side of the Jet Ski, like he was watching TV. He was singing this song about beer bottles on the shelf. The numbers were supposed to keep getting lower only he couldn't keep them straight.

"He didn't seem to get it, Mom," Ollie said. "It was like he still thought it was funny. I'm just a kid and I knew it wasn't funny."

Then Monkey Man hauled the girl out of the water and onto the boat. Cooper still wasn't doing anything besides watching.

The girl wasn't moving. She was just lying there, like a dead person. Then Monkey Man bent over and at first Ollie thought maybe he was giving her a kiss, but it turned out he just wanted to know if she was breathing.

"She's probably going to wake up in a minute," Monkey Man said to Cooper. "Meanwhile, we need to get you sobered up, buddy. Looks like you started in a little early today."

Then Cooper told his dad he'd had four bloody somethings. It didn't make any sense but he seemed to think this was funny. He thought everything was funny.

They tied up the Jet Ski alongside the boat. This was when Monkey Man started making Cooper drink all that water.

They sat around a long time then. Ollie said maybe they should call someone. Maybe his mom.

"My phone doesn't work out here," Monkey Man told him.

By this point, Ollie was feeling hungry. He'd been too excited to eat breakfast earlier. They never did go back in for their flapjacks, and now it was probably past lunchtime. But the girl still hadn't woken up. She wasn't like a normal person that's asleep, either. She was breathing, but not in the regular way, and she still wasn't moving.

"It's like that time I got hit with a lacrosse stick, junior year," Cooper had said. "I was knocked out for a while. They say you see stars and it's true. Then I was okay."

He wasn't laughing anymore. To Ollie, he sounded a little worried. But he was still talking funny, and Monkey Man was still telling him to drink more water. He had an old box of crackers in the boat. He told Cooper to eat those. Cooper said they were gross and soggy.

"I don't give a shit if you like them or you don't," Monkey Man told his son. "I want you to eat them all."

By this point, Ollie was so hungry he wished he could have one of the crackers, but Monkey Man didn't offer him one. It was really hot on the boat, and Ollie's hat had blown off, and since I had made such a big point of reminding him to keep his hat on, he was worried he'd get a sunburn and I'd be mad. They had covered up the girl with Monkey Man's jacket. Ollie was thirsty, so Monkey Man handed him the water.

"Don't take too much," he said. "My boy here needs to drink as much as he can. If you're thirsty you can have some of this." He handed Ollie a can of beer. Ollie knew kids weren't supposed to drink beer, but because he was so thirsty he took a sip.

They just floated there for a while then, the three of them. Four, actually, if you counted the girl. Ollie didn't know how long they stayed there, but it was long enough he had to pee so badly he thought he would burst.

"Pee over the side of the boat," Monkey Man told him.

But there was a girl on the boat.

"She won't notice," Monkey Man said.

Once again, Ollie told Monkey Man he wanted to call his mom. Monkey Man said, "Remember what I told you? We don't get cell phone service on the lake. And anyway, why would you want to call your mom? You aren't a baby, are you?"

To make the time pass, Ollie pretended he was watching *Toy Story 2* inside his head. Starting with the beginning and trying hard not to race ahead to his favorite parts. Only it didn't work very well. Then he tried to remember Shel Silverstein poems we'd read.

Two boxes met upon the road, he recited. Not out loud, just in his head. He forgot what came next, so he started in on a different one. *If you're a bird, be an early bird.*

"My brain was getting jumbled up," he said. "I couldn't remember anything."

Finally, he recited to himself the contents of *Goodnight Moon.* A baby book, but for some reason he still remembered all the words. *In the great green room, there was a telephone, and a red balloon . . .* It had made him feel better, he said, thinking about sitting on my lap, long ago, reading that book together.

It was getting late. He knew this because the sun was a lot lower in the sky than before—the time of day, he remembered, when I had told him photographers usually took their best pictures. Also, it wasn't so hot anymore. He had fallen asleep for a while, but then he woke up. Monkey Man and Cooper were still sitting on the back of the boat, talking.

"I think we can call someone now," Monkey Man said. This was strange, because all day Monkey Man had told him the cell phone wouldn't work on the lake.

For most of that day—except when Ollie asked him a question—it was almost like Monkey Man forgot all about him, but now he remembered.

"We need to talk about something, buddy," Monkey Man said to Ollie. "You and me. Man to man."

There were going to be some men coming over on a boat pretty soon, to help the girl wake up. She probably needed to go see a doctor. They'd have some medicine at the hospital to make her better.

"They might ask you a few questions, after," Monkey Man had told Ollie. "Like how she hit her head, and how the boat crashed into the Jet Ski.

Monkey Man had it backward. It was the Jet Ski that crashed into the boat. Ollie tried to remind Monkey Man about that.

"Some of the stuff from today . . . it wouldn't be a good idea to tell," Monkey Man told him. "The police might get mad at Cooper, if they thought he was driving a little crazy."

Cooper wasn't talking in that funny way anymore. He wasn't even smiling the way he had been before. He actually looked pretty serious, like a person who lost their money or their dog died.

"We aren't going to talk about Cooper driving funny on the Jet Ski," Monkey Man said. "The men that come on the boats to help us might not understand that part. Then they might not let Cooper drive the Jet Ski anymore and you wouldn't get to ride on the back next time."

Ollie didn't actually want to ride on the Jet Ski. Now all he wanted was to get back on dry land and never go to Lake Tahoe again.

"Another thing," Monkey Man told him. "We probably aren't going to mention about how we took our little rest. We'll probably just say we were out for a little ride, and we had this accident, and now we need to get our friend here to the hospital."

Ollie didn't understand what difference it made, whether they had the rest or not. Maybe his mom would be mad that Monkey Man let him stay out on the boat all this time without his hat on, getting a sunburn.

"Certain things," Monkey Man told him, "are just for us guys to talk about. Like that beer you drank, for instance. I wouldn't want you to get into any trouble about that. If you had to go to jail, for instance. You wouldn't get to see your mom."

Monkey Man took out his cell phone then and made a call, and the surprising thing was, the phone worked fine. A couple of minutes later another boat pulled up. It was some kind of water police. There were two men wearing uniforms, also a woman in a doctor suit.

The first thing they did when they jumped on the boat was check on the girl, who had been lying on the floor in the exact same position all this time. They put a cuff on her arm and listened to her heart.

They pulled up her eyelids and looked at her eyes with a flashlight.

Pretty quick, they said they needed to get the girl to the hospital. They put her on a stretcher first, then moved her onto their boat and drove away.

One of the boat policemen stayed on the Donzi with Monkey Man and Cooper and Ollie. The boat policeman rode back to the dock with them, towing the Jet Ski.

Ollie was hoping that once they finally got back on land, he could have something to eat. He knew he probably wasn't going to get those flapjacks anymore. But even some chips would have been good, or a peanut butter sandwich. Except the police officer told them they had to go to the hospital, too. They needed to get checked out, plus he wanted to write down the story of what happened.

When the police officer said this, Monkey Man looked at Ollie. He didn't say anything, but Ollie understood. He wanted to remind Ollie about their secret. The part of the story the police wouldn't understand.

Ollie nodded. Whatever Monkey Man wanted, he would try hard to do it.

After the doctor checked Ollie out, they told him he could sit on the couch in a waiting room. When he got there, Monkey Man and Cooper were already at the table. This was where I found them when I got to the hospital.

Then Monkey Man didn't talk to him anymore. Not then, or ever again.

My son and I had been lying next to each other on the bed while he told me his story. When he was done, I could feel something change. His whole body, which had been stiff and tense, suddenly softened, as if someone had just loosened the strings on a guitar. The whole time he'd been telling me the story of what happened, Ollie's voice had remained steady—quiet, and a little flat, but he had spoken with a surprising clarity and precision. Now he collapsed on my chest, weeping and trembling.

"I wasn't supposed to tell," he said. "Monkey Man told me not to."

"You didn't do anything wrong," I told him. "The wrong ones were Monkey Man and Cooper. I should never have let you go with him. I am so sorry."

"I don't ever want to go on any more boat rides," he told me.

I held him tight and sang him a song—"You Are My Sunshine"—that I used to sing to him when he was a baby. After a few minutes his tears stopped and his breath evened out.

"Mom," he said, just before he drifted off to sleep, "one more thing. I didn't tell Monkey Man, but I took some pictures."

71.

After he was asleep, I unzipped his fanny pack and took out the camera.

The first photographs were what you'd expect an eight-year-old would shoot on a long car ride. A picture of Swift, with his hands on the steering wheel and a cigar in his mouth. Pictures of road signs out the window. A McDonald's. A miniature golf place that Ollie probably hoped they could stop at on the way home, with a giant *Tyrannosaurus rex* in front and a statue of Paul Bunyan.

There was a picture of Swift's leg, and a close up of his earlobe, and one of Ollie himself: with only one eyeball and part of his nose visible, and his mouth making a goofy smile.

Then came the Tahoe house, which I recognized from my own trip there only a few weeks earlier. The yellow Viper convertible. The path down to the lake. The Donzi, next to the dock. Red and chrome and streamlined as a bullet, a boy's fantasy. Or an adult man's, evidently.

The next few photographs had clearly been taken while the boat was in motion. They were off-kilter, blurry. Most of what the pictures showed was water, and a little sky, though occasionally part of Swift's face would appear in a frame, and when it did he always seemed to be laughing. From the angle of the sun in these photographs it was easy to tell that it had still been morning when Ollie shot them.

Then there was a picture of a dot on the horizon, which must have been the Jet Ski.

Around this point, Oliver appeared to have discovered how to switch to video function. A short clip appeared—no longer than seven seconds—of the Jet Ski weaving toward the boat, with Swift's voice audible in the background, calling out, "Yeehaw!"

Then the video went haywire. Sky, water, the floor of the boat, sky again. A voice yelling "Shit!" Another voice: *"Help!"*

After this, Ollie had taken a couple dozen photographs. Each nearly identical—the work of a boy stuck on a boat for too many hours—hungry, thirsty, tired, scared—with nothing to do but point his camera at every single object within range of the viewfinder: The floor of the boat. The motor. The gas tank. The life jacket Swift had chosen not to put on. Swift himself, bent over the cooler, taking out another bottle of what he had told Ollie was their very limited supply of water.

There was a picture of Cooper, draped loopily on a boat seat, looking as if he had no idea where he was. Behind him—visible, though ignored—lay Estella's daughter, Carmen. Someone—Swift, probably—had put a life vest under her head and laid Swift's jacket over her like a blanket, as if she were peacefully napping. But even in my son's blurry photograph it was clear: Carmen was not simply sleeping. Something was terribly wrong.

There was a button on Ollie's camera that revealed the time each photograph had been taken. I pushed it and scrolled back through the images.

It had been just after ten o'clock when my son and Swift set out on the Donzi. The time on the photograph showing the approach of the Jet Ski read "10:27 A.M."

The photograph of Carmen—lying still, though not sleeping, her wet hair suggesting that she had recently been in the water—bore a time of 11:15 A.M.

In all the commotion, I doubt Swift had even noticed that Ollie was taking these photographs. In all those hours, he had barely made note of my son's presence on the boat.

But I knew who would take an interest. Officer Reynolds.

72.

C ooper was brought in for questioning. My son's account of his behavior, combined with the clear evidence that Swift and Cooper had delayed calling for help for more than six hours in an apparent effort to bring Cooper's blood alcohol level down to the legal limit, were sufficient that Cooper was charged with negligent operation of a vehicle (the Jet Ski) and driving while under the influence, along with multiple counts of reckless endangerment and failure to report an accident. The most serious of these, for which Swift was also charged, stemmed from the Havillands' apparently mutual decision to delay calling for help for an amount of time that might well have contributed to the level of brain injury sustained by Carmen Hernandez.

Swift had top-dollar legal counsel, of course. Not only Marty Matthias, but a whole team. To some cynical types—and perhaps I am slowly becoming one such person—it matters more in the end who a person's lawyer is and how much money he's prepared to throw at his defense than whether or not he actually committed the crime for which he stands accused. In the case of Cooper and Swift, at least, neither father nor son was found guilty of any crime besides—in Cooper's case—one count of reckless endangerment, for which the penalty was the one-year suspension of his boating privileges and the requirement to take a course in defensive driving of a watercraft. Swift was fined for operating an unregistered Jet Ski.

Based on the extent of injury to her daughter, Estella would have had grounds for a civil case, but here, too, nothing came of it. I can only speculate as to the reasons. A number of months after the accident, on a rare visit to the ridiculously expensive market where Ava and Swift got their groceries, I spotted Estella in the parking lot. She was at the wheel of a Mercedes SUV that was clearly hers; the bumper sported a sticker of the Guatemalan flag, and a little statue of the Virgin of Guadalupe stood on the dashboard.

In all this time, I had not heard from the Havillands. Naturally, once I decided to challenge Swift's testimony concerning the events out on the waters of Lake Tahoe that day—backed up with photographic evidence and my son's eyewitness testimony—I forfeited any possibility that Swift might assist me in mounting a new case for custody of Oliver. But as it turned out, in the midst of so much regret and so many losses, I didn't need Swift's expensive attorney after all.

I never had to mention to my ex-husband the information that Marty Matthias had disclosed to me that afternoon at my apartment. Life over in Walnut Creek had evidently gotten so difficult for Dwight and Cheri that Dwight was the one who suggested that maybe Oliver would do better living with me now. "If you're up for it," he said.

I was, of course. I still had the photograph in my drawer of that one bad night when I'd fallen off the wagon. I would take nothing for granted, but I wouldn't let that happen again.

And it hasn't.

I take no joy in the fact that the winter after Ollie moved back in with me, Dwight and Cheri lost their home to foreclosure. They moved in with Dwight's parents in Sacramento, where Ollie has continued to make regular visits—eventually driving up there on his own when he turned sixteen and, with his earnings from many summers of yard work and dog walking, bought himself an old Toyota.

He would probably make more frequent visits to Sacramento if it weren't for his swimming schedule. Between practice and meets, his weekends are generally full. He holds his swim team's number one spot in the five-hundred-meter freestyle. This, at least, we owe to Swift Havilland.

And other good things have happened. Ollie came to love being a big brother to Jared. Strangely enough—or maybe it's not so strange—Dwight's hard times served to make him a kinder and less judgmental person. He and Oliver seem to be forging a better relationship. Maybe one day they'll even be friends.

Friends. There's a loaded word for you. I know some people, when speaking of a particular relationship, may say "we're just friends," as if this were some lesser form of connection to that of lovers or so-called soul mates. But to me, there may be no bond that matters more, in the end, than friendship. True and enduring friendship.

Alice was a friend like that. "Loyal as a dog," she used to say. I wish I could say the same of myself.

I called her up one time. It was the summer after the accident, and there was a new Coen brothers movie out. I actually had to look up her number, it had been that long since I'd dialed it.

"I was an idiot," I told her. "Worse than that. I was a bad friend."

Silence on the other end of the line. How could anyone argue that point?

"I was thinking maybe we could get together and catch up," I said. "Becca must be graduated now. You wouldn't believe how tall Ollie's gotten."

More silence from the other end. Uncharacteristic for Alice, who always had something to say.

Finally, she spoke. "I wish I could say things could be just the same as they used to be, Helen," she said.

She had plans that night, she told me. That night, and every other one.

73.

Other than that one brief sighting in the parking lot at Bianchini's Market, I'd had no contact with Estella, and I had no idea how Carmen was doing. I didn't have a phone number, and of course the only people I knew who could tell me how things were going with Estella and her daughter were the people who no longer acknowledged my existence.

So one day, more than a year after the accident, I parked my car a couple of blocks down the road from Swift and Ava's house, remembering that this was the time of day Estella usually walked the dogs. Sure enough, there she was.

I jumped out of the car and ran to her. With the exception of the one time she spoke to me about Carmen's studies and her dreams of medical school, and the day she walked in on me when I had tried on Ava's clothes, Estella and I had barely communicated during all the time I'd spent at Folger Lane. Still, I had always felt a warmth and goodness coming from her. She had comforted me that day I feared for Ollie's life, had told me she would pray for my son. So I put my arms around her. All I had to do was say her daughter's name.

She shook her head. A person didn't have to speak Spanish to understand the universal language of grief.

In halting English, Estella gave me the news, such as there was. Carmen had been transferred to a nursing home, she said. A beautiful place. (I could guess who was paying.) She was receiving physical therapy, but so far, she did not seem to recognize anyone.

"I go every day to feed her," Estella said. "She don't eat much. Food for babies. She watch TV. Music videos. She's some salsa dancer, *mija*. She was."

I stood there on the sidewalk. Sometimes there is nothing to be said. All a person can do is listen.

"I sit by her bed," Estella said. "I sing to her. I pray. It's like she's an angel. One time she opens her eyes. *Gracias a dios*, she looks at me. But she's not like before, those bright eyes. The doctors can't make it better. Only God, one day."

I asked about Swift and Ava. They were helping her, right?

Estella nodded. "I got a cousin in Oakland. Right after the accident, she say I can get a lawyer. Make them pay big money." She shook her head again. "I tell my cousin no," she said. "Judge gonna listen to me? Judge see me, he send me back to Guatemala City. Where is my daughter then? Mr. Havilland takes care of us. He says we don't got to worry. They make sure Carmen's good."

The dogs were pulling at their leashes, impatient to get moving. Just Lillian and Sammy now.

"You don't come by no more," Estella said. She sounded unsurprised. This was not the first time Ava had a friend who suddenly disappeared from Folger Lane, I figured. "She's not so good these days. Mrs. Havilland."

"Ava's sick?" I asked.

"After Rocco died. She don't get over that. She blames herself."

For the death of her dog, Ava felt guilt. The brain death of Carmen, not so much. No need to point out the irony. Estella knew.

"This weekend, it's Cooper's wedding," Estella told me. "I take care of the dogs. The family's in Mexico."

Cabo San Lucas. As planned before all the rest happened. Whatever Virginia found out about Cooper—what he had done that day, or all the other days—she wasn't letting it interrupt her wedding plans. Now Estella and I stood on the sidewalk, reflecting on it all.

"My daughter loved that boy," Estella said. "He gave her a ring one time. From his team. They won the championship."

The rugby ring. I'd heard about it from Ava. Ava had believed Carmen stole the ring. That was her story. The idea that Cooper might actually have given it to Carmen—that maybe, once, he had actually cared about this girl—was beyond her imagination.

"I hope you get your boy back," Estella said. "The only thing that counts. Our children."

"I already did," I told her. "Oliver lives with me again now."

Sad as she was, Estella's face lit up then.

"Family," she said. "The only thing."

Time was, I believed I was part of the Havillands' family. Time was, they called Estella part of theirs.

She was partway down the block when I called out to her. I ran back. There was one more thing I had to ask her, I said.

"I know you've worked for the Havillands a long time. Since before Swift met Ava, right?"

"I know Cooper when he's a baby," she said. "Him and Carmen. I start at the other house, with Cooper's mom."

"Ava's accident," I said. "What happened?"

Estella shook her head. For a moment I thought she wasn't going to say.

"Bad time," she said. "Very bad time. Nobody talks about that."

I thought she might leave it there, but she didn't.

"They were on a trip. The road to Los Angeles? Not the big highway. They want to see the ocean."

"Going to Big Sur, probably," I said. "They love that place."

"He has a new car. No roof. Mr. Havilland likes to drive fast."

"I know," I said. What had I been thinking, letting Ollie get in a car with Swift? Had I been so desperate to win my son back that I risked his safety?

Yes.

"They say a car in front goes too slow. They need to get to the hotel. Big fancy place. Dinner reservations. Big news. Celebrating. He thinks he'll pass the car. The slow one. There's a truck coming. No place to turn."

The car had flipped over. Swift's car, the expensive one. Swift had emerged uninjured. But Ava was trapped.

"When the men come with the ambulance, they say be careful how you move her. One step the wrong way, they kill her. It's her cord. *Espina*. After, she can't move her legs no more. At first they don't believe it when the doctors tell the news. Mr. Havilland brings her to a big clinic. Two. They stay away a long time at the hospital. Then rehab. That's where they give her the chair."

Lillian was barking now. Up ahead, she'd seen another dog and she wanted to get going. Estella, too, looked as though she'd had enough.

"What can you do?" she said. "Some people are lucky. Some people not so much. That Mr. Havilland, he's always got good luck.

"She lose the baby that day, too," Estella said. "Five years they try, she don't get pregnant, then she does. That's why they go on the trip, they are so happy. After that day, you know what she tell me? 'He can do what he wants. I don't share my bed with that man no more.'"

"What do you mean?" I said. "They were always talking about their incredible sex life."

Estella looked at me. We were the same age, but at that moment, she was a hundred years old and I, born yesterday. She shook her head.

"People tell stories," she said. "You don't know that? You want to know the truth about these people, your friends, Ava and Swift? She hates him. She needs him, but she hates him."

74.

It had been more than nine years since the last time I walked through the door at Folger Lane. The last time I walked out. Eventually, I left Happy Times School Portraits and got a better job. A photographer in Piedmont who'd seen some of my work at a little pop-up gallery hired me to go into partnership with her. She said I had a real eye for capturing the true personality of my subject. She said I could always tell what was going on under the surface, behind the eyes.

Elsie and I run the studio together now, taking portraits—families mostly, the occasional wedding. Because the work we do is not cheap, our clients are generally the kind of people with plenty of money to spare—not as rich as the Havillands, in most cases, but you can tell from the clothes the children wear for these portraits, the smooth, well-tended skin and Pilates-trained bodies of the mothers, that these aren't the kind of people who drive around in a twenty-year-old car like my Honda Civic, or have a pullout sofa in the living room that serves as their child's bed. An upgrade from the air mattress.

Rare among our clientele—almost unheard of—are single parents. Single mothers, anyway. Judging by the photographs I take of our clients, you would think nobody ever had a problem bigger than a bad day on the tennis court. But of course I know well—better than I used to—that just because the image looks good doesn't mean it tells the real story.

Oliver, on the other hand, is exactly the person he appears to be. Still a little quiet, not a boy who has a million friends. Just two or three really good ones. He is loyal to his father and kind to his grandmother, adores his little brother, and is shy around girls. Though there is one now, Edie, who is crazy about him, and for Oliver, one is enough.

By the middle of his sophomore year, Ollie began receiving college recruitment letters from Division I schools. Never much for sports involving a ball, he is a wonderful, natural swimmer, which means that a good portion of one whole wall in our living room is filled with medals and trophies from meets. But one thing has been true all his life since that day out on the lake: For a boy who loves the water, he hates boats. He doesn't even want to ride the ferry to San Francisco.

75.

In the years since we said good-bye in the driveway of the house on Folger Lane, I thought of Elliot often, of course.

One night I found myself on Match.com again. Not that I intended to post a profile, I told myself. I was just curious about the people who still did believe in the possibility of that kind of thing working out, as I no longer could.

I had identified a demographic for this hypothetical search of mine: male, between the ages of forty-five and fifty-five, living within a thirty-mile radius, with the key words selected *movies, photography, outdoors,* and *sense of humor.* There was no place to put a check mark indicating a preference for constancy or kindness or integrity among one's romantic choices. As I well knew, nobody's better at pretending to tell the truth, or convincing another person of his upstanding qualities, than a brilliant liar and con artist.

I scrolled through more than a dozen profiles that night, almost relieved to see no one there with whom I could imagine having dinner. Then there he was—not smiling, precisely, because Elliot never smiles for the camera, but looking out from the screen of my laptop with a perplexed expression. Call it rueful amusement. *What am I doing here? Again?* His moniker, as before, read JustaNumbersGuy.

"To be honest," he'd written, "—and I can be nothing else, unfortunately—I'm probably not much of a catch. Fuddy-duddy kind of a guy. I like old movies and new dental floss. I study the annual reports of companies, sometimes for my livelihood but also, believe it or not, because that is my crazy idea of what constitutes fun. It's like a detective mission: The numbers may look dry, but the stories they reveal can be filled with drama and intrigue, even larceny.

"In my younger days, I labored in government as that dreaded individual: an auditor for the IRS. More recently—having recognized that chances appeared increasingly slim of my being called on to pitch for the Giants, or to play the new James Bond, I have maintained a private accounting practice, with an abiding commitment to the truth in numbers. Consider it fair warning that even if I fall in love with you, if I find out your Schedule C contains something fishy, the jig is up."

He had not added "LOL" after that line. If a person needed Elliot to explain that he was joking, she was not the person for him anyway.

It took a particular kind of individual to appreciate Elliot. I was one such woman. It had taken me a while. Too long. But here was the good news: He didn't have a girlfriend. We still had a chance.

"You might not guess it to look at me," he continued, "but I'm a hopeless romantic. Your basic one-woman man. I thought I found her one time, and it turned out I was mistaken. So I'll be careful with my heart. You might have an easier time gaining access to the vault at Fort Knox. But should you succeed . . . well, you'll never find a more loyal or loving man."

I sat for a long time studying Elliot's words on the screen of my laptop. No need to say how all of this struck me, I suspect. Loss is one thing. Regret over a loss that might not have happened had one known better is worse.

"You could give me a try," he wrote. "Think of it as a service to your fellow citizens—the ones trying to bamboozle the government. The longer I go on this way, staying home every weekend, studying numbers the way I do, the more crooks there will be out there (all of whom are probably a lot more fun to hang out with than I am) who'll be getting into hot water. All because I have nothing better to do than pore over their companies' annual reports."

All the rest of that evening, I thought about clicking "Reply" to JustaNumbersGuy's profile. The next morning I thought about contacting Elliot again. Rejected the idea.

That night—under the influence of three cups of green tea, my beverage of choice these days—I went online, resolved to write him a letter. Clicked the coordinates of Elliot's profile. It had been withdrawn.

I took this as a sign. He'd met someone. Things were going well. I remembered, in fact, the speed with which—after just one date with me—he'd taken down his profile.

"I'm not the dating type, really," he'd said. "Once I find a good woman, I won't be looking elsewhere."

76.

Just before the start of my son's senior year in high school, we left our old place in Redwood City for a real two-bedroom apartment in the East Bay. I had one year left with my son at home. I was finally able to afford a bigger place, and I wanted Ollie to have his own bedroom, at last. Before he was gone.

The day I moved out of our old apartment an odd thought came to me. I used to imagine that one night when I least expected it, I'd hear a knock at my door, and there would be Elliot on the step. Wanting to give it another try.

If he showed up now, I wouldn't be there anymore. Not that it was likely, I told myself. Not that he would ever do something like that. It was just something I might have wished for, only now it would never happen.

77.

We had been living in the new place for six weeks, which meant I never traveled to Portola Valley anymore. Ollie was turning eighteen that winter. He was due to graduate in June, meaning he'd be moving out soon. Not in the way he did back when he was five. This time, he'd be going someplace he wanted to be—college—and as sad as I would be to watch him go, I would be happy about that, too.

As for me, I'd be forty-nine soon. Pushing fifty with a short stick, as Swift would have put it.

We had just finished cleaning up the kitchen after dinner, and I was sitting down with my tea. In the next room, I could hear my son on the phone with his girlfriend. A bowl of popcorn beside him, probably. I heard hip-hop on the stereo and easy, happy laughter.

"No, really," Ollie was telling her. "We have to check it out. I could pick you up Saturday morning. Incredibly enough, I don't have a single meet all weekend. I bet my mom would even make us pizza if I ask."

It was nothing earth-shattering, but that's what I loved. Normal life. Ordinary nights spent with the person you love in reasonably close proximity, reasonably often.

We were a family of two. Two was enough.

I took my shoes off and set my feet on the footstool. I unwrapped the piece of chocolate that constituted my one nightly indulgence. I reached for that day's San Francisco *Chronicle,* set aside that morning. The headline caught my eye:

ANIMAL RIGHTS FOUNDATION HEAD
INDICTED FOR FRAUD

Under the headline: a photograph of Swift Havilland, executive director of BARK USA. Grinning, of course.

The newspaper story was not the kind of news I generally followed—and the complexities of the fraud it reported on were a little beyond me. The gist was that a Portola Valley businessman who'd made his fortune in a technology start-up appeared to have siphoned tens of millions of dollars from his family-run foundation (its board consisting of himself, his wife, and their son) after large losses in his personal portfolio. As a result of an extensive investigation recently come to light, Swift was now being indicted for securities fraud, wire fraud, racketeering, money laundering, and a long list of other charges.

"Swift Havilland surrendered at his attorney's office on Monday to face charges," the story went on. Because he was considered a flight risk, bail had been set at ten million dollars. Unable to make bail, the paper stated, Mr. Havilland was now being held at the federal correction facility in Mendota, California. Additional charges were expected shortly against Mr. Havilland's son, Cooper Havilland—a trader with DCY Capital Partners in Greenwich, CT—as well as his wife, Ava Havilland.

The newspaper story was a long one. I reached for my tea.

It seemed that Swift's financial troubles started slowly. Although he had a lot of assets, he spent a lot. To finance his lifestyle he'd taken out first and second mortgages on his family's homes and pledged some of the stock in his Silicon Valley company, Theraco, as collateral for more loans.

Swift's big problems had occurred in the stock market crash of 2008. That's when Swift had allegedly begun looting the BARK foundation he and his wife had established several years earlier.

He'd done it in a clever way, the story explained—arranging for millions of dollars from BARK to be put into an offshore company that he secretly controlled. After a complex series of mergers and name changes, Swift had liquidated that company and allegedly kept the money.

At this point in the story, a familiar name caught my eye: "Evelyn Couture, prominent San Francisco philanthropist." According to the reporter, Mrs. Couture appeared to have fallen under the influence of Swift Havilland's powers of persuasion, donating millions to his foundation. But she hadn't stopped there.

When Evelyn had died in 2006, the *Chronicle* story stated, she had left her twenty-million-dollar Pacific Heights home to BARK. In 2009, BARK sold the home to a Cayman Islands company for two million dollars in cash and eighteen million dollars in securities. That Cayman company was actually owned, through a web of other companies, by a Liechtenstein-based trust controlled by—here came another familiar name—Cooper Havilland.

The securites that BARK received for Evelyn's home were basically worthless. The trust then sold Evelyn Couture's mansion to a development company that was turning it into condominiums, and then funneled the money back to the Havillands, father and son, who had pocketed more than thirty million dollars.

Was I surprised or shocked? In a funny way, the part of the story that shocked me most was that Swift got caught. By his own proud admission, he was a man who knew all the angles, and he knew how to play the system. I could still hear Swift's voice—and that big laugh—as he dismissed the small-minded, unimaginative bean counters of the world. He would never have believed that any paper-shuffling bureaucrats could unearth the inner workings of the elaborate scheme he'd concealed behind the façade of his animal foundation. But apparently they had.

It was only in a smaller story that appeared farther back in the paper a few days later that I learned how the crime, now known as "Pooch-Scam," had come to light. No names were given, and the only source was "a high-ranking individual in the U.S. Attorney's office."

Evidently someone unaffiliated with the U.S. Attorney's office had been responsible for bringing Swift Havilland's alleged crimes to light. This person was a private citizen who had waived any remuneration under any state or federal laws.

"In an era in which stories abound of ordinary people seeking out their fifteen minutes of fame, not to mention the almighty dollar," read the editorial that ran in the *Chronicle* the same day, "this quiet unsung individual, troubled by the appearance of improprieties, had spent years sifting through tens of thousands of pages of obscure public documents and records to piece the details of the alleged scam together. This individual had presented his evidence to the U.S. Attorney's office. And when they ignored his evidence, he persisted until at last they paid attention."

Now, as a result of the hard work of this lone hero, the alleged perpetrator of a forty-million-dollar fraud had been indicted.

The newspaper described this person as having chosen to remain anonymous, but I knew his name, of course.

I sat there for a long time, holding the newspaper. I was studying the photograph of Swift, but the person I was thinking about was Elliot.

Many times over the years, especially at night—my son asleep in the next room, with no sound but the occasional creak of the hamster wheel—I had thought of reaching out to him. If I still drank, these would have been the moments I would have taken out the wine, and once I'd had a glass or two, writing to Elliot might have felt like a good idea.

But I didn't drink anymore. I didn't make up stories, either. Or fantasies that things were real that never were. I was once a woman who wanted, more than anything, to be part of a family, and for a period of eleven months I believed the Havillands had made me a part of theirs. I betrayed the love of a good man who would have stood by me forever, in favor of two people to whom I meant nothing more than an ice sculpture. Here today. Gone tomorrow.

How could I ask that Elliot trust me ever again, or believe anything I'd tell him, now?

That day at the hospital, though, as I sat in the lobby with my sleeping son wrapped in the blanket next to me, I had still believed we might find our way back to each other. For a few hours that night, I realized who the good man had been all along, and I still held out hope of a life with him.

After all this time, I had not forgotten a single moment of that night—the longest of my life.

It was sometime in the early hours of the next morning, probably, after the police officers and the child welfare advocate had concluded their interview with my son. Swift and Ava were long gone, back to their beautiful house on the shores of that beautiful lake, no doubt, delivering Swift's son back to the yellow sports car that would bring him to his beautiful fiancée. Carmen was gone, too, but to a different place, from which she would not be returning, her broken-hearted mother by her side.

Early that morning, I had placed the call to Elliot to ask if he could pick us up. He had answered on the first ring. He'd told me he'd be there to get us as soon as he could. Abiding the speed limit.

Sometime during the four hours it took Elliot to get to the police station, I had taken out my wallet. Inside, there was that card, the one on which Ava had written her name and number as the person to call in case of an emergency.

That night I'd crossed out Ava's name and written Elliot's.

I still had the card, and on it, the number.

I set down the newspaper. I picked up the phone.

Acknowledgments

I embarked on the telling of this story—though I didn't know yet what the story was going to be—in the spring of 2014. I'd moved into the home of the man who had recently become my husband, Jim Barringer—but there was a problem. (Or what passed for a problem, back in those days.) I had no place to work.

My friend Karen Mulvaney and her husband, Tom, made the most generous offer: to lend me the use of a wonderful little house they owned that was sitting empty at the time, for as long as I needed. They call it Bud's house, and now so do I.

One thing I have learned over my many decades of holing up in various cabins, motel rooms, attics—and, once, an underground parking garage—to write: The room doesn't have to be large or fancy (and probably should not be). But it needs to possess a certain feeling conducive to letting the imagination take flight. Bud's house—with its big sunny window over the desk; its red refrigerator; its wide front porch where I'd sit with my coffee, reading the previous day's work while a family of deer grazed under the fruit trees; and its little shed out back where the tractor sits, that Bud used to drive—has this quality in spades.

Just after dawn every morning, all that spring and into summer, I made my way over the hill to the town of Lafayette, California, to sit at the desk in that little red house and write this story. The first draft was completed there.

I should add that at the time I turned the key in the lock at Bud's and fixed my first pot of coffee there, I had no clue what I'd be writing about. The idea for this story came directly from my meditation on the great gift of friendship, as I had most recently experienced it from Karen, and the memory of times in my life when I had placed trust in a friendship that disappointed me—as I have no doubt disappointed others in my own life as a friend. Years after the loss, I still shudder to think of it. There are not many losses more terrible.

Two very different young women—both dear to my heart—provided another form of inspiration for this story. Melissa Vincel has been a part of my life since she was seventeen years old, when she stepped onto the stage at the Kennedy Center to receive from me one of only twenty national Scholastic Writing Awards. Years later, we re-met at my Guatemala writing workshop, and for more than ten years now, Melissa has helped run that workshop and much more—with the gift of her writing talents, good instincts, supreme organizational skills, and matchless common sense, as well as her boundless zest for life.

In a manner not unlike that of my narrator, Helen (minus the substance abuse and child-custody issues), Jenny Rein has worked for me—sometimes with pay, and sometimes not—taking care of the least glamorous details in a writer's life. When these details don't get taken care of, the writer may never get around to writing the book. Mailing off contracts and paying bills is one part of what Jenny did, but she also evicted a family of raccoons from my house, helped arrange for the cross-country transport of a gypsy caravan, delivered a pair of hiking boots to me in a parking lot, and once even—when she could tell I needed to let off some steam—brought me to her favorite batting cage and lent me her personal batting helmet so I could take a swing at a few dozen fastballs. Jenny created her own little traveling file cabinet of my life, the details of which she knows better than I do, in certain ways.

Hers is a phone number I call in case of an emergency. She always answers.

My sister, Rona Maynard, was—as she has been all my life—a deeply insightful reader of this manuscript. So, too, was my younger son, Wilson Bethel. It is a great day in the life of a parent (and I have many of these days now) when one of her children teaches *her* or points out something she had not seen herself. Many times, in his editorial suggestions, Wilson accomplished that.

When I needed to bring to life the character of a deeply lovable, somewhat uncool boyfriend for my narrator, Elliot—a man of great integrity who has made it his life's mission to rout out financial fraud that bilks honest citizens out of their hard-earned money—I found my model (with some details notably changed) in my longtime friend David Schiff, a man I'd trust with my money far more readily than I'd trust myself, and loyal as the day is long. The details of Swift Havilland's scam were constructed by David, who uncovers scams with as much zeal as others employ to perpetrate them.

At the age of not-yet-five, Landon Vincel contributed his choice of favorite Shel Silverstein poems, which not coincidentally also happen to be the favorites of the child in this novel, Ollie. Rebecca Tuttle Schultze and the gang at Mousam Lake, Maine—where I first encountered and rode in the Donzi—instructed me on the art of wave jumping on a Jet Ski. Margaret Tumas provided a key piece of veterinary advice important to my story concerning one food a person should never feed to her dog. The women of the Lafayette Library wrapped me in their warm embrace, as did Joe Loya, retired bank robber, writer, and my cohost for the Lafayette Library Writers' Series. A fierce and loyal protector if ever there was one.

To ensure that I was writing with accuracy about the life of an independent woman with a spinal-cord injury, I sought out the invaluable counsel of Molly Hale, quadriplegic martial artist as well as cofounder and coexecutive director of Ability Production, an organization committed to bringing information and resources to the community of those who use wheelchairs. I would never speak of Molly's constituency as "wheelchair-bound" or "confined to their wheelchairs," because Molly sees no limitations, only opportunities.

My gratitude as always to David Kuhn, of Kuhn Projects, and to his West Coast counterpart, my trusted adviser, Judi Farkas, and the team at William Morrow: Kelly Rudolph, Kelly O'Connor, Tavia Kowalchuk, and Liate Stehlik. From across the ocean, I feel the tireless encouragement and enthusiasm of the extraordinary team at my French publishing house, Philippe Rey. I also wish to single out—among the many foreign publishers who have supported my work—my lovely Hungarian editor, Eszter Gyuricza. Highest praise and thanks to my agent Nicole Tourtelot, at the DeFiore Agency, who read and reread my manuscript, offering invaluable editorial suggestions that helped to make this a deeper, richer novel than the one I first delivered to her, and when we were done with all that, took out a ukulele and sang.

As always, I leave to the end my treasured editor and, now, dear friend, Jennifer Brehl, who told me she believed in me as a writer of fiction back in 2008, and has remained unfailingly committed to helping me grow as a writer with every novel (and for this one, reminded me—as the months passed—that no publishing deadline matters more than the health of a person you love).

This will be the fourth book we have worked on together. Jennifer is one of that small and dwindling breed of editor who truly edits every single page—line by line, word by word, with thought given to the placement of every comma. Writing is a deeply solitary act, but working with Jennifer, I feel the presence of a hugely perceptive and generous collaborator at my side at all times.

Finally, to my husband, James Barringer, who has faced down the toughest adversary—pancreatic cancer—for ten solid months and counting, and never stopped urging me to go back to work, in the room of my own he made possible for me, at last. In our four years together, so far, Jim has taught me what it is to have a true partner, and to be one.

Your book is still being written in my head, Jim. Your name on my heart.

About the Author

Joyce Maynard is the author of eight previous novels, including *To Die For, Labor Day,* and *The Good Daughters,* and four books of nonfiction. Her bestselling memoir *At Home in the World* has been translated into sixteen languages. A fellow of the MacDowell Colony and Yaddo, and founder of the Lake Atitlán Writers' Workshop, she makes her home in Northern California.

THE NEW LUXURY IN READING

We hope you enjoyed reading
our new, comfortable print size and found it
an experience you would like to repeat.

Well – you're in luck!

HarperLuxe offers the finest in fiction and
nonfiction books in this same larger print size and
paperback format. Light and easy to read, HarperLuxe
paperbacks are for book lovers who want to see
what they are reading without the strain.

For a full listing of titles and
new releases to come, please visit our website:

www.HarperLuxe.com